Dearest Dvoyra,

I have read and reread your letter a hundred times. The news of your marriage took us by surprise. I pray your husband may change his mind about remaining in the old country. You must think about what kind of world it will be for your children, Dvoyra. I know this: there is nothing for people like us, like you and your husband, in Europe anymore—only misery.

While life is not easy in America, and we have to work very hard, it is better here. It took me some time to realize why. It is because there is no fear here. You never know how much fear there has been in your life until you wake up one morning and find it is gone. So please, please do not give up the dream of coming to America. Remember this dream. Tell your husband what I have written and beg him to reconsider. . . .

Write to me soon and send news of all the family. Think about America and what I have said. Tell everyone there we are well and send our love.

All my love,
Anna

Remember This Dream

Harold Gershowitz

BANTAM BOOKS
TORONTO · NEW YORK · LONDON · SYDNEY · AUCKLAND

REMEMBER THIS DREAM
A Bantam Book / November 1988

ISBN 0-553-26933-X

Published simultaneously in the United States and Canada

Bantam Books are published by Bantam Books, a division of
Bantam Doubleday Dell Publishing Group, Inc. Its trademark,
consisting of the words "Bantam Books" and the portrayal of a
rooster, is Registered in U.S. Patent and Trademark Office and
in other countries. Marca Registrada. Bantam Books, Inc., 666
Fifth Avenue, New York, New York 10103.

PRINTED IN THE UNITED STATES OF AMERICA
KR   0 9 8 7 6 5 4 3 2 1

*To Bayla and Steven, whose
memories I treasure so;*

to Diane, whom Heaven sent;

*and to our children,
Amy and Michael
and Larry, Danny and Jill.
They enrich our lives.*

Acknowledgments

I shall attempt to acknowledge a few of those individuals and institutions that helped make *Remember This Dream* possible.

There are simply no words to adequately express my gratitude to Coleen O'Shea, my editor at Bantam. Coleen's sensitive, insightful, and demanding guidance set a high standard and resulted in a final product vastly superior to the initial manuscript. The vitality of the story has been greatly enriched by her empathy for its characters. On behalf of them all, I thank her.

I must also acknowledge the contribution of Vivian Pearson, who working nights and weekends, typed and retyped this manuscript, often navigating through countless revisions and endless hand-edited text changes. She has been a dedicated and faithful partner in this effort.

I express my appreciation to literary agents Artie and Richard Pine for believing in this project and for shepherding this effort from my typewriter to the marketplace with such care and affection.

I am indebted to my good friends Linda Slan of Potomac, Maryland, and Fred Nolan of Chalfont Saint Giles, England, who were willing to read the original manuscript and share with me their considerable advice. *Remember This Dream* is an enriched beneficiary of the time they devoted to its review.

Indispensable assistance was provided by Shoshana Turk Germanow, of Rochester, New York. Shoshana interviewed those members of my family who represented a valuable link to the Old World and to the early days in the New World. With great skill and sensitivity she unlocked old and often painful memories that helped shape the world into which I placed my characters.

I also wish to express my thanks and appreciation to Mrs. Peninah Otiker of Kibbutz Yad Mordechai, Ashkelon, Israel, for so generously sharing with us recollections of her youth in Poland. Peninah was among the very last Jews to escape Poland before World War II sealed the fate of so many there. She left her parents and siblings behind when she fled to Eretz, Israel, in 1939. She alone survived.

The translating assistance provided by Mrs. Mildred Goodman of Washington, D.C., and Mrs. Pearl Kahan of Chicago, Illinois, was also indispensable.

When I traveled to Poland to visit, firsthand, the places about which I intended to write, I was impressed by the freedom I was accorded to move through the countryside, and I would be remiss if I did not acknowledge the assistance of the Polish Embassy and the staffs of the Auschwitz War Museum and the Treblinka War Memorial.

I wish to express my thanks and my appreciation to the United States National Park Service for their assistance in accompanying me on a tour of Ellis Island. Given the extraordinary role "The Island of Tears" played in American history, its state of disrepair at the time was deplorable. Its recent restoration will help an entire generation walk in the steps of its forebears.

I acknowledge with warm, deep, and tender thanks the role of my late wife, Bayla, who encouraged me to begin and who wanted so desperately to see me finish, and our children, Amy and Michael, for bearing with me through it all. And, in conclusion, I pay special tribute to my Diane, who was so willing to make *Remember This Dream* a part of her life when she married me.

Author's Note

While *Remember This Dream* is a work of fiction, the events that impact upon the characters are well rooted in history. One should not search for real-life counterparts to the central characters of this work, other than the historical personalities who are, from time to time, introduced throughout the text.

Most of the European episodes take place in the towns of Oleck-Podlaska and Biala-Podlaska. Oleck-Podlaska is purely fictitious. Biala-Podlaska is a Polish town situated west of the Bug River, located between the cities of Siedlce and Brest Litovsk.

Remember This Dream attempts to reconstruct life as it existed for millions of people. Through the story of two families, I have tried to re-create the realities that, for many, characterized an entire generation.

May we never forget.

REMEMBER THIS:

Everyone who came
left someone behind.

Prologue

The letter had been routed through Warsaw on its way to Oleck-Podlaska, a town near the city of Suwalki on the Polish-Lithuanian frontier. But the letter didn't leave Warsaw until a newspaper correspondent smuggled it out of a mail storage warehouse after the war. The letter had been written by my Aunt Becky on August 31, 1939, to her Aunt Dvoyra, who still lived in the old country.

World War II broke out right after the letter was mailed from the United States, and the Germans diverted it, along with millions of other letters, to a building in Warsaw where it remained until May 29, 1945.

The war correspondent, rummaging through the old building during a tour of Warsaw, snatched the letter at random from among the millions that had accumulated in the building and brought it back to the States. He returned it to Aunt Becky, who later gave it to me. I have always treasured it.

The letter from Warsaw is especially poignant because it represents the last attempt to contact a part of my family that no longer exists. And while the letter never reached my great-aunt Dvoyra, it miraculously found its way back to the family after its delivery was doomed by the Holocaust.

The letter was entrusted to me, and when I am certain my children can comprehend its significance, I will entrust it to them.

Its significance, I will tell them, is the communion it establishes with the past.

PART I

Chapter One

It was not a night for sleeping.

Shoule Appelavitch, overseer for Prince Josef Wollegian in the village of Oleck-Podlaska, lay weeping in his bed. Necha, his wife of thirty years, lay beside him and tried to comfort him, but he would not be comforted. Tomorrow their daughter-in-law, Anna, would leave the family home forever. Tomorrow she and her three daughters would begin the journey that would take them halfway around the world to join Anna's husband, their son Yakov, in America. Tomorrow was almost here.

So tonight was not a night for sleeping, but for remembering. A thousand memories, every one of which started an ache in the old man's heart that radiated throughout his entire body. The thought of never seeing his children or his grandchildren again was like a red-hot knife in Shoule Appelavitch's soul.

"Shoule, Shoule, it's not the end of the world," Necha pleaded.

He shook his head. She was a good woman, Necha. She loved him. But she still didn't see what he saw. They were going away, forever. In all the years of all the rest of his life, he would never see them again. Never. The word echoed in his mind like the tolling of a bell.

Shoule sat up, swinging his legs over the side of the bed and onto the wooden floor. He was tall and slight, but still stronger than many of the younger men. His gray beard added years to his appearance, but his pale blue eyes with their sparkle hinted at the warmth and kindness that lurked behind the serious expression he usually wore. Shoule's face was lined, more from the weather than from his years, and the winds that blew off the Masurian Lakes tinged his skin with a ruddy hue.

Necha could see her husband's face clearly by the light of the full moon streaming into the room. He put his face into his hands and sat motionless as he tried to control his emotions. Necha got out of bed and knelt in front of him. She felt him swaying, almost imperceptibly, from side to side. Tears ran between his fingers and down the hands that covered his face.

"Shoule, stop now," she said softly. "You don't want Anna and the children to see you like this."

He took his hands away from his face and clasped her fingers in his own. Shoule looked down at her and tried to smile. He knew how fortunate he was that God had selected Necha to be his wife. She had no commitment, no loyalty, no devotion, to anyone on this earth other than to Shoule, and he knew that. Her long gray hair nearly touched the floor as she knelt in front of him. He loved when she came to bed because it was the only time she released her beautiful hair from the chignon she pulled it into each morning. She, too, was tall and thin, and because she rarely smiled, Necha seemed to many to be an unhappy woman. But Necha Appelavitch was neither happy nor unhappy. She had been born in Oleck-Podlaska and had never traveled even so far as to Suwalki. Her life was her loyalty to her husband and to her God. Happiness, she knew, might be visited upon her, but not in this life and not in the Suwalki province of Russian Poland.

"Necha," he said. "Every day of my life I try to do what God expects of me. Every day, all my life, I've done that. I've always believed life should be lived to please Him. Is this how He rewards me? Is this what I get—a world so cruel that children must flee from their homes to find somewhere they can live unafraid?"

"It's just the way things are right now, Shoule," she murmured. "It will be better someday, you'll see. . . ."

"No. This is the twentieth century. It's 1911, Necha. If it hasn't gotten better by now, it will never be better. For them, maybe, in America. But not for us, not here. It's too late for that."

He sat there on the edge of the bed, shaking his head. Necha waited. She knew something else was bothering him. He had not said it yet, but it would come.

"So," he began slowly. "They will go, and we will stay. And we must bear it, because that is what God has ordained."

"Shoule, what is it?" she begged.

"Who will remember us, Necha?" he cried. "There will be no one left here to say *Kaddish* for us, to remove the weeds from our graves. If we have no one to remember us, what do we have?"

She put her arms around his shoulder and kissed his forehead as he wept anew. When she spoke, her voice was very gentle.

"They will remember us," she whispered. "In America."

It was time to go.

Anna looked around the room. She wanted to remember everything: the blackened old brick stove, the worn furniture, the broom she had used this morning. For more than ten years, she had lived here with her husband's parents in the middle of the province of Suwalki at the center of the mosquito-infested Masurian Lakes district near the Lithuanian frontier. The Appelavitch house, which stood at the center of the village, was small and simple, and while it had stood for nearly a hundred years, it seemed to creak more and more with the howling winds of each passing season. Anna looked at Shoule and Necha, her husband's parents, and could see that they were afraid to speak.

"I'm sorry, Poppa . . . Momma," Anna said.

"No." Necha shook her head. "You're doing the right thing, Anna. You're doing what's best for your family, your children."

Shoule nodded agreement. He took a deep breath, tapping the wooden tabletop with his fingers.

"Anna . . . you won't let the children forget us? Especially Rachel? She's so young, Anna! Sheara, Becky, they may remember, but Rachel . . . she's only four. She'll forget, unless you tell her about us. Will you promise, Anna? Promise to tell them about us?"

He couldn't go on. He turned his head away, and Anna saw he was struggling not to cry. She ran to him and threw her arms around his neck. She wanted to console him, but she knew there were no words for what she wanted to say. As they embraced, they heard a wagon creak to a stop in front of the house.

"It's Zaltzmann," Necha announced, looking out the window.

Nahum Zaltzmann was a trader who traveled frequently between Suwalki and Frankfurt. He had been making such journeys for many years, as had his father before him. For over fifty years the Jews of Suwalki had been trading with Germany, regularly transporting produce, timber, and even horses westward. Zaltzmann made a good living from carrying produce, and a second income from ferrying emigrants on their way to America through eastern Europe and across the German border. Tonight he would drive Anna Appelavitch and her children. Shoule Appelavitch had agreed to pay Zaltzmann nearly six months' earnings to deliver his daughter-in-law and grandchildren safely to the German port of Bremen.

Zaltzmann came in and stood blinking in the lamplight. He was a short, thickset man with a black beard striated with gray, his eyes narrow and wary. He looked at them all: Anna, her children, her two sisters, Dvoyra and Esther, who had come all the way from Berdichev to say good-bye, and the old people.

"Come along, come along!" he growled impatiently. "We have to be on our way. I want to be in Mazowiecki by daybreak!"

"A minute, a minute!" Necha said, clutching her husband's arm and looking beseechingly into his eyes. "Tell him to give us a minute together!"

Shoule looked at Zaltzmann and nodded. Zaltzmann shook his head, as if at folly, and stamped out into the darkness.

The enormity of what was about to happen overwhelmed them all. Anna and her daughters were about to begin their long journey. They would climb into Zaltzmann's wagon and leave forever the only world they had ever known. Forever was impossible to imagine.

The children stood silently, their eyes on Anna. Ever since their father had left for America, nearly five years before, Sheara and Rebecca, who were now eleven and nine, had known that one day they too would leave Oleck-Podlaska. The thought of the journey ahead excited them far more than the uncertainty of leaving home distressed them. Rachel, barely four, knew only that whatever was happening was making everyone very sad.

"Don't cry, Momma," she said, fighting her own tears. "I'll look after you."

Anna shook her head, unable to speak. She touched the old table with its scrubbed top, then one by one the worn chairs.

"You've got to go, Anna," Necha said, looking at her husband, fearful of interrupting his thoughts during these final moments. Still he did not speak. Dvoyra and Esther stepped forward and put their arms around their sister and nieces.

"Write to us often, Anna," Dvoyra said. "Make a vow that you'll write to us often."

Anna nodded, pressing her lips together to keep back the tears as Esther, her youngest sister, rocked the children gently in her arms, kissing them again and again. For many years now, Esther had been weakened by a serious kidney illness, and Anna knew she would never see her sister again.

They all left the house. It was bitterly cold, and there was snow on the edge of the January wind. Shoule carried out the two worn valises that contained everything Anna and the children were taking to America. He had bartered for the valises in the market at Suwalki a month earlier. The locks were broken and the surfaces scarred; Shoule had secured them with two old leather belts and a length of harness he had found in the road.

Zaltzmann, who was stamping his feet restlessly, lifted up the children one by one and put them in the baggage storage compartment just behind the front bench of the wagon. Anna embraced Necha and Shoule once again. They held on to each other until Zaltzmann's rasping cough of impatience separated them. Anna kissed Esther and then Dvoyra.

"You next," she whispered in her sister's ear. "You next!"

She climbed into the wagon and sat on the front bench beside Zaltzmann.

"Don't you people worry!" the trader called to Shoule. "I'll take good care of them!"

He shook his reins and clucked his tongue. The horse leaned into the harness and the wagon began to move. Anna heard her sisters calling good-bye, and the sound of Necha's voice.

They moved away from the house toward the edge of town. Shoule Appelavitch walked alongside the wagon. He reached up and took Anna's hand, squeezing and kissing it. Then he reached back and touched whichever of the children he could reach. He spoke their names one after the other: Anna, Sheara, Rebecca, Rachel.

As the creaking wagon picked up speed, he began to trot alongside, never taking his eyes off Anna. It was as if he could not bear to miss a second of seeing her during their final moments together. Then, up ahead, he saw the fork in the road that led toward Mazowiecki, and he knew he could go no further. Only now did he manage to say what was in his heart.

"Remember me, Anna!

"Remember me, Rachel, Sheara, Rebecca! Remember me!"

He stopped and stood in the middle of the rutted road, tears streaming down his face. The wagon began to pull away.

"Remember me!" the old man shouted as the distance between them grew greater. He stood watching as the wagon disappeared around the bend in the road, waving as if they could still see him. Then there was silence. He lowered his hand slowly. The wind sighed in the bare branches of the trees.

"Remember me," he whispered into the darkness.

Chapter Two

The miles fell behind them slowly, slowly. They passed through little towns whose names Anna had never heard. Often they had to get out of the wagon and walk beside it because the old horse could not pull them up a hill. The weather was hostile, the bitterly cold January winds driving snow and sleet in lashing torrents against the leaky canvas roof. In the mornings the world was white with frost. The children huddled against Anna for warmth, dark rings of hunger growing beneath their dark eyes.

"When will we be there, Momma?" they asked. "When will we get to Bremen?"

And Anna would tell them, "Soon, soon," and shush them to sleep. Sometimes it seemed to her that they had been in the back of Nahum Zaltzmann's wagon forever. She thought constantly of home: of Shoule and Necha, of her sisters, Dvoyra and Esther. And of her own mother, poor Momma, all alone in the little wooden house in Berdichev. *What have I done, Momma? What have I done to you?*

* * *

Chaya Sarah Engle had never approved of America, nor any of those who advocated going there. She viewed each wave of emigration as another insult to the Jews of Eastern Europe. "Families should stay together," she would say firmly whenever one of her daughters spoke of emigration. For her, the massive movement of Jews to America was not the escape to freedom they believed it was, but the abandonment of everything of value. She refused to accept the change her children saw as inevitable. Whenever the topic arose, she would turn away in anger.

"I don't want to hear it!" she would shout. "Don't talk to me about America! You'll be the death of me, all of you!"

It was no use. She was an old woman, and she was afraid. Afraid that if she went to America, she would lose her family to the new way of life. And afraid that if she did not, she would lose them anyway.

Then in April, 1903, a newspaper reported the absurd story of a Christian Youth who was allegedly killed by Jews, the victim of a ritual murder. The cry of *Snierć Zydom! Death to the Jews*, shrilled through the ghetto of Kishinev, two hundred miles south of Berdichev. More than fifty Jews were killed and hundreds wounded. Thirteen hundred shops, houses, and apartments in the Jewish quarter were sacked. When the reign of terror was over, the town looked as if it had been ravaged by war. There was a Russian word for this kind of terror, and every Jew knew it: pogrom.

When the news reached Berdichev, Shalom Engle, the eldest of the Engle children, abruptly announced that he was leaving for France and would never return. His mother's entreaties and his sisters' tears made no impression on him whatsoever. Three days later he was gone, and within weeks of his departure Deborah Korchevsky, the girl he planned to marry, followed him. They were married in Paris on Bastille Day.

To Chaya Sarah Engle this was further proof of what she had always said—that family meant nothing to young people anymore, and that the old ways were disappearing, the old values with them.

To her three daughters, however, Shalom's departure was a miracle. It was not that they wanted to leave Poland or wound their beloved mother as Shalom had done. It was that he had proved that there was a door, and you could go through it to escape the nightmare that surrounded them. *That* was the miracle.

"Yankle, Yankle," Anna thought as the creaking wagon lurched along the rutted roads of western Poland. She was far from home now, too far to turn back even if she wanted to. No, there was only one way to go—forward, to Bremen and then to New York and then to Baltimore, where her husband Yakov waited for her.

How can this be? she asked herself wonderingly. *How can it be that Anna Appelavitch from Oleck-Podlaska is on her way to America?* How did it all happen so soon, so swiftly?

The young couple met in a wretched furniture factory where they both worked painting tables and chairs. Handsome, with dark, serious eyes, Yakov was a tailor by trade, but there was no such work to be found. So he had gone to Rovno, where there were factories offering work during the winter months. He planned to return to Oleck-Podlaska the following spring. Then he met Anna.

Anna was a woman of uncommon beauty. She had long radiant black hair, which framed a delicate face that melted his heart. Her soft skin and pale complexion, her deep brown eyes, her straight and perfectly proportioned nose, and her broad and supple smile seemed more the creation of an artist's palette than the product of any of the nearby villages. There was a warmth in Anna's eyes and smile that caused people to pause an extra moment when they spoke with her, hoping the conversation would continue for just a while longer. Anna was a tall and slender woman of just over five and a half feet and, Yakov thought, proportioned like a goddess. She was simply the most beautiful woman he had ever seen.

The two young people took an immediate liking to each other. Yakov was gentle and quiet, the sort of man who carefully avoided argument or confrontation. He was a hard laborer. He told Anna he had been working since he was twelve. Yakov admired Anna's determination, her intelligence, her loyalty. He saw in Anna strengths he did not possess himself.

Soon Anna invited him home to meet her mother and sisters. She had no father, and only hazy memories of one, for he had died when Anna was nine. Yakov got on well with her mother, and within two months he had asked Anna to return with him to Oleck-Podlaska as his bride.

Chaya Sarah made no secret of her pleasure. Anna's impending marriage meant that her daughter would remain in the Jewish Pale of Settlement, the huge Russian territory where Jews were allowed to live—if not in peace, at least in common bondage. There would be children, and life would continue, and there would be no more talk about America.

Anna Engle Appelavitch had other dreams however. There was a door, there was a miracle—America. In America her children would grow up strong and unafraid. She did not want them to endure the life most Jews accepted as their lot in Poland. Anna knew Yakov hated Poland, a country that made him an outcast though he had been born Polish. He hated his miserable existence, the barely concealed hostility of the Poles toward the Jews, the stifling, ever-present stench of fear and humiliation.

On the day he and Anna moved into his parents' home, as was the custom, she told him she intended to save every kopeck they could scrape together for the next five or six years, and then he would leave by himself for America. Once he got there, he would find work and save until he could afford to send for her. Yakov was dumbfounded.

"Anna, Anna, we haven't even begun our life together, and already you talk of me leaving?"

"It would only be for a little while, Yankle," she said earnestly. "A year, two. Just a separation. Nothing. And it would be worth it, if . . . if we have children."

"America," he said dubiously. "I don't know, Anna."

"You always say how much you hate it here. You always say no matter how hard a man works, he can't get on."

"Yes, but how do I know I'd get a job? And find someplace to live?"

"Yankle, listen to me. I've heard people talking, people who have relatives over there. They say there's plenty of work, and the wages are good. If a man puts his mind to it, he can do well. And nobody cares where he's from or what his religion is. Can you imagine that, Yankle? Can you imagine a place where nobody cares if you're a Jew?"

"I don't know. What you say may be so. But if a man can't find work in America, or if he loses his job, who can he turn to? Here we have our home, our parents. In America we would have no one."

"It's a big decision," she said. "I know that. But it's the right thing to do. I'm sure of it!"

"Well, we'll see. There's plenty of time."

America, he thought. America was ten thousand miles away, halfway around the world. Who knew what such a place might be like? Just because a few people from the area had gone there didn't mean everyone who went would succeed. You never heard about the ones who failed, the ones who didn't make it.

But, he realized, there was also the certainty that a Jewish tailor would never get ahead in Poland. If you had the money to buy a tobacco retailer's license, if you could open a shop, if you became a horse or cattle trader or a moneylender, you could live decently. Otherwise there wasn't much to hope for, not if you were a Jew. In that, at least, Anna was right. Well, he didn't have to decide tonight. There would be plenty of time for that, years and years, he thought. He put his arm around Anna. When he was with her, he felt strong, confident.

"Of course," he said, "there would be many difficulties."

January 26, 1911

Dearest Dvoyra,

We have arrived in Bremen. I can hardly believe it. We have even seen the ship called the *Darmstadt*, that will take us to America. It is old and weather-beaten, but we have been told that it is a sturdy vessel that has made many, many safe crossings. God willing, it will make one more.

We arrived two days ago. Immediately on our arrival Zaltzmann took us to the *Hilfsverein der Deutschen Juden*, an organization set up to help emigrants. From there we were sent to an enormous center full of emigrants who will leave with us tomorrow on the *Darmstadt*. The first thing they did was to take us to a "delousing room." Can you imagine? I protested, but they explained that no offense was intended, and that such precautions were required by law. The center is a clean, warm place. They serve hot soup every night. The women who work for the *Hilfsverein* are wonderful. They were very kind to us and gave the children ice cream and cake. Few of the emigrants can afford to pay anything, but it doesn't make any difference. All are fed. I can't imagine what would have happened if all these people arrived in Bremen and there was no one to look after them. The women working here give their time as *tzedaka*, a duty of charity. Here in Germany many Jews have money, and they give generously to organizations such as the *Hilfsverein*.

The journey from Oleck–Podlaska took ten days. Zaltzmann seemed to know exactly what he was doing. Every night he took us to homes where we were made welcome. He must have paid some part of what Poppa Appelavitch gave him for our lodging. Sometimes the people seemed frightened of being caught helping us. It is hard to believe that the refuge they gave us was a serious crime. One night we had to hide in a barn when word arrived that border guards were coming to search the nearby village. Well, why write about such frightening things? We arrived here safely.

My dearest sister, we must get ready. Tomorrow we embark for our long journey to New York. I am both excited and frightened by the prospect. I could not make this journey if I thought I would never see you again. Don't let Momma talk you out of it, Dvoyra. Come soon, and make sure Esther comes with you. Poland is no place for young Jews. There is nothing there anymore for you. Please, please, come soon.

Tell Momma and Poppa Appelavitch and our momma that I will write them as soon as I arrive in America and am with Yankle.

God bless you all.

Love,
Anna

Anna felt her knees tremble as she looked up at the ship. She kept her daughters close to her to protect them from the crush of emigrants pushing forward toward the gangway. Steerage passengers boarded last; all other passengers were already aboard the ship. As she reached the gangway, Anna was horrified to see hundreds of them staring down from the upper decks, watching the emigrants coming onto the ship as if it were some sort of circus.

"Momma, why are they watching us?" Becky asked.

"Because they know we are the steerage passengers. They know we are the poorest people they've probably ever seen. They probably pity us," Anna replied.

"Watch your step!" a voice boomed from nowhere. "And mothers, hold on to your children!"

"Careful, going below!" another voice yelled.

The mob of emigrants had been funneled into one enormous line, often three or four persons wide, to be led up the gangways and along the starboard side of the ship. Old men and women, arms tightly linked, moved cautiously in the heaving press of bodies. A thin, cold drizzle made the steep gangway boards treacherous. All around Anna people who had been separated called to each other. Babies wailed in fear or weariness.

"Rebecca, Sheara, hold each other's hand!" Anna called, holding tightly to Rachel, whom she carried in her arms. She stood on tiptoe to peer over the heads of the crowd ahead. Several yards in front of her the line turned to the left and then disappeared into the interior of the ship.

"Watch your step!" the voice boomed out once again. "Hold on to children, please!"

"Careful, going below!" came the echo.

The shuffling line moved slowly, the people vanishing through the doorway as if it were a cavernous mouth. Finally Anna reached the opening. She gasped as she found herself staring down a steep, narrow iron stairway into darkness.

"Watch your step! And please hold on to children!"

Anna tightened her grip on Rachel and reached out for the cold handrail that ran along the steel bulkhead. The chorus of feet clanging on the metal stairway rang in her ears.

"Hold tight to the rail," she instructed Becky and Sheara, who were on the stair ahead of her.

Anna looked over her shoulder. It seemed as though a sea of bodies were descending upon her. She shuddered, trying to hide the fear she felt engulfing her. The arm holding Rachel began to cramp. Sheara and Becky were staring ahead, wide-eyed with fright.

"It's all right, girls, it's all right," Anna managed to say. "Don't be afraid."

Just when she thought she could not hold Rachel a moment longer, they reached a landing at the bottom of the stairway. She breathed a hugh sigh of relief. Thank God, it was over! The shuffling line made a sharp turn to the right just in front of her, and her heart sank as she reached the corner and faced another stairway plunging deeper into the bowels of the *Darmstadt*.

Where are they taking us? she wondered wearily. *How much further must we go?* Her arm ached unbearably. Her throat was dry, her heart banging. The narrow confines of the stairway were hot and poorly lit, and she tightened her grip on the slippery rail. Becky and Sheara looked back to Anna for reassurance.

"There's water on the walls!" someone wailed. "The ship is going to sink!"

"Quiet, you fool!" another shouted. "Do you want to cause a panic? The ship won't sink. It's just the walls sweating."

"And not only the walls!" a third voice remarked, causing a little murmur of laughter. A large black roach scurried along the wall, inches from Anna's face, and she flinched, biting her lip to keep from crying out. *Let it be over soon,* she prayed. *Dear God, please let it be over soon.*

They reached the bottom of the second stairway. Again the line turned a corner, and again they heard the now-familiar shouts.

"Watch your step!"

"Please hold on to children as you go below!"

They began descending the third stairway. Anna leaned against the wet wall for support, too tired now to care about moisture or roaches. She felt the dank chill as the water soaked through her coat sleeve. Her heart was pounding; her entire left side burned with pain as she struggled to keep her grip on her daughter. Beads of perspiration covered her forehead.

"Momma, Momma, are you all right?" Becky asked. Anna nodded and managed a smile. *Oh, God help me,* she thought as she reached the third landing.

"Watch your step! And please hold on to children!"

"Careful, going below!"

"There's more?" someone shouted in a voice full of anger and disbelief.

"Two more landings!" an authoritative voice replied. "Only two more landings!"

The sound of feet clanging on the metal stairs was deafening, and Anna, too tired to go on much farther, began to cry. In moments Rachel was sobbing too. They were now at the bottom of the fourth stairway, well below the flare of the hull.

"You all right, lady?" a crewman called to her as they began the fifth and final descent into the steerage compartment.

"I'll manage." Anna shook her head to dash away her tears. "Becky, Sheara, keep tight hold of each other!"

At the foot of the last stairway a yawning black hold gaped in front of them. Another sailor stood beside it.

"Please file in and select a berth!" the crewman shouted as they entered the hold. "Move right along, please! Don't block the doorway!"

Anna moved to the first tier of bunks she could reach. She put Rachel down on a second-level bunk. Her arm was numb and she rubbed it, trying to straighten it.

"Rebecca, you'll stay here with Rachel and me," she said. "Sheara, you take this bunk right underneath mine." She leaned against the bunks, her head on her forearm.

"Momma, are you all right?" Sheara asked. Anna swallowed her fear and nodded. The girls smiled at her, and Becky put her arms around her mother.

"The worst is over with, Momma. In two weeks we'll be in America," Becky said.

"Yes," Anna sighed. "Yes, that's right."

She looked at her children and managed a smile. *They're on their way to America,* she thought.

Good-natured Rachel looked tired. There was perspiration on her forehead and her black curls were turning limp just as they did when the humid air blew in from the lakes around Oleck-Podlaska. Sheara was pale, and her auburn hair, usually rich in tone and full of body, also looked matted and lifeless from the damp air. Her green eyes were red rimmed and Anna prayed that she wasn't ill. Meanwhile, Becky seemed to have recovered from the agony of the boarding. She was cheerful and anxious to be of help. Her hair was richly black like Rachel's, but nearly straight. It was parted on the side and fastened neatly with a clip. Her dark brown eyes darted curiously about the steerage.

Anna surveyed the compartment that was to be their home for the journey across the Atlantic. Tier after tier of bunks, three high and three berths wide, lined each side, enough for more than a thousand people. Rows of dim lights, protected by wire caging, ran along the ceiling. The walls were wet with condensation. She let her eyes wander over the throngs of people in the hold—single men and women, babies, old people, married couples. They spoke many languages, these passengers from Russia, Lithuania, from Germany and Poland. Many had collapsed upon the bunks, while moans and coughs and the cries of infants filled the air.

Crammed together like this, the people in steerage would

have no privacy, no quiet, no escape from each other, Anna realized. Like her, they would all be praying that the journey would pass quickly.

Without warning the ship lurched, and a woman screamed in alarm. Then a groaning shiver passed through the hull as the propeller shafts began slowly turning. Anna could feel the vibration through her feet.

"What is it, Momma?" Becky asked, her eyes wide.

"The engines," Sheara said. "We're moving."

An eerie silence settled over the steerage. Several people cried softly as the ship edged away from land, and some of the men stood to pray. Anna saw that they were weeping, too, as they bobbed and weaved in prayers of thanksgiving for their deliverance.

"Why is everyone so quiet, Momma?" Becky whispered. "I thought everyone would be happy."

"They are happy, really, Rebecca," Anna assured her. "But they're sad too. They're thinking about home. About all they're leaving behind them."

"Is that why you're so quiet, Momma?" Sheara asked.

"Yes," she said softly, and nodded, swallowing back the tears that again threatened.

The engine noise changed from a grinding rumble to a steady, beating roar. The *Darmstadt* began to roll slightly.

"We're moving!" someone shouted. "We're on our way!"

"Is it true, Momma?" Becky cried.

Anna nodded, hardly able to believe it herself. "Yes, children, it's true. We're on our way to America."

Chapter Three

Anna awoke an hour later to the sound of a woman's screaming in the aft section of the steerage compartment. It took her a moment to reorient herself. She leaned out of the bunk into the aisle to see what was happening. At the far end of the hold she saw a group of passengers knotted together in front of one of the bunks.

"Don't touch my baby, don't touch my baby!" someone cried.

"You can't keep the child here!" a male voice shouted.

"Stay away from me! Leave me alone!"

"You must be reasonable. There could be trouble. The authorities—"

"Keep away!" the woman screamed hysterically. "I'll kill anyone who comes near me!"

An elderly woman hurried away from the commotion and Anna called out to her, asking what was going on.

"There's a woman with a dead baby. I'm getting as far away from that mad woman as I can."

God in Heaven, Anna thought. She climbed down from her bunk, hesitating for a moment as she tried to clear her head. *I must have fallen asleep,* she thought. She remembered telling the older children they could go up on deck to watch the *Darmstadt* leaving harbor. Then nothing. Rachel was fast asleep alongside her. Anna made her way down the aisle toward the crowd. She pushed through and found herself facing a young woman sitting on a bunk, holding a baby.

The woman was slowly rocking back and forth, moaning as she clutched the dead child to her breast. She was young, thin, dark-eyed. Her fingers were long and very white, the skin almost transparent.

"Does anyone know her name?" Anna said.

"No, she's traveling alone," someone answered.

"What is your name?" Anna asked the grieving young woman.

Not replying, the woman continued rocking, moaning as if in pain.

Anna turned to a man standing nearby and asked in Yiddish, "Do you speak German?"

"I am German."

"Good. Go find an officer. Tell him what has happened. Tell him to tell the captain there is a dead child here. Ask him to find out if there is a rabbi on the ship."

"Are you crazy?" an old man hissed. "You want to bring an officer down here? We'll all get into trouble!"

"They'll think there's a disease down here!" a voice shouted. "They'll take us all back!"

"It's all her fault!"

"Bringing a dead baby on board!"

"Stop it—all of you!" Anna said sharply. "This poor girl's

baby is dead, and all you can think of is whether you'll get into trouble?"

"Why do you have to send for an officer?" a man asked angrily. "We can take care of this. A few of us will take the child up on deck tonight. Recite the *Kaddish*. Bury the baby in the sea."

"Bury the baby in the sea?" a woman standing beside Anna said, outraged. "Throw a baby into these cold, dark waves?"

"Better that than—"

"Please, please!" Anna cried. "Go do what I told you!" she said to the young German. He hesitated for a moment, and then turned toward the stairs. The man who had spoken of burying the child at sea turned angrily to Anna. He was narrow-faced, thin, balding. His clothes were shoddy, his manner furtive.

"It'll be your fault if there's trouble!" he said rudely. "It's very unwise, getting *them* involved in this. We could have taken care of it ourselves. Bury the child and be done with it."

"And what would you tell *them* when they discovered that a passenger was missing?" Anna asked sharply.

"Ach, they'd never know. It's a bad omen, starting a journey with a death."

Throughout this entire exchange the woman sat cradling her dead infant, oblivious to the crowd arguing over her.

Suddenly everyone fell silent. The young man had returned with an officer in a white uniform and an old Hasidic Jew. The fellow passenger led them directly to Anna.

"The Hasid is a Reb from Lublin," he said. "He was walking on deck when I found this officer."

Everyone stepped back as the officer approached. He looked at Anna and then at the young woman holding the baby. He was a dark and handsome man, no older than Anna, with gentle eyes and a refined expression. Taking the Reb by the arm, he brought him to the bunk where the woman was sitting, then knelt in front of her and removed his cap, gently taking hold of her arm.

"What is your name?" the officer asked. To the astonishment of the passengers he spoke in perfect Yiddish. The woman lifted her head and looked at him. Then a small smile touched her lips.

"My name is Chayides Lubaloff," she said quietly.

"I am Lieutenant Meyer Kramer. I want to offer you my deepest sympathy. The captain of this ship has asked me to also express his profound sorrow."

"Thank you."

"A Jewish officer!" someone whispered disbelievingly. The others were speechless.

"Chayides, will you tell me what happened?" Kramer asked. "When did your baby die?"

Tears filled her eyes again. "This morning," she whispered. "He didn't wake up."

"Had he been ill, Chayides?"

"No." She shook her head.

"Chayides, this is very important. Are you certain he had no fever? No other symptoms? Vomiting, diarrhea?"

She shook her head again. "No, nothing. He just . . . went to sleep."

"Why didn't you tell someone?"

"I wasn't sure . . . he was . . . I didn't want to believe."

"I understand," he said softly, touching the back of her thin hand. She looked into his eyes, tears streaming down her face. "I couldn't leave him behind. You can see that, can't you?"

Behind her, Anna heard several of the women crying. She watched as the lieutenant rose and reached out his hands.

"Chayides, come with me and the Reb," he said. "I'll take you to the clinic. The doctor will look at your son. You can rest."

She nodded, her eyes wide.

"Chayides, may I carry your son?" Kramer asked.

She stared at him for a moment and then lowered the baby from her breast. With infinite tenderness he took the dead child away from her and cradled it in his arms.

"Is there someone here you would like to come with you? A relative, a friend?"

The woman looked at Anna. "Will . . . would you . . . ?" she asked shyly.

Anna was taken completely by surprise. "I . . . I have a child sleeping back there."

"You go, Momma." It was Sheara. She and Becky were standing at the rear of the crowd. "We'll look after Rachel."

"Rebecca, Sheara, how long have you been there?"

"We came down behind them," Sheara said, pointing to Kramer and the rabbi.

"We had best go," Kramer said. "Will you come with us, please?" he asked, turning his attention to Anna for the first time.

For a fleeting instant she felt only his presence in the steerage. Unnerved, she replied, "Yes, yes, of course."

Anna put her arm around Chayides Lubaloff and followed the officer and the rabbi out of the steerage compartment.

When she returned an hour later, the other passengers clustered around and she told them what had happened.

"Chayides is resting. They've got a regular hospital up there. I've never seen anything like it. Lieutenant Kramer was very kind. He stayed with her the whole time."

"What will they do about the baby?"

"Chayides begged them to let her take his body to America and bury him there. The lieutenant said that was impossible, and the Reb said Jewish law requires burial as soon as possible."

"But how?" a woman asked.

"They'll bury the child at sea," someone replied. "If you die on a ship, they bury you at sea."

"The lieutenant and the Reb agreed that under the circumstances burial at sea was perfectly acceptable," Anna confirmed.

"When will they do it?"

"At sundown tonight."

"Did you find out anything about the mother?" a woman asked.

"She was married a year ago, just before her husband left for America. He is meeting her in New York, expecting to see his son for the first time."

A silence followed Anna's words as each person visualized that meeting. Death was always cruel, and the death of a baby seemed somehow crueler still.

At sundown on their first night at sea, with hundreds of upper-deck passengers staring curiously at them, the small group of Jews gathered on the stern to recite the ancient *Kaddish* for the infant son of Chayides Lubaloff. When it was over, Lieutenant Kramer took the bereaved mother's arm and led her back to the infirmary, where he had arranged for her to spend the night.

Many of the steerage passengers stayed on deck, preferring the fresh sea breeze to the airless hold, Anna among them. She turned toward the rail and saw Becky crying as she stared out at a spot in the ocean far behind the ship.

"Funerals are always sad, Rebecca," Anna said, putting her arms around her daughter. Becky nodded, the tears shining on her cheeks as she continued to gaze out across the moon-splashed sea. It was as though her eyes were fixed on some object far behind the ship's churning wake.

"What is it? Do you see something out there?"

Becky shook her head, never taking her eyes away from the sea. Anna strained to see what it was that so commanded her daughter's attention, but there was nothing there, absolutely nothing.

"Rebecca?" she said softly. "What is it?"

Becky closed her eyes and shook her head. Anna looked at her daughter and then back out over the water.

"I understand," she said, almost whispering. "You were looking at the place where they slipped the baby into the water."

Becky nodded, squeezing her eyes shut to fight off more tears. Anna tightened her embrace, murmuring her daughter's name.

"I just couldn't take my eyes off the spot," Becky said. "I didn't want him to be alone. It was as if, if I stopped watching, he would have been abandoned. As if we'd all abandoned him."

"Rebecca, that little boy hasn't been with us or his mother since early this morning, since before we left Bremen. It wasn't he whom we buried in the ocean, only the part of him that he left behind."

"But it seemed so cruel. All alone in this big, cold emptiness."

"It had to be done, Rebecca. At least it was done the right way, by a rabbi, with *Kaddish*."

"I know. I know."

Becky's tears had dried on her face. She looked thin and wan, and Anna hugged her closer, as if to impart some of her own warmth and strength.

"Are you hungry?" she asked, as Sheara crossed the deck from the opposite rail to join them.

"No, Momma. The food looked horrible."

"I know. They just served soup, cheese, and bread."

"Soup!" Sheara said, making a face. "It looked like dirty water with things floating in it."

"Those things were supposed to be beans and meat," Anna said, smiling.

"Bean and meat things," Becky said, laughing for the first time since they had boarded the ship.

"Hardly anyone ate it," Sheara informed them solemnly.

"I know," Anna said. "It's almost all *trayf*, not kosher."

"What will we do, Momma?" Sheara asked. "We haven't got any food with us."

"We'll manage."

Anna pulled her shawl over her shoulders. The wind was stronger now, and the waves rushing by the ship had white crests. The ship began to roll, and they reeled, off balance, against a bulkhead.

"We'd better go below," Anna said.

"Oh, Momma, must we?" Sheara said.

"Can't we stay in the fresh air?" Becky pleaded.

"No. Rachel is alone. I don't want her to be frightened if she wakes up."

The ship lurched again, and then again in quite another direction. They found themselves hanging on to the wet ironwork, trying to maintain their balance.

"That settles it. Come on, children."

"Why is the ship rolling about like this, Momma?" Becky asked.

Anna gave her a reassuring smile. "I expect it's just a rough patch. It won't last long."

"It feels like my body is going down and my stomach is going up," Sheara observed. They made their way down the stairway, holding grimly to the railing, taking each step as though it were a major obstacle. When they reached the first landing, they were panting as if they had run half a mile. As they stood there resting, Lieutenant Kramer appeared at the far end of the corridor. And walked toward them.

"It's you," he said to Anna. "Good evening."

"How is Chayides?" Anna asked.

"She's sleeping."

"When will these rough seas end?"

"Are you sick?"

"No. It's just that it's very hard to move about with the ship rocking like this."

"I'm afraid you'll have to get used to it. We are moving into the Atlantic. It will be like this for a long time. Keep one hand on a wall or railing whenever you can. It may help."

"How long is a long time?" Anna asked.

"We're expecting rough seas all the way to New York." At his words the ship heaved, hurling Anna and the girls against the bulkhead once again. Kramer hardly moved. He seemed able to steady himself by merely touching the bulkhead.

"Go back to your bunk," he suggested. "Above all, try not to think about the motion of the ship."

"What else should I think about?" Anna asked testily.

"I don't know." He smiled sympathetically. "But do your best."

"Children, come," Anna said.

Kramer watched them begin their descent down the second flight of stairs, his eyes riveted on Anna until she was out of sight. He continued on his way after dismissing the temptation to run after her and offer whatever assistance he could.

The family made their way to their bunks. The air was stale and heavy with the mingling aromas of cheese, fruit, garlic, perspiration, vomit, and the pervasive odor of the adjoining toilet area. Anna's stomach turned over.

"Momma, are you all right?" Becky asked. "You look pale."

Anna felt her skin turn clammy, her throat tighten. She swallowed to keep herself from gagging and broke into a cold sweat.

"I don't know what's the matter with me." She rubbed her temples. "It must be the rocking of the ship. I'll be all right in a minute. You just have to get used to it, he said."

She told the older girls they could go play—there were games and cards in the forward portion of the steerage compartment. Climbing onto her bunk she propped herself up on one elbow. Rachel, subdued by the droning vibration of the ship, was asleep. It was eight o'clock and well over half the bunks were filled, for many of her fellow passengers were already sick.

Try not to think about the motion of the ship.

It was going to be like this all the way to New York, Lieutenant Kramer had said.

Try not to think about it.

The children returned and Anna took Sheara and Becky to the toilet area. The tiny room smelled disgusting. Twelve washbasins were fastened to the walls, several dirty with scummy film, and one full of vomit. The girls found two reasonably clean basins and began to wash in the cold salt water that the single faucets delivered.

The toilets were even worse. Inside each stall was a trough with a hole in it, the area around each opening spattered with excrement. The girls each cleaned a stall as best they could, but it was impossible to use the toilets without putting their feet in the slopping pool of filthy liquid that had accumulated on the floor of each cubicle. Becky began to cry as she heard Sheara vomit in the next stall.

Try not to think about it.

Angrily Anna vowed to herself that in the morning she would find Lieutenant Kramer and tell him of these terrible conditions. She felt sure he would not tolerate such filth. She tucked the children in their bunks and kissed them good-night, noticing that Sheara was shivering, her skin clammy to the touch.

"Sleep, sleep," Anna told her, stroking her hair. "You'll feel better in the morning."

By midnight the seas were even more turbulent, and the *Darmstadt*'s steerage had been transformed into hell. Scores of men, women, and children were vomiting in their beds or in the aisles, their bodies racked by unrelenting nausea. Many fell helpless into the aisles as the ship tossed and heaved. A few feebly attempted to comfort their retching children. Anna clenched her teeth, praying for strength.

Try not to think about . . .

It was no use. She felt the inexorable upward heave inside her. *No, God, no,* she thought. She tried to turn her head and hang on to the side of the bunk and empty her stomach into the aisle. Her head dangled down toward the floor. Her entire body convulsed with pain and she emptied herself again. Vomit splattered on Sheara's hair. Becky grabbed Rachel, who had started to cry, and with her other hand wiped away the vomit that had soiled Sheara.

"Momma, Momma, are you all right?" Becky cried.

"Oy," Anna gasped. "That was terrible."

"Oh, Momma, I'm all dirty," Sheara sobbed.

Anna lowered herself off the bunk, steadied her quivering legs, and momentarily at least, regained control. She reached down and took Sheara by the arm.

"Rebecca, watch Rachel!" she said.

"Where are we going?" Sheara asked.

"To get cleaned up," Anna said, grabbing a towel from the foot of the bed and putting her arm around her daughter. Suddenly she felt better; perhaps moving around helped. They made their way to the toilets, where they splashed salt water on their soiled bodies.

"Oh, it's so awful, so awful," Sheara sobbed as they stood ankle-deep in swirling, filthy water. "I'm such a mess!"

"No one cares how you look. They're all too sick."

As Anna began to wipe Sheara dry with the towel, the ship lurched violently again. Anna managed to grab a nearby washbasin, but Sheara stumbled and fell into the cold, dirty water. The child began to sob hopelessly.

"Get up, Sheara!" Anna screamed, reaching down to pull her daughter to her feet.

"Leave me alone! Leave me alone!"

"Sheara, stop it!"

"We should never have left home! We're never going to get to America, never! We're all going to die on this filthy, stinking ship!"

"Sheara!" Anna grabbed her daughter's arms and shook her. "Stop it, do you hear me?"

"I want to go home," Sheara sobbed. "I want to go home to Oleck–Podlaska. I don't care if we never see Poppa again. I just want to go home!"

Anna's palm smacked against the side of Sheara's face. Sheara brought her hands to her face, her eyes wide with shock.

"Never let me hear you say a thing like that again!" Anna said, iron in her voice. "Do you hear me, Sheara? Never again!"

Sheara touched her cheek. It was the first time in her whole life that Anna had raised a hand to her.

"Momma," she whispered. "Oh, Momma, I'm sorry." She put her head on Anna's shoulder, crying softly. "I only want to go home."

"We're going home, baby. Don't cry anymore." She took Sheara in her arms. Wet, filthy, and weary, they held each other tightly, sharing their pain and strength.

By daybreak, the steerage passengers had grown desperate, unprepared for the severity of their sickness. Few of them had ever experienced such misery before. Old women wailed that they were being punished for leaving their homes and families for a heathen land. Others speculated that conditions at sea had turned so dangerous that their journey would have to be aborted. There were even rumors that the ship had already turned back and that by day's end they would all be safely back in Bremen.

Most of the passengers remained in their bunks that second morning at sea, although Anna and several others began organizing cleanup details to rid the steerage of the remnants of the last night's sickness.

Several crewman appeared briefly, walking through the area taking notes, and while they ignored questions and spoke to no one, mops and pails were delivered to steerage a few minutes after they departed.

Anna decided to find Lieutenant Kramer to complain about conditions. Sheara had fallen into a deep sleep after she and Anna had returned from the toilet area the night before, and she was not yet awake. Becky and Rachel were both awake, but too listless to leave their bunks. They were lying facing one another, Becky's arm affectionately over her younger sister's shoulder. Anna leaned into the bunk to make sure they were both all right and heard Becky singing softly to Rachel. She was singing an old children's folk tune, "Oif'n Pripichik," which she had learned from her mother, just as Anna had learned the song from Chaya Sarah so long ago. Anna listened as Becky sang about the oven the children sat on to keep warm while the village rabbi taught them their *Alef, Beys.*

This is how we bring our traditions with us, she thought with a smile.

She paused for several minutes to catch her breath after climbing the five flights of stairs to the top deck. The gray cold air assaulted her as soon as she stepped outdoors. The deck was deserted, and she had to hold on to a railing that ran along the superstructure of the boat to keep her footing. An unrelenting spray splashed up over the bow of the ship as it sliced through the water, and an aftermist drifted back over the entire length of the deck. Several hundred yards in front of the ship was a gigantic veil of fog. Anna clung to the railing as the ship approached the threatening cloudlike wall. Her breathing increased and her mouth turned dry as she watched the bow disappear into the fog before her very eyes. An instant later the first wisps of fog swirled around her as the fog horn suddenly blared out its ominous warning.

Anna gasped at the sound, fearing that it signaled disaster. She felt a hand on her arm and cried out in alarm as Lieutenant Kramer asked if everything was all right.

"God in heaven! You frightened me." She placed her hand over her heart.

"I'm sorry." He made little effort to conceal his smile. "What are you doing out on the deck on such a frightful morning?"

"As a matter of fact, I was looking for you," she replied, still gasping for breath.

He took her by the arm and directed her back into the interior of the ship.

"Well, you found me," he said, his hand still gently but firmly holding her arm.

"No, you found me," she replied with a smile.

"Now, what can I do for you?"

"Is everything all right?" she asked, brushing her hair from her forehead with her fingertips, the motion disengaging his grip.

"That is what I am supposed to ask you."

"No, really. I got so frightened when I saw the fog and heard the horn. Is that normal?"

"I'm afraid it is, but there is no danger. There are no ships that we know of anywhere near here."

"Then why the loud horn?"

He laughed. "Just in case there are any ships around that we don't know of. Really, you needn't worry."

"Do you still expect rough seas all the way to New York?" she asked, changing the subject.

He nodded. "I understand things were pretty rough down there last night."

"It was horrible. I never saw so many sick people before. How long does it take before people no longer get seasick?"

"It depends, Anna. Some never get seasick at all. Some stay sick the entire voyage, and some get used to the motion of the ship quickly and experience only a little discomfort."

"Is there anything we can do for the sickness?" she asked, aware that he had used her first name.

He sighed. "Not really. People often feel better if they eat, while others are nauseated by the very thought of food. Sometimes it helps to try to move around and keep busy, and it's best not to think about the motion of the ship."

"Lieutenant Kramer, if you could have seen what was happening down there last night, you wouldn't suggest that people could just 'not think about the motion of the ship.'"

He smiled. "Anna, I have seen it a hundred times. If something takes your mind off the seasickness, it often goes away. Tell me, you're not sick now. When did it pass?"

She thought for a moment before answering. "I'm not sure. I suppose the seas calmed down a little after midnight."

"Anna, it hasn't calmed down at all. It's rougher out there now than it was last night. Tell me the last moment you can remember being sick."

"Oh, I remember it well. I was literally hanging in the aisle and throwing up."

"And what happened?"

"My Sheara cried out. It was horrible. She was sick and it was just awful."

"And you came to her aid?"

"Of course! I had to pull her from her bunk and take her to the toilet area to clean her up. Lieutenant, it was horrible. She slipped and fell onto the filthy floor."

"But Anna, don't you see? You stopped being sick in order to help your daughter."

"Are you saying it was all in my head?" she asked incredulously.

"No, of course not. Seasickness is real and it hurts. But sometimes if something happens to take your mind off it, it goes away. I've seen it happen over and over again."

"Lieutenant, you have to do something about conditions down there. It is not fit for human beings."

"Anna, there is little I can do. We don't have enough crew to properly service the steerage, and the men hate to go down there. If you wait for our crews to keep the steerage clean, you'll be miserable."

"But what can we do?"

"You can organize your own cleaning details."

"But it isn't right. It's not fit for human beings," she repeated.

"It wasn't designed for human beings."

"What? I don't understand. What are you saying?"

"There are more than a thousand of you down there, Anna. You are in a hold of the ship that was originally designed for cargo storage. The *Darmstadt* will return to Europe with cargo. Because America ships more goods out of the country to Europe than it imports, the shipping companies had to find a product that they could bring to America so that they wouldn't have to go empty one way across the Atlantic."

"And we are the cargo they ship to America so they won't have to go empty? Is that what you are saying?"

He nodded. "Exactly."

"That is horrible. They can't treat people like cattle."

"Of course they can, and they do."

"It is an insult."

He shrugged. "Anna, all a shipping company has to sell is

space and the power to move it across the sea from one place to another."

"Did you really mean it when you said the *Darmstadt* would return to Europe with cargo in the very place we are staying?"

"Absolutely. No one is emigrating from the United States. So, we will go back with something else down there."

She shook her head. "I guess I never really thought about it."

"Do you have a few minutes? I'll have a cup of coffee with you while you have some breakfast."

"I'm afraid to eat."

"You may as well. If you are going to get sick, you are going to get sick. It doesn't feel any better on an empty stomach."

She shrugged. "All right then."

He accompanied her to the third-class dining hall, which was three levels down into the ship. It was nearly empty.

"I guess they are really sick," he said as he looked around the deserted dining room.

He poured them each a cup of coffee and showed her to a table. He pulled out a chair and held it for her while she sat down.

God, she is beautiful, he thought.

"Thank you."

He smiled. "Don't mention it. So, tell me Anna Appelavitch, what is waiting for you in America?"

She shrugged again. "My husband."

"Are you going to live in New York?"

"No. He lives in Baltimore."

He nodded.

"Have you been there?"

He nodded again. "It's not Berlin," he said with a smile.

"Yes, but it's not Oleck-Podlaska either."

"What does your husband do?"

"Yankle is a tailor."

His smile broadened into a grin. "We must have five hundred tailors on this ship."

"It is an honest living."

"I meant no disrespect, Anna. It is just that everyone says he will be a tailor. It would be better if they had other trades too."

"Why? What difference does it make?"

"With so many tailors to choose from, I just don't think the employers will pay very much for another tailor."

"Yankle makes much more than he did in the old country."

"Yes, I'm sure he does, Anna."

They sat sipping their coffee for a moment or two without speaking.

"Do you still have family in the old country, Anna?"

"Oh, yes. Almost everyone. I have two sisters in Poland and my brother lives in France."

"Are your parents still living?"

"Only my mother. She lives in Berdichev."

He nodded slowly.

"And what about your family?" she asked.

"All in Germany. I have two brothers and several aunts and uncles in Berlin and Hamburg. My parents are both in good health in Berlin."

"Do you have any family in America?"

"No. None at all. America has never appealed much to the Kramers. My family is quite comfortable. Germany has been good to us."

"You have no pogroms in Germany?"

"Not anymore, not the way you people have had them in Russia. It is barbaric the way they treat the Jews there."

She nodded her agreement. "And why do you think it is so different in Germany?"

"Germany is the most cultured nation on the face of the earth. She has outgrown such medieval behavior," he responded curtly. "Pogroms such as those that have occurred in Kishinev and Simferopol and Zhitomir, and God knows how many other places, would be unthinkable in Germany."

A silence fell between them. "I must get back to my children," Anna finally spoke. "I will try to remember your advice about keeping busy and not thinking about the seasickness. Thank you for the coffee, Lieutenant."

He bowed slightly, clicking his heels together. "Good day, Frau Appelavitch." He smiled inwardly at his own formality.

Anna's brief interlude with Lieutenant Kramer had lifted her spirits and she felt a soothing pleasure whenever she thought of him. She was confident the seasickness would not return, and that she would be better able to help her children cope with the balance of the journey.

Her return to the steerage, however, reminded her just ho[w] hard it would be to keep her mind off all that was sickenin[g] about the *Darmstadt*. The air was hot and stale from lack [of] ventilation and the stench was horrible. Most of the adul[ts] were still in their bunks. While few slept, most were just to[o] exhausted from the ordeal of their first night at sea to eve[n] contemplate moving about or trying to maintain their balan[ce] against the unrelenting roll of the ship. Many of the childre[n], faring somewhat better than their parents, had begun organi[z]ing games in the aft portion of the compartment.

Anna could see that Rachel was happily sitting on the floo[r] with several of the younger children. Sheara was lying on he[r] bunk, her eyes half closed. Her hair was matted fro[m] perspiration and she looked terribly pale, almost green, Ann[a] thought.

Anna gently brushed her daughter's hair away from he[r] forehead with her fingertips. "I'm sorry you feel so ill[,] Sheara."

Sheara nodded a weak acknowledgment.

"Can I do anything for you?"

Sheara shook her head weakly, suggesting she only wante[d] to be left alone.

"Sheara, I know how miserable you feel, but you must tr[y] to overcome the sickness. It will only get worse if you lie i[n] bed all day. Lieutenant Kramer says it is important to kee[p] busy and not think about the motion of the ship. He says—"

Sheara cut Anna off in mid-sentence by turning away fro[m] her. She lay there with her back to her mother, facing the stee[l] wall of the ship.

Anna sighed and then reached over and patted her daugh[t]er's shoulder sympathetically. "I'm sorry Sheara. I hope yo[u] will be better soon."

"Good morning, Momma," she heard Becky say behind[ ] her.

"Rebecca, how do you feel?" Anna asked as she got to her[ ] feet.

"I feel all right, Momma."

"What have you been doing?"

"I went to the dining room right after you left. I brough[t] back some cakes and fruit and some cheese. Rachel and I ate[,] but Sheara did not feel well enough to have any. I think th[e] sight of the food made her sicker."

"Your sister is not well this morning, but I'm sure she will feel better a little later. What else have you been doing?" Anna asked, changing the subject. "I didn't see you when I returned."

"I was in the toilet area with some of the other girls, trying to clean the place up. It was a mess in there, really horrible."

"I know Rebecca, I know. I'm proud of you. We will have to keep the entire area clean where we are staying. It's very important."

"Isn't the crew supposed to clean down here?"

"They are supposed to, but they won't, not the way we would clean it ourselves. Besides, with all the sickness we can't wait for the ship's crew to mop up."

"Some of the men and women began cleaning as soon as the crew brought the pails and mops," Becky said.

"I know, I saw them," Anna replied. "We should get as many people as we can to help every morning."

"Where did you go, Momma?"

"I was up on the top deck looking for Lieutenant Kramer. We spoke for a while."

"Do you like him?"

"Of course. He seems to be a fine young man." She wished she could see Kramer right at that moment.

"I can't believe he is really Jewish."

Anna smiled. "He's Jewish."

"I know. He just doesn't seem Jewish."

"He is not like the Jews we know, Rebecca. He is from a big city and I think he must come from a wealthy family. There are many Jews who would seem strange to us, since we come from a tiny village where almost everyone is poor. Few people ever left our village over the years, and fewer still ever came. We may think what we have known is all that there is to the world, but it isn't so. Soon we will know a world that is entirely different from the one we left."

"Will it be a better world, Momma?"

"Why, of course it will be a better world, my dear. That is why we are on this ship."

"But Momma, what will make it a better world? Will we be rich like Lieutenant Kramer's family?"

"No, we won't be rich."

"Doesn't Poppa have to work as hard in America as he did in Oleck-Podlaska?" TEMPLE ISRAEL LIBRA

"Of course Poppa has to work hard, but he is always able to find work in America."

"Is that why it is a better world in America, because Poppa can always find work?"

"That is part of it. In America, no one is afraid—"

"Afraid of what?"

Anna sighed. "Of them."

"Of who?" Becky persisted.

"Of the goyim!" a man's voice answered.

Anna and Becky turned toward the speaker, an old Jew who sat on a berth an aisle away.

"Every Jew on this ship is afraid of the goyim. That is why they are running halfway around the world. But there are goyim in America, too," the old man said.

Becky turned back toward her mother, her eyes wide. "Why are Jews afraid of the goyim, Momma?"

"Because they hate us," the man replied before Anna could say anything. "They blame everything on us. For two thousand years they have hounded us wherever we have gone. They think it will be different in America," he said, half laughing and half crying. "They think it will be different in America."

Becky huddled close to her mother. "What is he talking about? *Will* it be different in America?"

"He is full of Old World nonsense," Anna said firmly, making no effort to lower her voice. "Yes! It will be different in America. There may be goyim in America, but it won't be the same."

"Are you sure, Momma?"

Anna stared at Becky for several moments before responding to what should have been such a simple question. "Yes, I am sure," Anna said softly but with an air of finality in her voice. "It will not be the same in America."

Chapter Four

Sometimes it seemed as though the storm would never end. Hour after endless hour the *Darmstadt* pitched and wallowed on the thundering gray North Atlantic, punished by wind and rain that scoured her metal upperworks. In the fetid steerage the passengers no longer tried to fight off the unrelenting nausea. Men, woman, old, young—all eventually succumbed to the sickness. The floors were awash with vomit and there was nowhere to hide from the sight of people leaning out of their sodden bunks, retching into buckets already half-filled. Between the bouts of nausea people lay exhausted on their stinking bunks, families and strangers intermingled. The pain, the moaning, the hopelessness of trying to reach the crowded, filthy toilets, the sense of powerlessness against the lurching ship and the relentless sea, reduced them all to animals, stripped of thought, desire, or hope, stubbornly, miserably clinging to life and that alone.

And then, all at once, the gale eased. The wind still whipped white spume off the crests of the waves, but it no longer howled like a banshee. The huge seas no longer crashed over the blunt bows of the ship, rushing along the decks like boiling ice. Life began to stir once more aboard the vessel.

Several members of the crew came below, visibly shaken by what they encountered in steerage. Most of the passengers lay in their bunks, too ill to care how they looked or who saw them. The stench was so appalling that one sailor clapped a hand over his mouth and bolted for the stairway.

"The weather is clearing," a crewman announced. "The sun is coming out. All third-class passengers should come up on deck and get some fresh air."

"The sun is coming out," someone repeated wonderingly, as if this were the greatest miracle of all. "The sun is coming out."

"The third-class dining room is open. There is hot food. Please try to make your way to the upper decks. As soon as we can, we'll begin cleaning up down here. Try to come up on deck as quickly as you can. You'll be quite safe. The ship isn't pitching anymore."

"It's true!" one of the passengers said. "She's stopped rocking up and down!" This, too, seemed like a miracle. People climbed out of their bunks, even the feebler ones. They smiled at each other, for maybe the worst was over.

"Now they come to clean," one of them said. "Now they give us food. Why all of a sudden are they so concerned for our welfare?"

"Because we will be in America soon," a voice snapped. "If any of us is too sick to be admitted, the steamship company has to pay for our return passage to Europe."

"I heard that if a child under ten is refused entry, they have to pay for two return trips—one for the child, one for someone to go back with it."

"And what about children over ten?"

"A child over ten is considered an adult. Unless someone is prepared to pay for an extra ticket for someone to accompany the child, he or she must return alone."

A silence followed, then somebody broke in with a cheerful shout. "So why are we discussing such gloomy things? Upstairs the sun is shining. Let's go and see what American sunshine looks like!"

Slowly they began the long climb to the upper decks. Most of the families with children entered the third-class dining room, where bread and porridge were being served. Spirits soared as they realized that they had actually almost crossed the Atlantic. They poured out onto the decks, congratulating each other. They had done it! Europe was behind them forever! The promised land lay ahead, and the sun had never felt so good! Someone produced an accordion, someone else a fiddle. The passengers sang, and some even danced as the rear upper decks became the site of one great, spontaneous celebration.

Anna Appelavitch sat with her children, leaning back against a hatch cover, her face turned toward the sun, when she saw Lieutenant Kramer making his way through the crowd toward her. It had been ten days since she had seen him, and she made no effort to hide her pleasure as she rose to her feet.

"Anna!" he called. "Anna Appelavitch!"

She told the children to stay where they were and pushed through the happy throng of immigrants. When she reached him, he took her hand and drew her to one side, his face serious.

"Anna, I want you to come with me." She started to ask a question, but he laid a finger on her lips and shook his head. He led her to the barrier that divided the steerage area from the rest of the ship. A crewman snapped the bolts back and they went through.

"Where are we going?" Anna said. Passengers were watching her through the the windows of the salon, their faces white and curious, their expressions strained.

"This way, Anna, I'll tell you in a minute." They climbed a stairway, then another that brought them out on an upper deck. The breeze was stronger up here, and a loosely tied tarpaulin flapped on one of the lifeboats.

"It's Chayides Lubaloff," Kramer finally said. "She's threatening to kill herself! This is the boat deck. How she got up here I'll never know."

Anna glanced around her and saw the long, white-painted lifeboats along both sides of the upper deck, their blue tarpaulin covers drawn taut with looped ropes. A railing, perhaps four feet high, ran all along the edge of the deck.

"Where is she?"

"Over there." Kramer gestured toward the stern. They walked a few yards along the deck, and then Anna saw her. Chayides had climbed over the rail and stood now on the edge of the deck, holding the rail and staring down. Far below her the sea boiled past the sloping steel walls of the ship.

"Chayides!" Anna called, starting forward. Kramer grabbed her arm and held her as Chayides Lubaloff turned to face them. Her face was chalk-white, her eyes like two smudges of lampblack.

"Don't come near me!" she screeched. "Stay away!" The words were whipped away in the rising wind. *This can't be happening,* Anna thought. On the rear decks people were singing and dancing. In the heated salons below her feet the rich people were drinking tea and playing cards.

"Chayides!" Kramer said. "Listen to me. I've brought your friend to talk to you. Anna's here. Won't you talk to her?"

"Go away!" Chayides shouted.

"Chayides, please listen to me," Anna called. She edged a step forward so the girl could see her better. "Please let me talk to you."

"There's nothing to say," Chayides sobbed.

"Yes, there is, Chayides. There is. Tomorrow we'll be in New York. You'll be all right then."

"No. I'll never be all right again."

"Try to get closer," Kramer whispered to Anna. "Try to get near enough to grab her arm. If you can get hold of her, we'll pull her to safety."

Anna nodded. "Chayides," she said, edging forward another foot, "I can't see you. Let me come closer so we can talk."

"Tell him to stay back!" the girl shouted, her voice rising hysterically. "I don't want him!"

"Lieutenant Kramer only wants to help you."

"I don't want his help!"

Anna looked at Kramer. He reached out, touched her shoulder with his fingers. "Try, Anna," he urged her. "For God's sake, try."

"I'm coming nearer, Chayides," Anna told the distraught woman. "Just me, no one else. Is that all right?"

Chayides Lubaloff did not answer. She watched Anna with empty eyes, the wind whipping tendrils of her hair across her face.

"I'm coming, Chayides." Again there was no response. Anna took several tentative steps forward. She was three or four yards away when Chayides looked up and frowned. Anna stopped moving forward at once.

"Why are you doing this, Chayides?"

"My baby is down there." Chayides returned her gaze to the seething waters below. "Down, down, down."

"No, Chayides," Anna said softly. "He's not there. You know that. We both know it."

Again the girl was silent, but Anna could see the tears springing freshly to her eyes. *Help me, God,* she prayed silently.

"Oh, Chayides, I wish I could think of the right words to make your hurt less. I wish I were wise enough to answer the questions you must be asking yourself. But I can't. I don't know the answers. But I do know that your son left this earth the moment he died. He was at peace, in some other world we don't begin to comprehend, long before you boarded the *Darmstadt*."

Chayides shook her head. "What will I say to Shlomo?" she moaned. "What will I tell my husband?" Fresh tears rolled down her cheeks.

Anna did not speak. She did not know how to answer the question.

"He's waiting," Chayides continued. "There." She pointed at the horizon, and Anna's heart leapt with fear as Chayides swayed away from the ship. "Waiting to see his son. His firstborn. Waiting for me to walk off the ship with his little baby in my arms. Poor Shlomo. Poor, poor Shlomo. What will I tell him?"

"Tell him the truth, Chayides," Anna said. "Tell him your baby died before you left Bremen."

"I can't," the girl sobbed. "I can't tell him."

"You must." Anna moved forward another step. "It will be hard, I know. Hard for you to say. Hard for him to hear. But you must do it."

"I feel as though I've left part of myself back there. Back . . ." Her voice trailed away.

"We've all left part of ourselves back there," Anna said. "Home. Families. Friends. Every one of us."

"It's not the same. He was my baby. It's not fair."

"Listen to me, Chayides. I buried a beautiful daughter ten years ago. I was no older than you are now. I can never visit her grave again. I have left part of me behind, too."

"You lost a child? You?"

"I'll never forget my daughter, as you'll never forget your son. But I learned that we have to go on. It's hard at first. But you have to do it."

"I don't know. I don't know if I can."

"He loves you," Anna said, moving forward. "Tell him. He'll understand. He'll help you. One day you'll have another child. Maybe lots of children." She was no more than three paces away from the distraught girl now. *Oh, God, help me say the right thing. Help me, help me.*

"It will break his heart," Chayides said, as if to herself.

"I know. And you can't deny him that. But it's breaking your heart too. He will think how horrible it has been for you. He'll want to make sure you're not hurt any more. Give him the chance." Anna held out her hand, hoping Chayides would not notice how it trembled. "Give him the chance."

Chayides Lubaloff looked at Anna's hand and then at her face. For the first time Anna saw hope in her eyes.

"Come," she said. "Give me your hand."

She took the young woman's icy hand in her own, and in a few moments Chayides Lubaloff was in her arms, sobbing uncontrollably. Behind her Anna felt, rather than saw, the reassuring presence of Lieutenant Kramer.

"Oh, Anna, I am so afraid," the girl sobbed.

"We all are, Chayides," Anna soothed her softly. "Every one of us."

Kramer watched as Anna hugged and comforted the distraught, grief-stricken woman. This was, he would later remember, when his desire for Anna was born.

The sun did not shine for long. By three o'clock the next day rain drove the immigrants back down into the lower decks of the *Darmstadt*. They went reluctantly, their shoulders hunched against the chilling drizzle, pushing slowly toward the single staircase.

Standing in the lee of a lifeboat smoking a cigarette, Kramer watched them from the upper deck. He had seen so many immigrants—they were what they were. There was nothing he could do to alter their lot, even if he had wanted to. He was neither a philosopher nor a philanthropist. His job was to take them from Bremen to New York. What happened to them after that did not—should not—concern him.

Then he saw Anna Appelavitch in the crowd below, holding one of her daughters in her arms. He watched as she covered the child's head with the shawl she had been wearing around her shoulders. *She's lovely,* he thought. Almost as if she had sensed what he was thinking, Anna looked up toward him, her skin shiny with drizzle. Their eyes locked momentarily as something passed between them. She made no gesture, nor did she smile. He slowly raised his hand to his cap and saluted her. Haltingly she waved back. Then she looked away. He drew smoke deep into his lungs and exhaled it into the cool, wet wind. He watched her until she disappeared into the interior of the ship.

Why her? he wondered as he felt his heart race. He stared off into space, thinking about Anna Appelavitch. "I must see her again," he whispered as he flicked his half-smoked cigarette over the rail and into the icy waters of the Atlantic.

★ ★ ★

Anna felt her pulse quicken as she saw Lieutenant Kramer walking along the aisle inspecting the lights and pipework on the ceiling of the steerage compartment. She found herself brushing her hair back into place with her fingertips as he drew nearer and blushed as she realized why. He seemed at first to be oblivious to her presence.

"Is everything all right, Lieutenant?" she asked as he reached her.

"Anna!" he said, smiling. "And how are you this evening?"

"I'm well. What are you doing down here?"

"I have to keep an eye on things," he said with a wave of his hand. "Come, I'll show you."

Anna gestured for Sheara and Becky to look after Rachel, who was playing with a wooden hairbrush, and followed Lieutenant Kramer through the steerage compartment. As they made their way down the center aisle, he stopped occasionally to inspect the piping or one of the valves, explaining the function of each. When they reached the staircase in the corridor outside the compartment, Anna asked again why he'd come down to the steerage.

"I'm just . . . I came down to make an inspection."

She said nothing, but a small smile played around the corners of her mouth, and he saw mischief in her eyes.

"You don't believe me?"

"I don't know much about ships, Lieutenant. But I know they don't send officers into the steerage to inspect the piping."

He smiled and made a rueful gesture. "All right. It was an excuse to see you."

"To see me?"

He nodded. She did not know what to say. She felt suddenly breathless. Her hand moved to her bosom.

"Please don't be alarmed," he said. "I wanted to talk to you. To see you for a few moments."

She nodded and tried to smile. "I thought you were watching us from the upper deck this afternoon."

"You, Anna," he corrected.

"Me?" Why would you watch me?"

"I'll tell you the truth: I don't honestly know. There is just something about you that tells me you're a very unusual woman."

Now she smiled and shook her head. "That's nonsense," she said firmly. "I'm a nobody from a tiny village near

Suwalki. There must be hundreds of people on this ship far more interesting than I."

"No. No one more interesting."

"I don't understand."

He sighed. "When I came down here, my head was full of things I planned to say to you. I wanted to tell you that I think you are beautiful." He raised his hand to silence her protest. "I know, I know, I shouldn't be saying such things to a married woman. But there it is. I've said it. I only wish we'd met under different circumstances. In another place. Another time."

Anna bit her lip as she returned his gaze.

"In another place, another time, we would never have met," she whispered.

He gently took hold of her shoulders, drew her nearer, and kissed her on the forehead. Anna closed her eyes for a moment, and as she opened them again to look at him, he gently kissed her again, this time on the lips.

"Anna, come with me," he whispered softly.

"What do you want with me?"

"I want to be with you."

"I can't leave my children," she protested.

She felt his grip tighten around her arm as he spoke. "The children are perfectly safe here. Please come with me for just a few minutes," Kramer urged, leading her toward the stairs.

Oh God, what am I doing? Anna thought to herself. "Where are you taking me?" Her voice betrayed the panic she felt.

"Anna, one of the officers' cabins is empty. We can be alone there."

As they approached the stairs, she reached out and grabbed the iron railing that ran up the steel wall.

"Lieutenant, this is insane. I'm married."

"You are a woman, Anna, and I am a man. Our paths have briefly crossed between two worlds somewhere in the middle of the Atlantic."

"I have never been with another man. I don't want to do anything I'll regret later." She pulled back from his grip.

Kramer stood facing Anna and nodded his understanding. "Do you want to return to your children?"

"Can't we just stay and talk for a while?" she replied pleadingly.

"No, Anna, I can't just stand here and talk to you. I want to hold you."

"Nothing like this has ever happened to me before. I have never wanted to be with another man. I have never looked twice at another man, Lieutenant."

Kramer smiled and gently tightened his hold on her. "But you do want to be with me."

Anna stood there speechlessly for a moment and then nodded.

"You know I would never hurt you, Anna."

"I know," she whispered.

"Come with me," he said hoarsely as he stepped onto the metal staircase.

Kramer could sense Anna's fear as he guided her down the dark, narrow corridor. "Are you frightened?" he asked as they stopped in front of the metal cabin door.

"I'm scared to death."

"Of what I might do?"

She shook her head. "No, Lieutenant, of what I might do."

The cabin was small and, Anna observed, spotlessly clean. Kramer motioned for Anna to sit down in a small metal chair opposite the bunk where he took a seat. There was so little space between them that their knees brushed together softly as he sat facing her. Anna, too overwhelmed to speak, lowered her eyes self-consciously.

As she looked up to meet his gaze, he reached behind her neck and removed the clasp that bound her hair, and the warmth of his eyes revealed the depth of the affection he felt for her. As Anna's black silky hair fell over her shoulders, he moved his hands to the sides of her face and let the strands wrap around his fingers. He stood and drew her to her feet to take her in his arms. For a moment they just clung to one another. Then he cupped her chin and brought his lips down on her mouth.

"'*Ich liebe dir, ich liebe dich! Wie's richtig ist, ich weess es nich,*'" he murmured.

"What does that mean?"

He smiled. "It's a Berlin expression. It repeats 'I love you,' once grammatically correct, once grammatically incorrect. 'Either way, I love you,' the expression says."

She could feel her heart pounding in her chest as he tightened his hold on her. He lowered one hand to the small of her back and gently but firmly pressed his body against hers. Anna felt her own body thrust forward to meet his.

Kramer, still holding her tightly around the waist, slowly

slid his free hand over her breast. He carassed her softly and then began to unfasten the buttons on the front of her dress. She did not speak, and moments later she stood vulnerably before him, her clothing lying on the floor around her feet.

Kramer, stunned by her beauty, just stared. Her radiant hair cascaded down across her shoulders, framing her face and falling gracefully to her full and perfectly shaped breasts. But for the faint blush of color on her cheeks, her skin looked like porcelain in the dimly lighted room.

Anna watched, her senses reeling, as Kramer undressed without taking his eyes from her. He stood confidently before her, his muscular frame superbly proportioned, his chest blanketed with wiry black hair.

The fear Anna had known only moments before was suddenly swept away as they fell into one another's arms again. She had never before experienced the feeling that now raced through her, and as Kramer lowered her onto the bunk, she reached up to hold him and awaited his next move.

"I want you to feel what you are doing to me," he whispered, taking her hand in his and moving it down between them. Anna's eyes searched his as her fingers closed around him.

"This is what you do to me, Anna."

"Oh, God," she whispered.

Kramer took his time with her, sensing, correctly, that while she had shared a bed with her husband, she had never known the touch nor the tenderness of a lover. By the time she was ready for him, her body was rhythmically responding to every stroke of his skilled caress. When her response to his touch was strong enough, he entered her. She held him with all her strength as she thrust upward against his body. Again and again in perfect and unrelenting unison they thrust themselves at one another, and soon Anna could feel the well of passion begin to build deep within her. Then, just as the tension seemed more than she could bear, Anna felt the sudden throbbing release pulsate through her entire body. She cried out in pleasure, and a moment later, following Kramer's own convulsive release, the two of them lay spent and breathless, entwined in one another's arms.

Anna sat on the edge of her bunk, her hands clasped in her lap, staring blankly ahead. She was stunned from the sense of loss she had felt when she and Kramer had parted only hours before.

"Momma? Are you all right?" she heard Becky ask.

"What? Yes, yes, Rebecca, I'm fine."

"You looked funny. Dreamy."

Anna smiled briefly. "I expect I got a bit dizzy from the rocking of the ship. It seems to have become worse again."

The smile was a lie, the words were a lie. She had never lied, ever, to her children. Or to her husband.

"Don't worry, Momma," Becky said, putting her arms around Anna's neck. "Someone was saying we'll be there tomorrow. In New York. Won't that be wonderful?"

"Yes," Anna said absently. "Wonderful."

And I will never see him again.

At seven-thirty the next morning a man ran through the steerage, shouting excitedly, "I have seen it! I have seen it! We are in America!"

A roar of excitement and emotion erupted throughout the compartment. People rushed wildly for the stairs, shouting, laughing, some even crying. Within minutes the steerage was nearly emptied.

When the first crush had subsided, Anna sent the girls ahead of her, warning them to wait for her at the head of the stairs. For some reason she did not understand, she wanted to be alone for a few moments. When they were gone, she let her eyes roam around the cavernous hold. She thought of her family back in Poland, and tears welled in her eyes. She stood up and walked down the aisle through the steerage. Refuse was strewn everywhere—an empty bottle, a piece of black bread, dirty linen, children's drawings. She reached out and gently touched the bunk where she had first seen Chayides Lubaloff, holding her dead son.

Then she focused on Meyer Kramer and could no longer hold back the tears. He towered in her mind at that moment, crowding out her halfhearted attempts to think of Yakov, her husband of more than twelve years, the father of her children and, after four years separation, a veritable stranger. Kramer had given her the most profound, exhilarating moment of her life, and she ached at the thought of never seeing him again.

Finally she went up the stairs to the deck where a crowd had clustered against the rails, talking excitedly. Anna lifted Rachel into her arms. Becky and Sheara tugged at her dress.

"Momma, Momma, can we go by the rails and see America?" Sheara said. "Oh, Momma, can we please?"

"Please, Momma!" Becky begged.

Anna smiled and nodded. They ran ahead of her to the rails at the side of the ship. They were just entering New York harbor. The land lay low on the horizon, the city merely a dark smudge. A hush fell over the crowd as off to their left a huge statue came into view. Men and women alike began to cry as they gazed at the torch-bearing woman towering over the harbor.

"Anna!" she heard Meyer's call.

She searched for him but did not spot him.

"Oh, Momma, what is it?" Becky cried in awe.

"What?" Anna replied, distracted by Meyer's voice.

"It's called the Statue of Liberty, child," said an old man standing by the rail. "It was a gift to the people of America from the people of France. It was placed here in the harbor to welcome travelers such as us."

"Anna! Over here," he called as she finally spied him making his way through the crowd toward her.

"Thank God I found you," he said, grabbing her hands.

"I was afraid I wouldn't see you." She tried to ignore the twinge of guilt that had troubled her since succumbing to Meyer's embrace.

"I will pray for your happiness, Anna."

"And I for yours."

"I will never forget you, Anna."

"Nor I you," she said, her heart pounding.

"I must go, Anna. I can't stay. I am supposed to be on the bridge."

She nodded her understanding.

"Wherever life leads, God be with you," he said, squeezing her hands.

"God be with you, too."

"Anna—"

"Go," she interrupted. "Go, before it becomes impossible to say good-bye."

He stood for a moment, desperately wanting to embrace her. As if reading his thoughts, but held back by the curious eyes of her fellow passengers, Anna offered him her hands.

"God love you, Meyer Kramer," she whispered as they clasped each other's hands tightly.

After a moment's hesitation he pulled away and smiled sadly before he turned and walked away.

"It's beautiful," Sheara said. "Momma, isn't she beautiful?"

Anna nodded, her heart too full to speak. *Oh, God, we are in America!* she thought, her attention slowly returning to the scene surrounding her. She and her children had actually arrived in the New World. It was like being born all over again. "Thank you, dear God," she cried aloud. The *Darmstadt* slowly drifted past Liberty Island, on which the statue stood, and they heard the rattling thunder of the anchor chains as the old ship came to a stop. A strange silence settled over them as another island appeared as if from nowhere. Its buildings resembled a fortress, giving it a forbidding air. The immigrants watched as two wooden ferries pulled away from their moorings on the second island, about a quarter of a mile away, and headed across the water toward the ship.

"The Island of Tears!" someone hissed.

Anna looked at the faces of those around her. Their joy seemed to have evaporated at the sight of the turreted, rectangular structures.

"What is that place?" she asked the old man. "Why do they call it the Island of Tears?"

"Its name is Ellis Island," the man said. "Everyone coming to America must first go there, so that the authorities can make sure they are healthy, that they have the necessary papers, that there is someone to meet them. Sometimes they turn people away. That is why they call it the Island of Tears."

"Ellis Island," Anna said. "I remember now. My husband wrote to me about it. He said it was a hateful place."

"They won't send us back, will they?" Becky asked.

"No, no, child," the man said kindly. "They won't send you back."

Sheara and Becky smiled, reassured. But Anna, like the hundreds of other immigrants standing on deck looking at the island, was less confident. What could one do if they turned you away? To whom could you appeal?

"It will take forever for all the people on this ship to get to that island on those little boats," Becky said as the ferries drew close.

"The boats are only for us," someone said bitterly. "The third-class passengers. We're the only ones who have to go to the Island of Tears."

Anna glanced up and saw that the first- and second-class passengers were now clustered at the rails, gawking down at them as they always did whenever they were on deck. She concealed her anger by telling the girls they would have to go downstairs now and get their belongings together.

There was no need for haste. It was a long time before the immigrants, carrying everything they owned, were permitted to inch their way toward the gangways. Along the deck, crewmen with megaphones shouted instructions.

"Everyone must have a landing card to leave the ship! Make sure your landing card is attached to your outer clothing!"

The landing cards identified the immigrants by their own name, by the name of the ship that had brought them to America, and by their language. Anna took out the landing cards she had been given when they boarded and tied her card to the front of her own coat, helping Rebecca and Sheara do the same.

"Come, Rachel, let's tie this to your top button," she said, kneeling down to attach her youngest child's landing card. Her eyes blurred with tears as she read the words on it and realized that the formal procedure of processing her children into America had begun.

> APPELAVITCH, Rachel
> *Darmstadt*
> Yiddish

It seemed an eternity before they reached the sloping ramp leading to the ferry for Ellis Island. "Hold tightly to the rail," Anna called out to the girls. "Here we go, Rachel. Hold on to Momma!"

The shuffling procession making its way down the ramp halted every few seconds. Before she stepped off the ramp and onto the ferry, Anna turned once to look back at the towering steel sides of the ship. *There is no return,* she thought, *for me and my children, or their children who will follow. Europe belongs to the past.* She turned her face toward the approaching island, putting the past behind her.

Chapter Five

It took the ferry less than ten minutes to get to Ellis Island. The immigrants filed off and were told to line up in front of a huge red brick building. Officials in uniforms milled around conferring with one another while the immigrants stood waiting in the bitter cold, holding on to their bundles and suitcases and to their children.

"Okay, okay, let's move!" one of the uniformed men shouted in Yiddish, waving the line forward. The immigrants shuffled in the direction he had indicated, entering a large, poorly lighted hall. As Anna looked about, she saw suitcases and trunks lined up in rows against the walls. From the center of the room a long, wide staircase led to another floor.

"You may store your baggage here!" another man in uniform shouted. "You may store your baggage here!" Although he spoke Yiddish, no one moved to turn their baggage over to him.

"Can't we keep our belongings?" someone shouted. "Can't we take them with us?"

"You can if you want to, but it's a real schlepp, I warn you!" the man shouted back. "You either check your belongings now, or you'll have to carry them with you at all times till you leave here!"

"I didn't bring everything I have in the world all this way just to give it to someone else," a voice muttered. "Even if he is Jewish."

Some of the immigrants, including Anna, chose to turn their luggage over to the baggagemen for safekeeping; most did not. Who knew who could be trusted in this strange new world? Now they had to go up the stairway to the next floor, and once again Anna and her children became part of a mob, pushing their way upward a step at a time. Hundreds of immigrants were crammed on the stairway, lugging their bundles and suitcases with them. Tempers flared as people were jostled on the stairs, as suitcases banged shins or jabbed into the ribs or backs of the weary travelers.

There were forty stairs; Anna counted every one of them for it took nearly an hour to get to the top. She was exhausted as she put Rachel down and sat on a step to catch her breath.

"That was worse than boarding the *Darmstadt*," Sheara said.

"Yes, it was," Anna agreed, looking around. They were in what was called the Great Hall. It was the biggest room she had ever seen, and it was packed with people. *There must be over a thousand*, she thought, *perhaps more*. She looked up a the three huge chandeliers that hung from the ceiling, and from them to the balcony that ran along the walls. It, too, was packed with immigrants making their way from one room to another. Above the din Anna thought she could hear the sound of a woman shrieking, somewhere above, in one of the rooms on the balcony. Was someone being sent back to Europe, refused entry? It was a terrifying thought. No wonder they called it the Island of Tears.

"Hurry up and move to the line!" a voice yelled in Yiddish. "Come on, come on, hurry up!"

Anna saw that the throngs of immigrants were being channeled through a maze of aisles formed by rails that led them across the room to inspection stations set up along the west wall. Through the big windows she could see the buildings of Manhattan. So near, she thought—how awful to actually see the promised land and then be told you may not enter it.

Anna held Rachel tightly and nudged the other girls forward, crushed in the lurching press of the crowd around them, toward the first inspection station. The solid, endless noise beat down on them, punctuated by shrill cries, the sound of male voices raised in quick anger, the wails of fretful children, and the barked commands of the immigration personnel.

"How old is the child?" a voice blared in clipped English.

Anna could not see who had asked the question. She was not even sure to whom it had been addressed since she was unable to turn her body to face the speaker.

"Is the child lame?" the same voice demanded impatiently. "You, madam! I am talking to you!"

She managed to turn enough to see a uniformed official glaring at her from the other side of the barricade. She had no idea what he was saying. He tried some Yiddish.

"Der kinder!" he yelled, pointing to Rachel. *"Der kinder!"*

"I don't understand. Are you talking to me?" Anna asked, pointing to herself.

"Yes, yes, I'm talking to you. Why are you carrying the child?"

"Can I be of help here?" a man asked in English as he approached the inspector. He wore a jacket and a tie and a hat with letters HIAS embroidered on it. He said a couple of sentences to the inspector that Anna did not understand, then turned to her and asked in perfect Yiddish, "Why do you carry the child?"

"Why?" Anna shook her head. What a stupid question! "So she won't be crushed in this crowd."

"The inspector asks if she can walk."

"Of course she can walk," Anna said impatiently.

"It would be better if you put her down and let the inspector see," the man said. "Just put her down here, on this side of the rail, so we can see her walk."

As Anna moved to put Rachel down, her daughter tightened her grip on her mother's shoulders, shaking her head.

"Rachel, it's all right. Let me put you down. The nice man wants to see how well you walk."

Rachel clung to Anna tightly, her eyes wide with fear. As Anna tried to loosen her grip, she began to scream. The inspector glared at them both. He took a piece of chalk from his pocket and reached for the lapel on Rachel's coat.

"Wait!" the man with the HIAS cap shouted, snatching Rachel from Anna's arms. Anna froze, then screamed.

"My baby! Give me back my baby!"

The man ignored her, walking a dozen steps carrying the screaming Rachel in his arms, then turned and faced Anna. The crowd watched, silent, astonished. He put the screaming child on the floor, and Anna, realizing what he was doing now, called out to her daughter. Rachel looked up in bewilderment and then ran into her mother's arms. Anna scooped Rachel into the air as dozens of onlookers cheered and applauded. The inspector turned on his heel and walked away without a word.

It took Anna and her children nearly five hours to complete the prescribed medical and legal inspections that morning, an exhausting, frightening, and humiliating experience. Inspectors peered into their ears and eyes, yanking up the eyelid to check for trachoma. Their hair was examined for lice. They were made to open their blouses so that nurses could listen to their hearts and check their lungs for the "Jewish disease"—consumption. They were passed from doctor to doctor, nurse to nurse, and finally past the review board, where their papers were checked. Sharp-eyed men asked Anna questions about where she would live in America, how much money she possessed, her employment status, and her reasons for leaving her native land.

Finally it was over, and Anna and the children were allowed into another large room, one wall of which was completely lined with railway ticket windows. Here, relatives and friends awaited the arriving immigrants. The clamor was overwhelming, a wall of noise, of laughter, of shouts of joy, of tears brought on by the first physical contact of loved ones reunited after years of waiting. All around Anna people were embracing, sobbing, laughing and shouting, clinging to one another. She stood amid this pandemonium, trying to catch a glimpse of her husband. For the first time she realized how alone she was: if Yankle failed to meet her, she simply had no idea where to go or what to do.

"Listen, Momma!" Sheara said. "Someone is calling your name."

Anna heard it, an unfamiliar male voice, calling her name. She began to push through the crowd, holding the children tightly. Her heart was pounding. Then she saw him—an utter stranger. He was tall and bearded, dressed in a black suit and a blue cap with the Hebrew letters for HIAS embroidered on it, like the man who had helped her in the Great Hall.

"I am Anna Engle Appelavitch," she said in a voice that betrayed her fear.

"Do you speak English?" he asked in Yiddish.

"No."

"My name is Avrum Greenstein. I am with the Hebrew Immigrant Aid Society. I'm going to help you meet your husband."

"He was supposed to meet me here. Is something wrong? Is he ill?"

"Your husband is waiting for you in Baltimore. You must go there by train. I have your tickets already."

"Why isn't Yankle here to meet us?"

"It's expensive to come to New York from Baltimore. Your husband would have had to pay for a ticket to New

York, another back. So he asked us to help get you there instead."

Too tired and too disappointed to stop the tears, Anna buried her face in her hands and began to sob.

Avrum Greenstein took her gently by the shoulders. "Anna, you're almost home. Soon you'll be with your husband. Don't begin with tears. Here, blow your nose." He took a handkerchief from his pocket and handed it to her. Hesitating for a moment, she used it and handed it back.

"Feel better?" he said, smiling. "Listen, I'll come with you to the train station, make sure you and the children are safe on board. You'll be able to sleep a few hours, and before you know it, you'll be in Baltimore. Come on now, smile. You've much to be happy about."

Anna smiled feebly. "I know. It's just . . . I don't think I've ever been so tired."

"Here, let me take the child." He lifted Rachel, who was fast asleep against Anna's shoulder.

"A moment, please," Anna said.

"What is it? Is something wrong?" he asked, seeing the look of concern on her face. Becky looked to see what had attracted her mother's attention.

Across the room, Chayides Lubaloff, tears streaming down her face, was talking to a frail, ashen-faced young man.

"Oh, Momma, she's telling him about their baby!" Becky whispered, grabbing Anna's arm.

Anna nodded. They stood silently, watching the heart-breaking conversation they knew must be taking place. Chayides's husband's face was twisted with pain, then he began to cry, clenching his hand into a fist and biting his knuckles in an effort to maintain his composure. Chayides stared silently at him, her eyes haunted. He lifted a hand, shook his head. Then as they fell into a sudden embrace, clinging to one another as they shared their grief. Anna wiped tears from her own eyes as she watched the man lift his right hand from his wife's shoulder and tenderly stroke the back of her head.

"Shall we go?" Avrum Greenstein asked softly.

As he had promised, the kindly man from the Jewish agency accompanied Anna and the girls on the ferry across the harbor to New Jersey. As they made their way across the Hudson River, Anna saw that two more ships had anchored in the harbor, and the ferries were bustling to and fro, taking hundreds more immigrants to Ellis Island.

"It's wonderful that America gives them all a new home," she said.

Greenstein looked out across the choppy water toward Ellis Island and sighed. "I'm afraid it won't continue. There are strong voices calling for an end to open immigration."

"Why? Why would they want to keep people out?"

"Mostly fear."

"What is there to fear from them? From us?"

"If thousands of foreign workers arrive every day, foreigners willing to accept lower wages than American laborers, some are afraid there won't be enough work to go around."

She nodded. "I hadn't thought of that."

"Others say there are too many foreigners here already. They say they don't fit in. They don't believe immigrants will ever become Americans like themselves."

"We will," she said firmly. "My children will all be Americans."

At 5:45 Avrum Greenstein put them on the train for Baltimore. He instructed the porter who helped them find their seats to be sure they disembarked there. Anna and the girls stared in amazement at the porter as he talked to Greenstein. He was *black:* they had never seen a Negro before.

At six precisely the conductor shouted, "All aboard!" and the train lurched and jerked into motion. Anna caught a final glimpse of Avrum Greenstein, raising his hand in farewell. For a moment she recalled her father-in-law's standing on the road, waving good-bye to Anna and the children. *Remember me,* he had shouted. As if she could ever forget.

Then her thoughts drifted to Lieutenant Meyer Kramer, and she saw him reaching up to loosen her hair before he made love to her in the dimly lit cabin aboard the *Darmstadt.* She smiled tremulously, sighed, and closed her eyes.

"Ma'am." The porter was shaking Anna's shoulder gently. "Ma'am, you're in Baltimore."

"What? Where?" Anna sat up, completely disoriented. Rachel had fallen asleep within minutes of their leaving the train depot, and by the time they reached Trenton, the monotonous rhythm of the wheels had seduced all of them into the deepest sleep they had experienced since leaving Oleck-Podlaska.

"I said, you're in Baltimore, ma'am. We're gonna be there in a few minutes."

She could only understand one word. "Bal-ti-more?" she said excitedly, pointing out of the window. "Bal-ti-more?"

"That's right, ma'am. You're in Baltimore. You're home, ma'am."

Anna's heart pounded with excitement as she woke the children and the train slowed to a stop. She could barely manage to put on her coat and help the children with theirs. They stared out of the window, silent with anticipation.

The night air was cold as they gathered their bags and stepped out onto the platform. Anna held Rachel tightly at her shoulder, while Becky and Sheara carried the two old valises as they made their way across the platform.

Then Anna saw her husband standing beneath a post light. He was thinner than she remembered and looked considerably older. Anna stopped in her tracks, tears filling her eyes.

"Yankle?" she whispered as he took off the wide-rimmed felt hat he wore and clutched it nervously.

She was not prepared for the sight that greeted her. He had written to her that his hair had grown thin, but she had never visualized him to be so bald or to look so tired. And while he smiled broadly at the sight of his family, his deep-set eyes were full of sadness.

Becky and Sheara did not recognize their father, but they saw Anna's tears. Then the man standing beneath the light walked forward, tears streaming down his face too, and embraced their mother. The couple clung together wordlessly for several minutes while the children stood silently to one side, waiting, watching.

"Yankle, Yankle," Anna cried, holding her hand to the side of his face. "I can't believe we're really here!"

"You're here, you're here," he said, kissing her, patting her shoulder clumsily.

He released her from his embrace, knelt down, and opened his arms to the children. He enveloped them in hugs, kissing them, saying their names, laughing, crying.

"Rebecca, Sheara, Rachel—little Rachel who I've never seen, look how pretty you are—and now you're here, we're together at last, all of us. Oh, if only you knew how I've been longing for this moment!"

He stood again, embracing Anna, kissing her over and over. For an instant an icy tightness gripped her insides as the smiling image of Meyer Kramer flashed through her mind.

"So, we're all together, we're a family again," he said. "And these are your bags, not so heavy, not so bad. I'll carry them now. Come, come. Your journey is ended. You're home."

The new home was really a second-floor apartment in a three-story row house on High Street, not far from the harbor. The house was clean and warm enough, but terribly crowded with two families sharing the second floor and another two families sharing the third. The entire first floor was occupied by the owner, Mr. Seymore Cohen, and his wife and two children.

Anna and Yakov would share a small bedroom furnished with an old double bed, a rocking chair, a chest of drawers, and a wooden crib that the sisterhood of the Ohev Shalom Synagogue had obtained for Yankle when they learned of Anna's impending arrival with a child and two older girls. The sisterhood also sent a large jar of beet borscht and a loaf of black bread, which the Appelavitches devoured in silence shortly after arriving. There was also a room containing a stove, a sink, a small icebox, a table with four chairs that didn't match, an old piano bench, and two sagging cots for Becky and Sheara. Anna helped Yakov drag the crib into this room. There was no bathroom in the apartment itself, but there was a small room with a toilet and sink at the top of the stairs leading from the first floor, which the four tenant families had to share.

Anna lay in bed and watched as Yakov undressed. Though she guiltily reminded herself he was her husband of twelve years, she thought of the young Jewish-German lieutenant who had taught her so much about love in such a short time.

"It's been so long, Anna," Yakov said as he lay down beside her.

Anna managed a smile, but did not speak.

Yakov reached out and gently pulled his wife closer.

She turned on her side to face him and put her hand on his shoulder. Yakov, excited by her touch, pulled her closer and in the same motion raised her nightgown above her waist.

He reached down, not to caress her, but to see if she was ready for him. "Are you too tired, Anna?"

"No, I'll be all right. I just need a moment."

"I understand. It's been a long time."

Anna closed her eyes and thought of Meyer Kramer. She

could feel his fingertips gently but skillfully caressing her, and as she dreamed of Kramer, Yakov could feel that his wife was now ready for him. A moment later he entered her, and after a minute of thrusting he reached his climax.

Anna stared at the ceiling, tears in her eyes, as he rolled off her.

"It's going to be so wonderful having you here with me," Yakov said tenderly.

"Yes," she whispered.

Chapter Six

Baltimore, February 11, 1911

Dearest Dvoyra,

Thanks be to God! We have arrived! How can I tell you, my dear sister, our excitement on reaching Baltimore? Now you must plan *your* journey, and we will be together here, just as we always dreamed.

The trip was far more difficult than I ever imagined, but we all came through it in good health. I cannot tell you very much about America yet, because we are still resting quietly after the long journey, but Yankle is fine, although he is thin. He works from early morning until evening in a shop where they make men's clothes. It is owned by a Jewish man from Germany named Rosenberg. Yankle says he will bring home work that I can do. In this way I can work here while he works at the shop, and between us we can earn more wages. Who knows, my dear sister? Maybe we will grow rich in America!

The children are healthy. They have all grown since you last saw them. They were all good travelers, and they will soon be good Americans. Dvoyra, I will count the days until you, too, are here. Please promise me that you will come soon. You must come, Dvoyra.

Give all our love to everyone, and let Momma and Poppa Appelavitch know that I am with Yankle, and that he is well. Also tell Momma it is a blessing that we are here, and that she should understand it will be a blessing for you to come too. I can't wait until I hear from you.

Love,
Anna

Anna sealed the letter in an envelope and ran her hand gently over its surface. She sighed and looked around at her new home.

Glad as she was to be in America, Anna was dismayed by the Spartan living conditions on High Street, though she said nothing about her feelings to her husband when he left for work. She pictured the seemingly endless row of identical houses and wondered if all of them were as crowded as this one, and if the women who lived in them felt the same unnerving sense of confinement. *It's too small for five of us*, she thought.

She shook herself into action, for the children were beginning to stir. To her dismay she discovered there was very little food in the kitchen. The icebox contained only half a loaf of black bread and a jar of herring. She opened the door of the cupboard hanging on the wall over the stove. It contained a collection of unmatched dishes, cups, saucers, a few grimy glasses. On the top shelf she found a box of tea and a bowl half-filled with sunflower seeds. She sighed and shook her head.

After the children had picked at the makeshift meal, they asked if they could go outside to play. They told her they had seen a playground through the window in the bathroom. It was actually a vacant lot that had been converted to a neighborhood play area. After she had looked for herself and had seen the scores of children playing there, Anna told them they could go. They pushed back their chairs and bolted from the table, running to get their coats, shouting happily as they ran down the wooden stairs.

"Watch after Rachel!" Anna shouted as the door banged behind them, and she was alone. *Oh, God, please don't let me be disappointed in America,* she prayed. She stood silent in the center of the room, the sense of isolation swamping her. Then without warning the silence was ruptured by the sound of someone's pounding on the door.

Tightening the belt of her robe, Anna pulled open the door to find a tall, heavyset, dour-looking woman staring down at her.

"Good morning," Anna said in Yiddish, smiling nervously.

The woman looked at Anna for a moment, then pushed past her into the apartment. Swallowing hard to suppress her fear, Anna pulled her robe more tightly around her. "Is something wrong?"

"You are the wife of Yakov Appelavitch?" the woman asked in crude Yiddish. She appeared to be in her middle or late fifties, her skin lined with tiny reddish-blue veins and peppered with ugly freckles. Her eyes were puffy, and her rust-colored hair hung down in ringlets that would have looked comical but for the harsh expression on her face. Hostility radiated from her like heat.

"I am Anna Appelavitch."

"I'll speak frankly, Mrs. Appelavitch, it's always the best way. It's the noise. I told your husband it would never work. I told him we didn't want noisy people living above us. He said not to worry, he'd keep the children quiet. Well. We see what that was worth, don't we?"

"I'm sorry, I don't understand. Who are you?"

"Who am I? I'm Ida Cohen, that's who I am. My husband and I own this house. And we don't want a bunch of wild children running around over our heads."

"My children aren't wild. They—"

"Listen, Mrs. Appelavitch. I'll get right to the point. I think you and your family better look for somwhere else to live."

Anna felt as if she had been punched in the pit of her stomach. She stared at Mrs. Cohen in disbelief.

"But what have we done?" she protested. "My children just went out to play."

"I know that," Mrs. Cohen said sarcastically. "I heard them leave. A deaf man would have heard them leave. And I'm not deaf, Mrs. Appelavitch. I heard them scraping their chairs on the floor, running across the room, banging down the stairs, slamming the door. I can't have a racket like that over my head, I'll go crazy."

"We didn't know. We only just got here. They're only children, Mrs. Cohen, please, give them a chance. I'll make them take off their shoes when they come in. I'll tell them to talk quietly in the apartment. We've never lived in a house with other families before."

"There's plenty would be glad to take your place," Mrs. Cohen said, glaring at her. "Quiet people, with no children. I should have known better than to let your husband talk me into renting to a family with three children. I should have known."

"Please, be patient with us, Mrs. Cohen," Anna pleaded. "If you feel we're making too much noise up here, just let me know."

"Oh, I'll let you know all right, Mrs. Appelavitch. I'll let you know. If I hear the sort of commotion up here I heard this morning, I'll bang on the ceiling with a broom handle till the windows rattle!"

Without another word she stomped out of the room, slamming the door behind her.

Stunned, Anna stood for several moments staring at the door. As the momentary shock turned to anger, she decided to get out of the apartment and into the brisk fresh air of the Baltimore morning in order to think.

She dressed quickly, wincing each time the floor creaked as she walked or shifted her weight. She pictured Mrs. Cohen sitting in a chair, staring at the ceiling and waiting for the first tiny sound from the apartment above.

As she pulled open the door to step into the hallway, she nearly collided with a short, gray-haired woman about her mother's age.

"You must be Yakov Appelavitch's wife," the woman said. "I'm Rifka Moscowitz. I live upstairs, and I was coming down to say good morning and welcome. I think I've been looking forward to your getting here almost as much as your husband has."

"I'm happy to meet you, Mrs. Moscowitz."

"Are you all right, Mrs. Appelavitch? You look so very pale."

"No," Anna said hastily. "I'm fine. Really. I think perhaps I haven't quite adjusted to being here yet. Come inside please. Sit down, won't you?"

"The old lady give you a hard time?" Mrs. Moscowitz asked as she sat down at the table. "I heard her lecturing you."

Anna nodded. "She upset me. I will not make my children sit in chairs all day without moving."

"That woman! Hmph! Well," Mrs. Moscowitz said, rubbing her chin furiously, "you just send them up to me to play during the day, my dear. I'd love to have them."

"Oh, I don't know what to say. It's so kind of you—"

"It's nothing. That woman . . ." She rubbed her chin again with her right hand, a habit Anna would become very familiar with. "To be so rude to you, and on your first morning here. It's terrible, that's what it is."

"Mrs. Moscowitz, I'm so happy we met. I was beginning to feel very sorry for myself."

"Now, now, there's nothing for you to feel badly about. Things will get better, you'll see. My late husband used to say, 'It's not an easy place to live, America, no. But where, I ask you, is it easy?' You'll see, Mrs. Appelavitch, things will get better."

"Please call me Anna."

"Only if you agree to call me Rifka. Is it a deal?" Mrs. Moscowitz extended her hand.

"I'm sorry, I don't—"

"We make a deal, you and me. I'll call you Anna, you'll call me Rifka. We shake and make a deal."

"Ah . . . a bargain!" Anna laughed as she took hold of the older woman's hand. "Yes, we make a deal."

"Now, you were going out?"

"Yes, but can you tell me where I can find a market nearby?"

"Better than that, I'll take you myself. Fink's Grocery is just around the corner. I'll introduce you. Fink's a good man. He'll look out for you. Put your coat on while I go get mine. We'll take a little walk together."

"I'd like to stop by the playground and see that the girls are all right."

"Why not? I'm dying to meet your kids."

They collected the girls at the playground and spent the next couple of hours walking through the neighborhood.

The streets were a maze of red brick walls, punctuated by the ever-present white marble four-step stoops that were lined up with military precision as far as the eye could see.

Every three or four blocks they came upon small corner grocery stores, and on one corner Rifka pointed out a place called Reid's Drug Store.

"Let's go in. It'll be my treat. You kids haven't tasted a coddie yet," she said.

Anna and the children stared curiously at the soda fountain before the girls eagerly climbed up on the stools that lined the counter. They waited with anticipation as Rifka ordered each of them a small fried codfish cake on a saltine cracker and a mug of root beer.

"It's a Baltimore special," she said. "You can't find them anywhere else and they are absolutely delicious." They had, indeed, never tasted anything quite like them before, and the coddies were the first really appetizing food they had tasted since arriving in America.

Later, Rifka took them by the harbor, which was rimmed with factories and warehouses, and explained that thousands of people worked in the area.

"There is one of the biggest employers in Baltimore," she said, pointing to the huge McCormick Spice Factory.

"What smells so good, Momma?" Sheara asked.

"Vanilla," Rifka answered before Anna could respond. "They make vanilla extract there."

They moved on to Fink's Grocery, and the unfamiliar mingled aromas of pickles, herring, cheese, and fresh vegetables assailed Anna's senses as she walked into the store.

Fink's Grocery was long and narrow, and the shelves on the wall behind the counter opposite the entrance were lined with the largest assortment of canned and packaged goods Anna had ever seen. It was nothing like the squalid shops in the market in Oleck-Podlaska.

Mr. Fink himself was standing behind the meat and fish counter at the rear of the store, sawing bloodred cutlets from a loin of lamb. Wooden buckets three feet high lined the front of the counter. Some were filled with kosher pickles and others with green tomatoes, and one with pieces of mackerel floating in a pungent salt brine. Baskets of fresh produce sat in a two-tiered bin near the huge plate-glass window at the front of the store. The wooden floors were swept clean, although Anna noticed the sawdust on the floor under the produce bin and behind the meat counter, thrown there, she assumed, to absorb the dripping water from the melting ice.

"Fink feeds half the Jews in Baltimore," Rifka said loudly enough for the round-faced proprietor to hear.

"Rifka, what did I do to deserve you so early in the day?" he lamented, smiling as he came out from behind the counter. "Don't I wish I really did feed half the Jews in Baltimore! What a rich man I'd be!"

"You're rich enough already," Rifka said briskly, "feeding

half the Jews on High Street." She beckoned Anna to come closer. "Max, this is my good friend and new neighbor, Anna Appelavitch. She just came over, got in last night, a real greenhorn. Her husband is Yakov Appelavitch. They live in the apartment below us."

"Such luck." He smiled. "To live in the Cohen house. You like it there?"

"Max, Max, don't tease the child!" Rifka said.

"All right," the shop owner said, unabashed. "You listen to me, Anna. Cohen, he's a regular guy. But that wife of his, she's a real pistol."

"A pistol?"

"Take no notice of him, Anna," Rifka said. "He's just saying he doesn't like her any more than anyone else does."

"And what have we here?" Fink bent down until his face was level with Rachel's. "What's your name, my little beauty?"

"This is Rachel," Anna said. "And these are my other daughters, Rebecca and Sheara."

Max Fink eagerly shook the girls' hands. He delved into a glass jar and gave each of them a little stick of rock candy. "To welcome you to Baltimore," he said, smiling, "and to hope you'll be happy here."

"Look at him, the ambassador," Rifka said, patting Max on the back. Then her voice became businesslike. "Max, Anna needs food in the house. Her husband is a hardworking man. You can rely on him to pay his bills. I'm going to help Anna shop for what she needs. And you'll put it on the book, yes?"

"Rifka Moscowitz says I put Anna Appelavitch on the book, I put her on the book." He threw up his hands in a gesture of mock helplessness. "Who am I to argue? Do I own the place?"

"Tsk, tsk, man, out of the way," Rifka said, pushing past him. "Come, Anna, let's shop!"

Half an hour later, walking back to the apartment with a bulging bag of groceries, her face flushed with happiness, Anna asked Rifka how Mr. Fink could give so much food to a stranger and not take any money.

"Pooh, its not such a big mitzvah," Rifka told her. "Look, child, instead of selling you a loaf of bread and whatever else you could have brought with the few cents you have to spend, he let you have what you really need. He makes a bigger sale, and you wind up with what you want. Fink knows he will get paid when Yakov gets paid. This way everybody's happy, except maybe your Yakov."

Rifka's mischievous grin was infectious, and for the first time since she had arrived in America, Anna found herself laughing out loud.

Dinner, thanks to Rifka and Mr. Fink, was almost festive. Anna served cold beet borscht and a main course of thick chunks of well-done beef brisket, boiled potatoes, and fresh Russian black bread. The drab little apartment began to take on the real feel of home.

Yakov was anything but unhappy about her obtaining credit from Fink's; in fact, he was astonished. "You got all this food on credit?"

"Mr. Fink wrote my name on the top of a page in a book he keeps somewhere under the counter. He says I am 'on the book' now. We can shop there when we are low on money and pay him when you get paid. From what Rifka says, I think most of his customers are on the book."

"I know they are," Yakov said. "I used to see housewives buying on the book all the time. I used to wish I could."

"Why didn't you?"

"I never had the nerve to ask," he said sheepishly. "I was too embarrassed."

Anna looked at her husband, puzzled by his response. Because the children were at the table, however, she said nothing.

Following dinner, she sent the girls up to the Moscowitz apartment. She did not want them to hear about her encounter with Mrs. Cohen. Yakov listened intently as she described what had happened.

"I promised her we'd be quiet," he said without looking up from the table. "I said it wouldn't be a problem."

"Yankle, they're children! They can't live in silence. Neither can I!"

"Listen to me, Anna," he said firmly, raising his eyes to meet hers. "I only earn about nine dollars a week, sometimes ten. I had to borrow money for the train tickets to bring you and the girls here from New York. I have to work almost two weeks just to pay the rent, and this is the cheapest apartment I could find. Now I owe Fink three dollars for the food you bought. We have to make ends meet, whether we like it or not. If that means we have to be quiet up here, you'll have to keep quiet. I don't want any trouble with the Cohens!"

She was shocked at his tone. It was the first time he had ever raised his voice to her. "Yankle, Yankle, what are you saying? Did we come all the way to America to be afraid to walk around in our own home?"

"We live in the Cohens' house. They make the rules."

"Then let us find somewhere else to live where the rules are more reasonable!" Anna said spiritedly. "I want our home to be full of happiness, Yankle. I want to be able to dance around the room with Rachel in my arms. We didn't have very much in Oleck-Podlaska, but at least we had happiness, we had singing, dancing."

"Couldn't you just try to keep the children from running around the apartment?" he asked wearily, resting his head in the palm of his hand. "Is that too much to ask?"

"Yankle, what's come over you? Are you afraid of them?"

He leaned back in the chair and closed his eyes. She sensed that he was near tears and moved quickly to his side, kneeling down beside him.

"Don't fight me, Anna. I'm so very tired."

"I'm sorry, Yankle. I didn't mean to argue with you. Why don't you lie down for a little while and rest."

"Just let me sit here for a few minutes and rest my eyes," he replied wearily.

Anna left him sitting there and quietly walked into the bedroom to be alone. Sitting on the edge of the bed, she lowered her head into her hand and slowly rocked back and forth while she collected her thoughts.

What am I to do? Nothing is as I dreamed. Not this city. Not my home and, she thought, squeezing her eyes shut as though to confine her infidelity, *not my husband.* Then unbidden, she thought of Meyer Kramer and embraced her body with her own arms and choked back the tears.

Chapter Seven

The following morning Anna enrolled Becky and Sheara in the Calvert Elementary School, where they were placed in an Americanization program with other immigrant children recently arrived in Baltimore. The school was located in a congested business area near High Street.

"The children here are speaking Yiddish," Sheara observed as Anna accompanied her and Becky up the white marble steps in front of the school.

"Do you feel better?" Anna asked.

Becky smiled. "I thought we would be the only ones who couldn't speak English."

"Becky, there is an entire generation of children here in America who must now learn to read and speak English for the first time. You and Sheara will have lots of company."

That night Yakov returned home from work carrying a sewing machine. It was a loan from Mr. Rosenberg, he told Anna excitedly, explaining that she could finish the garments he worked on during the day.

"I could turn out twice as much if you did the finishing, Anna. I get paid for each piece of work I complete. With you helping me, I could make twelve, maybe fourteen dollars a week. That's as much as they earn in New York!"

"Wonderful, Yankle, wonderful!" she said, sharing his excitement. After supper she hurried upstairs to tell Rifka the good news. To her surprise, her neighbor did not seem pleased for her.

"But don't you see?" Anna said. "We'll earn much more money this way!"

"Is that what you want, Anna? Money?"

"What do you mean?"

"Everyone wants to make more money," Rifka sighed. "Ask yourself, do you want to give up your life for it? I'm an old woman, I've seen it happen too many times, families turning their homes into factories. First the wives take in work. Later they give work to the children too. I know homes where the entire family spends all its waking hours at the sewing machine. What kind of life is that?"

"No, no, you don't understand. It would only be temporary."

"It doesn't always work out that way, Anna."

The following evening Yakov returned home with thirty-two unfinished vests. His eyes sparkled as he explained to Anna how to sew buttonholes on the vests.

"Anna, Mr. Rosenberg will pay two and a half cents a vest for finishing buttonholes. You should be able to do four vests an hour. You could earn eighty cents, maybe even a dollar a day, right here in our kitchen. Think of it, Anna, an extra four or five dollars a week!"

"Four or five dollars!" Anna exclaimed. It was a fortune, half of what Yankle was earning now. By the time they went to bed that night, Anna had mastered the technique of buttonholing, practicing on a yard of waste fabric. She fell asleep thinking of the new clothes she would be able to buy for the children with the extra money they would make.

As soon as she had gotten Becky and Sheara off to school the following morning, and settled Rachel down to play with an old stuffed doll, Anna sat down at the sewing machine. She completed the buttonholes on the first vest in well under fifteen minutes and smiled as she held up the garment to inspect her work.

"Perfect!" she said out loud. By noon she had completed fifteen vests. Her eyes were beginning to smart, and her back was aching horribly. She decided to do just one more garment before taking a break. She was finishing the third buttonhole of the sixteenth vest when the muscles of her upper back cramped, sending a bolt of pain from her spine across her right shoulder blade. Anna jumped in her chair, and as she did, the steel needle ran through the tip of her forefinger. She jerked her hand back in pain, and her injured finger ran across the fabric, leaving a smear of blood perhaps a quarter of an inch in length.

Anna did not see the stain at first. She sat with her eyes squeezed shut, sucking on the injured finger. When she opened them, the first thing she saw was the narrow bloodstain on the tan fabric.

"Oh, why didn't I stop to rest five minutes earlier?" she chided herself, fighting back tears. She stood up. Her back was a solid mass of pain, and her finger was throbbing wildly. She examined the small gash in the flesh at the very tip; the needle had split part of the nail away from the skin. She squeezed the finger and a surge of blood emerged. She put her finger in her mouth again and ran upstairs to find Rifka Moscowitz.

"I'm so angry with myself," Anna said as Rifka bandaged the finger. "How could I be so clumsy?"

"Rain falls, accidents happen," Rifka replied.

"I was doing so well. I'd already made forty cents. I was finishing four vests an hour, and now I'll be lucky if I can do three."

"Three days you're here, and already you're chained to a sewing machine," Rifka chided her. "That's why you came to America?"

"I'm doing it to help Yankle, Rifka. There's nothing wrong with that, is there?"

"You've only been doing it for a few hours, child. Let's see how you feel after four days. Or four weeks."

"If it gets too hard, I'll stop."

"They all say that. At first. But you'll find within a month you'll be depending on whatever extra money you can earn at the machine. It will not be so easy to stop."

The work went much more slowly in the afternoon. By three o'clock Anna had completed twenty-three vests. Her back was stiff and sore now, and her heavily bandaged finger throbbed painfully. Soon Becky and Sheara would be home from school. Anna had wanted to finish the vests before starting to prepare dinner, but she knew she had at least three more hours of work to do, not counting the time she would lose when the girls came home. She decided not to even think about what it would be like to spend all the next day at the sewing machine.

When she heard their footsteps on the stairs, she got up to greet her daughters. Becky's eyes widened when she saw her mother's bandaged finger.

"Momma, what happened to your hand?" she cried.

"It's nothing, a silly accident." Anna hugged and kissed her daughters. "How was school today?"

"It was good," Becky said.

"We learned 'The Star-Spangled Banner,'" Sheara added.

"It's America's most popular military song," Becky told her mother. "The teacher says it was written right here in Baltimore, at a place called Fort McHenry."

"Then you must sing it for me." Anna smiled, trying to ignore her discomfort.

With that brief word of encouragement Becky and Sheara broke into the first stanza of Francis Scott Key's hundred-year-old poem. Anna watched and listened to her daughters singing the strange words she did not understand. When they were finished, Anna applauded but the sharp movement of her hands increased her pain.

"Wonderful, children, wonderful! Now, I must get back to my work."

"Can we help, Momma?" Sheara asked.

"Can we sew too?" Becky said, kneeling down to play with Rachel.

"No, but there are lots of other things you can do," Anna told them. "Sheara, I want you to iron Poppa's shirts. Becky, fold the wash and put everything away."

By four o'clock Anna was busy at the sewing machine and the girls at their chores. "Mind Poppa's collars, Sheara!" Anna called over her shoulder. "Mind Poppa's collars."

It was nearly seven o'clock before Yakov returned home from work. The minute he walked through the door, Anna could see that something was wrong. She went to her husband and kissed him on the cheek.

"Yankle, are you all right? You look upset."

"I'm fine, Anna," he muttered wearily, taking off his coat. "Don't fuss, now. Just let me sit down and look at the paper."

She nodded and took his coat from him. Sheara, who had stopped ironing, had watched the exchange between her parents. She, too, could see that something was amiss. She approached her father and kissed him, though he barely acknowledged her. Becky and Rachel had come in from the bedroom to greet him, but stopped when they saw how indifferently he accepted Sheara's kiss.

"Hello, Poppa," Becky said hesitantly.

"Hello, Rebecca," Yakov said, hardly glancing up to look at his daughter. Becky looked at her sisters, and the three girls went quietly into the bedroom.

"Yankle, what's wrong?" Anna whispered. "Can't you even kiss the children when they've been waiting for you to come home?"

He sighed deeply and laid down the paper, his expression a mixture of exasperation and self-pity. "I've got more on my mind than kissing the children, Anna," he said wearily. "I almost lost my job today."

Anna felt the color drain from her face, and she sat down to brace herself for bad news. "I don't understand. You say you almost lost your job. Does that mean you still have it?"

He sighed again. "Yes, I still have it. In a manner of speaking."

"What do you mean?"

"When I got to work this morning, Mr. Rosenberg called me into the back room. He said the large clothing stores told him they would not be buying from our shop anymore. They said they can get the same goods cheaper elsewhere. Mr. Rosenberg had already fired three of the younger men before I arrived."

"Go on."

"He told me he'd promised the big stores finished work at cheaper prices than our competition."

"So they will continue to buy from Rosenberg?"

"Yes, they will continue to buy from Rosenberg. But—"

"But what?"

"Anna," Yakov said patiently, "Mr. Rosenberg said he could only keep me on, and not reduce my wages, if I could produce more work." He stared down at the tabletop, avoiding her eyes.

Anna drew in a deep breath. "How much more work?"

He bit his lips as he looked up at her, tears in his eyes. "He says he'll let me stay on if I include the work you do at home."

Anna could feel the strong throb of her heart in her chest, the matching throb of pain in her hand. Her lips trembled as Rosenberg's proposal became clear to her.

"You mean we will be paid nothing for the work I do?" she cried.

"He says he can't meet the lower prices demanded by the stores any other way. Maybe it will only be temporary. I suppose I can be grateful he's keeping me on at all."

"Grateful!" Anna exclaimed angrily.

Then Yakov noticed her bandaged finger for the first time. "Anna, what happened to your hand?"

"I ran the needle through the tip of my finger," she said quietly.

"Oh, God. Did you get the vests finished?"

"Yankle, I just told you I ran the needle through my finger, and all you can ask is whether I finished the work?"

"I'm sorry, Anna. I'm sorry about your finger, but I must have those vests back in the shop tomorrow!" he said, his voice rising. "Don't you understand? I must! Now, did you finish?"

"No!" she cried angrily. "No, I didn't finish! I've still got at least two hours more work to do!" Yakov jumped to his feet bringing his hands to the side of his head in frustration.

"I couldn't work as fast after I hurt my hand. I'll finish the vests after dinner."

"Oh, Anna, Anna, I'm sorry, I'm sorry," Yakov said weakly. "I shouldn't have yelled at you. But Mr. Rosenberg has to deliver thirty-two suits with vests tomorrow, and we've got to have them ready when I go to work."

Anna felt a wave of dread course through her body as she suddenly remembered the bloodstained vest.

"Yankle," she began hesitantly. "I don't think that will be possible."

"Why not?" He frowned. "You said you'd be able to."

"One got . . . soiled, Yankle."

"Soiled?" he echoed, his voice growing loud again. "What do you mean . . . soiled?"

"I bled on the vest when I hurt my finger. It's only a small—"

He turned white. "Let me see the vest!" he hissed.

Anna pulled the tan garment from the pile of finished work she had stacked on a nearby chair. Her hand shook as she held it out to him.

"This is terrible," he whispered. "Terrible."

"It was an accident, Yankle. Surely Mr. Rosenberg will understand?"

"And the customer? You think he'll understand too? He may not even take the suit at all."

"So Mr. Rosenberg will have you make another vest. It's not the end of the world."

"You just don't understand, do you?" he shouted. "Don't you realize this could cost me my job? Don't you understand there are dozens of men who'd be happy to take my place, Anna, men with wives who help them instead of making careless mistakes!"

"I didn't do it on purpose!" she shouted back, shocked to

hear her voice raised in anger, but somehow she couldn't stop herself.

"You should be grateful! He loaned us the machine! He's doing us a favor by letting you help me!"

"A favor? I've worked at that machine all day. As soon as we're through eating dinner, I'll be back over it again, even though my arm is throbbing with pain and my back is stiff as a board. For this, and for my work, you tell me we'll be paid nothing—and now you want me to believe Mr. Rosenberg is doing us a favor?"

"You'd prefer I lost my job?"

"Yankle, he's taking advantage of you!" she cried, forcing herself to lower her voice.

"Nobody takes advantage of me!" He continued to yell. "Nobody!"

"You tell him he has to pay for the work I do or you'll find a job elsewhere!"

"Are you crazy, Anna? He'd let me go in a minute, then give the machine to someone else to take home."

"He can't expect me to work all day for nothing, Yankle. He can't!"

"It's not for nothing! You're helping me to do my job!"

Their argument was suddenly interrupted by the sound of Mrs. Cohen pounding furiously on her ceiling. The noise brought the frightened girls running into the room.

"What is it, Momma? What's happening?" Becky cried. Her eyes were wet with tears, as were Sheara's. Anna realized the children had been listening to the argument. She looked at Yakov, who was staring helplessly at the floor as the angry pounding continued.

Anger choked Anna. *That woman!* she thought. She jerked open the door and ran down the stairs to the Cohen apartment and began beating on the door with the palm of her hand. Mrs. Cohen opened the door, her face slack with astonishment.

"Stop pounding on the ceiling, do you hear me?" Anna ordered, waving her bandaged finger in front of the startled woman's face. "Stop it this minute!"

"Mrs. Appelavitch, do you realize how much noise you were making up there?" Mrs. Cohen asked coldly, regaining her composure.

"My husband and I were discussing a problem. We were—"

"Yelling, Mrs. Appelavitch," Mrs. Cohen broke in, her

face haughty. "You were both yelling. I've said it before and I'll say it again, I won't have yelling over my head, and that's final!"

"I don't care what you want!" Anna snapped back. "Don't you dare terrify my children again by pounding on the ceiling like that, do you hear me?"

"I'm sorry if the children were frightened, Mrs. Appelavitch," Mrs. Cohen said frostily. "But you brought it on yourselves. You can't say I didn't warn you. I think all things considered, the sooner you find yourself somewhere else to live, the better!"

"I don't plan to live here any longer than is absolutely necessary, Mrs. Cohen," Anna said levelly. "But as long as you are taking our money, let us understand each other. If you have something to say to me, come and knock on my door like a *mensch,* and we'll talk. If an apology is due, I'll apologize. But no more of this warfare, Mrs. Cohen, please!"

Ida Cohen said nothing, but animosity lit her eyes like a coal fire. Anna turned and walked briskly back upstairs. She heard the landlady vent her feelings by slamming the door of her apartment.

Following a tense and silent dinner, Anna returned to the sewing machine. She worked quickly and neatly, occasionally lifting her eyes to glance at Yakov, who was sitting across the room, his eyes fixed on the *Daily Forward.* She knew he wasn't really reading the newspaper, which he held before him like a shield.

It was nearly ten-thirty before she finished. Wordlessly she prepared for bed. Ten minutes after she retired, Yakov put down his paper and came into the bedroom. He approached her side of the bed as if to speak to her, but Anna pretended to be asleep. She heard him walk to the rocking chair and sit down. After a while he put his head in his hands. Her heart went out to him, but something held her back.

"I'm sorry," she heard him whisper, to her or himself or both of them. "I'm sorry, I'm sorry."

"You want my advice? Tell your husband to tell this Rosenberg he can have his machine back, that Anna Appelavitch doesn't work for nothing," Rifka Moscowitz said the next day when Anna told her what Yakov's employer had proposed.

"Yankle would never do that," Anna said, biting her lip. "He is afraid he might lose his job."

"I doubt he would lose his job," Rifka said. "Rosenberg isn't doing him a favor by keeping him on. Yankle is a hardworking, no-nonsense employee, and workers like that aren't so easy to find. But he has to stand up for himself. He has to go to Rosenberg and demand fair treatment."

Anna sighed. "I know what you're saying is right, Rifka. I don't know if we can risk it."

"I can't tell you what to do, you have to make up your own mind. But if you let Rosenberg exploit you now, he will do it again. And next time it will be worse."

All the rest of that day Anna thought of Rifka's advice. By the time Yakov got home that evening, she had decided that she would insist on being paid, although she dreaded the argument they would have if Yakov disagreed with her decision.

She was setting the table for dinner when she heard his footsteps on the stairs. She turned to face the door, brushing back her hair with her fingertips as he came in. To her astonishment he was carrying a big bundle of unfinished vests.

"Well," he said, putting them down, "it looks like you're going to be busy, Anna."

"Yankle," she said, her heart like lead in her chest, "I can't . . ." She shook her head in dismayed confusion. "I won't work for noth—"

She stopped in mid-sentence; her husband was grinning at her. "What is it?"

"He'll pay, Anna!" he exclaimed, embracing her. He danced her a few steps around the room. "He'll pay, he'll pay, he'll pay."

"Yankle, what happened? What made him change his mind?"

"Me!" Yankle said, tapping his chest with his thumb. "I told him I couldn't ask you to work for nothing. I said before I'd do that, I'd quit."

"You told him that, Yankle?"

"I thought about it last night, after you went to sleep. I was thinking about your telling off Mrs. Cohen last night. I thought, if you can do that, I can face Rosenberg. So I told him."

"What did he say?"

"Anna, I couldn't believe it. He went white. He said I should think it over and not do anything hasty."

"And he said he'd pay for my work?"

"Yes, yes, even though it would cost him money from his own pocket, he said. He looked at all the vests, and he said, 'Yakov, this is fine work your wife does.'"

"What about the one with the bloodstain?"

"Nothing about the one with the bloodstain. I'm telling you, Anna, he was a different man."

After dinner Anna called on Rifka to tell her the good news, repeating what her husband had told her about Rosenberg.

Rifka looked dubious. "Rosenberg's no different, Anna. That type never changes. Know what I think? I think he was afraid you and your husband were going to sell your work directly to the stores without him."

"Why on earth would he think that?" Anna laughed at such a preposterous notion.

"Anna, all it takes to be a contract garment-maker is a sewing machine and someone who knows how to use it. You two don't need Rosenberg half as much as he needs you. He knows you could produce for the stores just as easily as for him. My guess is, when Yankle came in and threatened to quit, he jumped to the conclusion that Yankle already had such a plan in mind."

"But we couldn't think of starting our own business." Anna smiled. "We have nothing."

Rifka grinned. "You know that, and I know that. But Rosenberg doesn't know it, not for sure anyway. Maybe you can turn that fact to your own advantage."

"How do you mean?"

"Tell him you're not satisfied with the wage he's paying you. He can pay a lot more than two and a half cents a vest and still make a handsome profit."

Anna shook her head. "Rifka, Rifka, yesterday we were worried that Mr. Rosenberg wasn't going to pay us anything. Now you're suggesting we tell him he's not paying enough?"

"Strike while the iron is hot," the older woman advised. "It's not as if he can't afford it—he's making a good profit. If he wasn't, he wouldn't have reacted the way he did. Another few cents for each finished suit wouldn't hurt Rosenberg one little bit."

The more Anna sewed the next day, the more she thought about what Rifka had said. Finally she decided her friend was right. Two and a half cents a vest was not enough. She would tell Yankle so tonight.

Chapter Eight

April 4, 1911

Dearest Anna,

I was thrilled to receive your letter and to know you are with Yankle in America. Please write often, as I will always want to hear about you and the children and life in America. Momma and Esther are well, and so are the Appelavitches. Everyone sends their love.

You know, dear sister, how much I love you, so I hope you will understand how difficult it is for me to write what follows.

Immediately after you left for America, I met a very fine man from Oleck-Podlaska. He is Berl Hoffman, the son of Isaiah Hoffman, whom I believe you know. We were married three weeks after he asked for my hand, and we now live here with his family.

Berl believes strongly that his place is here in Poland with his family. He will not even consider emigrating to America. So I have given up my steamship ticket.

Berl is a good man, Anna, and he will be a good husband to me. I would be completely happy were it not for the fact that my heart is not here in Oleck-Podlaska, but in America, with you and your children.

I am not altogether sure I could explain to myself, let alone to you, the chain of events that brought about our marriage and resulted in my giving up our dream of being together in America. I want so much to be happy, and to make Berl happy, but it is hard when all I can think about is America, and the fact that you are living there, so far away from me and Oleck-Podlaska.

I do not want my first letter to you in America to make you sad, Anna. I shall try to write about Berl and our new home in future letters. I know you will understand my obligation is now to him and to making him happy. Already he has asked me to give my word that I will not leave him to go to America, and I have done so. All the same, my thoughts and dreams have been with you and the children since you left. They will always be with you, my dearest Anna. Please give my love to Yankle and hug and kiss the children for me. I think of all of you every day. Write again soon. Please, please write again soon.

> Your loving sister,
> Dvoyra

Although it was barely the first week of June, the breeze felt hot and humid as it gently blew through the open bedroom window. The apartment was quiet. Rachel had gone upstairs to visit Rifka, as she did most days. Rifka adored the child and looked forward to Rachel's knock on the door almost as much as Rachel enjoyed visiting her.

Anna lay on the bed with a damp cloth over her eyes. Beside her lay the letter, which had arrived that morning, bringing her the news that Dvoyra was not coming to America after all. *I would never have come here if I had known things were going to turn out this way,* she thought. *Now I am truly alone.* She knew she must get on with her work, but she needed a quiet moment to rest, to gather her strength and courage. Bad news never traveled alone, she thought.

She was pregnant.

Her pregnancy did not make her happy. It wasn't that she didn't want more children; it was the effect the arrival of a baby would have. While Mrs. Cohen had kept her distance since their confrontation, she would insist they move once she learned a baby was on the way. In addition, the presence of a baby would reduce the amount of work she could do—and their income.

Finally Anna got up and returned to her sewing machine, where she stayed until Yakov returned from work. He laid down the bundle of vests he was carrying, and a frown touched his forehead as he looked at the stack of trousers yet to be finished.

"Anna, are you all right?"

She looked up at him with puffy, tired eyes. "I'm fine." Then she shook her head. "No, I'm not. I'm not fine at all."

"What's wrong?"

"Everything. I heard from Dvoyra today."

"What's wrong, Anna? Is it bad news? Is it my parents?"

"No, no, everyone's well." Anna drew in a deep breath. "It's Dvoyra, Yankle. She isn't coming. She married Isaiah Hoffman's son, Berl, and she's going to stay in Poland."

"Oy, you frightened me." He put his right hand over his heart. "I thought something bad had happened."

Anna was speechless—how could he be so unfeeling?

Yakov walked past her to the icebox, reached into the upper compartment, and took out a mason jar filled with cold water. "It's hot on the street." He poured himself a glass of water. "Going to be a long, hot summer."

He did not see his wife close her eyes and breathe deeply, fighting for composure.

He set the glass down on the sink and turned to see Anna sitting at the sewing machine, her hands crossed over her stomach. He frowned. "What is it?"

"Didn't you hear me say Dvoyra isn't coming to America? Don't you realize I'll never see her again?"

Yakov grimaced. "Anna, I'm sorry, I just didn't think." He put an arm around her shoulder.

Anna twisted away from his touch. "You're not sorry!" She got to her feet. "It doesn't matter to you. You don't care about any—anything!" She had nearly said "anyone." "You are a different person. I don't feel as though I know you. Maybe I never really knew you."

"Don't say that. I love Dvoyra as if she were my own sister."

"You didn't even blink when I said she wasn't coming."

"I know, I know, it was thoughtless. But for a moment I thought you'd had news about my parents. I could see you were upset when I came in."

"You could see I hadn't finished the trousers when you came in," Anna corrected him. "That's what you were concerned about—why I hadn't done more work!"

"How could you say such a thing?" he protested. "You know that's not true. I'm sorry about Dvoyra, really. But it's not the end of the world. Maybe she and her husband will come to America someday."

Anna shook her head. "She says her husband wants to stay in the old country."

"Then her place is with him, Anna. And you know, maybe it's better this way. Where would we have put another person in this apartment? We're too crowded as it is."

She felt her heart skip a beat. "We would have moved. We need a larger apartment anyway."

"A larger apartment! Anna, we've got to stay here and save every penny we can put away. We'll never get ahead otherwise."

Anna sat down again and lowered her head into her hand. She sighed, knowing there would be no good time to reveal her news.

"We're going to have a baby, Yankle," she said softly.

He stared at her, then began shaking his head as if to deny her words. "No," he whispered.

"Yes. I'm pregnant."

"How long have you known?"

"Over a month."

"Why didn't you tell me?"

"I was waiting for the right moment. Somehow it never came."

"This is terrible," he muttered, closing his eyes and rubbing his temples with the heels of his hands. "This will be a big setback for us, a real setback."

Anna felt her anger returning. "Yankle, what is the matter with you? I'm going to have your baby, our first child born in America! And all you can say is it's a 'setback'? What is wrong with you? What's happened to you?"

"There's no room for a baby in this apartment," he said wearily.

"Then we'll find a bigger one!"

"Don't you understand, woman? A baby, a larger apartment, all cost money. We'll have nothing for ourselves, nothing!"

"Then ask Mr. Rosenberg for more money."

"Why should Mr. Rosenberg pay me more because we are going to have another mouth to feed?"

"Yankle, we would have to have more money even if there were no baby. Rosenberg has never increased your wages."

"Have you forgotten we demanded more money for the work you do here and that he agreed?"

"We're not talking about what he pays me, we're talking about what he pays you."

"He could give my job to someone tomorrow who'd be delighted to do it for a lot less than I get," Yakov snapped.

They had little to say to each other during dinner as Yakov silently brooded over the news of the baby. The children were subdued. As usual, they had heard every word of their parents' argument. As for Anna, between Dvoyra's letter and Yakov's reaction to her pregnancy, she felt totally defeated. She found herself looking forward to the solitude she would have once everyone had gone to bed.

She did not immediately return to the sewing machine after Yakov's morose departure to the bedroom. She sat down in the rocking chair, picking up an old glove that Rachel had been playing with before she went to bed. Anna smiled sadly as she fondled it. It had once belonged to her mother. What neither Rachel nor the other children knew was that it had, long ago, been the favorite plaything of Anna's second child, Miriam, who had died nearly ten years earlier of an illness the doctors could not identify. The old glove had made the journey with her all the way from Oleck-Podlaska. She closed her eyes and slowly raised the old glove to her lips. As she kissed the soft calfskin, a tear trickled down her cheek.

Chapter Nine

Nobody had ever heard of Mendel Beilis until the spring of 1911. He would have remained anonymous had not a young boy named Yushchinski been murdered and his body dumped near the Kiev factory where Beilis was employed. When Beilis was charged with murdering the young child in order to obtain Christian blood for one of those totally secret Jewish rituals that everyone knew about, anti-Semitism erupted and spread throughout Eastern Europe. While a small but vocal faction in Russia protested the absurdity of the ancient charge of ritual murder, the Polish Jews had no such defenders.

As summer neared, tensions mounted. Even in Suwalki, five hundred miles from Kiev, Jewish shops and stalls were vandalized. The windows and walls of Jewish buildings were daubed with the word *Beilis*.

Berl Hoffman, who had been hired to repair some farm buildings in Suwalki owned by absentee landholders, doggedly refused to get involved, one way or the other. He believed the way to stay out of trouble was to stay away from it.

One could tell that Dvoyra was Anna Appelavitch's sister. They were of the same height and build and they had similar coloring, except that Dvoyra's hair had a gentle wave to it and touches of amber could be seen streaking through her hair when the light was just so. Dvoyra's face was slightly more round than Anna's, but she had the same warm eyes and smile.

"Berl," Dvoyra asked him one evening before dinner, "do people really think we kill Christians for their blood?"

He sighed. "Dvoyra, I've had a long, hard day. Let's not discuss the Beilis thing. It will pass. These things always do."

"I'm not sure," Dvoyra said as she laid the table. "It seems to me they are always finding some new way to victimize us."

"Dvoyra, please, let it rest." He sat down. "It's best to keep out of such things."

"Berl, maybe we should leave. Go to America—"

"No!" he yelled angrily, banging his fist on the table so the plates jumped. "I've worked hard so that we could have a home of our own. I'm not going to let some pranksters drive me away from my home!"

Berl—a handsome man, tall, muscular, strong—had straight black hair that sometimes reached below his collar, and eyes that burned like hot coals when he was angry, as he was now.

"It isn't pranksters, Berl. It's the government—the Czar, the Duma, the politicians, the newspapers. Even ordinary people. It's like a disease."

"I tell you it will all blow over," he said firmly, putting an end to the conversation. "You'll see."

At dawn the following morning he set out for Suwalki, nearly twenty kilometers away. Berl wanted to do as much work as possible before it got too hot, and be on his way home well before sunset.

The farm was on the south side of town, and from the top

of the barn he was repairing, Berl could see all across the rooftops of the old town. He was a good worker, conscientious and thorough. So engrossed was he in his work that he did not notice the group of men down by the gate of the farm until he heard their voices drawing nearer. They were coming down the dirt path beside the barn, eight of them, strapping young men in rough clothes and heavy work boots. Two or three of them were smiling. The others simply stood looking up at him, their arms folded across their chests.

"What do you want?" Berl shouted down.

"We want you, Beilis!" a voice answered menacingly. Berl frowned, running his tongue over his lips, which had suddenly become dry. He looked about to see if there was anyone around who might come to his aid. There was no one in sight.

"Get down here, Beilis!"

"My name isn't Beilis!" Berl yelled hoarsely. His heart was pounding. "I'm from Oleck-Podlaska. My name is Hoffman. Berl—"

"Down, Beilis!" One of them, a burly fellow with a heavy mustache and long, greasy hair, shook the ladder violently. "Or do we have to shake you down?"

"Leave me alone! I've got work to do!"

"What, killing children?" one of them taunted. The big man with the mustache shook the ladder again, and Berl clutched at it to avoid falling. He started down, and as he did, he spied two young peasant women approaching the path leading to the farm.

"Hey!" he yelled, waving to them in the hope the men below would think they knew him. "Hello!"

"Why are you waving to our women, Beilis?" one of the men shouted up at him. "Do you murder Christian women too?"

Berl felt nausea sweep through his body. He was going to have to fight, and he had no hope of winning. He took a deep breath and jumped to the ground. The men formed a ring around him, the two women standing to one side.

"Who is he?" one of the women asked.

"He's a Jew, aren't you, Beilis?"

"My name is Hoffman."

"You're a Jew," said a man with a pitted face and sly, close-set eyes. "A Jew child-killer!" Without warning he stepped forward and smashed his fist into Berl's face. Berl staggered backward but did not fall. As the man rushed forward to hit him again, Berl swung his own fist, catching his assailant squarely in the middle of his face, driving him to his knees, bright blood spurting from his broken lips and nose. Before Berl could even lift his fist again, another man hit him from behind, sending Berl facedown into the dust. Two more pinned his arms behind him, while a third held his head in a viselike grip with his face inches from the dirt. The weasel-eyed man Berl had hit stood over him, wiping the blood from his face with the back of his hand.

"Jew bastard!" he snarled. He put his foot on the back of Berl's head and ground his face into the earth.

"That's right, Jozef, clean your boots on him!" a woman shouted, her face alight with excitement. "Filthy Jew!"

"You girls ever see a Jew's prick?" the man shouted, his foot still on the back of Berl's head.

"Do they really cut the end off it when they're born?"

"Let's take a look!"

The man took his foot off Berl's head. The men who were holding him rolled him over, and as they did, the one called Jozef smashed his fist repeatedly into Berl's face. His brain numbed by the crushing blows, choking on his own blood, Berl felt them tugging at his trousers, powerless to fight them.

"Look at that!" a woman's voice taunted.

"There, Jew!" someone shouted, and Berl felt a boot smash into his groin, and vomit filled his throat. The men who had been holding him let go, and as Berl curled up, groaning in agony, and humiliation they began kicking him in the ribs and back. When he rolled over to try to protect himself, they kicked him in the groin again and in the head. When they were tired of him, they swaggered away, laughing.

It was a long time before Berl regained consciousness and had enough strength to sit up. His entire body was a mass of pain. He was covered with blood and his clothes were soiled with vomit. Finally he managed to drag himself to the barn. It took him over an hour to hitch up the wagon, so it was almost midnight before he stumbled through the door of his house and collapsed on the wooden floor. Dvoyra ran to him, cradling him in her arms. He looked at her through eyes that were mere slits in the swollen mess of his face.

"What happened, Berl?" she cried. "Who did this to you?"

"Beilis," he whispered. "Beilis."

* * *

June 10, 1911

Dearest Dvoyra,

I have read and reread your letter a hundred times. The news of your marriage took us by surprise. You know, dearest sister, that nothing is more important to me than you happiness, and that is why I still pray your husband may change his mind about remaining in the old country. Soon the two of you will bring children of your own into the world. You must think about what kind of world it will be for them, Dvoyra. I know this: there is nothing for people like us, like you and your husband, in Europe anymore—only misery.

While life is not easy in America, and we have to work very hard, it is better here. It took me some time to realize why. It is because there is no fear here. You never know how much fear there has been in your life until you wake up one morning and find it is gone. So please, please do not give up the dream of coming to America. Remember this dream. Tell your husband what I have written and beg him to reconsider.

Well, I don't want my letter to become a lecture. Let me tell you our news—I am going to have a baby. Our first American-born child will arrive early next year, perhaps in time to celebrate our first year here. Yankle is worried because we will have another mouth to feed, but you know Yankle, he always worries.

The girls are fine. Rebecca and Sheara are doing well in school and have already learned to speak English. I have begun to go to school at night to learn English, and already I can make conversation like an American. Yankle is well. He works too hard and lets his employer take advantage of him, but that is the way he is and I don't think he could change if he wanted to. Sometimes we argue over the way Mr. Rosenberg treats him, and that upsets me even more than seeing how hard he has to fight for a decent wage.

Write to me soon and send news of all the family. Think about America and what I have said. Tell everyone that we are well and send our love.

All my love,
Anna

* * *

September 1, 1911

Dear Anna,

Your letter just arrived, and it lifted our spirits more than you can ever know. It has not been a good summer for us.

Berl was attacked by a gang of goyim on a farm near Suwalki. They nearly killed him, but he still refuses to consider moving away. He says leaving his parents behind would be unthinkable, especially the way things are.

But I want to tell you the good news. Esther married a man from Berdichev two months ago, and already she is pregnant. She writes that she will have the baby next spring. I must tell you, dear sister, that I am concerned for her. She has had two very bad kidney attacks. We must pray all will go well for her. Her husband Azriel Agronski, will look after her. He is a good man.

Momma is fine and, of course, delighted that Esther and I are married and staying here.

Tell Yankle his parents are well and send their love. Your father-in-law has not been the same since you left. His mind always seems to be somewhere else, and when I mention you or the girls, tears come to his eyes. He misses you all so very much.

Now I must close. Take good care of yourself so you will have a strong and healthy American baby. Kiss Yankle and the girls and write again soon.

Your loving sister,
Dvoyra

Whenever he had a problem, Yakov would drum his fingers on the tabletop. He had done so tonight, all through dinner, and it unnerved Anna, because she knew that until he would reach a decision, he would be difficult and unapproachable. She waited quietly. Becky and Sheara looked at each other, sensing the tension. Dinner was eaten in silence.

Following the meal, Yakov buried himself in the *Daily Forward*. Not yet, then, Anna thought. She saw how the children were watching her and Yakov.

"Come, girls, we've got work to do," Anna said, breaking the stony silence. "I'll clear the dishes. Sheara, you can finish the ironing, and Becky—"

"Fold the wash, I know," Becky replied with a mock groan.

"Mind Poppa's collars, Sheara," Anna said as she worked over the sink. Sheara looked at her sister and they both grinned. After Anna had finished washing the dishes, she pulled a kitchen chair across the room and sat down opposite her husband. She reached out and let her hand rest gently on his arm. He looked up, frowning.

"Can't you see I'm reading?" he said wearily. "Can't a man have any time to himself?"

"I'm sorry, Yankle. I thought you were worrying about something."

He looked up again, and decision hardened his expression. He folded up the newspaper. "All right. You want to know, I'll tell you. It's Sheara."

"What about her?" Anna asked, confused. "What has she done?"

"She hasn't done a thing." Yakov leaned forward in his chair. "That's just it. It's time she did."

"Yankle, what are you saying? The child is in school until three. She comes home, she does her studies, she has chores after dinner. What more could she do?"

"A lot more!" Yakov exclaimed, his voice rising. "She could be earning good money in the garment trade. Rosenberg would give her a job tomorrow. She could bring home another five dollars a week."

"She has to go to school, Yankle!"

"School, school!" he said scornfully. "Sheara knows the language now. She's learned all she needs to know. What's the sense in keeping her in school when she could be bringing in good money. The girl is twelve years old, Anna."

"She's just a child. What's the hurry to turn her into a worker?"

"We need the money!" Yakov snapped. "I can't sleep at night worrying how we're going to pay for everything. We're moving to a new apartment. I owe Fink for over a month's groceries. In two months we'll have another mouth to feed. That's what the hurry is, Anna. We need the money!"

"If we need money so badly, why don't you ask Rosenberg for a raise?"

"I did! And you know what he said? He said I was overpaid as it is. And you know what else he said, Anna? He said I was crazy to work the way I do to provide for a family as big as mine when I have a grown daughter wasting her time in school!"

"She's not wasting her time!" Anna said firmly. "She's getting an education so she'll have a chance to be whatever she wants to be! Isn't that why we came here? To make a better life for our children?"

"Momma, don't fight. I'll go to work."

Anna turned to see Sheara standing behind her, her face pale and tense.

"No, you will not!" Anna said.

"I want to do it, Momma. I want to help. I don't want you and Poppa to argue over me."

"You see?" Yakov nodded sagely. "You see? Sheara agrees. She's smart. She doesn't want to waste any more time in school."

"She wants us to stop arguing," Anna said, struggling to control the dread and anger welling inside her. "She's even prepared to give up school if that will do it."

"No, Momma. Poppa is right. Lots of children my age are leaving the school to start work."

"Sheara, listen to me. If you leave school now, your whole life will be different!"

"Different," Yakov scoffed. "Yes, it will be different, Sheara. You think how different it will be if we can't pay our bills. Think how different it will be if Fink cuts me off, if we're thrown into the street because we can't pay our rent. Think how different life will be, then!"

"Yankle, that's a terrible thing to tell the child! You make it her responsibility to keep us from starving?"

"It's no use arguing. If we had sons at school, maybe I would feel differently. But what use is it to have girls sitting in school all day learning poems and ancient history when they could be earning money? Do you know what the men at work say? They say they wish they had daughters Sheara's age. They say to me, Appelavitch, you're throwing away ten, maybe fifteen cents for every hour that child sits in school. You must be wealthy, Appelavitch, if you can afford to do that!"

"Momma, I don't mind," Sheara pressed. "I'd really like to

work." She stepped forward and put her arms around Anna's shoulders. Anna lowered her head into her hands, fighting back the tears. *No,* she told herself angrily, *I will not weep. It will get me nowhere.* She looked up as Becky crossed the room toward them.

"Will I have to leave school too, Momma?" she asked plaintively.

"You won't have to do anything you don't want to do, Becky," Anna said calmly, looking at her husband as she spoke. He glared at her, his expression frightening her. *My God,* she thought, *I have never seen him look at me like that before.*

"Now you let ten-year-old children make the decisions in this house?" he asked acidly. "Is this how you teach them to respect their father?"

"Didn't you let Sheara decide what she wanted?" Anna cried, her temper flaring.

"That's different."

"Yes, different," she shot back scornfully. "She agreed with you instead of me. That's what's different!"

"The matter is closed!" he said resolutely. "We agreed that Sheara is wasting her time at school."

"*We* agreed nothing of the sort!" Anna protested.

"The child wants to work. I will arrange it."

"She wants us to stop fighting, Yankle." Anna pleaded with him, "Don't you see that? She is willing to go to work because she thinks it will bring peace to our home."

"Then let her have her wish!"

"And what next? Will it be Rebecca next?"

"If I had my way, she would begin work tomorrow."

"No!" Anna protested. "No, Yankle, no!"

"Momma, Momma, it's all right!" Becky cried, running into Anna's arms. "Don't fight over me. If Poppa wants us to work, we'll work. We'll do what Poppa wants, Momma. Only please, please stop fighting now!"

"Shhhh, Becky," Anna whispered, stroking her daughter's head. "Shush, it's all right. It's all right."

She looked at Yakov. He stood up, smiling.

"This is wrong, Yankle," Anna said, softly, looking at him over the heads of their children.

His face changed again, darkening with anger.

"You aren't going to make me feel guilty for this, Anna!" he snapped. "I won't feel guilty for wanting to stay alive!" He snatched up his sweater from the back of a chair and stormed out of the apartment without saying another word.

Sheara left school in October and went to work at Rosenberg's shop, sewing buttons on men's suits and vests. She was a good worker. He paid her ten cents an hour.

Chapter Ten

Spring came late that year, but it had finally arrived. The warm breeze entering through the open window was soothing, and the rise and fall of the baby's back against her hand as he slept increased Anna's feeling of contentment. They had called him Shmuel, after the father whom Anna could hardly remember. He was a healthy baby, placid and good-natured.

It had been a miserable winter. Yakov's growing despair sapped the Appelavitch household of any fragments of happiness. Sheara's departure from school was a blow to Anna, shattering much of her vision of life in America. Her pregnancy was uneventful, but with every passing week her fear over the burden of a growing family increased. And then came the devastating news that her sister Esther had died of kidney failure while delivering her first child. Anna sometimes thought that if it had not been for Shmuel, she would have spent that entire bitter winter grieving for Esther.

Yakov's voice broke into her reverie, and she turned away from the window to face him.

"I asked you what you were thinking," he said quietly.

Anna smiled. "I was thinking, poor Yankle, I haven't been much of a wife to you lately."

"Anna, don't say such things. I know how much Esther's death affected you. But you have to stop brooding about it."

"I wasn't. I was only thinking of the old country, of everything we left behind."

"Like what, in heaven's name?"

"Foolish things," Anna said, shaking her head. "Your father's smile. The old wooden synagogue. The well in the center of town. The commotion on market day. I miss all

hat, Yankle. I miss visiting my father's grave. And I miss
Dvoyra so."

"You keep saying that, as if you will never see her again. I
say she'll come yet. One of these days she'll sway that
husband of hers; Dvoyra is too smart to stay there."

Anna shook her head. "I don't think so. I don't think I will
ever see her again."

Yakov sighed. "It's not in our hands, Anna. What will be,
will be," he said, fetching a sweater and pulling it over his
head. "I'll be back shortly. I'm going to Reid's to buy a
paper."

"All right," Anna said with a weary smile. She laid the baby
in his crib and went into her kitchen, where Sheara was
ironing. "Mind Poppa's collars, Sheara."

Sheara laughed. "You know, Momma, every time I iron
Poppa's shirts you tell me the same thing, mind Poppa's
collars."

"Well, it's important that Poppa's shirts be ironed just so."

"Why?"

"I . . ." Anna looked at her daughter and began to laugh.
"I don't know. But it's still important, you'll see. One day
you'll be ironing your own husband's shirts and you'll
understand why. Tell me," Anna continued, suddenly serious. "How do you like your work?"

Sheara shrugged. "It's work. I don't have any feeling about
it. But that man Rosenberg—"

"You don't like him?"

"He's an evil man, Momma. But what can you expect? He's
an employer. He lives off other people's sweat. I think all
employers are evil."

"Oh, Sheara, come!" Anna remonstrated. "There are good
ones and bad ones. You and Poppa just happen to work for
one of the bad ones."

"You don't know, Momma, the way they treat workers
here in America. At the factory the men tell stories about
things that have happened to laborers in other parts of the
country. Bad things."

"You shouldn't listen to such stories. I'm sure they're not
meant for the ears of young women."

"Young women are active in the labor movement," Sheara
said defiantly. "Why shouldn't we hear what is happening to
workers in other cities?"

"What is this labor movement you're talking about?"

"Workers are forming unions in a lot of shops and factories. It's a way to protect themselves against the employers."

"Such matters are not for women." Anna's expression grew more serious. "You leave such talk to the men."

"It's not just men, Momma. One of the most popular people in the labor movement is a woman, Elizabeth Gurley Flynn. She has fought for the rights of workers all over America. Last year she chained herself to a streetlamp in a city called Spokane, on the other side of the country."

"God in heaven!" Anna exclaimed. "Why would she do such a thing?"

"She found out some workers had been thrown into jail for protesting against men who had sold them jobs that didn't exist. It was her way of drawing attention to what was happening to them, and other workers like them."

"This is happening in America?" Anna asked with a frown. "How can that be? People came here from all over the world to escape such things."

"They escape nothing, Momma. Only yesterday Rosenberg deducted five cents from a boy's pay because he said the boy, Aaron, went to the toilet too often. When Aaron protested, Rosenberg told him if he didn't like it, he could go find work someplace else. Aaron had to accept the wage cut or lose his job. That's your Rosenberg, Momma. That's the way employers treat workers. He's a tyrant, a real Jewish cossack. You should have heard him scream at me when I put up the notice honoring the hundred and forty-one girls who were killed in the Triangle fire in New York."

"You put up a notice about these girls?" Anna said, remembering the horrible Triangle Shirtwaist Company disaster.

"I thought we should bow our heads in silent prayer for five minutes on the anniversary of the disaster. Rosenberg called me a socialist troublemaker. He said my stupid five-minute prayer would cost him two solid man-hours of work. He said if I didn't take down the notice, he would fire me. So I took it down."

"Did Poppa know?"

"Yes. He was cross with me. He said I could have lost both of us our jobs."

"Why wasn't I told about this?"

"You know Poppa doesn't like to talk about such things. And he gets very upset when the men talk about joining the union. He says no possible good can come from it, they should all be thankful they have a job at all."

"It's very important to Poppa to have work, Sheara. It gives him pride, confidence. He has never been without work. I met your father in a factory in Rovno, did you know that? He came there to find work because things were bad in Oleck-Podlaska. Plenty of men were out of work there, but your Poppa isn't the type to sit and wait for work to come to him. He went out and found it. That's why he feels as he does, Sheara. That's why you mustn't cause any trouble for him. All he wants to do is an honest day's work. Let others do the fighting, if they want to."

"He'll have to one day, Momma. All of us will. For a decent wage, a decent place to work in."

"Poppa knows what he's doing, Sheara. You must do as he tells you."

"No, Momma," Sheara said firmly. "He is wrong about this, and I'm not."

"You're just a child!"

"If I'm old enough to work, Momma, I'm old enough to think for myself."

That night after the children had gone to bed, Anna asked Yakov if Sheara's stories of unrest among the workers at Rosenberg's factory were true.

He said yes. "It's dangerous talk, Anna. Rosenberg could get rid of all of us in a minute."

"But you would find work elsewhere."

"I'm not so sure. Employers don't hire people who have been let go for making trouble. Besides, Rosenberg says times will be harder next year, there won't be so much work."

"How can he possibly know that?"

"Because it's his job to know. He talks to the retailers, he talks to the textile mills. He says business last year was bad and next year will be worse. Do you know what else he said? 'Just wait, Appelavitch,' he told me. 'Just wait. Next year all these troublemakers will be standing in line outside my office begging for work.'"

"Sheara says workers are protesting about wages and working conditions all over the country."

"Sheara is going to have both of us in trouble if she doesn't learn to hold her tongue!" Yakov snapped. "Her job is to do the work she is paid to do, and not meddle in things that don't concern her!"

"Have you told her so, Yankle, for her own protection—and yours?"

"Tell her so!" Yakov threw his hands into the air in frustration. "You think she listens to me? She's like the rest of them, she has no respect. All I want is to do my work and be left in peace. Is there anything wrong with that?"

"No, of course not, Yankle," Anna placated him, wanting desperately to avoid another argument.

"Then she should stop making trouble!" he reasoned. "If times get hard, it will be the troublemakers who get fired first. And I don't want to be one of them!"

"No, of course not," Anna soothed as she began to undo Yakov's necktie.

"Anna, what are you doing?" he asked, momentarily confused by her behavior.

"I am untying your tie, Yankle." She smiled. "This conversation is getting much too serious."

"I am perfectly capable of taking off my own clothes."

"Good, then take them off," she whispered, smiling playfully.

"Anna, what's gotten into—"

"You know, sometimes you talk too much," she murmured.

"Anna . . . ?"

"Much too much." She cut him off with a kiss.

Yakov was both delighted and confused by what was happening as Anna pulled him into bed. Their lovemaking had always been quiet and serious and at his beckoning. He had never seen Anna behave so brazenly, but she looked radiant and her excitement was contagious.

As he continued with his lovemaking in the only manner he knew, she took him by the arms and pushed him over onto his back, rolling over until she sat atop his hips, straddling him.

"Anna!" he exclaimed. "What are you doing?"

"Shh!" She touched her finger to his lips. "You'll wake the children."

He lay there in wonderment as she eased herself over his body, taking all of him.

He could not believe this was his Anna. Her hair, now loosened, hung sensuously over her shoulders, and each time she moved above him, a willowy smile blossomed briefly across her face. Her eyes were barely open and she seemed to be floating hypnotically in another place.

But Anna was not in a trance. She was, instead, in exquisite control. And as she soared, bringing Yakov to new heights of pleasure, her thoughts played on long-buried images of love-making in a cabin of the *Darmstadt* as it steamed through the icy night toward America.

Despite that brief interlude of happiness, life did not get easier for Anna and Yakov, but the tension between them finally began to subside. More and more they found themselves facing life as a couple and less and less as antagonists who complicated each other's existence.

Summer wore into fall, and it looked as if Rosenberg would be proven wrong. There was plenty of work at the factory, and the long tables in the shop were piled high with unfinished garments. But as winter passed and the days lengthened into another spring, the work dropped off noticeably. And the more it slackened, the more tense Efraim Rosenberg became as he tried to hide his secret.

Last year Rosenberg had borrowed twenty-five thousand dollars from the bank, ostensibly to renovate his shop and buy new equipment. Instead, he had quietly invested most of the money in a new textile mill. But an unexpected strike had closed the mill, and Rosenberg couldn't cover his bank debt. Worse, he could not produce title to the equipment he was to have purchased, nor show any evidence of renovation of the dilapidated building he had pledged as security. At best, Rosenberg was facing ruin. At worst, prison.

It was the middle of April. Two weeks had passed since Yakov had brought work home for Anna.

"I don't know what's happening," he said. "Every day there is less and less work to do."

"It's probably just temporary," Anna said. "Things will improve, you'll see."

"I'm not so sure. The men at work all say the same thing, bad times are on the way. I ask them why they say such things, and they shrug, who knows? Nobody knows, and yet you feel it in the air. Something, they say. Something bad is going to happen."

"No, Yankle," Anna soothed him. "Nothing bad. Something good." She swallowed nervously and tried to smile. "Something good is going to happen . . . to us. We're going to have another baby."

He stared at her in disbelief. Anna held her breath until she felt a pain in her chest. His eyes closed slowly, like a curtain coming down between them.

"God in heaven," he whispered. "Not another child, Anna. Not another child."

"Please, Yankle, it will be all right," she pleaded. "We'll manage. We always manage."

He shook his head, sinking into the chair as if the strength had been sapped from his legs.

"Oh, God, oh, God," he whispered, "what are we going to do?"

Yakov and Sheara always walked to work together, though rarely talked much on the way. Since Anna had announced her pregnancy, Yakov had become even less talkative, worrying constantly about how they would manage without his wife's income.

Today was May first, and as they hurried along, Sheara remarked how strange it was that only America failed to honor its working masses on May Day.

"You can celebrate May Day by working," Yakov told her gruffly, "and be grateful you have a job."

As they rounded the corner of the street, they saw a crowd of people gathered around the entrance to Rosenberg's building. Recognizing the faces of their coworkers, they knew something was wrong. Yakov pushed his way through the crowd and stood dumbfounded in front of the sign nailed to the wooden door.

This Vacated Building
For Sale or Rent
Contact
Union Bank and Loan Co.
Mr. Pheiser, Loan Dept.

"What does it mean?" Yakov asked.

"It means Rosenberg has gone broke," someone replied.

"But he owes us all a week's wages!" Sheara said.

"Ha! Try and get it!" a small, angry-eyed man snapped. "The bank will snatch up everything he owns."

Yakov felt his knees begin to shake as panic overtook him. For the first time in his adult life he was without work. He grabbed Sheara's hand and pulled her away from the crowd, away from the building where he had worked for the best part of five years.

"Where are we going, Poppa?" Sheara asked as he hurried

her down the street, running to keep up with him as they crossed the road.

"We're going to look for work—before every former Rosenberg employee gets the same idea."

The story was similar wherever they went. None of the shops were hiring, and in fact many of them were reducing their own work forces. It was the same at the big factories in East Baltimore: there was just no work.

They returned to the apartment exhausted.

"Has something happened? Has someone been hurt?" Anna asked, her face full of worry when she opened the door for them.

"Rosenberg has gone out of business," Yakov said dully, collapsing into his chair and leaning back with his eyes closed.

"Sheara and I have been looking for work all day. There is nothing. Nothing. I have no job, Anna."

Anna looked at him over the top of her daughter's head. Yakov had always been a worrier, but this was truly serious. She could see fear in his eyes as she searched for something comforting to say, but no words came.

Sheara straightened her shoulders. "Everywhere we went, Momma, they all said the same thing. 'There is no work. We are letting people go. We can't help you.' We didn't even get paid for the work we did last week."

Anna gasped. "Surely Rosenberg—"

"Rosenberg is finished, Anna," Yakov said wearily. "He owes everybody money, the mills, the bank. We're the least of his worries."

"This is America," Anna said, trying to hide her fear. "You will find something tomorrow. It will be all right, you'll see. Come, eat something, try not to think about it any more tonight. Tomorrow, you'll see."

Yakov made no reply. He sat silently in his chair, staring at the wall, his eyes empty. Ever so often, he shook his head slowly from side to side.

The following afternoon Yakov and Sheara were told by a friend from Rosenberg's factory that there might be work at Kohn's Ready-to-Wear Fashions, down on the waterfront. The man gave them a name, Carl Marman. They thanked him and set off eagerly, traveling nearly an hour to get to the harbor area. They found the building, a large warehouse-factory combination. The first floor was filled with racks of cheap clothing. Someone, an employee, told them they would find Mr. Marman on the top floor. As they moved through the hot, dingy building and made their way up the four flights of stairs, Sheara and Yakov were conscious of the hostile stares they drew from the workers.

On the top floor they went into a drab office where a heavyset man sat behind an old wooden desk. He had droopy, tired-looking eyes and oily, black curly hair. He neither stood to greet them nor offered to shake hands. He didn't even bother to take the cigar out of his mouth.

"I'm Marman. What can I do for you?"

"I am Yakov Appelavitch. This is my daughter, Sheara."

"We're looking for work," Sheara put in quickly.

"I see." The man let his eyes slowly roam from Sheara's knees to her face and back again. Sheara, nearly fourteen, could turn a man's head faster than many women. She still wore her hair in a girlish braid, but her green eyes held a worldly maturity. Her figure was youthful and inviting, hinting at a sensuality yet to come. Marman got to his feet and came around the desk without taking his eyes off her.

"And what makes you think you'll find any work here?" he asked, as if he were angry with them for wasting his time. "I don't know of a goddamned place that's hired anyone in over a goddamned month!"

Yakov was shocked and embarrassed that a Jewish businessman would use such language in front of a young girl. "We heard you might be hiring," he said tentatively.

"Appelavitch, did you see the racks of clothes down below? That's inventory, Appelavitch. Inventory."

"They looked like fine clothes," Yakov lied.

"Fine, shit!" Marman snapped. "Didn't you understand what I said, Appelavitch? They're inventory. You can't make a cent out of inventory unless you've got customers. And you can't get customers unless you've got the lowest price. Are you getting my drift?"

"I'm sorry, you're busy," Yakov mumbled. "We shouldn't have bothered you."

"You, girl!" Marman said loudly. "How long have you been at the machine?"

"Over a year and a half."

Marman ran his hand across his forehead and down the rest of his face, removing the cigar from his mouth for the first time since they had come into his office. "Where?"

"Rosenberg's."

"Ha, that fart!" Marman snorted. "What did he pay you?"

Yakov stood opened-mouthed, horrified at the man's

crudity, astonished at his daughter's equanimity in the face of it.

"Twelve cents an hour," Sheara said.

"All right, I'll pay you the same. You can start tomorrow."

"I thought you said you weren't selling any merchandise," Sheara said boldly. Marman grinned, then stuck the cigar back into his fleshy mouth.

"I'm not. So what?"

"So how can you hire us if business is so bad?"

Marman laughed out loud. "I'm hiring you *because* business is so bad, sis."

"I don't understand."

"Explain it to her, pop," Marman said to Yakov.

Yakov shrugged. "I don't understand either."

"Jesus Christ, did you two just get off the boat?" Marman exclaimed, rolling his eyes in exasperation. "Look, I'll spell it out for you. I pay the men who work here twenty-five cents an hour. I'm willing to bet you can do the same amount of work they do. If you can, you've got a job, and I save thirteen cents an hour."

"And what happens to the man?" Sheara said angrily. "You throw him out, is that it?"

"That's the way it is, sis. This ain't no charity we're running here."

"I'd never take another person's job!"

"You want to bet?" Marman leered. "You will, Sheara, and so will pop, there. Things are going to be very tough out there on the street before long. Anybody who's got a job sure as hell isn't going to worry over who had it before him!"

"No," Sheara said, turning for the door.

"Suit yourself," Marman said. "You just remember you could have had a job at twelve cents an hour today. Come back tomorrow, maybe you won't be so lucky."

"No," Sheara said again. As they started down the stairs Marman came lumbering after them. Yakov turned, hesitating.

Sheara tugged at his arm. "Let's get out of here, Poppa. Come on, let's get out of this place."

"Talk some sense into her, pop!" Marman shouted down the stairwell. "And if you got any more daughters, send them along too, long as they're over twelve."

Carl Marman grinned around his wet cigar as he looked up

from his desk and saw Sheara and Rebecca standing in front of him.

"So, you got a sister. Well, well." *Jesus Christ,* he thought, *one is prettier than the other.* Becky, dressed in a white blouse and a dark gray cotton skirt, reminded Marman of the Catholic kids on the way to Saint Mary's. *She even looks Irish,* he mused to himself.

"We had a family discussion last night," Sheara said, looking him right in the eye. "We decided it was time for Becky to leave school and go to work."

"You did, did you?" Marman leered. "And what time do you think we start work here, midday?"

"We got here as early as we could," Sheara said.

"But not early enough!" Marman snapped. "Show up late again and I'll fire you so fast it'll make your head spin!"

"I didn't even know we'd been hired!" Sheara protested.

"I told you yesterday I'd hire you, didn't I? You can start right away, at eleven cents an hour."

"You said twelve cents an hour!"

"That was yesterday, when you walked out of here with your nose in the air, sis. Today, it's eleven cents. Take it or leave it."

Sheara clenched her jaw, but did not speak. Marman shrugged. "You better say something, sis. In ten more seconds your pay will be ten cents an hour. You want to stand there and argue, or do you want to work?"

"We'll work," Sheara replied. "Where do we go?"

"You go up to the sixth floor, report to Mr. Cohen. He'll put you to work basting."

"What about my sister?"

"You let me worry about her."

Sheara looked at Becky, hesitating to leave her alone with Marman.

"I'll be fine, Sheara," Becky said calmly. Satisfied, Sheara nodded and left Becky to face her new employer.

"You know how to sew buttonholes?" Marman asked.

"I used to help my mother."

"Good. Go see Mr. Finestein on the fifth floor. He'll put you to work right away."

"How much?"

"What?"

"How much are you going to pay me?"

"Eleven cents, same as your sister," he said, his surprise tinged with impatience.

"No," Becky said firmly. "I want twelve."

"Are you crazy? Didn't you just hear me tell your sister I'd only pay her eleven cents? Who the hell do you think you are?"

"I am Becky Appelavitch," Becky said, her eyes hard with determination. "Not Sheara Appelavitch. It was Sheara you argued with yesterday, not me. I never walked out on you, so I don't see why you should penalize me."

Marman couldn't believe his ears. No employee had ever talked back to him and gotten away with it.

He shook his head in unwilling admiration. "All right. You win. Twelve cents it is."

"I want you to give the extra penny to Sheara. Let her get twelve cents an hour. And I'll take eleven."

"I can't do that. I already told her—"

"You can do anything you want, Mr. Marman."

He stared at her for several moments before speaking. "Tell me something, young lady, how old are you, anyway?"

"I'll be twelve next birthday."

Marman shook his head. "Twelve, twelve. Well, Becky Appelavitch, all I can say is—God help us all when you're twenty!"

Chapter Eleven

At seven-thirty Becky burst into the apartment, her face alight with excitement.

"Poppa! Momma! It's going to be all right!" Becky cried. "We've got work, both of us! We'll be earning nearly as much as you do, Poppa!" Sheara, her entrance more subdued, winced, knowing Becky had said the wrong thing. Anna also caught Becky's remark and saw that Yakov had turned his face away from his smiling daughter as she crossed the room to kiss him.

"Yankle, Becky meant no harm," Anna said softly. "She's just excited—"

Cutting her off, Yakov stood up and left the room, shutting the bedroom door behind him. The girls looked at each other, and then at their mother.

"Shall I go to him, Momma?" Sheara asked.

"No, maybe we'd better leave him alone for a little while."

Becky stood beside the empty chair where Yakov had rebuffed her and closed her eyes in frustration. "I thought he would be happy. I thought he would be proud of us."

"He is, Becky, he is." Anna went to her daughter and took her in her arms. "It's just that he feels he's let us down. He's never been out of work before."

"But it's only been a few days, Momma," Sheara said. "He'll find work. We did."

"I know, I know," Anna said. "That's what I tell him. But you know Poppa worries."

Becky went to the bedroom door and slowly opened it. She saw Yakov sitting in the rocker, shoulders hunched, holding his head in his hands in the darkened room.

"Poppa!" she whispered. Slowly he lifted his head and looked at her, defeat in his eyes.

"Poppa, I'm sorry. I didn't mean to upset you."

He shook his head and did not speak.

"Poppa, it will be all right. You'll find something. Maybe we can ask Mr. Marman—"

"You think I would work for that *goniff*, thief?" Yakov said angrily. "You think I'd slave fifty hours a week for half of what I was getting before?"

"Poppa, you'll be all right, you'll—"

"All right?" he snapped bitterly. "How can a man be all right when he has to send his children to work so he can live?"

"I don't mind, Poppa. I told you that when we decided. Lots of the girls at school said they would go to work if only they could find jobs."

"And every one of them that does puts a man like me on the street. You don't know what it's like, walking the streets all day."

"You mustn't worry so much, Poppa. We'll manage."

"Child, we couldn't manage when we lived at Mrs. Cohen's, before Shmuel was born. That's why Momma had to work at home. That's why Sheara left school. Now we have a bigger apartment, we have Shmuel, there's another baby on the way, and we have less than half the wages coming into the family than we had a year ago."

Becky bit down on her lip as her eyes filled with tears. She had never seen her father like this before, and it frightened her.

"Poppa, don't give up," she whispered. "Don't lose hope."

"Hope?" he said with a cynical laugh. "Can we use hope to pay for our groceries? We can't even pay for what we've already eaten." He shook his head again. "No, it's my fault. All my fault."

"Poppa, what are you saying?"

"You would have been better off staying in the old country," Yakov muttered dully. "I brought you all here too soon. I wasn't ready. I wasn't ready."

"Poppa, no! We all belong together!" Becky said, the fear rising in her as he lowered his head into his hands again.

Anna watched Yakov pick at his breakfast. Becky and Sheara had left for work moments earlier, and their departure seemed to plunge him deeper into his depression. He scooped tea from his cup with a spoon, then let it dribble back into the cup. It was as though she were not there.

"Where will you look today?" she asked hesitantly.

He did not lift his head. He turned the spoon over, the tea pouring back into the cup. He seemed mesmerized by the pointless ritual.

"Yankle, what is it?"

"I don't know what we're going to do, Anna," he said, still not looking up. "I just don't know what to do."

"You're going to find a job. Things have got to get better sometime."

"You keep saying that"—exasperation put an edge on his voice—"as if saying it will make things change! But it doesn't help me to find work, or tell me what we will do if I don't!"

She sighed, restraining her own frustration. "All right, Yankle, I don't know what we'll do, either. But I do know you won't find work sitting here stirring your tea and wishing you'd never brought us to America!"

He flushed angrily and got to his feet. "You never let up, do you? Never! Never!" He seized his sweater, then stormed out of the apartment, slamming the door behind him.

Dismayed and afraid, Anna sat staring at nothing. It was as if Yakov were building a wall between them. Every time she tried to give him strength and hope, she alienated him still further.

She was waiting for her husband when he came in early that evening, ready to do anything that would heal the rift that was growing between them. But she could tell the moment he came through the door that his job hunt had been unsuccessful. She went to him and put her arms around him, kissing him on the temple and then on the forehead. He sighed and put his arms around her.

Anna pressed her cheek to his and held him tightly. "My poor Yankle, are you exhausted? Walking the streets all day like that. Come sit, rest."

He sighed again, slumping into his chair. He looked at her and shook his head. "Nothing, Anna," he said wearily. "Nothing."

"How many people did you talk to?"

"I can't remember," he lied. "I didn't count."

He had spent the entire day walking the drab streets of south Baltimore, oppressed by the dingy buildings and the gloomy factories. *Why did we come here?* he asked himself over and over. He found himself pining for the old country and the old ways, his parents, his old *shtetl*. He had come to America with so much hope, but it was all gone now, destroyed by cruel reality.

"I'm tired, Anna." He closed his eyes. "I'm so tired. No more questions now, please."

Anna felt the fear coiling itself inside her. She closed her eyes and put her arms around him again. *Please, God,* she pleaded silently, *don't let this go on.*

Her prayer was answered only hours later when Becky and Sheara came home from work, talking excitedly. Kohn's Ready-to-Wear Fashions had an opening for an experienced tailor. Carl Marman had told them he would pay their father twenty cents an hour, or by the piece, whichever Yakov preferred.

"That thief, that crook, he knows my wage is twenty-five cents an hour!" Yakov protested.

"Mr. Marman said you could earn more if you did piecework," Becky said.

"Yes, working in a sweatshop," he replied sullenly.

"Yankle, maybe it would give you time to find something else," Anna ventured. "At least you would be working."

"You think he's doing me a favor?" Yakov burst out. "He's

taking advantage of me. He wants me to work twice as hard and get less money for it."

"It's still better than nothing, Yankle."

"Is that why we came to America, Anna? To spend our lives working to make men like Marman rich?"

"Poppa, Mr. Marman says if you're not there tomorrow when the plant opens, he'll give the job to someone else," Sheara said quietly.

"I don't want to work for that *shtunk*!" Yakov said angrily. He knew, of course, that he had no choice.

It was raining when Yakov and the girls left for work. There had been little conversation at breakfast. Yakov was miserable at the thought of working for Carl Marman, and he had been especially cross with Anna when she tried, once more, to convince him he was lucky to have any sort of job at all. The steady sound of the rain falling against the windows deepened her somber mood. She watched through the window as her husband and daughters made their way along the street, her eyes fixed on their distorted images until they were out of sight. She drew in a long, deep breath—her way of fighting back the too familiar urge to cry. She had vowed long ago there would no more be tears, and she was determined to fight for a better life for her family. She glanced across the room. Shmuel and Rachel were still asleep. She sat down at the table and listened to the rain, picturing Yakov and her daughters moving along the drab gray streets in the morning shower. *Will it never end?* she thought, rubbing her eyes. *Will we never be free from this endless worry?*

The knock on the door startled her. She got up, hoping Rifka Moscowitz hadn't picked this particular morning to visit. She pulled open the door and gasped when she saw him standing there.

"Meyer Kramer!"

"Ah, you speak English," he said, smiling. "I am proud of you."

He was wearing a dark blue suit, a neat white shirt, and tie. He looked clean and elegant, a complete contrast to Yakov with his shabby clothes.

"Come in," she said, half-laughing and half-crying. "Come in, oh, please, come in!"

He took in the drab apartment, trying to imagine what life was like for Anna.

"You look well, Anna," he said, almost too quickly.

"And you, Meyer, are a liar," she said with a smile. "But tell me, how did you find us?"

"The HIAS people were very helpful. They gave me your address on High Street, and a Mrs. Cohen there told me you had moved to this new place several months ago. It was really quite simple."

"I'll make some tea. Please, sit down."

Meyer could see that Anna was flustered and he desperately wanted to put her at ease. "Please, the tea can wait, Anna. I want to hear about you and your children. What has happened since we said good-bye on the *Darmstadt*?" She smiled and blushed slightly as he took the chair Yakov sat in each morning to read his *Daily Forward*.

"Well, to begin with"—she sat down opposite him—"Shmuel and Esther arrived."

Two more babies? he thought.

"Shmuel was born early in 1912, Esther a short while ago."

"And the other three, the ones who were on the boat with you?"

"They're all well."

"Are they at school?"

Anna shook her head. "Sheara went for a year. Becky nearly two, but they are working now."

"There was a baby. Rachel, wasn't it?"

"Ah, Rachel. She started second grade just this month."

"And your husband, Yakov?"

"You remember everything," she said, laughing.

"Yes," he said, meaningfully. "Everything."

His tone made the color rise again in her cheeks, and she looked down at her lap.

"Anna," he said, nearly whispering. "Are you all right?"

She nodded, still avoiding his eyes.

"Anna, look at me," he pleaded.

Slowly she raised her head to meet his gaze.

"What is it, Anna?"

"It's nothing," she lied. "Really."

"If I thought for a minute my coming would upset you, I would have never left Washington. I wouldn't do anything to upset you."

"Your coming hasn't upset me. It's just that I haven't gotten over the surprise of seeing you standing at my door. That's all."

"I couldn't come all the way to America again without trying to find you."

Anna smiled. "And so you found me."

"Yes, I found you."

"And now what?"

"I . . . I don't know. I guess an old friendship has been renewed," he said simply, reaching out to take her hand.

Anna did not pull away from his grasp.

"You will never know what our brief time together has meant to me these past years," she said, tightening her grip on his hand.

"It has meant a lot to me too, Anna," he said after a moment, distracted by her subtle assertiveness in squeezing his hand.

She smiled. "You gave me a different world I still escape to when the reality of our life here becomes more than I can bear," she admitted after a brief pause.

"Has it been bad, Anna?"

"Nothing has been as I dreamed. Life here is hard, Meyer. Very hard."

"Did your sister ever come?"

She shook her head. "No," she whispered. "Dvoyra married and chose to stay with her huband in Oleck-Podlaska. And my younger sister, Esther, died earlier this year."

"I'm sorry. I'm so sorry."

"It's like a fairy tale, your actually being here. Never in a million years did I believe I would see you again," she said, once again squeezing his hand.

"Well, I'm here. You were wrong."

"Are you glad you came?"

"Yes, Anna. You see, I never doubted that I would see you again."

"Are you pleased with what you've found?"

"I would have liked to have seen a happier Anna Appelavitch," he answered truthfully.

"Happiness," she mused, nodding longingly. "There's been no time for happiness."

"Oh, Anna," he whispered, pulling her into his arms as he stood.

"No, Meyer. Please don't. The children are in the other room," she whispered, pushing gently away from him as he held her.

"Anna, we had such happiness once. It was brief, but it was wonderful. We can have it again, Anna."

"No, no, we can't. We're no longer two people between two worlds, drifting on a sea. We're in my home, my world, and soon you will return to your home and your world. Do you really believe I could survive if you . . ."

"Made love to you," he said, finishing her sentence for her.

"And then walked away," she continued, "leaving me to manage with Yankle and our five children and the constant struggle we have just to survive? I couldn't go on."

"Can't I do anything for you?" he pleaded.

"You have. You have given me a very special moment that I have relived over and over again. Don't spoil it by becoming too real. I can manage the memory, the dream. It has its place in my heart. But not again, not now."

He nodded. "Can I tell you how I feel?"

She answered with a pained smile.

"I love you, Anna. I always will."

"And I you."

Just then a baby's cry broke the quiet, and the sweet magic of the moment was gone. He watched her as she went to calm the crying baby. Kramer shook his head and thought of Anna standing naked and frightened before him in the small and softly lit cabin of the *Darmstadt*.

God, she is beautiful, he thought.

A few moments later Anna returned, carrying her baby. Kramer stood up, and Anna cradled the child in her arms so he could see her better.

"This is Esther? She's beautiful."

"We named her for my sister."

"I'm sorry for your loss." He wanted to reach out and touch her as he saw the sorrow in her dark eyes. "But Anna, never regret your decision to come here. Life holds no promise at all for Jews in the old country. Life will never get better for them, especially if there is a war."

"War?" she said, surprised. "Is there going to be a war?"

"Everyone prays it won't happen. But it could. The fighting in the Balkans seems to have settled nothing. The Treaty of Bucharest has done nothing but create frustration. Serbia has all but doubled in size yet still hasn't got the seaport she so much wants. The Bulgarians lost as much as they gained, Turkey has been embarrassed by the Serbs, and Austria-Hungary is ready to go to war against Serbia tomorrow. All they need is an excuse. One incident and all Europe could be in flames."

Anna closed her eyes and shook her head. "I read about it in the newspaper. It's all so frightening, this talk of war."

"You have nothing to be frightened of, here in America."

"I'm thinking of my family. Yankle's parents."

"You should write to them, tell them to come to America while there is still time."

"And what should I tell them? We have no money. They have none. What should I tell them? That they should walk to America?"

"I'm sorry."

"It's not your fault. It isn't anybody's fault."

He looked at his hands, and Anna could see there was something he wanted to say, something he was having difficulty putting into words.

"I'm—I'm sorry things have been hard for you. I so hoped I would find you were happy and thriving here in America."

"Forgive me. I didn't mean to complain. We're better off than most. We are healthy. My husband has work. We manage."

He took a watch from his pocket. "I must go. I have to be back at our embassy in Washington by four o'clock."

"Come see Shmuel first," she urged, suddenly not wanting him to go.

He got to his feet and followed her to the cradle.

"The girls call him Sol. That would be his name in English. Even Yankle calls him Sol."

"Solomon in all his glory," he said, gazing at the sleeping child.

Later, he stood at the door preparing to leave, he reached out and took her hand. "I'm glad I found you."

"Will you come again?"

"I hope so. One day."

They stood looking at each other. He gently reached down and took her chin in his hand. He tilted her head up and kissed her softly on the lips. When he drew back, he saw that her eyes were closed. He smiled and gently kissed her on each eyelid. He could taste the salt from her tears.

"I don't know if we shall ever meet again, Anna, but I will go on hoping. And I want you to do the same. Promise me, Anna. Promise me you'll keep hoping. Will you do that?" he asked.

"I'll try," Anna said. "I'll try."

Anna sat quietly for a long time after he had gone, trying to decide whether to tell her husband about Lieutenant Meyer Kramer's visit. In the end she decided not to: Yakov would not understand. She was not altogether sure she understood herself.

Chapter Twelve

Yakov was in a particularly dark mood at dinner the evening following Meyer Kramer's visit. Marman was demanding more production from the workers than was reasonable, he complained.

"The man won't be happy until someone keels over dead," he predicted quite seriously.

"Poppa, you wouldn't have to work so hard for your wages if we had a union," Sheara said defiantly.

"Keep talking like that and I won't have to work at all," Yakov replied sarcastically.

"If you think like a peasant you will be treated like a peasant," Sheara shot back.

"Sheara!" Anna cried.

Yakov glared at his daughter from across the table. "You won't be happy until we are all out of work, will you?"

"Poppa, don't you understand what is happening here? The employers are stealing our labor, our energy. The more they hold us down, the more they put in their own pockets. They are thieves."

"Sheara, they are Jews like us," Anna interrupted.

"No, Momma, they are not Jews like us. They are employers and they are from Germany and they treat us like dogs. Ask Poppa how many Jews from Germany work by the piece instead of by the hour."

"I don't understand."

"Tell her, Poppa!"

"It's true," Yakov sighed. "Only laborers from Poland and

Russia are made to do piecework. The German laborers all seem to be paid by the hour."

"And they are paid a higher wage by the hour than the others," Becky put in.

"Listen, we are lucky to have work. Have you all forgotten so quickly how it was when we were without it?" Yakov asked.

"No, Poppa, it is not we who are lucky to have work. It is Marman who is lucky to have us. Besides, the panic is over. The last thing Marman wants or needs is a strike now that business is finally improving."

"A strike!" Yakov gasped, as though Sheara had uttered a word forbidden to all living things.

"Yes. A strike. It's the only weapon we have. The workers can close Marman down."

"Don't you ever use that word again. Don't even think that word," he said, fury in his voice.

"Yankle!" Perhaps what Sheara says has some truth to it," Anna interjected.

"I forbid it. I will not listen to talk of a strike in this house."

"Workers all over America are standing up to the Marmans and the Rosenbergs. Why are you so loyal to men who mock you every day?" Sheara cried.

"They are troublemakers."

"No, it is the employers who make the trouble. They make trouble by starving their workers, and the more trouble they make, the more money they make."

"You are a dreamer and a fool if you believe the workers can fight the employers and win."

"The workers can win. They are winning. Without us the employers have nothing."

"They control the jobs."

"Only if we let them. If we don't work, they don't sell."

"Sheara, do workers at Kohn's want to start a union?" Anna asked.

"Some of us do."

Yakov glared at his daughter but did not speak.

"Men from the Confederated Garment Workers of America have been talking to some of us."

"Sheara, you stay away from them!" Yakov shouted, jumping to his feet.

"They are good people, Poppa."

"They are radicals! You will be the ruin of us all," he warned.

"You don't even know them. You are repeating what the employers say."

"Why don't you go listen to what they have to say, Yankle?" Anna suggested, her expression thoughtful.

"Because I never want to be without work again, Anna. Is that too hard for you to understand? You can be fired for just talking to the union organizers."

"Then I will go listen to them, Yankle. What they say sounds interesting. Mr. Marman can't fire me because I don't work for him."

"You stay away from them! Do you hear me? You stay here where you belong."

Anna looked about the tiny apartment that all but imprisoned her. "What did you say?" she asked defiantly.

"I said you stay here where you belong," he snapped, knowing full well she had heard him the first time.

She stared at him for a moment and then slowly turned to Sheara. "When will you next go to hear the men from the union, Sheara?"

"Sunday afternoon, Momma," Sheara replied, barely able to conceal her excitement.

"Then I will go with you."

It was the first time Anna had been with so many people since her arrival at Ellis Island. The diversity of the crowd that packed the union hall that Sunday afternoon reminded Anna of the Great Hall on the Island of Tears. While Yiddish seemed to be the predominant tongue spoken in the room, there were many that Anna could not understand at all.

"God in heaven, Sheara, there are many children here," Anna said as she surveyed the union hall.

"They are not children. They are young workers like me."

"And they all work in the garment trade?"

"Yes, everyone here works for men like Marman."

"Some of the workers could be the grandparents of the younger workers."

"The shops are full of old men and women and, as you say, children."

"And every age in between too."

Anna focused all her attention on the union organizer taking the stage in the front of the hall. "He does look a bit like a radical," she mused to herself as she listened to the young man. While she was not close enough to see him well, she guessed his age to be about twenty-three or twenty-four. He was tall and his close-cropped black beard framed a strong and handsome face. His dark eyes seemed to sparkle with the fierceness of his stare.

Ivan Wollmack silenced the crowd by lifting his long muscular arms high above his head. Wollmack was indeed an imposing figure. He wore a black suit and vest. He had removed his jacket as he approached the center of the stage and dropped it over the back of a chair. He loosened his tie, rolled up his sleeves, and stood there looking out at the crowd. Then he held up his hands, and as the crowd grew still, he shouted the first of his questions at them.

"Do you want a fair hourly wage?" he boomed.

"Yes!" the crowd roared in unison.

"Do you want a fair work week?" he shouted.

"Yes!"

His message was simple and, Anna thought, so entirely just. He told the assembled crowd they would undoubtedly succeed. "When you realize the power you have, and when you are ready to use it, there is nothing you can't accomplish," he said confidently.

"Use your power wisely," he warned them. "A fair wage for a good day's work. Fair hours and equal treatment for all—that's our cause. That is our only cause."

Anna looked around at the mass of workers surrounding her. *They're all immigrants,* she thought. *They are asking for so little, yet they have to fight so hard for it.*

"Poppa belongs here, Momma," Sheara whispered in her ear. "If the workers strike at Kohn's, Poppa will become a scab. I know he will."

"A what?"

"A scab. One who does not belong to a union and who betrays his fellow workers by working even though a strike has been called. The employers use scabs to try to break a strike and defeat the union."

Anna looked back to the stage where Ivan Wollmack still stood. He seemed to tower above them as a commander towers above his army.

"Poppa will not betray the union," Anna said firmly, refusing to accept Sheara's predictions.

Ivan Wollmack excited the crowd that Sunday afternoon, his words expressing what they all felt in their hearts.

"Oh, Momma, isn't he wonderful?" Sheara said, more a

statement than a question. Anna smiled and nodded in agreement. "Do you see why I get so upset with Poppa?" Sheara asked as they began making their way from the room.

As they moved slowly toward the door, Anna saw that Ivan Wollmack was standing at the side of the room talking to two men whom he seemed to know well.

"Let's go over and shake his hand, Momma."

"Why not! Yes, I would like that."

As they approached the three men, Ivan Wollmack looked up and caught Anna's eye. He watched her as he continued to speak to one of the men.

"Excuse me," he said as he turned his full attention to Anna, who now stood facing him.

"How do you do?" He extended his hand to her.

"You were quite impressive. I am Anna Appelavitch, and this is my daughter Sheara.

"Hello, Sheara.

"Hello, Mr. Wollmack. I work at Kohn's. I hope everyone there joins the CGWA."

"It won't be easy. Marman is tough. Tell me, Mrs. Appelavitch, where do you work?"

"I work at home. My husband Yankle brings me work to finish."

Wollmack nodded knowingly. "May, I ask what you make an hour?"

"I average ten cents an hour."

"God," he sighed.

"But it's in addition to what Yankle earns. He gets paid by the piece. He can finish more work with my helping at home."

"It's criminal, Mrs. Appelavitch. Why should Marman pay you half of what he pays others for the same job in that sweatshop of his?"

Anna didn't reply.

"He probably has a hundred women just like you working all over Baltimore for a lousy dime an hour. They think they're helping their husbands earn more. It's a joke."

"What can be done?" Anna asked.

"Someone has to organize the women who are working in their homes. If everyone would simply say 'enough' it would stop. Labor must always speak with a single voice and that includes the home workers. If we could reach them we could turn the garment industry in this town upside down."

"Are you going to visit the women in their homes?" Anna asked.

Wollmack laughed. "No, that wouldn't do. I'd be accused of all sorts of scandalous things and I would infuriate many of the men if I visited their wives at home."

"What will you do?"

"I am not sure. We may have to recruit a woman to call on the home workers."

"You could do it, Momma."

"Me!"

"Yes, and I could get the names of the women who work at home for you."

"What did you say?" Wollmack asked, suddenly showing great interest in what Sheara had just said.

Sheara repeated what she had said.

Wollmack turned to Anna, and she saw the urgency in his eyes. "Would you?" he asked.

"Would I what?"

"Work for the union by calling on the women in their homes?"

"God in heaven!"

"You are perfect for the job, Mrs. Appelavitch."

"I am no such thing," she protested.

"You are a woman. You have a man and a daughter working for Marman."

"Two daughters," Sheara interrupted.

"And most important you, yourself, do work at home."

"I know nothing about union organizing."

"Do you agree with what I have said here tonight?"

"Yes, yes, I do."

"Then you know all there is to know."

"Mr. Wollmack . . . ."

"Please, my name is Ivan."

"Ivan, as unfair as it may seem, I can't afford to lose the ten cents an hour my work brings in."

"If you are willing to work for ten cents an hour for the likes of Marman, you should be willing to work for the CGWA for ten cents an hour," he snapped.

"Momma, you've just been offered a job," Sheara said with glee.

"You would offer to pay me?"

"I just did."

Anna searched his eyes and found the honesty and warmth she sought.

"Momma?"

"Yes, yes. I'll do it," she finally replied without taking her eyes from his.

His stare seemed to burn with even greater intensity as his face broke into a wide grin. "Welcome to the CGWA, Anna." He extended his hand once more and she accepted his handshake, momentarily taken aback by the firmness of his grasp and the extra moment he held on to her hand.

Predictably Yakov was enraged when Anna told him she would no longer be finishing work at home and that she would now be organizing for the CGWA. "Marman will fire me if he hears you are working for the union."

"Yankle, if he tries to fire you because I have taken a job with the union, Ivan Wollmack will have pickets in front of Kohn's within an hour."

"Do you think Marman is afraid of Wollmack?"

"Yes, I do, and if he isn't, he should be."

"Anna, we don't need this trouble," he protested.

"Yankle, Yankle, our trouble isn't caused by a union that is trying to help the worker," she responded, exasperated. "Our trouble is caused by employers like Marman who take advantage of workers like you. Why do you think Wollmack fights with men like Marman? He is fighting for a fifty-hour week. He is fighting for a fair hourly wage. He is fighting for safe working conditions. Why do you see him as a trouble-maker? Are you against those things?"

"You are a dreamer, Anna. Marman has the power."

"No, he doesn't! The Marmans only have the power because you give it to them. The workers have the real power if they would only use it."

"Anna, I just want to be left alone so that I can work. I don't want to join with the radicals."

"I'm no radical, and neither is Ivan Wollmack. You should have come to the meeting. There were hundreds of men and women there just like us. All they want is work without anyone's taking advantage of them. They want exactly what you want. I didn't see any radicals there."

Yakov knew it was useless to argue with her. He also knew that Anna was probably right, though he was too ashamed to concede to her.

"I hope you know what you are doing," he said.

* * *

Anna waited anxiously for Rachel to return home from school each day so that she could stay with the younger children while Anna called on the women who worked at home for Marman. Anna was better than good at her job. She was, as Ivan Wollmack was to say many times over the years, simply superb.

As efforts to organize Kohn's progressed, the union believed Marman would continue to court the "at home" work force. By doing so, he would be able to maintain production even if half his factory workers walked off the job. In a real emergency he figured he could get them to double their hours, and the home workers would be his ace in the hole.

What Marman didn't know was that Anna had already courted them. And when the union was ready, Wollmack would pull the rug out from under Marman.

Sheara had no difficulty compiling the list of women who finished work in their homes. All she really had to do was watch to see which men brought finished work with them in the morning and which men took work home with them in the evening. During the day she asked those on her list for their addresses. Oddly, very few of the men even asked why she wanted the information.

Ivan Wollmack instructed Anna to concentrate on those women whose husbands were either neutral or anti-union, explaining that the wives of the pro-union workers could be counted on to honor a strike should one be called. Marman would be counting on the wives of scabs to make up for the lost labor of the strikers. These were the women she had to convince to honor the picket lines, even if their husbands continued working.

The union organizer also learned that Marman had recruited dozens of women who had no ties to Kohn's whatsoever to work at home. It was evident that Marman believed it would be difficult for the union to identify these independent women, and even more difficult to convince them to honor a picket line. After all, they were working for themselves and would not be influenced by husbands who were not employed at Kohn's.

By the end of the first month of the effort to unionize Kohn's, Wollmack knew that reaching and convincing these independent "at-home" workers would be critical, and he often shared his theories with Anna.

Ivan Wollmack was the most charismatic person Anna had ever known. They met frequently to discuss union strategy, and Anna soon found herself looking forward to every opportunity to talk with Wollmack. He was interested in everything she had to say, and she admired how much he knew about so many issues. He spoke with authority and conviction about almost everything. But mostly it was his eyes that so intrigued her. They would sparkle and dance during moments of light conversation and burn with searing intensity when the conversation grew more serious, as it did when he talked of the employers' exploitation of labor.

"Anna, there are probably forty to fifty of these independent women working at home for Kohn's. They could really make a difference if we call a strike."

"But we don't even know who they are, let alone where they live."

"I know. I know," he mused. "But there must be a list somewhere. They have to get paid. Someone has to deliver their pay to them."

"If you can find out who they are, I will start calling on them. I am sure I can convince many of them to support the union."

"See, if Sheara can find out who takes the pay to them."

"Oh, Ivan, I couldn't think of involving Sheara in this. Yakov is worried enough as it is. He just would not hear of letting her get further involved."

"Why don't we let Sheara make that decision?"

"She's just a—"

"Don't say it. Sheara is as much a member of the labor movement as I am. She works as long and as hard as anyone at Kohn's. She is as committed as we are."

"What do you want her to do?"

"For now, I would just like to identify those who have access to the list. My guess is that it's just Marman and maybe one or two others. Someone has to deliver the garments and their wages to them."

"I'll talk to Sheara," Anna finally agreed.

Carl Marman knew how valuable his list of independent workers was. He entrusted their identity to only one other employee at Kohn's, the young, sixteen-year-old woman who made up the payroll and delivered their pay. She had never worked for anyone other than Carl Marman, and he was more certain of her loyalty than that of any other employee.

The payroll clerk at Kohn's was Clara Louise Marman, Carl Marman's only daughter.

Carl Marman was dumbfounded when he was told that the wife of Yakov Appelavitch worked for the CGWA. One of his employees, Menasha Apter, hoping to curry favor with his boss, was waiting at his office door one morning when Marman arrived at work. He explained to his employer that Anna Appelavitch, whose two daughters and whose husband had been fortunate enough to have been given work by Carl Marman, was working for the very union that was trying to destroy the company. Why, the woman had even called on Mrs. Apter to urge her to honor the strike when it was called. Of course Mrs. Apter would have no part of this and was anxious for Mr. Marman to know the truth about the Appelavitch family, he assured a shocked Carl Marman.

Yakov felt a sickening twinge in his midsection as Carl Marman entered the large workroom where dozens of tailors sat at their machines. Yakov knew he was coming to see him and his pulse quickened. As the angry Marman rushed toward his bench, Yakov looked up from his work, determined to remain calm.

"Appelavitch, come with me!" Marman barked as he passed Yakov's bench without breaking his stride.

Yakov stopped working. Taking a few deep breaths, he slowly picked up his wire-rimmed glasses from the benchtop and put them on. He rose to follow Marman.

As they entered the poorly-lit hallway outside the workroom, Marman spun around and confronted Yakov. "What the shit are you up to, Appelavitch!"

"What are you talking about?" Yakov tried to mask his fear.

"You know damm well what I am talking about. That wife of yours is working for the union."

"It's an honest job," Yakov replied, surprised at his even response.

"Don't you know those bastards are trying to break us?"

"That isn't true! The union wants Kohn's to prosper."

"Yeah, like the cotton mill wants the boll weevil to succeed. What the hell is wrong with you, Appelavitch? Don't you know the CGWA is the enemy?"

"Their demands are reasonable," Yakov said, remembering Anna's words.

"Fuck their demands! They want to organize my work force. Who the hell do they think they are?"

"Why shouldn't the workers have their own organization, Mr. Marman? I don't understand."

"It's un-American, Appelavitch. We don't conspire against the people who employ us in this country."

"I would never listen to any union that made unreasonable demands, Mr. Marman."

"Listen, Appelavitch, you've got a gripe, you come see Marman. You don't need a whole union talking for you."

Yakov thought of his very first conversation with Marman and raised his shoulders. "What do you want of me?"

"Tell that wife of yours to stay away from the union," Marman snapped.

"Anna has a mind of her own. She believes in the union."

Marman could have fired Yakov on the spot, but didn't. He had a hunch he would have better luck if he could talk directly with Anna. "Tell your wife that I would like to see her at ten o'clock tomorrow morning."

"I will tell her."

That evening Anna went to the union hall to find Ivan. Wollmack was not surprised to learn that Marman had demanded to see Anna.

"Yankle said Mr. Marman was very upset," Anna said.

"Frankly, it sounds as if he was more restrained than I would have expected. I think you should go see him. You can tell him there will be pickets if he threatens to move against Yakov."

"He said we were un-American."

Wollmack smiled and took Anna by the shoulders. "You are as American as apple pie, Anna Appelavitch."

She beamed with pleasure at his compliment. "Thank you."

His expression grew more serious. As he stood facing her, his hands still holding her shoulders, his grip tightened ever so slightly. "Anna—" he whispered.

"I . . . I must go, Ivan," she answered, not letting him finish.

He nodded his understanding. "I know," he acknowledged, releasing her. As Anna turned to leave, Ivan snapped his fingers as though he had just remembered something.

"Anna, if he gets rough, tell him you know about the weak roof."

"What are you talking about?"

"Last winter when we had so much snow, the roof at Kohn's began to leak. One of the laborers he hired to repair the roof told me it would never stand another accumulation of snow like the one we had last year. He said the whole roof could fall in."

"Does Marman know?"

"He knows. The laborer told him too. Know what he said?" She shook her head. "He said it hadn't snowed like that for a hundred years and it won't snow like that for another hundred years."

"God in heaven." Anna's mind flashed back to the tragic Triangle Shirtwaist disaster.

"I was going to play that card at the right time. I think this is as good a time as any."

Carl Marman waited anxiously for his secretary to bring Anna into his office, looking forward to intimidating Yakov Appelavitch's wife. She was not what he expected, and for a moment he just sat there staring at her. *How in the hell did a weasel of a greenhorn like Appelavitch wind up with a beauty like this,* he thought to himself.

"Mrs. Appelavitch, sit down, please," he said with false warmth, gesturing for her to sit in one of the two metal chairs that faced his desk.

"You wanted to see me?" she asked politely, as if she were innocent of his motives.

"Yes, I thought we should talk. You are well?"

"Very well, thank you."

"The children are well?"

"Oh, yes, thank you."

"And Yakov?"

"We are all well."

"You know it is really wonderful how a family thrives when everyone has work. I can still remember when your husband and children first came to me. Things were bad back then."

"Yes, it was a bad time," she agreed, continuing to go along with him.

"But I liked those kids. I felt terrible for your husband. I said to myself, 'Carl, you have to help these people.'"

"Oh, come now, Mr. Marman," Anna said with a smile,

ready to make her move. "That isn't what you said to yourself at all."

The smile quickly faded from Marman's face. "What do you mean?" he asked sharply.

"What you really said was, 'Now, here are three people I can really take advantage of.'"

"Now just a sec—"

"What you really said," she broke in, raising her voice to cut him off, "was, 'I can let two twenty-five-cents-an-hour men go and hire these girls for about ten cents an hour, and the man I can put on piecework.'"

Carl Marman sat back and studied the defiant but striking-looking woman who sat before him. After a moment he rose without taking his eyes from her.

"I demand that you stop seeing the wives of my employees."

"Are they not allowed to have guests? Does the prison you run here extend to the homes of your employees as well?"

"How dare you!" he hissed, taken aback at her boldness. "I've tried to be civil with you."

"You have tried to intimidate me."

"What you need is to be reminded of what it's like when there is no work."

"Please don't threaten me, Mr. Marman."

"You know, if I fire your husband and those kids of yours, they will never find work in Baltimore again." Anna did not take her eyes from him as he fumed at her. "It's ten-fifteen, Mrs. Appelavitch. Push me too far and all four of you can leave here together at ten-thirty."

"Sit down!" she said in a quiet, level voice.

"What!"

"Sit down! I have something to say to you and it would be most unfortunate if you weren't paying attention."

He stood there for a moment, hardly believing his ears. Then slowly he sat down once again.

"So much as threaten my family with loss of their jobs because of me, and you will see a picket line at Kohn's quicker than you can say your name."

"My workers will laugh at you."

"They won't laugh."

"You think they will stand with you rather than with me?"

"They'll be with the union."

"They trust me, Anna Appelavitch. They know I look out for them. Most of those men wouldn't have a roof over their head if it wasn't for me."

Anna leaned forward, relishing the opening he had just given her. "And will there be a roof over their heads, Mr. Marman, the next time it snows?"

Carl Marman's mouth dropped open. "You don't know what you are talking about," he said haltingly.

"Oh, we know, Mr. Marman. We know." She rose to her feet.

"Just a second!" he yelled as she turned toward the door. "You can't go around saying things like that. You can really hurt someone that way."

"How *dare* you lecture me about how something I say can hurt someone. What did *you* say when you learned your roof was in danger of collapsing? How many people's lives were you willing to risk to save the cost of repair?"

"Please, Mrs. Appelavitch," he said, suddenly conciliatory. "Please. Sit down. I meant no harm."

"Who would believe that, Mr. Marman?"

"So help me, I intend to fix the roof before next winter."

"Good. That's one of the demands the CGWA will make that should give you no trouble."

Yakov couldn't believe his ears. "You actually talked like that to Carl Marman?"

Anna nodded. "I had more to frighten him with than he had to frighten me with."

"He'll still fight the union." Yakov said.

"Oh, yes. He will fight as a matter of honor if nothing else. The very idea of men organizing into a union drives him mad. He'll fight all right."

"I bet he won't fight with you again, Momma," Sheara said proudly.

"Oh, Carl Marman is not afraid of the likes of me. Today he was taken by surprise. Tommorrow might be a different story."

"Momma, I know who takes the pay to the women," Becky broke in.

"Who?" Anna asked as Yakov and Sheara turned their attention to Becky.

"Clara Louise Marman, Carl Marman's daughter. Today I

watched her fill a satchel with pay envelopes and leave the shop with it."

"Could you tell how many envelopes there were?" Anna asked.

"I tried to count. She arranged them by address. It looked as though she arranged the envelopes in groups of six."

"Could you tell how many such groupings she made up?"

"I think it was either eight or nine."

"That means he has between forty-eight and fifty-four workers," Anna said. "That's a lot. Do you know this Clara Louise?"

"Not real well, but we talk sometimes."

"Would she ever let you go along with her?"

"I don't know, but it wouldn't matter. She goes during the day. I could never leave work just to keep her company."

"But you are friendly with her?"

"Sort of." Becky paused for a moment. "Momma, she is very nice. I wouldn't want her to have any trouble with her father because of me."

Anna smiled at her daughter. "I understand. I wouldn't want you to take advantage of her either."

Ivan Wollmack listened carefully as Anna repeated her conversation with Carl Marman. "He was going to fire Yankle and the girls. The information about the roof stopped him."

"It was a victory today, Anna. The cost was high, but it was a victory nonetheless."

"What do you mean, 'the cost was high.' What was the cost?"

"We used up valuable information. Just as he caved in over the issue of job security for Yakov and the girls, he might have caved in on some other critical issue—perhaps to allow a union at Kohn's."

"If the information about the roof worked for me today, why won't it work for us again?"

"Believe me, it won't work again. First, you took him by surprise. Second, he will have dealt with the problem before we can raise it again. He'll never let us use that issue again."

"We need another issue."

"We need that damn list."

"We know who takes the women their pay."

"How did you learn that?"

"Becky saw Marman's daughter putting pay envelopes in a satchel. She carried between forty-eight and fifty-four envelopes out of Kohn's yesterday afternoon."

"Does Becky know the girl?"

"Somewhat."

"Anna, this could be very important."

"Ivan, I am not going to ask Becky to betray this girl. She says Clara Louise is very nice, and Becky doesn't want to cause trouble between the girl and her father."

"Anna, all the workers are nice too. They all have children who are also nice. We need that damned list."

"Becky is not going to trick Marman's daughter."

"For Christ's sake, Anna—"

"No, Ivan! I will not ask Becky to do that."

Becky knew how important the list was to the union, but she would not use deceit to obtain it. She just couldn't. But the following week Clara Louise Marman confided to Becky that she was going to have to miss a party because of her father's stupid insistence that she—and she alone—deliver the payroll to a bunch of seamstresses at their homes, and Becky found herself wavering.

"I have been waiting for Morris Rothstein to ask me out all year, and he finally asked me to a party in College Park and I can't go."

"Why not?" Becky asked.

"Because we would have to leave early Friday evening, and I would never have time to get ready since I must deliver the payroll on Friday."

"Do you go out on Shabbos?"

"We don't observe the Sabbath. We don't observe anything at our house. Besides, Morris is much too sophisticated for religion."

Becky's mouth turned dry as she pondered over the opportunity Clara Louise had given her. "Can I help?" she asked nervously.

Clara Louise laughed. "Are you volunteering to go to the University of Maryland with Morris Rothstein?"

Becky forced a smile. "I'll do the deliveries for you, Clara Louise."

The young girl suddenly grew very serious. "My father would kill me," she whispered.

"Oh, then you shouldn't—"

"Oh, but would you, Becky? I'd pay you!"

"No. No, I'll do it because you're a friend. Someday you'll do me a favor."

"Becky, you can't tell a soul. My father is crazy when it comes to that list."

"Why is it so special?"

"I don't know. He thinks it would be valuable to the union radicals. It's crazy. Most of the women on the list are tired old ladies. You're not a radical, are you?"

"Do I look like a radical?"

Both girls laughed.

"Meet me at three o'clock at the statue on Charles Street."

At two forty-five Becky told her shop foreman that she was ill and had to go home. Fifteen minutes later she stood in front of the memorial to George Washington, waiting for Clara Louise Marman. Clara Louise arrived a moment or two later and handed her the envelopes and the list, which Becky put in a bag she'd brought with her. Clara Louise explained that there were nine packets numbered one through six, and each was arranged in the order in which she would need them as she made her way from one address to the next.

As they were about to part, Clara Louise reached out and hugged Becky. A moment later she was on her way, having deceived her father, and Becky was on her way, having deceived Clara Louise.

Yakov and Sheara were surprised that Becky was not home when they arrived from work, and Anna was now beside herself, having been told by Yakov and Sheara that Becky had left work early because of illness.

It was seven-thirty when Becky finally arrived, grinning.

"Momma, Momma, I have the list! I have the list!" she said excitedly as she held it out to Anna.

"Becky! How did you get this? Where have you been?" Anna asked.

"My god, Marman will go insane if he hears of this," Yakov murmured.

Sheara watched speechlessly as Becky danced around her mother with delight and explained what she had done.

Anna took the list from Becky and glanced over it. "Oy," she whispered to herself. "Becky, Clara Louise will learn sooner or later that your mother works for the union. She will be furious."

"I know," Becky said nervously.

"Her father will kill her," Yakov said. "He will absolutely kill her."

It took ten days for Anna to call on the fifty-four workers on the list. After explaining what was at stake and how the CGWA could help them, none of the women had any intention of letting Carl Marman use them as strike breakers. Miraculously, no one told Marman that they were on to his scheme.

When the call for a strike went out, Marman was confident he would win and that Ivan Wollmack's power with the workers would be crushed. He was feeling so cocky that he agreed to a meeting with the labor organizer.

For over an hour the men argued, neither conceding an inch. Finally, Ivan Wollmack grew very serious and spoke slowly and deliberately without moving his eyes from Marman. "Now, you listen to me. You want a strike, you'll have a strike. If you think that's the way to survive, fine. But those workers of yours have had it up to here with the inequitable pay scale and the long hours." He raised his hand to his throat. "They're ready to send a message to the entire garment trade, and they are prepared to use you to do it. You think you'll outlast them, but you are wrong. They're ready to walk and so are their wives and children."

Marman grinned. "I'll win, Wollmack. You think you have all the cards, but I'll win. We'll see how the workers support you when they learn you can't offer them jobs."

Ivan ignored his taunt. "We want thirty cents an hour, a fifty-hour week, and an end to any preferential treatment for workers from one country over workers from another country."

Marman's grin seemed to spill over into a low guttural laugh. "Wollmack, I'll win."

Now it was Ivan's turn to grin. "No, Marman. You've already lost. Nearly all of your employees will honor the picket line, and so will their wives and children who work at home."

Marman sat there, drawing a long puff on his cigar. He slowly exhaled and studied the glowing ash for a moment. "You think you have all the answers don't you, Wollmack."

"I think we have covered all the bases."

"First, second, third, and home plate, huh, Wollmack?"

"First, second, third, home plate, and the other fifty-four as well, Marman," Ivan said calmly as he rose to his feet.

Carl Marman's mouth dropped open.

"Marman, your ash just fell on your tie," Wollmack said from the doorway, glancing back at Carl Marman's ruined silk necktie. "Sometimes everything goes wrong, doesn't it? The strike starts tonight at midnight."

"Jesus, Wollmack, don't do this to me!"

"Tonight! Marman."

"Sit down, Wollmack."

Wollmack silently studied the factory boss for several long minutes before he returned to his seat.

"Will you settle for a fifty-four-hour-week, thirty cents an hour, and fifteen cents an hour for the kids?"

"No, but we can talk."

"No strike?"

"Not for the time being," Ivan Wollmack said as he rose to his feet and strode from the room.

The CGWA had won. Kohn's became a union shop and the workers began to enjoy a little more money in their pay envelopes and a little more time with their families. Carl Marman brooded for a short time but wanted no more trouble with the CGWA or with Ivan Wollmack. Ironically Marman, in defeat, had secured the only period of tranquility Kohn's had ever known.

Now that a temporary settlement had been reached at Kohn's, there was less for Anna to do, although she did stop by the union hall every Sunday afternoon to help in the office. She saw less of Ivan during the month following the campaign to organize Kohn's, and Anna stopped going to the CGWA union hall shortly after Ivan left Baltimore late that spring. He had been asked by the union to go New York to run the New York local of the CGWA. Where Anna once had felt exhilaration upon entering the CGWA offices, she now felt only an unexpected emptiness and sadness. The hard fight was over—and they had won it. She returned to her Singer in the apartment finishing trousers and occasionally sewing buttonholes for Kohn's. Nothing much had changed except the wage she now earned. Anna was paid fifteen cents an hour to do the same work that had paid a dime only two months earlier.

Chapter Thirteen

She laid the newspaper down, noting the headline about the disorders in Haiti and Santo Domingo. She shook her head. The world was full of trouble spots this summer: crisis in Ulster; revolution in Mexico; Greco-Turkish hostilities; and the fateful assassination at Sarajevo, which was pushing Europe to the brink of war—just as Meyer Kramer had predicted nearly a year earlier.

Americans seemed to consider all these events much less important than what would next befall Pearl White in the *The Perils of Pauline,* or the craze for dancing the tango. It was as if they felt that what happened in Europe had nothing to do with them. It was very strange. Anna avidly read the news in the Baltimore *Sun* every day. She knew about the growing clamor for prohibition, and film stars such as Mary Pickford and Charlie Chaplin. But these things were not as important to her as they seemed to be to almost everyone else in America.

Day after day Anna devoured the sketchy news reports from Europe. It was odd how all the terrible words were small ones: hate, death, kill. War. The Germans were advancing through "little Belgium." There was fighting in France, from Switzerland to the sea. The Western Front, they called it. When would war erupt in the East? Day after day Anna anxiously read the newspaper. Day after day there was nothing.

It was some time during the last week of August that Sheara ran into the apartment waving a copy of the Baltimore *Sun.* The headline read: "Russian First Army Attacks Germans."

Her parents stared at the map on the front page in horror. It showed the Masurian Lakes district, with its principal city, Suwalki. Ominous arrows streaked westward through an area bordered on the south by Suwalki and the north by Czerniachowsk. The southernmost arrow cut through an area both knew contained the village of Oleck-Podlaska. They could only pray that Yakov's parents and Dvoyra and her family were safe; pray that the war would not touch them.

Their prayers were not answered. The early Russian breakthrough was due more to surprise and luck than superior planning or leadership. Two Russian armies, the First led by General Pavel Rennenkampf, the Second by General Alexander Samsonov, pushed into East Prussia, where there were few German troops. The German commander, General von Prittwitz, took flight at the appearance of "the Russian steamroller" and fell back, proposing to stand behind the Vistula. Had Rennenkampf put his First Army into hot pursuit, a rout that might have altered the course of the war could have ensued. But Rennenkampf had moved his ill-equipped and badly trained troops without coordinating their movements with those of his counterpart to the south. He moved slowly and carefully, consolidating his gains.

Prittwitz was dismissed, and the coming man of the German General Staff, Erich Ludendorff, was sent to replace him. When it was discovered Ludendorff did not hold high enough rank for supreme command, the elderly General Paul von Hindenburg was brought out of retirement to cover for him.

Ludendorff made the most of the wide gap separating the two Russian armies; he also made the most of the casual Russian practice of sending wireless messages *en clair*—code was too difficult for them. He not only knew where the Russians were and what they planned to do, but exactly how their forces were deployed.

The Germans pulled all their troops away from Rennenkampf's tentative advance and fell upon Samsonov's Second Army to the south, slaughtering it. This victory achieved, the Germans turned their full attention to Rennenkampf's First Army, breaking it and sending it reeling back toward Russia. This was the battle of Tannenberg, August 29. Russian troops would not set foot inside Germany again for the duration of the war.

With the German armies pressing ever closer to the borders of their country, the Russians turned their fury upon the Jewish civilian population, whom they were convinced were not only sympathetic to the Germans, but actually providing them with information about troop movements. A new policy for dealing with this collaboration was formulated forthwith:

> Our experience during this war has clearly revealed the hostile attitude of the Jewish Population, particularly of Galicia and the Bukovina. As soon as there occurs some substantial change in the location and movement of our troops, and whenever we temporarily evacuate one or another district, the enemy, because of the intervention of the Jews, adopts cruel measures against the loyal non-Jewish population. In order to protect the population faithful to us from reprisals by the enemy, and to safeguard our troops against the treason that the Jews employ along the entire front, the Supreme Commander of the Russian Armed Forces considers it necessary that the Jews be banished as soon as the enemy retreats. It is necessary to take hostages from among the rich or well-to-do or other persons holding important positions. The most influential rabbis of the respective communities must also be seized and deported as prisoners to the interior of our country. This will in the first instance be to the province of Kiev, where they are to be held in concentration camps.

> —Grand Duke Nikolai Nikolaievich

Chapter Fourteen

Berl Hoffman's hands trembled as he read the pamphlet. It had been given to him in Oleck-Podlaska by a refugee who had fled from Galicia.

"They are banishing Jews from their homes, all over Galicia," the man had told him. "They say we are spies for the Germans."

"Read it, Dvoyra," Berl said, handing it to his wife. "Read it. It is signed by the Grand Duke himself."

Dvoyra read the Russian field order, her eyes wide with disbelief. "But Berl, when the goyim see this, they will turn on us as never before. We must leave."

"Leave? Where would we go? To the east is Russia, to the west, Germany. The Austrians and Germans are fighting the Russians in the south. Where would we go?"

"I don't know. But we must think of our child. Of our children.

He turned to face her, frowning. "What did you say?"

"I think I may be pregnant, Berl," Dvoyra said softly. "I'm sorry."

He shook his head. "Don't, don't be sorry."

"It will make things more difficult for us, I know."

"Then they'll just have to be more difficult," he said, trying for a reassuring smile. "When have they ever been easy?"

"I know." She touched his hand. "That's why I wondered whether . . ."

"Dvoyra, we can't just go without knowing where or why."

"Why is easy. To protect Peninah and the baby. Where? North, I suppose. That's where everyone will go if they are ordered to leave their homes. Vilna, maybe."

"Vilna?"

"If we wait until everyone leaves, it will be impossible to find somewhere to stay in Vilna. We mustn't wait, Berl."

"But who do we know in Vilna? What would we do when we got there? Besides, the Russians control Vilna too."

"There are tens of thousands of Jews in Vilna. They can't empty out the entire city. We would find help there, I'm sure."

"What about Poppa? What about the Appelavitches?"

"We could all go together."

He shook his head again. "They won't leave, Dvoyra. It would be different if we were being ordered out. But the old people won't leave because we *think* they might order us to leave."

"Then we will have to go alone."

During the last week of October word began filtering into the village that Rennenkampf's First Army was retreating back through the Masurian Lakes district toward Suwalki. Berl and Dvoyra knew that as the Russians retreated, they would draft as replacement troops every able-bodied man they could find. Finally Berl agreed that it was time to go. By the eve of their departure he was as anxious as Dvoyra to get away.

They discussed their decision with Berl's father. Isaiah Hoffman gave them his blessing and told them they were doing the right thing, but refused to join them. Dvoyra talked to Shoule and Necha Appelavitch as well. Like Isaiah Hoffman, they told Dvoyra that she was making the right decision. And like Berl's father, they declined to leave. There were Jews in town who believed they would fare better at the hands of the Germans than they had under the rule of the czars; in fact many were waiting eagerly for the Germans to drive the Russians out. But Shoule and Necha were not among these—they were staying simply because Oleck-Podlaska was, and always had been, their home. They talked of Yankle and Anna, agreeing sadly that they would probably not hear from her again until the war was over. Dvoyra promised them she would write her sister from Vilna. It wasn't much of a hope, but it was the only one she could give them.

Now Berl spread out the map he had drawn on the kitchen table, and together they traced out the route they would travel. First to Suwalki, then northeast along the main highway to Kapsukas. They would cross the River Nemumas at Prienai, passing through four more small towns before they reached the end of their journey, two hundred and eleven versts, a hundred and forty miles.

"Do you think we'll be able to find places to spend the night as we travel? Dvoyra asked her husband.

He shrugged his shoulders. "We'll just have to see. For a few kopecks we can always—"

He stopped at the sound of a fist pounding on the front door. Alarmed, they looked at each other as Berl quickly folded up the map. He went to the door and opened it just wide enough to see a man standing outside, a sleeping child cradled in his arms.

"Azriel!" Berl exclaimed. "Dvoyra, come quick!"

They had not seen Esther's husband since the week following Esther's death, almost two years ago. He looked worn out, his clothes covered with dust as if he had been on the road for a long time. His eyes were red and irritated, either from the dust of the road or because he was badly in need of sleep. He had the face of a Russian officer in the czar's army—square, proud jaw, high cheekbones, coal-black eyes, and straight chestnut-colored hair. However, he was a poor farmer who, like Berl, believed his home and his place was in Poland near the banks of his beloved Bug River.

"I didn't know where else to go," he said as Dvoyra took the child, Yitzhak, from him. She laid the child on the old sofa, covering him with Berl's coat. Her brother-in-law almost fell into a chair. His face was haggard, dark shadows of exhaustion were visible beneath his deep-set eyes.

"You've come from Berdichev?" Berl asked, astonished. It was a journey of nearly five hundred miles.

"I have to report for duty in the Russian army in less than a week," Azriel said, his voice flat with fatigue. "I have brought Yitzhak to you for safekeeping." He looked first at Dvoyra, than at Berl. "You'll take care of my son while I'm gone? I don't know whom else to ask."

"Azriel, why didn't you take him to Momma?" Dvoyra asked as a sickening premonition tugged at her. He looked up at her with tear-filled eyes, his face twisted with pain.

"I wrote to you, Dvoyra," he whispered. "I wrote and told you everything. The mail . . . I suppose nothing got through because of the fighting. There's been chaos in Berdichev since it started. You can't imagine . . ."

Dvoyra sank into a chair across the table from Azriel Agronski, her eyes wide. "What has happened?" she whispered.

"Chaya Sarah is dead, Dvoyra. I'm sorry. I thought you knew.

"When was this?" Berl asked quietly, standing behind his wife and placing his hands on her shoulders.

"We buried her a month ago. I did write to you, Dvoyra. I really did."

"I'm sure you did, Azriel," Dvoyra said softly, tears rolling down her cheeks. "Did she—"

"She died in her sleep. She was never sick, not even for a day."

"Thank God for that at least," Dvoyra whispered. She looked at Berl. He took her hand in his and held it against his heart.

"Do you still want to leave in the morning?" Berl asked her.

"Leave? You're leaving Oleck-Podlaska?" Azriel stared at them uncomprehendingly.

"We are going to Vilna," Berl said.

"Vilna?" Azriel repeated in a whisper, dread in his eyes. "Why?"

"Azriel, they are deporting Jews all over Galicia. They are forcing our men to fight in their army. I am pregnant and we don't want to wait until we are forced to leave."

Azriel closed his eyes. He put his head in his hands. "What about my baby? What about Yitzhak?"

Dvoyra looked at her husband, who nodded. "We must protect the children, Dvoyra," he said. "We will take Yitzhak with us, if you want us to, Azriel."

Azriel did not look up. "Vilna, Vilna," he murmured. "He will be so far away."

"The farther away he is, the safer he will be," Berl told him. Azriel nodded. He walked across to where his son lay sleeping, staring down at him. He knelt down and took the child's tiny hand into his own, kissing the tips of his son's fingers.

"I'll come for you when the war is over, Yitzhak," he whispered. "I'll come as soon as God lets me."

"Azriel, you don't intend to leave tonight?" Dvoyra protested. "You need some food, rest. You can't—"

"I must, Dvoyra." Azriel stood up. "If I do not get to Berdichev in time, they could shoot me. Besides, I couldn't bear to leave if he were awake. It's best this way."

"But he's only two years old," Berl said. "What will we tell him when he wakes up?"

"He knew he was coming here. I have told him about his Tante Dvoyra many times."

He took Dvoyra's hands in his, looked deep into her eyes, as if searching for something.

"My Esther always said that if I was in trouble I should come to you, Dvoyra. 'She is the best one of us all,' she said. I know you will take good care of my son, I know that. But Dvoyra—"

"What is it, Azriel?"

"Don't let him forget me," he whispered. "Please don't let him forget me."

"Well," Berl said as he brought the wagon to a stop on a knoll overlooking the old city. "There is Vilna, the Jerusalem of Lithuania." He smiled, gesturing toward the gray, brooding city that lay before them.

"It doesn't look much like Jerusalem to me," Dvoyra

replied dubiously. Vilna stretched as far as the eye could see, roofs glistening in the early-morning rain. Off to the left the mighty River Viliya bent through the northern part of the city, joining the smaller River Vileika below a hill crowned with the ruins of an old castle.

"It's enormous," Dvoyra said. "How many people live here?"

"I don't know. A hundred and fifty, two hundred thousand maybe. Jews, Lithuanians, Poles."

"It looks so depressing."

"Cities always look depressing in the rain," Berl replied, trying to reassure her, putting his arm around her shoulder. "it will look better when the sun comes out."

The road led downhill through the suburb of Pogulyanka toward the center of the city. Peninah and Yitzhak woke up and climbed onto the seat between Dvoyra and Berl, watching wide-eyed as trolleys clanged past and people in fine clothes went by in splendid carriages. By the time they got to Jatkowa Street on the edge of the Jewish quarter, the sun was shining. The streets were much narrower here, paved with cobblestones, and pushcarts lined the sidewalks, offering old clothing, sticks of furniture, battered books for sale. The sidewalks were quite crowded, but few of the pedestrians showed any interest in the Hoffmans. They seemed preoccupied, scurrying from shop to shop, pausing only to peer quickly into the front windows and then hurrying on without going inside.

"The shops are all empty," Dvoyra said.

"Most of them appear to be meat markets," Berl observed. "There probably isn't any more meat here than there was in Oleck-Podlaska."

"Hey, you!" someone shouted. "Have you anything to sell?"

Berl turned. A short, well-fleshed man of about fifty, a two-day stubble on his chin, was waving from the doorway of one of the shops. Berl regarded him suspiciously as the man approached.

"I said, have you got anything to sell?"

"No, nothing." Berl frowned. The man looked at him for a moment, and then at Dvoyra and the children.

"Where are you from?"

"Oleck-Podlaska. We came here to get away from the war."

"You brought nothing to sell? No grain, no fruit, nothing?"

"It never occurred to us," Berl said. "We came here looking for a safe place to stay until the war is over."

"And you came to Vilna? Ha, that's a good one!" the man said with a harsh laugh. "Listen, my friend, it's only a matter of time till the Kaiser gets here. Meanwhile there's no food worth the name to be had. As you see, all the shops are closed. We can't get anything to sell."

"You're a butcher?"

"I would be if I had any meat. That's my shop there. Isaac Levin's my name."

"I'm Berl Hoffman. This is my wife Dvoyra. Maybe you can help us, Mr. Levin. We've been on the road for a long time. Can you tell us where we might find a place to rest?"

Levin shook his head ruefully. "I told you, things are bad here. Your best bet is to go to the Great Synagogue. Maybe someone there can help you."

"Can you tell me how to get there?"

"That I can. You keep going straight ahead until you come to Niemiecka. Nyemetzkaya in Russian. They both mean the same thing, German Street. Go one block and on your left you will find Zydowa. Yevretskaya in Russian."

"Jew Street?" Dvoyra gasped.

"It's the Jewish quarter." Levin smiled. "Why should't there be a street named for the Jews?"

"First left, Zydowa," Berl said. "What then?"

"You'll see the Great Synagogue. You can hardly miss it. If the gates are closed, go around to the alley on German Street."

"You're very kind," Berl said. "Thank you for your help."

"I wish you luck." Levin waved them on. "And you'll need it," he added under his breath.

They had no trouble finding the Great Synagogue of Vilna. It stood in a courtyard, protected by a huge iron gate. Two stone pillars, each supporting its own lamp, flanked the gate, creating an aura of security. They went into the courtyard, stopping to read the tablets near the two doors at the entrance to the sanctuary. The one on the right bore the legend:

Gift to the Lord
From the Holy Society of Psalm Sayers
1642

The one on the left had, according to the inscription, been presented by the Tailors' Society in 1640.

Berl helped Dvoyra and the children from the wagon, and they went through the doorway. Immediately inside they saw stone steps that descended in a long curve, lit by lamps in sconces on the wall.

"Strange," Berl muttered. "Why do the steps go down, instead of up?"

Dvoyra shrugged. "The synagogue is very old, Berl. Maybe they—"

"Can I help you?" a voice interrupted. They turned to see an old man step from the shadows. His hair and beard were streaked with gray, but there was a youthful twinkle in his dark eyes.

"I didn't intend to startle you." He smiled. "My name is Grobman. I am the sexton of this synagogue."

"My name is Berl Hoffman. This is my wife Dvoyra, our daughter Peninah, and nephew Yitzhak. We are looking for somewhere to stay, and I need a job. A man called Levin directed us here."

"Where are you from?"

"Oleck-Podlaska. It's near—"

"Suwalki, I know. You have come to escape the war?"

"We were worried about the children. And my wife—"

"Yes, I see," Grobman said, nodding after glancing at Dvoyra's gently swelling belly. "Well, Mr. Hoffman, what can I tell you? Things are bad here. The charity rolls are bulging. There is very little work to be had. What can you do?"

"I'm a craftsman. I can repair or build anything."

"A leaky roof?"

"Of course."

"Then we might be able to help each other."

"How?"

"It's simple enough. You need a place to stay, food for your family. We need someone who can fix our roof. We will make a trade. The community, the Kahal, has opened a free kitchen near here. We also have a building a few doors farther on, which we use for storage. I think there is an empty room there. If you repair our roof, you can stay in the empty room, and you can get soup and bread from the kitchen for your family."

"I'll do it," Berl said immediately. "Thank you."

"Don't be so quick to thank me. When you see how much work has to be done, and the room and food you will receive in return, you will probably curse my name."

"Berl, Berl," Dvoyra said under her breath, "are you sure you are doing the right thing? You want us to live in a room in a warehouse, eat in a charity kitchen?"

"I want to be sure we do not have to sleep on the streets," he said quietly. "Don't you see how things are here, Dvoyra?" He turned to Grobman. "Where is this warehouse of yours?"

"It's on Pohulanka Street. Not far, I'll take you there." Grobman led the way out of the synagogue, through the courtyard, and down narrow, badly paved streets where the buildings leaned so close together that they shut out the sunlight. The air seemed full of the sour smell of poverty and fear.

"There's something else I'd like to know," Berl said as they made their way toward Pohulanka Street. "Why was the synagogue constructed so that the floor is so far below ground level?"

"A craftsman's question," Grobman said. "The synagogue was begun in 1573. In those days there was a law that forbade the Jews from building their synagogue higher than any of the Christian churches."

"I see. So the floor was constructed below ground level, making it possible for them to have the interior height they desired without breaking the law!"

"Jews are renowned for finding solutions to seemingly impossible problems." Grobman smiled. "I hope you have a resourceful mind, Mr. Hoffman?"

"Why do you ask?"

"We have no tools for you. No nails. No lumber. You might as well ask for gold. That's why I ask if you have a resourceful mind."

"But how can I work without tools or materials?"

"Come back to the synagogue tomorrow, and I'll give you a list of the membership. You'll have to find people to contribute whatever you will need."

"But nobody knows me here," Berl protested. "How will I do that?"

"You're the craftsman, Mr. Hoffman."

The old man handed a key to Berl and took his leave, leaving the Hoffmans standing outside the dilapidated Kahal storage building. Berl opened the door and they went inside.

There were three rooms on each of the three floors. All but one room on the first floor were piled high with old furniture, cartons of clothing, and boxes full of books and papers. The building stank of mildew.

"Berl, it's a pigsty!" Dvoyra said, appalled. "We can't possibly live in this mess!"

"We have to stay somehere until we can find a better place." Berl lit an old kerosene lantern that hung from a hook on the wall of the first room they had entered. The children looked about them, whimpering in fear.

"We'll freeze to death!" Dvoyra said.

"No, there's an old stove in the corner." Berl pointed at a blackened, potbellied woodburner across the room.

"The old man said you might as well ask for gold as lumber," Dvoyra said.

"He also said we'd curse his name when we saw this place, and he wasn't far from wrong."

"Maybe we won't have to stay here." Dvoyra looked around the filthy, barren room. "Will we?"

"Of course not." He smiled to allay her fears. "It's only temporary. We'll find something better soon, you'll see. Come, don't fret now. Come, children. Let's go back up the street to that kitchen and get something to eat!"

He led his family out into the narrow, shadowed alley, where he swung Yitzhak up onto his shoulders and marched along singing songs and making both children laugh. Dvoyra followed silently behind, listening to her husband's voice bouncing off the walls of the drab buildings. She wondered whom he thought he was fooling.

As time went by, Yakov seemed to spend more and more of his leisure time hidden behind the pages of the *Daily Forward*. He followed the progress of the war almost obsessively. He had found a new word: "significant." He used it to describe some of the events happening in Europe. The German blockade of Britain was "significant," as was their announcement that all shipping destined for enemy nations would be sunk wherever intercepted. The first reports, in the spring of 1915, that the Germans had used poison gas during the second battle of Ypres in France were, Yakov pronounced sagely, of enormous significance. Poison gas was a new weapon, a terrible one. It would be interesting to see whether they used it in the East, on the Russians.

Anna shuddered whenever she read the war news in the

Baltimore *Sun*. She did not want to think of such things: she was consumed with fear for Dvoyra's safety. She held the new baby, Benjamin, closer to her breast, and tried to forget her fears in the pleasure of watching her youngest child grow.

Yakov took little or no interest in the child. Anna had come to expect that—as time passed, he seemed not to want to have anything to do with any of his children. The newspaper was erected nightly as a barrier between him and them. The effect of this was to bind the children ever more closely to their mother.

Once in a while Sheara or Becky would bring home an American newspaper so Anna could read it. As always, Anna was surprised by the lack of interest shown by Americans in the war. There was as much news about baseball as there was about what was happening in France or Poland. The girls knew all the names of the new sports heroes: Ty Cobb, Jess Willard, Walter Hagen. There was news of the new musical rage, "ragtime." A man named Edison had spoken into a telephone in New York and had been heard clearly by a man in San Francisco, on the other side of the continent. Sheara told her mother about another miracle, the nickelodeon, where you could go and see pictures that actually moved. And Anna realized that her daughters were becoming Americans, that the war was to them, as to most Americans, something that was happening a long way away.

Then on May 7, 1915, an event occurred that changed all that and brought the grim reality of war into every parlor and onto every street corner in America.

"Anna, Anna!" Yakov shouted, waving the *Forward* as he came through the door. "A terrible thing, terrible! The German U-boats have sunk a big ship, the *Lusitania*!"

Her first thought was of Meyer Kramer. Could he have been on the German ship? It was obvious now that they were on different sides of this battle. It was almost impossible to think of the man who once held her with such love as her enemy now. She forced herself to listen to Yakov reading aloud.

". . . largest and fastest steamship in passenger service . . . at least twenty minutes after the explosion . . ."

Over a thousand had perished as the great ship slid beneath the waves off Old Head of Kinsale, not far from the port of Cork.

"This is a very significant event, Anna," Yakov said sententiously, rattling the paper. "The Germans may have made a big mistake in sinking the *Lusitania*."

"In what way?"

"Americans have been killed. More than a hundred. This could be construed as an act of war against America. Those Germans must be mad, mad! To risk bringing America into the war! Mind you, anybody who would serve in submarines would have to be out of his mind anyway!"

Anna closed her eyes, seeing Meyer Kramer, and remembered the love in his eyes. *God be with you, Meyer Kramer, it is over between us* she thought.

"I read somewhere that they're working on a new defense against the U-boats," Yakov was saying. "Depth bombs or something. They drop them into the water where they think the submarine may be, and the U-boat is crushed by the blast and sinks."

"Please, Yankle, don't talk about such things!"

"Why do you care what happens to men in U-boats?"

"They have mothers too, Yankle. Brothers, sisters, people who love them."

"You care too much. You have to be more detached, Anna. There's nothing we can do about what's happening out there."

"I can't help it. No matter who is right or who is wrong, innocent people die. How can I help but care, when it might be my sister, your parents?"

Yakov sighed, wishing now he had never brought up the subject. No matter which aspect of the war he wanted to discuss, it always came back to the same thing: her family, her sister.

"We just have to hope, Anna," he said, returning to his newspaper. "It's all we can do."

Hope. That was what Meyer had said. *Keep hoping, Anna. Will you do that?*

"The Russian army seems to be collapsing, Anna. They say thousands have been made homeless in Eastern Europe."

Keep hoping, Anna.

"The German army is converging on Lithuania. They say Vilna will be captured soon."

Keep hoping.

"They say the average life expectancy of a U-boat crew is less than a year."

Promise me you'll keep hoping.

And silently within herself she screamed: *How? Somebody tell me how!*

Chapter Fifteen

As the German advance across Poland formed a great encircling "C" whose jaws would soon close on Warsaw, the Russian army fell back, taking with it anything and everything that might be of value to the enemy, leaving the people whose towns and villages they sacked nothing but deprivation, disease, and despair.

In the Jewish quarter of Vilna private homes, schoolrooms, public buildings, and synagogues were jammed with the tens of thousands of refugees expelled from the provinces of Kovno, Grodno, and Suwalki by the Grand Duke Nikolai's decree. Parents abandoned their children, hoping some family with greater means might take them in and provide for them, or that their children would be placed in orphanages and there be fed and clothed. Throughout that abnormally dry summer, starvation and cholera decimated the population.

For Berl and Dvoyra the warehouse that had become their home no longer seemed a filthy hovel, but a safe island in the sea of misery outside. The Kahal continued to find work for Berl and to provide his family with food. In a city where there was no work and food was scarce, they had a degree of security almost unknown to the rest of the Jewish population.

Berl had managed to collect a bed of sorts, a makeshift table, a stool, and some boxes for the children to sit on. Peninah and Yitzhak slept on a mattress made from old blankets stuffed with paper, in a corner of the room that Berl had partitioned off with pieces from boxes and crates.

Like many of the Vilna Jews, the Hoffmans hoped that the German advance toward Lithuania would not only mean the end of Russian oppression, but perhaps of the war itself. The Germans had hammered three times upon the gates of Warsaw without success. It could not be long till their efforts were crowned with victory.

That victory had not yet come by June 21, when on a hot and windless night, by the flickering light of the kerosene lamp Berl had suspended above her, Dvoyra was delivered of her baby. Wet with perspiration, biting hard into a water-soaked cloth to keep her from crying out and waking Peninah and Yitzhak, Dvoyra felt her husband gently pull the baby from her womb, and smiled as he told her it was a daughter.

"Annette," she sighed as he laid the squalling child in her arms. They had agreed upon the name if the baby was a girl. A boy would have been named after Berl's father.

Annette was not a month old when the Germans began their fourth assault on Warsaw. The city fell on August 4; next day, the fortress of Ivangorod capitulated. The "Vistula line," the barrier to the German advance created by the great river, was breached, and the Russian armies fell back in disarray.

The mighty Reichswehr moved forward like a lurching colossus, crashing against the walls of Kovno in an eleven-day battle that resulted in formidable German losses. On June 17 the great fortress, last bastion on the River Neman, surrendered. The Germans took Brest Litovsk on August 25, Bialystok at the end of the month. By September 7 they were encircling Vilna, their forward units in Novo Troiki, and Volkovysk to the south. Thirty thousand German cavalrymen looted within ten miles of the city. As the Jews of Vilan went to their synagogues on Yom Kippur to pray for deliverance from the pestilence and war that dominated their lives, the Russians abandoned the city to its fate.

Berl Hoffman did not stay long at the Great Synagogue that afternoon. He was not a deeply religious man, and although he would not work on Yom Kippur, he knew the Kahal had several properties in need of repair in the quarter. There was no reason he could not go and look at what needed to be done.

German Street was filled with people, an air of excitement in the crowd so electric that it was almost tangible. Berl stopped and asked a passerby what was going on.

"Someone says the Germans have entered the city," the man said.

Berl thanked him and hurried down German Street to Theater Square. There were crowds in front of the town hall and the Cathedral of St. Nicholas opposite. Down Ostrovorotnaya—Town Gate Road—Berl heard music, drums, the sound of cheers. Then he saw them, halfway down the street—a column of marching German soldiers preceded by a band wearing spiked coal-scuttle helmets, led by a rotund, black-booted officer. The officer was flanked by a soldier carrying a brass pole surmounted by a tasseled canopy; from its crossbar hung horsehair tails, sleigh bells, and crescent-shaped pieces of glass that tinkled and jingled in time to the martial music. An officer on horseback rode alongside the procession, his expression haughty.

Berl pushed his way through the crowd on the square and ran back up German Street and all the way to the warehouse at 11 Pohulanka, where Dvoyra and the children were waiting.

"The Germans are here!" he shouted as he burst into the room. "They're marching up the Bolshaya right now!"

"Is the war over?" Dvoyra asked, her eyes sparkling with excitement. She ran to his side and put her arms around him. "Oh, Berl, do you think we'll be able to go home?"

He shrugged. "I don't know. The Russians are all gone. We'll have to wait a day or two, see what the Germans do."

"They can't be any worse than the Russians."

He shrugged again. "We can't be so sure about that, yet."

Two days after the German occupation, Berl was summoned to the Kahal. Dr. Jacob Wygodski—a man of almost sixty, tall, austere, and dignified—motioned Berl to a chair, then sat down himself, his face serious.

"Hoffman," he said without preamble, "we have a disaster on our hands!"

"Who is 'we'?"

"When the leaders of the Jewish Central Committee fled from Vilna, we formed a Citizens Committee to deal with the Germans. It consists of myself, Arthur Littauer, Joseph Izbicki, and Dr. Nemah Shabad."

"I know Dr. Shabad," Berl said, remembering having seen the man at the Kahal.

"We had hoped the Germans would help us. Instead, they are requisitioning everything they can get their hands on."

"But we have nothing. The people of Vilna are starving as it is."

"I know." Wygodski ran a hand through his long, black beard. "And it's going to get worse."

"It could get worse?"

"Take my word for it, it will. That's why I've sent for you.

Hoffman, we're going to have to open free kitchens all over Vilna. The few we have now just won't be enough. Before the war began, there were maybe sixty thousand Jews living in Vilna. There are now eighty-two thousand. On top of that, there are ten thousand Christian refugees who need feeding."

Berl did some rapid mental arithmetic. The free kitchen on Pohulanka Street could serve about a hundred people at a time. In the course of a full day perhaps nine hundred people passed through its doors. "You're talking about close to a hundred kitchens?" he asked in disbelief.

"A hundred." Wygodski nodded. "Otherwise there'll be bodies piled ten feet high in the streets of Vilna next winter."

"It can't be done. There aren't enough vacant buildings. Enough stoves. Enough anything."

"It must be done, Hoffman. The Germans won't lift a finger to help us," Wygodski said grimly. "That's why I sent for you."

"Me? What can I do?"

"You probably know more about the buildings in the Jewish quarter than anyone else in Vilna. You're the ideal man to do a survey of the city, to find suitable places and decide what will be needed to make them usable."

Berl stared at the old man. "Have you any idea what you're asking me to do?"

"The impossible," Wygodski said without smiling. "And I want you to get started right away."

"How long do I have?"

"How long can a hungry child go without food?"

Winter laid its iron hand upon the land. From the Baltic to the Danube, women and children tramped the icy streets of village and town, searching or begging for food. The great hunger spared no one, soldier or civilian, friend or foe. In Germany they called it the "turnip winter," because that humble food was the best that could be had. The levies imposed on the conquered lands by the occupying armies grew heavier. Farmers began to slaughter milk cows for meat.

In the West, the Great War had reached a grisly stalemate. Throughout 1915, four million men, burrowed in trenches that stretched from the English Channel to the Swiss frontier, spilled rivers of each other's blood without altering the line. Seeking to resolve that deadlock, Germany laid siege to Verdun in February 1916. When that endless siege was lifted five months later, nearly three quarters of a million Germans and Frenchmen lay dead. France had not fallen. The front had not moved.

On July 1 the British launched their greatest offensive of the war. By October it too had ground to a halt, with more than a million dead on both sides of the largely unaltered battlefront.

In the East, Russia responded to the Allied request for relief offensives. The Russian response, ill-conceived and ill-executed, was to attack Vilna. The offensive was launched in the middle of March, just as the thaw came, smothering the attack in mud. As the battle concluded, the frosts reappeared, swallowing up whole companies in the stiffening swamps. One hundred and twenty thousand Russian soldiers were lost, and General Evert pulled back his central army group to lick its wounds and await a second chance. It was never to materialize. Although they did not yet know it, the Imperial Army, and its commander the Czar Nicholas, were to be a factor in the Great War for only a little longer.

Throughout this momentous year Berl Hoffman worked like a man possessed. He was awake at daybreak and on the street shortly thereafter, moving from block to block, building to building, searching for enough space to install a kitchen in which to serve soup to the starving people of Vilna. He commandeered plots of land at the Botanical Gardens and the Bernadinski Garden, erected makeshift huts on them, and installed Jewish families to live on and cultivate the allotments. He bargained for seeds from merchants in the spring in return for the promise of vegetables in summer and autumn. Of every dozen cabbages, every twelve leeks, he got but three for the kitchens. One went to pay for the seeds; one to the Jews who had grown the vegetables and protected them by living on the allotments; three for the soup kitchens. The balance was levied by the Germans. It was an offense, punishable by death, to falsify or evade the levy.

Every night after dark Berl went to Wygodski's room at the Kahal, and they reviewed the day's survey: a basement storage area in an abandoned house on Steklyanskaya, Glass Street; a looted shop owned by Jews who had fled from Vilna when the Germans arrived; a stable; a building on the Vokzalnaya, opposite the railroad station, once used by maintenance workers. Within a day or two the Committee would have obtained permission from the German Occupation Control to use the buildings, and somehow a free kitchen would be put into operation.

By the end of the year the Jews had opened nearly a hundred kitchens in Vilna. As winter took hold, however, it became increasingly difficult to find food and fuel. Black marketeering, theft, smuggling, and the ever-increasing levies of the Germans made it nearly impossible to keep all the kitchens open. In all his life Berl had never experienced anything as difficult as the realization when faced with the scarecrow figures silently, stoically waiting in the bitter autumn winds that whipped across the city, that the kitchen on which they depended for life itself must close.

"I'm afraid, Dvoyra," he told his wife. He had come home, as usual, too late to talk to the children, who were already asleep. He was gaunt with hunger and exhaustion and looked many years older than he was.

"What do you mean?" Dvoyra pushed back the lock of hair that hung over his eyes and kissed his forehead.

"The Germans . . . they don't care what happens to us. I don't think they hate us, the way the Russians did. But they aren't going to help us either. If it comes down to a choice between a German starving and a Jew starving, that is no choice at all to them."

"Have you talked with Dr. Wygodski?"

"He agrees with me. He's trying to form cooperatives to buy and distribute food. God knows where he'll find any. Or what he will use for money. The community is in ruin, Dvoyra. Over thirty-two thousand Jews are completely dependent on charity.

"Surely there are still some with money?"

"Those who have any are using it to buy food from the black marketeers."

"But where do the black marketeers get it?"

"Look, suppose you have a cow and she drops a calf. You know if you tell anyone, the Occupation Control will come and take them both. So you arrange to smuggle them to a dealer, who will sell them to the highest bidder. They sell on the black market for ten times what they paid."

"How could anyone do such a thing when people are dying of starvation in the street?"

"Money," he said flatly. "And what is worse, the smugglers are Jews. I keep my eyes open. I suspect the identities of several of the black marketeers. I've shared my suspicion with Wygodski, and he and the Kahal are investigating it."

"I don't believe it!" Dvoyra cried.

"I didn't believe it either," he said sadly. "But it's true."

"They should be named," Dvoyra said hotly. "Their names should be made public! They're no better than jackals!"

"They're powerful men, Dvoyra," he warned, rubbing his eyes. It could be dangerous to antagonize them."

"God in heaven, Berl!" she cried. "What is happening to our people?"

January 28, 1918

Dear Anna,

I wish it were possible to send you good news, but I fear this letter will bring you little but sadness. We have come back home to Oleck-Podlaska. We had to leave Vilna. Berl's life was threatened because he discovered some black market dealers and denounced them to the Kahal. The Kahal provided us with rail tickets to Suwalki, and we left just after Christmas. I was not sorry to leave that unhappy place.

The first thing we discovered was that Berl's father's house was empty. Even worse, the Appelavitch house is a blackened ruin. No one knows what has happened to Mr. Hoffman or to the Appelavitches. We can only assume they left at the same time everyone else did. Many of the local people came back when the Germans drove the Russians out, but Poppa Hoffman and the Appelavitches were not among them. We go on hoping that they will return one day.

We had very little to carry, which was just as well, for the snow was a foot deep on the road between Suwalki and here. From the train we saw many ruined farms and houses. At Suwalki the old Yevropeiska restaurant in the railroad station was in ruins, the result of a direct hit from a German artillery shell. Do you remember Rospuda, the great house owned by the Pac family at Raczki? The Germans used it as their field headquarters during the fighting. They stabled their horses in the family chapel.

While we were in Vilna, the Russians expelled all Jews from territories occupied by the Russian armies. Thousands and thousands of refugees came to Vilna in the spring of 1915. But there was little food and housing was very dear. The Germans, in an effort to reduce the number of mouths to be fed, began rounding up unemployed men for conscription into labor battalions. It was rumored that the work was back-breaking; conditions were unspeakable in the Silesian coalfields far to the south where they were sent and the pay was outrageously low. While many Jews had signed up rather than starve, most stayed off the streets rather than risk being sent away to do sixteen hours of forced labor a day for thirty pfennigs.

They say it was much worse further east, so we did not know what to expect when we got back here.

We have moved into Berl's father's house, and we will try to rebuild our lives. It will not be easy. Food is scarce, and the soldiers killed most of the animals. I am planting a garden so we will have vegetables to trade for bread and milk. The children are happy here—at least they have open air, room to play. Peninah and Yitzhak are just like brother and sister. Annette is growing up, going on three. It seems impossible that the time has gone so fast since she was born in that dingy warehouse in Vilna. I wrote you soon after she was born, in July of that year, but perhaps you never received the letter. Conditions were chaotic at the time.

Berl is very busy. He has all the work he can handle right here in Oleck-Podlaska, where everyone is repairing or rebuilding their homes. Not everyone can pay cash, so he brings home a chicken or some cheese as often as Polish marks.

Please write and send us news of the family. You are all we have now, Anna. Everyone else is gone.

Love,
Dvoyra

Chapter Sixteen

Anna blew out the candles she'd lit to celebrate the Sabbath meal and looked across the room at her husband. As usual, he was completely hidden behind his *Daily Forward,* which he held up like a barrier to the world around him. *And to us,* she thought. She watched as Martin climbed down from her lap and crawled over toward his father. Clutching at Yakov's trouser leg for support, he hauled himself to his feet, smiling triumphantly, looking up at Yakov for praise. Yakov cast an annoyed glance at the child, then returned his attention to the paper. *He doesn't pay any more attention to the boys than he did to the girls,* Anna observed.

She wondered if he knew how unhappy she was, how unhappy she had been this last year. All the way back to the day he had come home from work and told her about the new immigration laws. The government had decided there were enough immigrants in America already, he said. From May, 1921, only three percent of the number who had entered from each country in 1910 would be allowed in. The news had devastated Anna, shattering her cherished dream that Dvoyra might yet come to America.

She looked across at Yakov again. He read on, oblivious to her presence, or her feelings. Even when she had struggled with her own emotions, when her whole being had ached with supressed longing to be with Meyer Kramer, he had never sensed that anything was wrong. How many times she had wanted to tell Yakov, how many times she had wished she could unburden herself of the secret she had kept all these years! But of course she remained silent, knowing the truth would destroy him.

She sighed. If only there were someone with whom she could share her secret thoughts as she had shared them once with Dvoyra! Much as she loved them, she could not bare her innermost heart to her daughters. And anyway, close as they were to her, Sheara and Becky had their own lives now.

Sheara had met a fine young man, Lou Wollman. Lou was a welder with the Baltimore & Ohio Railroad who had come with his parents from Poland fifteen years earlier. He was short, dark, intense. He talked enthusiastically about his work and prospects, the good future he would make for Sheara, for their family. Well, thought Anna, Sheara was a woman. It was time for her to build her own home, raise her own family.

Becky, too, was in love. Joe Fineman worked with her at Sonnenborne's Women's Wear Emporium. Joe was tall and thin, as quiet and thoughtful as Lou was volatile, originally from a small town to the north of Warsaw called Chorzele. His parents were still there. He had been saving to bring them over, but now he was sending them money every week out of his pay. He was a simple, honest man, and it was clear that he adored Becky.

Both daughters were married at the end of 1921, and while Anna was happy for them, they were gone and she missed them. Into that empty place in her heart moved Rachel, with her quiet determination and her immense sensitivity. Frequently, after Yakov and the younger children had gone to bed, Anna and Rachel would sit and talk, of the old country, of the nightmare existence Dvoyra wrote about, sometimes of Anna's dreams for her own family. Someone, perhaps Rifka Moscowitz, had once asked her what she wanted for her children, and she had replied unhesitatingly: *Everything!* It was still true—she wanted them to have the good life so many Americans unthinkingly accepted as their natural due.

Anna looked at Yakov again. He did not seem to miss Sheara's no-nonsense way of going at things, or Becky's cheerful resolve. She sensed that, if anything, his reaction to their going was regret at losing the income they had brought in, mixed with relief that they were off his hands. The responsibility of providing for his family never ceased weighing on him. He worked so hard; perhaps it was unfair to criticize him because he distanced himself from them.

How will I ever tell him? she worried. Her period was a week late, and the thought of another pregnancy terrified her. *How will we manage with another baby?* she asked herself. It was hard enough to make ends meet now, and she was so utterly tired. She looked up and saw Yakov staring at her over the top of his paper. She managed a faint smile. He smiled back automatically and returned his attention to the paper.

Martin tottered from Yakov's chair and suddenly sat down with a bump. The baby's smile dissolved into a look of surprise, followed by a wail of tears. Anna stooped to pick up the child as Shmuel and Benjamin tittered in the corner. Yakov glanced up in annoyance.

"Isn't it time these children were in bed?" he snapped, his voice impatient. "It would be nice to have a bit of peace."

She had no clear recollection of crossing the room, yet she did so in two strides, the anger erupting inside her as never before. She brought back her hand and slapped the paper from his grasp with all her strength. Yakov's head jerked back as he stared at her in astonishment.

"Are you crazy?" he gasped. "What's wrong with you?"

"That!" she snapped, gesturing at the sheets of newspaper strewn on the floor. "That wall you have built between yourself and your children!"

"God in heaven, not that again!"

"Yes, that again! Someday you will need them, Yankle. Or God forbid, they will need you. And you will be like strangers."

"Anna," he said wearily, bending down to retrieve the scattered pages, "I won't listen to this stupidity! You've said things like this before, and I don't know why, Anna. There is no wall between us!"

"There is, Yankle." She struggled to control herself. "There is."

"Well, I don't see it!" He shook the paper together and lifted it in front of his face. "I don't see it at all!"

Realizing it was futile to try to reach him, she sighed, "I know, Yankle." She looked at him sadly. "That's the trouble."

Later, when he had gone to bed, she cried a little. Rachel sat with her, holding her hand. Anna was sorely tempted to confide in her, but she knew it was unfair to unburden herself on the child. Instead they filled the silence by speaking about Dvoyra and the old country. Day-to-day events in America—Prohibition, bootlegging, gangland violence, women's suffrage, movies, automobiles. She nodded and listened, knowing these were things for Rachel and her generation.

She had followed every twist and turn of the turmoil that enveloped Poland and the Ukraine during the Polish-Russian war, sighed over the new lines drawn between them subsequent to the Treaty of Riga. Dvoyra's letters were few, and the news in them contributed further to Anna's deep sense of unhappiness.

"Dvoyra says she does not think Azriel, Yitzhak's father, will ever come back," she told Rachel. "They will raise the boy as their own son."

Rachel nodded and said nothing. She had a vague memory of Tante Dvoyra. The names of the towns—Oleck-Podlaska, Berdichev, Vilna, Suwalki—were no more than the little circles on the map in the atlas she had brought home from school. But she loved to listen to her mother talk about the old days.

"You met Poppa in Berdichev, right, Momma?" she asked. "Was he very handsome?"

"Yes, he was. I liked him right away. He was sweet and gentle then. But it was in Rovno, Rachel, not Berdichev. was working in a furniture factory. I remember I could see the fortress through the window. There were lots of soldiers in the town, stationed there. They used to wait outside the factory and call to us as we came out. Your father got angry and told me not to look at them," she said with a smile.

"And when you were married, you left Rovno and moved to Oleck-Podlaska."

"Poppa hated going back. I always thought that was where he began to change. He hated being in Poland, hated the hostility toward the Jews.

"Are you sorry you came, Momma?"

"Sorry?" Anna's radiant smile changed her face completely. "Of course not!" The smile faded. "It's just . . ."

"I know," Rachel soothed, touching her mother's hand. "We all know, Momma. How could we not know? Why do you think Sheara and Becky couldn't wait to set up their own homes?"

"Rachel, I won't hear you speak about your father disrespectfully!" Anna said sharply.

"Why doesn't he love us, Momma? Why doesn't he love us?"

"He loves you, Rachel," Anna said softly, taking her daughter into her arms. "He loves us all. Sometimes it's harder for a man to show his love than it is for a woman. And you know Poppa, he worries all the time, how we will make ends meet."

"But we always do! We always have, haven't we?"

"Yes, we always have, and we always will. And one day we'll have a better life. That's my dream, all of us together. You'll see. One day, you'll see."

She held her daughter tight against her breast. She wanted to tell Rachel to hold on to the dream, to tell her that one day it truly would come true for them. But all the time, hammering in her head, the same question repeated itself: *How will I tell him? How will I tell him I am pregnant again?*

There was a smear of blood on the toilet paper.

Anna stared at it. She drew in a long, deep breath to steady her nerves. *Oh, please God, let this be the end of it,* she begged in a whisper. Immediately she felt guilt wash through her for wishing the tiny unborn life inside her dead. And yet, what a blessing it would be! She got up and went about her chores, trying to put the thought out of her mind. *Nature will take its course,* she told herself, teetering between hope and dread.

Within an hour the bleeding had increased. It was almost like a normal period, except that she had begun to discharge scraps of fetal tissue. *Thank God,* she thought. *I know I shouldn't say it, but thank God, thank God!*

"Shmuel, watch the children for a while," she called as she went into the bedroom. "Momma is going to lie down for a few minutes."

She took a deep breath and smiled to herself as she lay back against the pillow. She decided not to tell Yakov that she had been pregnant. What good would it do? It would only depress him further. Thank God, she whispered again, for she would not have been able to conceal it from him much longer. She wiped her forehead with the back of her hand; it was wet with perspiration. Alarmed, she touched her cheek, then her throat. A fever, she thought, exasperatedly. As if all this weren't enough, she was coming down with a fever. *Well, I'll just have to get on with it. The dinner isn't going to cook itself.*

"Are you all right?" Yakov asked her over the top of his newspaper after dinner. He had not mentioned her outburst of last evening; it was as if it had not happened. Anna saw Rachel glance across the room at her. She smiled. This was Yakov's way of proffering the olive branch.

"I'm just tired. I'm having a little bit of a problem with my monthly sickness. You know."

"Ah," he said, nodding as he returned to his paper. "That explains it."

That explains why you acted the way you did—that's all right, then. Sometimes Yakov was so transparent, so patronizing, so disappointing.

"I'll be all right in the morning," she said, certain he was no longer listening to her.

He awoke just before six next morning. He lay on his side facing the open window, annoyed to have awakened so early when he could have slept for another half hour. What had awakened him? All at once he realized the bed was shaking. He turned over, propping himself up on his right elbow.

"Anna?" he said, dread rising inside him like a flood. She was shivering uncontrollably, clenching her teeth in an effort to stop herself. Yakov took her in his arms and pulled the blanket folded at the bottom of the bed over her. He held her tightly against his body. How could she be shivering like this when it was so hot? he wondered.

"Anna, Anna," he said softly as the shivering began to subside. "What is it? What's wrong?"

"F-f-fever." She struggled to catch her breath. "I must have had a f-f-fever. It's all right. I think it's . . . b-breaking."

"God, you frightened me. Lie down, keep still. There, is that better?"

"Yes," Anna sighed. "Poor Yankle, I'm sorry. I've woken you."

"I think Rachel had better stay home with you today."

"No, Shmuel can look after the children. Tell Rachel to give them some breakfast before she goes to work. I'll be all right if I can get some rest."

"Are you sure, Anna? You look so pale."

"It's the fever," she said, patting his arm. "Don't worry. Just bring me a towel."

"What do you want a towel for?"

"I'm bleeding a little more heavily than usual. Go on now, it's nothing."

"You're sure?" He frowned.

"Sure."

She was fast asleep by the time they left for work. Not until she felt Shmuel tugging her arm did Anna awaken.

"Momma, Momma, it's two o'clock," he said as she tried to focus her eyes on him. "We're hungry, Momma."

Anna felt as if she were drugged. She tried to prop herself up, but her head felt too heavy to lift from the pillow. Her lips were parched, and her skin felt as if it were on fire.

"Shmuel, fix some bread and butter. . . ." she whispered, startled to find herself breathless and weak from uttering those few words. "I'll . . . see to it . . . later. . . ." She was asleep again before Shmuel reached the doorway.

Yakov sat in a chair beside Anna's bed most of that night, watching her sleep. *I should have sent for the doctor,* he thought, *no matter what she said*. He reached out and gently touched her forehead. The skin was hot and dry.

Rachel had been waiting for him when he got home from work. He could see that she was frightened.

"What's wrong?" he said, dreading the answer.

"It's Momma, Poppa," Rachel said, her voice thin with anxiety. "She's burning up. Shmuel said she's been asleep all day. She didn't even get up to make them lunch."

"My God!" Yakov exclaimed, pulling off his jacket and throwing it on a chair. He rushed into the bedroom and sat down on the edge of the bed, gently touching his wife's shoulder. Anna opened her eyes and smiled feebly. Her skin was hot, her lips cracked and dry.

"How do you feel?" he said, his eyes filled with worry.

"Exhausted. I don't think I've ever felt so tired."

"You must have been." He tried to smile. "You've been asleep ever since I left for work."

"The children—?"

"They're all right, don't worry." He put his hand on her shoulder as she weakly struggled to rise. "Anna?"

Her eyelids were drooping; she opened them with visible effort.

"Anna, are you still bleeding? Like you were this morning?"

She frowned, as if confused by his question. With considerable difficulty she rolled onto her side and pulled back the light blanket that covered her.

"Holy God!" Yakov whispered. The towel she had placed between her legs early that morning was saturated with blood, as was all the bed linen beneath her.

"Anna, we have to get the doctor!" He started to get up. She caught his sleeve, held it.

"No," she whispered. "No. Just bring me another towel."

"Anna, you're still bleeding!"

"It will stop." She tried to catch her breath. "It's all right, Yankle, it will stop. It just looks worse than it is because I didn't change the towel. It can't go on like this . . . much longer. Please." She struggled for breath. "Another towel."

"I think we ought to get a doctor."

"If I'm still bleeding in the morning"—she nodded—"but not now, Yankle. I know it's nothing serious and we don't need the expense of a doctor. Please, I don't want a lot of fuss."

He brought her two towels, one to replace the blood-soaked one, a second to place between herself and the bedclothes. "You've had nothing to eat. I'll have Rachel fix you something. A bowl of broth, maybe?"

"Yankle, I'm not hungry." Her eyelids fluttered with exhaustion. "I just want to rest," she whispered as sleep claimed her once more.

I should have sent Rachel for the doctor, he thought as he sat in the darkness listening to his wife's uneven breathing. The first light of dawn was visible in the sky. He must have dozed. He jumped from the chair in panic as Anna called out incoherently in her sleep. Her breathing had changed and was harsh and labored.

"Anna!"

She moaned softly.

He jumped to his feet, his hand trembling as he reached for the light switch. He rushed into the other room and shook Rachel's arm.

"It's Momma!" he cried. "Come quick!"

He ran back to the bedroom with Rachel on his heels. They stood by the side of the bed. Anna was drenched with perspiration again, moaning with every breath she took.

"Poppa!" Rachel cried. She pointed a trembling finger at the bedclothes where the towel Anna had stuffed between her legs formed a mound beneath the white sheet. A red stain was spreading through the cotton fibers. Yakov stared at it in horror. Rachel covered her face with her hands for a moment, then, with a glance at her father, pulled back the sheet covering Anna. They both cried out, frightened by what they saw. Anna was lying in a pool of blood, and their stricken eyes locked on the rivulet flowing freely between her legs.

"She's bleeding to death!" Rachel screamed. "Stay with her, Poppa. I'm going for help!"

She ran from the room, her eyes wild with fear and anguish.

"Don't leave me!" Yakov called after her.

She did not hear him.

★ ★ ★

It was two miles to Mount Sinai Hospital. Rachel ran the entire distance. Panting, sweating, crying, she described her mother's condition to a startled nurse. The nurse summoned a doctor, who had an ambulance on the street in five minutes. Even so, almost an hour had elapsed before they got to the apartment.

The young doctor took the stairs three at a time, pushing Yakov gently aside as he bent over the bed to examine Anna.

"I'm Dr. Hillman, Paul Hillman. When did she start to bleed?" he asked Yakov, his voice tense.

"I don't know," Yakov faltered. "I think it was the day before yesterday."

"The day before—!" The doctor bit off whatever he was going to say. "How long had she been pregnant?"

"Pregnant?" Yakov said, bewildered. "I didn't know she was pregnant. Is that why—?"

"I think she has had a missed abortion."

"What's that?"

"I'll explain later," the doctor said briskly. "Right now we have to get her to the hospital. She's hemorrhaging badly, and there are signs of septic poisoning."

"She said it was only a female problem," Yakov whispered, staring at the doctor, who shook his head and sighed. The doctor went to the top of the stairs and called down to the ambulance men waiting below. They ran up carrying a stretcher and gently lifted Anna onto it.

"You'll save her, won't you?" Rachel sobbed, tugging at the doctor's sleeve as he directed the transfer. "You've got to save her!"

"We'll do everything we can." He watched the attendants wheel Anna from the room. "Do you want to come with us in the ambulance?"

"Yes, of course. Come on, Poppa!"

"No," Yakov mumbled. "You go, Rachel. You go with her. I'll stay here with the children."

The young doctor stared at Yakov for a moment as if he couldn't believe his ears. He made an angry sound and went out of the room and down the stairs. Rachel looked at her father, her eyes desperate.

He was shaking his head back and forth, tears streaming from his eyes. "No, no, no," he kept repeating.

Yakov now knew Anna was critically ill, and the thought of losing her terrified him. Life without her was unthinkable.

She had always been his salvation throughout these years of frustration and despair. He truly intended to make up to her with kindness for all the years of intolerance and indifference. That was his intention. That had always been his intention.

Rachel ran into the other room. The children were huddled together on the bed, eyes wide with fear.

"Shmuel!" she said. "At nine o'clock go to Sonnenborne's. Find Becky and tell her to come to Mount Sinai Hospital. Can you remember that?"

"Mount Sinai," he repeated, his wide eyes moving from her to the doorway, where Yakov stood weeping. "What's happened, Rachel?" Shmuel asked.

"Find Becky!" she shouted before she bolted from the apartment. The last thing she saw was Yakov, staring at the empty, bloodstained bed.

Becky arrived at the hospital shortly after ten that morning. A nurse led her to her mother's bedside, in a ward with five other women. Her bed was in a corner of the large room, shielded by two large white screens standing at right angles to each other. The nurse, a tall, thin woman with a grave expression, pulled back the screen.

Rachel was by the bed, her face white and tense, holding Anna's hand. Anna lay almost motionless, only the slight rise and fall of her chest indicating that she was alive. Her face was as white as paper, her lips bloodless, a thin line drawn by pain. Rachel looked up at her panic-stricken sister and tried to speak, but began to cry instead.

"Shhh, now," the nurse whispered. "You mustn't disturb her."

"Can I stay?" Becky asked.

"Of course. Of course. But please be very quiet. Your mother is seriously ill." The nurse pulled the screen back into place, shutting them off from the rest of the ward, and left the girls alone with Anna. Becky sat down on an upright chair next to Rachel.

"What happened, Rachel?" she asked, her voice shaking.

"Yesterday morning Poppa said Momma wasn't feeling well." Rachel wiped the tears from her eyes. "He said she was going to stay in bed for a while. But when I got home that night, she hadn't been out of bed. She had a fever, and she had been bleeding."

"Why didn't Poppa send for a doctor?"

"Momma told him not to. She said she would be all right."

"Where's Poppa now? Why isn't he here?"

"I tried, Becky. He wouldn't. He wouldn't come."

Her sister shook her head in disbelief. "What did the doctor say?"

"He said Momma had been pregnant. She hadn't told Poppa. I don't know exactly what the doctor said, but the baby died. And her insides became infected. Septic poisoning, he said it was. Oh, Becky, you should have seen all the blood—" She shook her head, sobbing.

"It's all right, Rachel." Becky rocked her sister in her arms. "Momma will be all right, just you wait and see."

Becky gently brushed a few strands of damp hair from her mother's forehead. Anna's eyelids flickered, and her head moved slightly on the pillow, as if in response to Becky's touch. The sisters moved closer to her as they realized she was trying to say something.

"Dvoyra?" Anna whispered, calling out to her sister.

"It's the fever," Becky said. "Momma is delirious. Momma, it's Becky. And Rachel's here too."

"Dvoyra, is it you?" Anna's voice was no louder than a sigh. "Dvoyra, bring Esther. Then we'll all be together."

Becky leaned over and stroked her mother's forehead. "Shhh, Momma," she soothed. "We're all here. It's all right. Rest now, rest."

"Everyone together," Anna sighed. A faint smile touched the colorless lips, and for a moment she was quite beautiful.

"We'll always be together, Momma!" Rachel cried. "I promise you!"

"There must be some medicine they can give her?" Becky said.

"The doctor said there isn't. He said they managed to stop the bleeding, but they have nothing to fight the septic poison inside her. All we can do is wait, and hope. It's up to Momma now."

"She won't die!" Rachel said fiercely. "She can't!"

"We have to get Sheara." Becky fought to keep her voice level. "Momma's resting comfortably now. Why don't you go fetch Sheara and bring her back with you? I'll stay here till you come."

"I don't want to leave her."

"It will be all right. I'll be here. Go fetch Sheara."

After Rachel left, Becky laid her head down on her mother's outstretched arm. The flesh felt cool and clammy.

"Oh, Momma, please don't die," Becky whispered. "Not after all you've been through. Not when we all need you so much."

Her head on Anna's arm, Becky's thoughts drifted back across the decade. They had all been through so much together. Becky recalled memories of the past ten years, all the way back to their departure from Oleck-Podlaska when they were huddled, shivering, in the back of Mr. Zaltzmann's wagon. She could see her grandfather standing in the road, waving to them. "Remember me!" he shouted, his voice growing fainter. "Remember me!"

She remembered the foul air of the steerage, the wonderful fresh salt smell of the sea, and the first day they were allowed on deck. A smile touched her lips as she recalled the sight of her mother on the deck of the *Darmstadt*. Her dark hair blew in the cool breeze as she tilted her head back and closed her eyes to the sun, and Becky remembered thinking, *My momma is beautiful*.

She heard Anna's voice telling her never to forget the steerage. And Ellis Island and the train journey to Baltimore and Poppa waiting at the station. And the yells of the children in the schoolyard that first day, when Anna told them they would have a lot of company becoming Americans.

She heard her mother moan and sat up quickly. Anna's complexion had turned even paler. Sliding aside the screen, Becky called urgently for the nurse, who came hurrying down the ward, a frown of concern on her face. She reached for Anna's wrist and checked the pulse against her watch. She slowly shook her head and went to get the doctor.

"No!" Becky cried, urgently.

"Becky?" Anna said in a tiny whisper. Her eyelids flickered, as if she might open her eyes.

"Yes, Momma, I'm here," Becky said, struggling to control her tears and taking Anna's cold hand into both of hers.

"Becky, come close," Anna breathed. Becky leaned down until her cheek was touching her mother's.

"I'm here, Momma." She choked back her tears.

"Mind," Anna sighed.

"Yes, Momma, what is it?"

"Mind . . . Poppa's collars." She sighed again, as if she were falling asleep. A graceful smile crossed her face and then vanished.

"No," Becky whispered. "It couldn't be. *No*."

The doctor touched her shoulder in a small gesture of sympathy. Blinded by tears, Becky could not see him.

"Momma!" she cried. "Momma!"

Chapter Seventeen

Anna's funeral took place on an oppressively hot and humid July day nearly twelve years after her arrival in Baltimore. The simple service was performed, for a fee of one dollar, by the sexton of Beth Shalom, a neighboring synagogue on Charles Street. Both Sheara and Becky signed notes for halves of the twenty-five-dollar fee that purchased a plot in the cemetary of the synagogue.

It was not until the two bearded men from the burial society began lowering the plain pine box into the grave that the finality of their mother's death came home to them. Becky saw her father wince, as if in pain, when the first shovelful of earth slammed with a hollow thud on the top of the coffin.

"What now?" she heard Sheara whisper to her husband. Lou shook his head, as if to say he didn't know.

None of us knows, Becky thought. She reached for Joe's hand, needing his strength and reassurance. She looked up at him and his eyes met hers. *He looks as if he is crying inside,* she thought.

Becky looked at her father and recoiled at the resentment she felt. *She deserved so much more,* she thought. *From Poppa, from us, from life.*

Yakov was all but oblivious to his children. Mesmerized by his own misery, he looked down at Anna's grave, sick with guilt over his failure to have bestowed upon Anna the kindness, the appreciation, the warmth, he had always intended to eventually reveal. Her death had robbed him of his intent to make up for all that he had denied her. Once again he was preoccupied with the injustice of life.

The children eyed Yakov expectantly as he entered the apartment after the funeral. He looked at them blankly, as though they were strangers. Becky and Sheara embraced their younger siblings. Only Rachel stood aside, her eyes dry, her expression unreadable, as Yakov walked over to his favorite chair and slumped into it, lowering his head into his hands.

The family did not sit *shivah,* the traditional seven-day mourning period. None of them could afford to stay away from work. Apart from Rifka Moskowitz, there would be no callers. Instead, the Wollmans and Finemans came to the apartment every night after work, Sheara and Becky helping Rachel prepare dinner while Lou and Joe played with the younger children. Yakov showed no interest in any of this. Each night he came home from work, ate his supper, read the paper, and then sat silently, staring into space. The children watched him uneasily and realized that he was not going to be any more attentive to them now than he had ever been.

The weekend following Anna's funeral, Becky and Sheara discussed the crisis they saw looming. Rachel had left work the day Anna fell ill and had not returned. Yakov's income, twenty dollars a week, meant there was only three dollars and thirty-three cents for each family member. It would be more difficult than ever to run the household.

"Poppa is no help at all," Becky said.

"I know, I know," Sheara agreed wearily. "He's like a child. I feel as though the whole family is falling apart."

"Did you notice the way the children won't go near him?"

"It's hardly surprising," Sheara said. "He shuts them out, the way he always shut us out. When did he ever play with us or take us for a walk like other fathers?"

"He was working all day, Sheara."

"Most men work all day. Some even have two jobs. That doesn't mean they ignore their children. He doesn't even talk to the boys. He's been the same with them as he was with us. He just left all that to Momma. The only time he took any interest in us was when he thought it was time for us to go out and earn money."

"Yet Momma always insisted that we respect Poppa." Becky shook her head. "Do you know the last thing she said to me? She told me to 'mind Poppa's collars.'"

"Right to the end," Sheara whispered. "She must have loved him right to the end. Even though he never shared the most important thing in her life with her—us, her children."

"Well, I know one thing, I'll never let Joe be like that with our children."

Sheara looked up at Becky's words.

"Are you . . . ?"

"Yes," Becky whispered. "I'm pregnant."

"Oh, I'm so happy for you!" Sheara exclaimed, putting her arms around her sister and kissing her.

"I wish I was happy for myself. This isn't the best time to be having a baby. Joe wasn't exactly overjoyed when I told him. You know how much he wants to bring his family over."

"What are we going to do, Becky? About Poppa, and the family?"

"I don't know. Joe and I talked about it after the funeral. I just don't see how we can do anything. We need every cent he earns."

"There's something I must tell you about us too, Becky," Sheara said hesitantly.

"What is it?" Becky asked, sensing trouble.

"Lou and I are leaving Baltimore."

"What!"

"Lou's been offered a better job, in Hagerstown. They need welders there."

"Where is Hagerstown?"

"It's west of here, about seventy miles away."

"Seventy! Sheara, how can you do this when things are so bad for the family?"

"We've got to think of ourselves too, Becky. Lou was told that if he didn't move, he'd probably lose his job here—they're making cuts. This is a good chance for us. We'll be able to save some money. That way, we can help with the children."

"From seventy miles away? Oh, God, this is like a bad dream."

"Lou says we should call Mrs. Klovens at the Jewish Welfare Aid Society, the woman Mr. Sternman told us about."

Paul Sternman was the hospital administrator at Mount Sinai. While they had been finalizing the arrangement to pay the eighteen-dollar bill for Anna's treatment, Sternman had asked them how they would manage. He suggested that if they needed assistance, there was an organization in Baltimore that could help them. He wrote down the address and the name of the woman they should contact and gave it to Sheara.

"I'd forgotten about that," Becky said. "Maybe they could

send someone to help Rachel during the day. It's a good idea, Sheara. Let's go see them first thing in the morning."

Edith Klovens, chief administrator of the Jewish Welfare Aid Society, was a motherly woman about Anna's age, her dark hair drawn back into a neat chignon. She wore a white blouse and a dark gray serge skirt. Her office was airy and sunny, and there were fresh flowers on her desk.

"So you are the Appelavitch girls!" she said as she stood to greet them. She smiled at their surprise. "Oh, I've been hoping you would come to see me. Paul Sternman called me and told me about your family. Now, let me see, you must be Sheara, and you are Rebecca, Becky, yes? Tell me, how are you managing? How is your father taking things?"

"Badly," Sheara said bluntly.

Edith Klovens nodded. "That often happens. When the wife dies, the widower just can't cope. Everything collapses. So, have you come to any decisions about the future?"

"No. We thought maybe we could each take two of the children," Sheara said.

"I thought there were five?"

"Rachel, the oldest, should stay with Poppa, but she wants to come and live with me," Becky said. "She'd be more help to me. I'm pregnant, you see."

"How old are you, Becky?"

"Twenty."

"Do you think it would be a good idea to take on the responsibility of three children when you are expecting a baby yourself?"

"What else can we do?"

"You could let us help. We can find the children fine foster homes with caring Jewish families who will look after them like their own children. People we know, people we have worked with for years."

"No," Becky said firmly. "I could never agree to breaking up the family."

"Becky, dear, let me ask you a question. You too, Sheara. Please don't think me prying, but how much do your husbands earn?"

"Twelve dollars a week," Becky said.

"Twelve-fifty," Sheara added.

"And with your combined wages, can either of you save anything?"

"Joe sends two dollars to his family in Europe every week," Becky said.

Sheara shook her head. "We haven't been able to save a penny."

"Then how would you manage if suddenly each of you had two or three more mouths to feed, and you can no longer bring in any money?"

"Poppa would have to pay something to help with the children."

"Becky, my dear," Mrs. Klovens said gently. "I think you must be prepared for your father's being a little unpredictable for a while."

"He wouldn't—" Sheara began, then stopped. "I don't know, though," she said thoughtfully. "Maybe you are right, Mrs. Klovens. Maybe he would."

"Would what?" Becky frowned.

"Forget his responsibilities to his children. Out of sight, out of mind," Sheara said.

"Have you talked all this over with your husbands?" Mrs. Klovens asked.

"Joe is worried he wouldn't be able to bring his family over," Becky admitted. "That's the most important goal in his life right now."

"And you, Sheara?"

"My husband has taken a job in Hagerstown, Mrs. Klovens. We're moving."

"My dears, listen to me. Think about what I said. Let us help you. It's a way of keeping the family together. They'll be well provided for, until you and Sheara can take care of them."

"No," Becky said. "We can't let them go live with strangers."

"You can't take on all five of them, Becky," Mrs. Klovens said quietly.

"Momma said something," she said quietly, "before she died. Something about us all staying together. It was always her dream. For all of us to be together, and happy. That was all she ever wanted."

"I understand," Mrs. Klovens said softly. "And we would be the last people on earth to break up a family if there was any other way. But Becky, Sheara will be seventy miles away. Even if she took two of the children, they would still be separated. We can at least try to place them as near to each other as possible."

"What would you do," Sheara asked, "if you were in our place?"

Mrs. Klovens smiled sadly. "I don't know, Sheara. I think I would be just as confused and angry as you girls are. But I do know this—we have placed scores of Jewish children in foster homes. I would say most of them have done better that way than they otherwise would have done."

"Do you know which families you would place them with?" Becky asked.

Mrs. Klovens shook her head. "It could take a few months. We have to find the right families. Until then, we would take the children of course. They could stay at Sachshaven."

"Sachshaven?"

"It's a home for children in similar circumstances to your brothers' and sisters'. A lovely place, out in the country south of Baltimore."

"How many children live there?" Becky asked, a note of suspicion in her voice.

"About two hundred."

"It's not a home, it's an orphanage. You're talking about putting my brothers and sisters into an orphanage!"

"I'm talking about trying to help, Becky—"

"No!" Becky shouted, jumping to her feet. "No, no, no!" She rushed to the door and out of the room, her footsteps echoing in the corridor outside.

"Becky, come back!" Sheara called.

"Let her go, Sheara," Mrs. Klovens said gently. "I know how she feels. She needs some time to think. You both do. Go after her, talk it over. Then come back and see me and tell me what you have decided."

That evening the girls went to their father's apartment to discuss their meeting with Mrs. Klovens. Becky was still angry, but she had spent the day thinking, and she was beginning to realize that what Edith Klovens had suggested might well be the only solution to their problem. They waited until the children had been put to bed, then sat down at the table with Yakov and Rachel.

"Well," Yakov said expectantly, "did they say they can send someone to help us, these Jewish Welfare people?"

"No, Poppa, but they suggested something else," Sheara said. Rachel glanced at Becky in time to see her biting down on her lower lip, just as their mother had done when she was apprehensive. Becky saw Rachel's quick glance and tried to smile.

Something's wrong, Rachel thought. "If they can't send anyone to help, what else can they do for us?" she asked, her voice betraying her unease.

"Mrs. Klovens said she could arrange for the children to stay with very nice families," Sheara explained evenly. "She said they work with such families all the time."

"There are really people who do this?" Yakov asked, raising his eyebrows. "Take in other people's children?"

"Yes," Sheara said. "Good families, with nice homes in the country. People who could give children everything they need."

"Everything," Rachel said, "except their own family."

"Rachel, what's the matter with you?" Yakov snapped irritably. "Listen to what Sheara is saying."

"I hear what she is saying, Poppa," Rachel said, her voice controlled but hostile. "She's saying we should give the children to someone else to raise."

"We haven't got a choice, Rachel!" Sheara said, her temper fraying. "Nobody else is going to do it!"

"What about us? What about their own family?"

"Rachel, Rachel, you don't understand," Sheara said. "Lou and I are leaving Baltimore. We're moving to a place called Hagerstown. Lou has been offered a better job there."

"Sheara, you never said anything!" Yakov said, shaken by the news.

"It happened just before Momma died, Poppa. There was no chance to discuss it."

"When will you go?" Rachel asked.

"In about six weeks."

Rachel lowered her head into her hands. Yakov stared at her, then frowned. "This is a big problem," he said. "A big problem. How are we going to manage now, Rachel? If Sheara goes?"

Rachel did not lift her head or reply. Yakov became impatient. "Rachel, answer me! What are we going to do?"

"I don't know, Poppa," Rachel said wearily. "Maybe Becky could take Esther and Sol. I'll stay home and look after Benjamin and Martin."

"Becky's got a baby of her own on the way, Rachel," Sheara said. "How well do you think she could provide for three children? And even if she could, how could you take care of four of you on just Poppa's wages?"

Rachel closed her eyes, thinking desperately. "Maybe we

could rent a bigger apartment. Then Becky and Joe could move in with us, and . . ."

"Oh, Rachel, I don't think Joe would like the idea of us doing that," Becky said sadly. "He's trying to bring his own family over from Europe."

"Are they more important than us?" Rachel asked bitterly, and Becky flinched, as though her sister had struck her.

"It's difficult, difficult," Yakov said, nodding. "So perhaps Sheara is right, Rachel. Maybe we should ask these Welfare people to help us."

"What's wrong with you, Poppa?" Rachel said, her voice rising. "What's wrong with all of you? Don't you realize you're talking about sending the children away?"

"Rachel, these are people who will help us as if we were family," Sheara said.

"But they're not family!" Rachel shouted. "They're strangers who want to take the children away from us!"

"They're not going to *take* the children, Rachel!" Sheara said with exasperation. "They're going to provide a home for them until we can take care of them ourselves."

"And when will that be?"

"I don't know!" Sheara was shouting now. "As soon as we can!"

"You mean never, and you know it!"

"Rachel!" Sheara protested. "Don't say that!"

"Tell me it isn't true, then! Becky and Joe can't have them. You and Lou are going to be gone altogether. Poppa can't wait to get rid of them as it is—"

"Rachel!" Yakov shouted, jumping to his feet. "That is unforgivable!"

"Stop it, stop it, stop it!" Becky screamed. "Stop it, all of you!" Everyone turned to stare at her in surprise, for she rarely yelled. "Rachel is right! We all know she is right," Becky said into the silence. "So let's stop pretending."

"She said I couldn't wait to get rid of the children," Yakov grumbled, sitting down again. "That's not true, not true at all. A girl should not say such a thing about her father."

"You're right, Rachel," Becky said, ignoring Yakov's protest. "If the children go into one of these foster homes, it may be years before we can bring them home, and perhaps by that time they may not even wish to come. You're right, and I agree with you. I was upset as you are when Mrs. Klovens first suggested this. I ran out of her office, Rachel, I wouldn't even listen. Now . . . now I'm not so sure anymore."

"Why?" Rachel whispered.

"Rachel, we can't manage it. You haven't worked since Momma died, Rachel, and you can't work and take care of four children at the same time anyway. It's painful for all of us, but we have to face reality. We need help and Mrs. Klovens wants to help. Mrs. Klovens says she's seen lots of families going through what has happened to us. She says these foster homes are there to help a family, not to replace it. That's what you must keep in your mind."

"I still say we could manage," Rachel said stubbornly, "if we really wanted to."

"You think we don't want to?" Sheara snapped. "We're not in a position to help, but that doesn't mean we don't want to help." Anger reddened her cheeks.

"I'll tell you what I think," Rachel said, suddenly calm. Her eyes rested on each one of them in turn. "I think I'm the only one here who believes there is nothing more important than keeping this family together." Her voice was level, frank, unafraid.

Becky closed her eyes and remembered her mother's words before she died. *Then we'll all be together, everyone together.* "Maybe you should talk to Mrs. Klovens, Rachel," she said softly.

"I don't need to talk to her," Rachel said quietly. "I'm sure everything she says makes very good sense. As long as you don't mind sending your family to live with strangers." She turned to Yakov. "Poppa, don't you have anything to say?"

"What do you want me to say?" Yakov asked irritably. "We have no one to turn to except this Mrs. Klovens."

"Even though you know nothing about the families to whom the children would be sent?"

"Oh, that wouldn't be for a few months anyway," Sheara said, immediately regretting her answer.

"What does that mean?" Rachel asked sharply. "What happens to them in the meantime?"

"They take them to a place in the country called Sachshaven," Becky said, her voice trembling.

"A home?" Rachel said, her own voice beginning to shake as she fought back the tears. "An orphanage?"

"Rachel, don't make this any worse than it already is," Sheara pleaded.

"How could I possibly do that?" Rachel said bitterly. "Tell me this, Sheara. Would you suggest sending the children to an orphanage if you thought Momma could hear you?"

The room fell silent as the weight of Rachel's question descended on them. Yakov looked anxiously from Sheara to Becky and back again.

Becky finally spoke. "Momma can't hear us, Rachel," she said softly. "Momma's dead."

"Yes, I know," Rachel whispered. "And so is this family."

This is almost as bad as watching Momma die, Becky thought. The children were huddled together in Edith Klovens' office, weeping. When Becky tried to comfort them, they shrank away as if her touch would burn them.

"I think it would be best if you left now," Mrs. Klovens told her kindly.

"We'll come see you on Sunday," Becky said to the children.

Sol looked up, tears streaming down his face. He was breathing rapidly and his teeth were clenched. Then he turned away, covering his face with his hands.

"Don't want you to!" he shouted. "Don't want you anymore!"

"Don't leave us here!" Esther screamed. "Rachel, Becky!"

"Esther, it's all right," Rachel said. "We'll see you every Sunday. I promise you. It will be all right."

Benjamin and Martin were crying now as well. Mrs. Klovens put her arm around Esther's thin shoulders. Esther twisted away, her face sullen.

"It's all right, Esther," Mrs. Klovens said. "I understand." She put her hand on Becky's arm and gently but firmly coaxed her toward the door. Sheara and Rachel followed. The three sisters walked along the corridor and out into the street, fighting back their tears. It was no good. As they stood on the steps outside the agency, Becky and Rachel broke down, weeping uncontrollably.

"Rachel, Rachel, it's all right, it will be all right," Becky sobbed, her arms around her sister.

"All right!" Rachel cried. "How can anything so wrong ever be all right? How, how?"

"Stop it, you two!" Sheara said, struggling to keep a tight rein on her own emotions. She gritted her teeth tightly, and told herself over and over that this was neither the time nor the place for tears. "Stop acting as though we had abandoned them!"

"Isn't that just what we did?" Rachel demanded. "Isn't that just what we did in there?"

"We did the best we could," Sheara said firmly. "All we could. Now let's go. We're making a spectacle of ourselves."

"Sheara's right, Rachel," Becky said, wiping her eyes with a handkerchief. "The children will be well looked after."

"Let me ask you something, Becky," Rachel said, her voice bitter. "Suppose it was your baby, the one you're carrying. What would it take to make you leave your child in there?" She made an angry gesture at the doorway of the Jewish Welfare Aid Society. "Tell us, Becky. Tell us now, so we'll know!"

Her words fell on Becky like blows, leaving her momentarily speechless. "Rachel," she managed finally. "That's not fair—"

"That's right, Becky, it isn't!" Rachel said, sobbing once again. "Because it would be *your* child, wouldn't it?"

Stunned by the tension of the moment, Becky and Sheara could only stare at their sister as she turned away from them and ran down the white marble steps, leaving them standing together in silence. After what seemed like a long, long time, Becky touched Sheara's arm. Without another word they turned and walked away.

After discussing it with Mrs. Klovens, Sheara, Becky, and Rachel decided to wait two weeks before making the train trip to Sachshaven to see the children.

The journey to Laurel, a small rural town about halfway between Baltimore and Washington, took only twenty minutes, and the sun was already high as they stepped off the B&O train. A bus with the word "Sachshaven" painted neatly on its side in yellow letters stood opposite the small, square station. They made their way toward the bus and climbed aboard.

The brief ride took them through serene farm country interspersed with dense forest. There was no signpost to identify Sachshaven, and only when the bus turned off the highway onto a long straight driveway did they know they had arrived. Ahead of them they saw the house, an imposing, three-story red brick building. It was not at all the depressing place they had expected it to be. It looked like the house of a rich family.

The bus stopped in the circular driveway and the girls alighted. The sound of children at play carried clearly on the still summer air, reminding Becky of her first day at school in Baltimore.

They were greeted by an attractive, middle-aged woman who told them her name was Edna Goldschmidt. Becky immediately noticed her eyes: they twinkled brightly, as if they held a childish mischief. Edna Goldschmidt looked capable but not hard, gentle without weakness.

"I'm the director here at Sachshaven," she said, warmly, extending her hand. "You must be the Appelavitch girls, yes? Sheara, isn't it?"

"Why yes," Sheara said, as Mrs. Goldschmidt took her hand and squeezed it warmly. "These are my sisters—"

"Becky and Rachel," Mrs. Goldschmidt finished. "I've been hearing a lot about you. All of you. Come, I know you're anxious to see the children, but let's take a few minutes to talk, yes?"

She led them into the house, opening the door of her office and ushering them in. It was a small room with a window that looked out on a flower garden, its delicately patterned wallpaper and chintz curtains giving it a cool, restful ambience. Mrs. Goldschmidt gestured them to chairs and sat down at her desk, smiling.

"I take it Mr. Appelavitch didn't come with you?" she began.

"He didn't feel well," Sheara said quickly. Mrs. Goldschmidt smiled sympathetically, not missing Rachel's grimace of impatience. Edith Klovens had told her all about the Appelavitch family, with special emphasis on the father.

"How are the children, Mrs. Goldschmidt?" Becky asked eagerly.

"I think you'll be pleasantly surprised. They're doing very well." She saw the doubt on their faces and smiled again. "You'll see for yourselves in a moment. But I don't want you to be misled by what you see."

"What do you mean?" Sheara asked.

"You brothers and sister are happy here. Oh, it took a few days to adjust, but that passed. That part is easy. They're surrounded by children their own age. They play hard all day, they eat well, they might as well be on vacation."

"Then what concerns you?" Sheara asked.

"You do. What we're doing for your brothers and sister will be worthless if you don't do your part. You are their family. You must keep that bond as strong as possible."

"But that's why we're here!" Becky said. "We know how important it is to them."

"It's important to you too, Becky. That's what I'm really

trying to tell you. It's important to you. And important that your father not lose contact with the children now, because he may never reestablish it. Do you know what I am saying?"

The girls stared uncomfortably at each other as a silence fell over the room. Each of them knew that Mrs. Goldschmidt was right; just as each of them knew how difficult, if not impossible, it would be to persuade their father to come to Sachshaven.

"They looked well," Sheara said as the train rattled north toward Elkridge. They had hardly talked at all since boarding the train.

"It was so . . . I can't describe it," Becky said. "Almost as if we were strangers. Did you feel that?"

"Sol hardly spoke."

"And Esther, it was as if she couldn't wait till it was time for us to go."

"Did you notice they never asked for Poppa?" Becky said.

"I noticed," Sheara said.

"Mrs. Goldschmidt was right, we must persuade him to come with us," Becky said. Sheara nodded.

"He won't come," Rachel said, finally speaking. "He'll never come."

"Rachel!" Sheara exclaimed. "You don't believe that!"

"You'll see," Rachel said with a shrug.

Chapter Eighteen

September 12, 1922

Dear Rachel,

Your letter arrived today. I have read it a dozen times, but I still cannot believe what it says. It is like a nightmare from which I am unable to awaken. Not a day has passed since you all left Oleck-Podlaska more than ten years ago that I have not thought of you. The knowledge that my beloved sister is dead is almost more than I can bear. I loved her more than anyone else on earth, and I will cherish her memory for as long as I myself live.

Forgive me if I do not write much today. I pray that God will give us all the strength to overcome this terrible loss. We will write to each other again. Let us make a promise that we will be the ones who ensure our family remains united.

I cannot advise you, my dear neice. I know nothing about life in America. I can only hope you have found a way to keep the family together, and that things will get better for all of you. This much I do know: you must never regret your parents' decision to take you to America. There is still hope there, for you and the children. Here there is only hatred and fear. Those of us who were not killed or starved to death in the wars survive only to be scorned. My greatest regret is that I didn't go to America, and I pray that when they can, my own children will try to get there. Taking you to America was the greatest gift your mother could have given you. Never forget it.

Write and let me know what is happening with all of you. I pray that God will look after you, and that he will take care of your momma now that she is in His hands.

Love
Tante Dvoyra

"Becky, you're going to have to talk to Rachel," Joe Fineman said as he helped his wife clear the table after dinner. "She can't go on working seventy hours a week."

"She says she loves it at Korman's."

"That's beside the point. It isn't right for a child to work that hard."

Rachel worked at Hutzler's Department Store during the day as a sales clerk in the children's department, earning twenty-five cents an hour. She set aside ten dollars a month to defray expenses at Becky and Joe's and to buy whatever clothes or other necessities she needed. The rest, almost half of what she earned, she saved.

Rachel had taken on a second job at Korman's, a garment

manufacturer, soon after she moved in with Becky and Joe. Rachel was anxious to move out of their father's apartment, and everyone agreed she would be a big help to Becky, whose first child had been born shortly after the first of the year.

The Sunday that Aaron, named for his grandfather, was circumcised in January 1923 was the first Sunday that Rachel did not visit the children at Sachshaven. During the brief ritual, as her smiling father held his first grandchild in his arms, she decided she would take the evening job at Korman's Men's Wear. It paid well—twenty-cents an hour, four hours a night, ironing clothes that had been purchased and altered during the regular daytime hours.

"She isn't a child anymore, Joe," Becky said. "She may only be sixteen, but she's a woman in every other respect. She took that job as a way of making more money, to bring the children home faster. It's been six months since they moved to Sachshaven, and it's all she thinks of. Nothing else matters to her."

"And what's going to happen when she learns my sister and parents are coming to live with us in May, and there won't be room for the kids even if she does manage to get them back?"

"She'll be disappointed," Becky admitted.

"Heartbroken, you mean. You know she's set on it."

"I know. She'd have them here tomorrow if it was possible. She's always hated their being at Sachshaven."

"Oh, don't start that again," he said wearily. "We had no choice but to send them there. You know that, Becky. Becky? Are you listening to me?"

"What? Oh, yes, of course, Joe."

"You weren't listening. You were off somewhere else."

"Just thinking."

"About the children? What else could we have done?"

"We could have gotten a larger place, taken them in with us."

"Becky, I earn less than fifteen dollars a week," Joe said patiently. "I can't afford this place, let alone a bigger one."

"Rachel works. Poppa works. It could have been done."

"Poppa!" Joe said, contempt in his voice. "He ought to be ashamed of himself. He hasn't been to see the kids once since they went to live up there last August. Not once!"

"I have gone so seldom, myself," she whispered.

"You were pregnant. And you know how sick you were at first."

"Sheara and Lou haven't gone since they moved to Hagerstown last September. Only Rachel goes all the time. She hasn't missed a Sunday except for Aaron's *Bris*."

"Rachel hasn't got any other responsibilities. We have. We'll have to tell her my family is coming, Becky. She has to know."

"She knows. She's known for years you were saving to bring them over."

"Yes, but that's not the same as knowing they will actually be here, living here, on May seventeenth. And that there'll be no room for the children."

"You're right," Becky sighed. "I'll tell her tonight."

Korman's was considered one of the better places to work in Baltimore's garment trade, and Rachel was fortunate to have found a job there. Ben Korman was a progressive and maybe even a socialist at heart. His was one of the very first of the major shops to go union nearly twelve years earlier. The spacious workroom was always kept clean, well lighted, and well ventilated. Everyone in the business thought he was crazy, but his level of productivity was consistently the highest in the trade. "Happy workers are better workers," he would tell his critics.

Rachel was scanning the bulletin board that hung alongside the time clock by the door of the alterations rooms at Korman's. Most of the notices pinned to the cork surface by various employees announced used furniture for sale, Hebrew lessons, piano lessons, social gatherings, or union meetings.

Rachel was a member of the CGWA but had never participated in union activities. Ordinarily the notice of a union meeting would not have caught her attention. But tonight one had. She focused on the notice and read it more carefully.

Confederated Garment Workers of America
National President-Elect Ivan Wollmack
To Address Baltimore Local
CGWA Union Hall
2:00 P.M.
Sunday, February 13, 1923

"Who is Ivan Wollmack?" she asked the night supervisor, Paul Abrams.

"Wollmack? He's the new president of the union. He's from New York, supposed to be quite a speaker. Why? You thinking of going?"

"No, I never go to union meetings. I have other things to do on Sundays."

"Yes, I know. You visit your sister and brothers every Sunday, don't you?"

"Yes. I never like to miss a Sunday."

"Come to think of it, Wollmack was once from Baltimore. He led the local here about ten years ago. He made such a name for himself they sent him up to New York. He was only twenty-two or twenty-three when he went to New York."

"My mother must have known him. She worked for the union ten years ago."

"Who knows?" Abrams shrugged. "It's possible."

Rachel didn't give the matter any further thought and probably wouldn't have had it not been for her father's comment the following evening. Yakov had joined them for dinner as he did from time to time and was talking about a major remodeling project being undertaken at Kohn's. Carl Marman was installing new ceiling lights in the workrooms.

"I tell you it's the most money Marman has spent at Kohn's since your mother and Ivan Wollmack made him repair the roof back in 1914," Yakov said, laughing.

"Momma knew Ivan Wollmack?" Rachel asked excitedly.

"Oh, yes," Yakov replied. "Wollmack and Momma worked together to unionize Kohn's. He couldn't have done it without Momma. He told her that too."

"They really worked together?" Rachel asked.

"Yes, yes. Becky, you helped too, don't you remember?"

"You knew Wollmack?" Joe asked, surprised by what he was hearing for the first time.

Becky smiled broadly as she nodded. "I was just a child, but I guess I really did play a part in the campaign to unionize Kohn's."

"Play a part!" Yakov said, slamming the table so hard with the palm of his hand that the silverware and dinner dishes clattered on the table. "Rachel, your sister Becky actually obtained the list of women Marman was going to use to break a strike. She got it from Marman's daughter. Your mother, may she rest in peace, called on every one of those women and got them to promise to support the union if a strike was called. Momma really did that. And Wollmack used that to force Marman to back down."

Rachel felt her flesh tingle with excitement as Yakov described Anna's relationship with Ivan Wollmack.

"It's true, Rachel," Becky said. "Momma was really the hero of the union's fight against Kohn's."

"Wollmack would remember Momma if he heard her name?" Rachel asked.

"Oh, yes," Becky said. "He would remember."

"I wonder if he ever learned Momma died," Rachel wondered aloud.

"Who knows," Yakov sighed, the exuberance gone from his voice.

"I doubt it," Becky said sadly.

"How would he know?" Joe asked into the silence that rapidly descended upon the room.

Rachel decided to attend the CGWA meeting the following Sunday afternoon. She took the seven o'clock train to Laurel, spent the morning with the children, and caught the one o'clock B&O back to Baltimore. It would be tight, but if the trolleys were running on time, she could get to the union hall close to two o'clock.

The hall was crowded and Rachel started to make her way to the rear of the room where she planned to stand for Wollmack's address. She was a little late, but fortunately Wollmack had not yet begun to speak. He was sitting on the stage at the front of the hall with other members of the local, listening to the president of the local deliver a report on the union's finances to the membership.

"Are you alone?" a volunteer usher asked her.

"Yes," she whispered.

"You're in luck. There are some single seats in the front row. Come with me."

Ivan glanced up from his notes as the usher escorted Rachel to the front of the hall. He shifted ever so slightly to see the girl better. He was about to rise to his feet when he saw that it wasn't Anna.

"My God," he whispered aloud.

"What did you say?" asked the union secretary sitting at his right.

"Who is that woman?" Ivan asked, cocking his head toward Rachel, who was about to take her seat.

"I have no idea. I've never seen her before. Do you think you know her?"

"No, I don't know her, but I would bet anything I know

her mother. She bears an absolutely astounding likeness to Anna Appelavitch, who used to work here when I did."

Rachel had indeed grown into an enchanting image of her mother. The contours of her face, the way she wore her hair, her deep penetrating brown eyes, and the inviting, almost smiling shape of her lips, all stirred a memory Ivan treasured.

The labor leader dropped his notes on the vacant chair to his left and waited for the conclusion of the generous introduction that was being delivered by the president of the local. Then he rose and walked to the podium, holding up his hands to acknowledge the enthusiastic welcome by the crowd.

"It's good to be home!" he shouted, setting off another wave of thunderous applause and loud cheering. "We began a great crusade in this very hall just one decade ago." The crowd settled down to hear him. "It was a glorious time and it was a victory for the union, and it was a victory for right and it was a victory for working men and women everywhere!"

His timing was as masterful as ever, and with each point the crowd responded with ever-growing cheers of approval.

Ivan outlined the progress of the CGWA during the prior ten years and evoked, as he had done so many times before, an enormous sense of pride and power among those in the audience.

Then toward the end of his address he paused and looked directly at Rachel.

Her heart pounded as the young bearded union leader peered down at her.

"We have a lot to remember," he said as the room grew silent. "We must never forget the struggles, the anguish, the injustice and the sacrifice that freed us all from the oppression we knew so well. We are better off because of those sacrifices, and our children and their children will be better off too. Ours was a struggle of people, of ordinary people who believed they could make a difference.

"The soldiers of the CGWA campaign of 1914 were working men and women and children joined together—in union." He raised his voice and extended his clenched fist toward the heavens. "Women such as Anna Appelavitch, who single-handedly called upon every laborer who worked at home and who as a group could have crushed our crusade, and Anna won them over to our cause and stole from our opponent his greatest weapon."

As the room erupted with deafening applause and cheers

and whistles, Ivan saw that tears were streaming down Rachel's face, and he knew that the daughter of Anna Appelavitch stood before him in the front row of the CGWA union hall.

Afterward, as the crowd of well-wishers that encircled him after his address began to thin, Ivan saw that Rachel had remained behind and waited her turn to approach him. He excused himself from a small group of men who were standing with him and walked over to her.

"Hello, I'm Rachel—"

"Appelavitch." He could see her eyes widen in wonderment at his recognition of her.

"How did you know?"

"Rachel, you are the image of your mother." Ivan took her hands in his. "How is she?"

He saw her expression change and an instantaneous dread washed over him.

"Momma died six months ago, Mr. Wollmack."

"I'm sorry."

Ivan closed his eyes and Rachel sensed the depth of his pain.

"I had no idea," he whispered.

"You lost all contact when you left Baltimore?"

"Yes, we lost touch since I left Baltimore ten years ago."

"I would love to hear about Momma's work with the union," Rachel said enthusiastically.

"Well, I'm the man who can tell you. We worked together. We were a team."

"She was really important?"

"Rachel, can I buy your dinner? I can't think of anything I would rather do than talk about Anna Appelavitch with her daughter."

She smiled warmly. "I would love it."

They left the union hall as soon as he had said good-bye to the local's leadership, and they walked the short distance to the Lord Baltimore Hotel and were shown to a table in the nearly empty dining room.

"I guess it's too early for dinner," he said.

"I'm starved. I came here by train from Laurel. I haven't had lunch."

"You live in Laurel?"

"No. It's a long story."

"Well, let's order something to eat first. Then I want to hear your long story." Ivan signaled for a waiter.

"And I want to hear about Momma and the CGWA."

They talked for over two hours. Rachel told Ivan about how her mother's death had changed the entire family, surprised at how readily she opened up to this stranger who'd once known her mother. Later, Ivan walked with Rachel to the eastbound streetcar stop and waited until she boarded. As she was about to step into the trolley, she turned and hugged him and kissed him on the cheek.

"I had a wonderful time!" she yelled as the streetcar began moving.

He stood on the platform for several minutes, watching the streetcar glide away from him along the steel track that would take it all the way to the harbor. As he drove along Route One toward Washington where he now worked, Ivan's thoughts were consumed with memories of Anna. He would have been devastated by the news of her death had it not been for Rachel. Somehow Anna seemed to be so present during his afternoon with her daughter.

As he entered Laurel, about midway between Baltimore and Washington, he pulled into a truck stop and asked the attendant for directions to Sachshaven.

He pulled off the road as soon as the stately building came into view and turned off the engine of his new Ford. *She really would turn over in her grave,* he thought, staring at the orphanage.

"Trust me, Anna. I'll do something. Trust me," he whispered into the darkness.

Rachel loved her job at Korman's. Although most of her coworkers were older than her, she got along well with all of them, especially Paul Abrams, the night-shift supervisor. She would never forget how moved he was when she told him why she wanted the job.

Paul Abrams, had taken an instant liking to Rachel. She was a good worker, turning out more finished work than any of the others. She was always cheerful, a favorite with everyone in the shop, unpretentious, and he admitted it to himself, very beautiful.

Paul, the son of a once-prosperous trader from Odessa, had come to America with his parents and two brothers in 1919. Within a short time he became an assistant manager at Korman's Men's Wear, and in less than a year he had been promoted to night-shift supervisor, earning sixty cents an hour with a bonus for productivity. He was a tall man, warm and likable, quietly handsome but painfully shy, and seemingly older than his thirty years.

There was another reason Paul liked Rachel Appelavitch. She did not make him feel awkard or intimidate him as most women did. But he knew it was inconceivable that she could think of him in any way other than as a friend. She was only seventeen, and she probably thought of him as an old man. She would probably be repelled by any hint of his interest.

He could tell as soon as Rachel arrived at work that night that something was wrong. She looked troubled and dejected, and at the end of the shift he went over to speak to her. "Let me help you with your coat." He held it open for her to slip into.

She looked at him in surprise, then managed a faint smile.

"Are you all right, Rachel?"

"Fine." Her fragile smile faded. She shook her head. "A family thing. Something I've got to work out on my own."

"Is it money? I've saved a bit. I'd be glad to help out."

Rachel looked into Paul's eyes and could see he was serious. She smiled at him and touched his forearm gently.

"It's really very kind of you, Mr. Abrams, but no, it's not money. Thanks, anyway."

"Please, it's Paul," he told her. "Look, I'll walk home with you. We can talk. You know what they say, two heads are better than one."

She looked at him for a long moment, just the hint of a frown on her forehead.

"It . . . I . . . it's just an idea," he said almost apologetically. "You don't have to—"

"You're sure it's not out of your way?"

"What?" he asked hastily. "Me? I've somewhere else to be?"

They left the shop and started walking across town toward the Patterson Park area where Rachel lived with Becky and Joe. It was bitterly cold and Rachel walked quickly, her shoulders hunched against the biting wind. Time and again Paul tried to summon the courage to put his arm around her shoulder, but every time he thought of it, he imagined her pulling away from him, revolted by his touch. They were approaching the street where Rachel lived before he finally got up the nerve to speak to her.

"I wish you'd tell me what's wrong, Rachel."

She stopped and turned to look at him. Her eyes were unreadable in the light of the streetlamp.

"It's good of you to ask, Mr. Abrams, I mean, Paul. But there's nothing you can do. Nothing anyone can do. Thank you any—"

"It's the children!" he interrupted, struck by sudden realization and angry with himself for not thinking of it sooner. She had told him all about her family when she had applied for the job. They were always uppermost in her mind. "It's the children, isn't it?"

She nodded and he saw the pain in her eyes. He lifted his hands, the desire to hold her momentarily overcoming his fear. But as he realized what he was doing, he quickly dropped his arms down at his sides again.

"They're sick?"

"No, nothing like that."

"Tell me. Maybe I can help."

"It's my brother-in-law, Joe. He's bringing his family over from the old country, in May. They're going to move in with us."

"And there won't be enough room for your brothers and sister, is that it?"

He saw the tears trickle down her cheeks as she shook her head. "Oh, I want to bring them home so much!" she cried.

Again he reached out for her, and again he checked himself. "Rachel, it will be all right."

"I'm so scared. I'm so scared they'll never come home. I'm . . . just so scared!" She reached out and grasped him by the shoulders, her touch electrifying him, and Paul astonished himself by taking her in his arms. Rachel laid her head on his shoulder and wept as she had not wept since her mother's death. He held her close, stroking her hair, until he felt her stir against his body and she stepped back, smiling through the tears.

"I'm sorry," she whispered, her face flushed. "I got you all wet."

"Rachel—"

"Thank you for being so kind. Good night, Mr. Abrams."

"Paul," he said hoarsely. "It's Paul."

"Good night, Paul," Rachel said before she turned and ran down the street toward the apartment.

Paul Abrams made his way home, caught in a turmoil of conflicting emotions. He knew he was attracted to this girl as he had never before been attracted to any woman. The soft warmth of her body pressed against his own had seemed so natural, so right. He was shaken by the strength of his own feelings. He wanted to make everything right for her, protect her, see to it that she never again stood on a street corner in the icy wind and wept because she could not have what she wanted most in all the world.

On the way up to Sachshaven the following Sunday, Mr. Applebaum, the bus driver, told Rachel that Mrs. Goldschmidt wanted to see her. She spent the entire journey agonizing over whether one of the children was sick or injured.

"Ah, Rachel," she said as Rachel stepped through the doorway of her office. She smiled and came around her desk. "We've got good news for you."

"There's nothing wrong with the children?" Rachel asked immediately.

"Good heavens, no! Just the opposite. We've found two wonderful families who are ready to have the children come live with them."

"So soon?" Rachel said, stunned by the news.

"It's not so soon. It's taken longer than usual. But it's all arranged. Sol and Esther will go to the Gordon family in Reisterstown, west of Baltimore. Benjamin and Martin will be living with the Ackermans in Glen Burnie."

"Is that near Reisterstown?"

Mrs. Goldschmidt hesitated. "Ah, no, I'm afraid it's on the opposite side of Baltimore."

"Then, they'd hardly ever see each other," Rachel murmured.

"Not as often as we'd like," Mrs. Goldschmidt admitted. "But it's still far better than their staying in an institution. Even one as fine as this."

"Have you told them?"

"No, not yet. I wanted to tell you first."

Rachel said nothing, devastated as she was by the news.

"We've taken a lot of trouble to find families who could take all four children at the same time, Rachel." Mrs. Goldschmidt's voice reflected the compassion she felt for Rachel at that moment. "We didn't want to send two of them away and keep the others behind."

"I know." Rachel took a deep, shuddering breath. "It's

just . . . it's just . . ." It was no good. She just shook her head.

Wordlessly Mrs. Goldschmidt put her arms around Rachel. "It's for the best," she whispered. "They need a proper home. A family."

"When will they go?"

"In a day or two."

"You couldn't wait a week?"

Mrs. Goldschmidt frowned. "What would that accomplish?"

"I think Becky and Joe will be able to take them, in a week or so."

Mrs. Goldschmidt released Rachel and looked her straight in the eye. "Did they tell you that, Rachel?"

"A week?" Rachel pleaded, ignoring the woman's question. "Please, Mrs. Goldschmidt. Let them stay another week."

"I don't know. I know how you must be feeling, Rachel, but some things can't be changed."

"Can't you please, won't you give me just a few more days, Mrs. Goldschmidt? My sisters and I think we have a way to bring them home," she lied.

"I know I shouldn't—"

"Oh, thank you, Mrs. Goldschmidt!" Rachel said quickly, flinging her arms around the older woman's neck and kissing her. "You won't be sorry, you'll see."

"There, there, child. You're the last person in the world whose feelings I'd want to hurt. But Rachel, a week is all I can allow. You understand that, don't you?"

"Yes, yes, of course!" Rachel's eyes shone. "Can I go see the children now?"

"Of course." Mrs. Goldschmidt smiled. "But Rachel, you won't mention anything about this?"

Rachel shook her head. Her visit with the children was going to be difficult enough without her telling them that unless she could find a way to bring them home in a week's time, they might never live together as a family again.

As soon as she got back to Baltimore, Rachel decided to go and see her father. She discussed her decision with Becky, who tried to discourage her. "You will only make him miserable," Becky warned. Rachel, however, was determined to try once again to persuade her father to help with the children. Surely now, faced with the knowledge that the children were actually going to be split between two different families on opposite sides of the city, he would face up to his responsibilities.

In spite of Becky's warning that Poppa was no answer, Rachel could see no other solution to their problem. Becky was waiting for her when she returned from her visit with Yakov.

"It's late," Becky said as Rachel took off her coat and sat down at the table. "I was getting worried."

"I walked around for a while."

"In this weather? You must be frozen. I'll make you some coffee." Becky bustled about, filling the kettle, lighting the stove, putting cups on the table. She did not need to ask how Rachel's talk with Yakov had gone. It was written on her sister's face.

"So, how's Poppa?" she said, just to start the conversation.

"The place is such a mess, Becky. It looked as if every dish Momma ever bought was piled up in the sink. There were dirty clothes everywhere. Poppa didn't look as if he'd shaved for two or three days. Even his collars were dirty."

Mind Poppa's collars, Becky. Becky heard her mother's voice and swallowed hard. "Did you clean up for him?"

"I threw out old copies of the *Forward*, washed all the dishes, put his clothes in the tub to soak."

"I'll go around tomorrow," Becky promised. "How was your talk?"

"Horrible. Poppa wants nothing to do with the children."

"And what did you expect?" Becky sighed as she poured two cups of coffee and joined Rachel at the table.

"How can he turn his back on his own flesh and blood?"

"You asked the question, Rachel. Now answer it."

"What?"

"Answer your own question."

Rachel frowned. "It's simple. He's too selfish."

"That's *too* simple, Rachel. No one would put himself through what Poppa is going through out of selfishness."

"What are you talking about?"

"It's not that he won't, Rachel. He *can't* do it. He's not capable of taking the responsibility for children without Momma there. He was being honest with you. I believe him. You should too."

"I can't accept that. It isn't right."

"I agree." Becky, folded her arms and leaned back in her

chair. "It's not right that a father run away from his responsibilities. But is it right to make him do something he isn't capable of doing?"

"You'd prefer they are sent to live with strangers?"

"We're not in a position to do anything about it, Rachel," Becky said slowly, keeping a firm rein on her own temper, but recalling all the times when she wanted to scream at Rachel, *Enough! Enough!* "Look, we've been over this ten thousand times. We can't do anything. It makes me miserable, but I understand it. Poppa knows his limitations. They make him miserable, but he understands them. You've got to understand them too."

"I can't," Rachel whispered. "I won't. And I'll never forgive him. Never!"

"Then maybe he'll forgive you."

"Me? What have I done to be forgiven for?"

"You've made Poppa—you've made all of us look at what we are doing, Rachel. You've made us realize none of us has acted admirably. Sheara and I can deal with our guilt better than Poppa. We can justify what we did by saying we had our own problems. Poppa has nothing but his own weakness to blame for what happened to the children. He would like to pretend to himself that he acted for the best, but you won't let him. I think he will always feel ashamed and guilty."

Rachel shrugged. "He could soon cure that if he wanted to make the effort."

"No," Becky said softly, shaking her head. "He can't."

"How can you be so sure?"

"Let me ask you one last question. When you left him after your talk, what was he doing?"

"Sitting at the kitchen table."

"He was crying, wasn't he?"

"Yes," Rachel sighed. "He was crying. And asking Momma to forgive him."

Chapter Nineteen

Rachel left the apartment earlier than usual the next morning. She detoured through Patterson Park and walked briskly to the offices of the CGWA.

"Can I help you?" asked a middle-aged woman from behind the front desk.

"Yes, thank you. I have to get a message to Ivan Wollmack in Washington."

"Well that's a bit unusual. Is it anything we can help you with."

"No. It's personal. I have to reach him and I don't have a telephone."

"Would you like his address in Washington. Perhaps you would like to write to Mr. Wollmack?"

"No, it's urgent. Please tell him Rachel Appelavitch has to talk to him. I'll stop by later in the day—maybe you'll have a message for me."

"Appelavitch? Are you one of Anna's daughters?" asked the receptionist.

Rachel nodded and managed a smile.

"I knew your mother. I was so sorry to hear about her passing."

"Thank you. Will you contact Mr. Wollmack for me?"

"He'd have my head if I didn't." The woman laughed. "You stop by before six and maybe there'll be a message."

Rachel returned to the CGWA offices shortly before six o'clock. The receptionist greeted her with a smile, but said she'd been unable to reach Ivan Wollmack.

"Mr. Wollmack left this morning for New York," she explained. "You know he's just moved down from the union's offices there. He had to go back today to clean up some things."

"Can you try to reach him there?" Rachel asked, a note of desperation in her voice.

"I already have. They said he's closing up his apartment in New York. He's not expected at the office, but if he calls, his staff will give him the message."

"Do you know when he will return to Washington?"

"They said he should be back in Washington on Wednesday or Thursday."

"Wednesday or Thursday!" Rachel exclaimed.

"I don't know what else I can do, Rachel," the receptionist said sympathetically. "Mr. Wollmack had his New York number disconnected. If he calls either the New York or the Washington office, he'll get the message."

"I'll stop by tomorrow. Maybe you'll have word."

"I hope we'll hear," the woman said kindly.

Rachel nodded her appreciation. "Thanks a million," she said as she turned to leave.

By the time the New York–bound train reached Aberdeen, Maryland, Ivan Wollmack had made up his mind. Over the years he had accumulated nearly seventy-five hundred dollars in his union pension account, and while he could not withdraw any of the funds before his retirement, he could borrow from the CGWA Credit Union an amount equal to his retirement account.

Ivan could not wait to see the look on Rachel's face when he told her of his plan to help the family. Indeed, he realized he could not wait to see Rachel. He was troubled by how much he'd thought of her since their dinner together. He wondered—was he being drawn to Rachel because she so resembled Anna, or was he really simply captivated by this beautiful young woman?

You've been on ice too long, Wollmack, he murmured under his breath as the train roared along the tracks of the Pennsylvania Railroad through Havre de Grace and on toward Philadelphia.

On Monday night Rachel went straight to her bench at Korman's without so much as a glance in Paul Abrams's direction. He had spent most of the weekend rehearsing what he was going to say to her when he saw her again, and her apparent indifference threw him off balance.

The four-hour shift seemed endless. Unsuccessfully he tried to think of excuses to speak to her. *I'll wait till the end of the shift,* he decided. *I won't bother her now.* Finally the women finished their ironing and hung the suits on the rack that held the evening's work. Rachel continued to work on an additional suit, and Paul's heart leapt—she was staying late so they could talk! He watched her unplug the iron and look around her bench one more time to make sure everything was in order. His heart pounded as she put on her coat and walked across toward his desk. He smiled and started to get up.

"Good night, Mr. Abrams," she said absently, walking quickly past the desk and down the stairs that led to the street.

"Rachel!" he yelled after her. "Rachel!"

He grabbed his coat and ran for the stairs. When he got to the top, he stopped abruptly. Rachel was staring up at him from the bottom of the stairway, a frown creasing her forehead.

"Did I forget something?"

"No, Rachel, but could I walk along with you?"

She gave him a polite half-smile, and he thought he saw just the suggestion of a shrug as she pushed open the heavy steel street door. He rushed down the stairs. A blast of freezing air struck him as he ran out into the street after her, pulling his topcoat tightly closed under his chin. A thin, icy drizzle was falling, and the sidewalks gleamed tar-black. Paul fell into step alongside Rachel, who was walking at her usual rapid pace.

"Hey wait, slow down a bit!" Paul said, smiling. "I want to talk to you."

"About what?"

"I noticed you seemed a bit upset tonight. I thought . . . if you had someone to talk it over with. Whatever is bothering you?"

"You're very kind, Mr. Abrams, but—"

"Paul, please call me Paul. Rachel, I want to help. I told you that the other night. Is it something to do with the children again?"

"Yes. I went to see them yesterday. They're being sent to foster homes next Sunday. I won't even be able to visit them at Sachshaven anymore."

"Oh, Rachel, I'm sorry. Is there any way I can—"

"No." She pressed her lips firmly together. As they crossed Fayette Street, a sudden blast of icy wind blew in from the harbor a few blocks away, and Rachel automatically turned her back to the gust. Without thinking, Paul reached out and put his arm around her. To his surprise she didn't pull away. They continued down the street and he gently tightened his grip on her shoulder. She didn't seem to mind; he thought it a miracle.

Suddenly he stopped and faced her. "Rachel, listen to me," he said nervously. "I think I know a way to bring the children home."

She looked up into his eyes. His heart was racing as he looked down at her, afraid to speak, yet determined too.

"How . . . what do you mean, Mr. Abrams?"

"Paul," he said again. "Please, Rachel, call me Paul. Will you do that?"

"Yes, yes, but what are you talking about?"

His lips moved soundlessly. He swallowed and tried again. "There is a way to bring the children home," he whispered, his voice choked with emotion as he spoke his well-rehearsed words. "You could marry me."

There, he thought, *I finally said it.* But he saw that Rachel was trembling with emotion and immediately read her astonishment as rejection.

"Rachel, I know what you're thinking," he said hastily. "I know I'm nearly twice your age. But I would consider it to be an honor to be your husband, and to provide a home for your brothers and sister. I've got some money saved, and I make a good living. It would be a privilege, a mitzvah, to make a home for them."

"Oh, Mr. Abr—Paul," Rachel finally said, in a small voice. "I don't know what to say. You're one of the nicest people I ever met, but . . ."

"But what?"

"I don't know if I'm ready to get married. I don't know anything about being a wife," she said, her face flushed.

"You wouldn't have to worry about . . . that," he said gently. "I'd wait, Rachel. I'd give you all the time you wanted."

She looked into his eyes. "I hardly know you, Paul. How can you be asking me to marry you?"

"You think I'm mad, don't you?" he asked miserably. "Maybe I am, at that."

"No, it's not that. It's just that no one has ever asked me out. Outside of my father and my sister's husbands, I've never really talked to a man."

"Rachel, there's something I want to tell you. Something very important. I want you to know I have never asked any other woman to become my wife. You are the very first, the only one."

She smiled, shaking her head in disbelief, overwhelmed by

this conversation with a man she hardly knew. Paul put his arm around her and held her close.

"Will you consider it, Rachel? Will you consider becoming my wife?"

She looked up and touched his face with her fingers, her eyes full of wonder. "I can't believe this is actually happening," she said softly. "But . . . yes, Paul. I will consider it."

"You won't regret it," he vowed. "Rachel, you'll never regret this." He closed his eyes and sighed.

"Um . . . Paul?" she whispered, her voice muffled against his coat. "You don't know how strange it is for me to be calling a man by his first name. When . . . when would we. . . ?"

"Get married?" he filled in. "Whenever you say. Next week, tomorrow, this instant if you like!"

"And we'd bring the children home right away?"

"As soon as we found a place to live."

"Have you ever lived with children? What if you don't like the arrangement?"

"Arrangement!" He laughed. "Rachel, I'm asking you to be my wife. Your family will become my family. I will treat your brothers and sister as though they were my children—as I will one day treat *our* children."

He touched her cheek gently and stroked her hair, smiling reassuringly.

"In time, Rachel," he said quietly. "In time, when you are ready and unafraid."

"I don't know anything about *that*," Rachel said, swallowing nervously. "It seems frightening."

"You mustn't worry, Rachel. Not now, and not ever. We have all the time in the world."

"You don't think I'm too young?"

"You're seventeen, Rachel. Many girls get married at your age, and most of them aren't nearly as intelligent as you or nearly as mature. Nearly as special."

"Is that what you want in a wife?"

"I want a wife who is a good person, Rachel, someone who cares about other people. That's the most important quality I can think of in a woman. And I know that you are good, Rachel, just as I know that you are beautiful."

"I've never thought of myself as beautiful," she whispered. "Or anything, really. Just me, Rachel, doing the best I could. Trying to make things better."

"We'll make things better, Rachel." Paul held her closer. "Together."

"Married?" Becky shouted moments later. "Are you crazy? Are you out of your head?"

"I'm not crazy," Rachel said defiantly. "And I'm not deaf either, Becky, so stop shouting!"

"Whom? Whom are you going to marry?"

"His name is Paul Abrams."

"Who is he?"

"The man I work for, the night-shift supervisor at Korman's."

"And he asked you to marry him? You're just a child, for God's sake. How old is he, this Paul Abrams?"

"He's older than me," Rachel said hesitantly.

Becky frowned, sensing Rachel's evasion. "How old?" she pressed.

"Thirty," Rachel said, steeling herself for the reaction.

"What?" Joe gasped.

"My God, Joe, he's older than you!" Becky said. "Rachel, what's got hold of you? Why would you want to marry a man thirteen years older than you?"

"Because he is good. Because he cares about other people."

"Ah," Joe said with a smile, suddenly understanding. "I think I begin to see what this is all about." Rachel looked at him uneasily.

"It's the children," Joe said, "Isn't it, Rachel?"

Rachel stared at the floor and said nothing.

"I thought so," Joe said with a nod. "He's agreed to have the children come and live with you, hasn't he, Rachel?"

"Yes," she whispered.

"And when was all this decided, Rachel?" Becky asked.

"Tonight." Rachel's voice was almost too soft to be heard. "He proposed after we finished work."

"Tonight!" Becky exclaimed. "And you said yes, just like that? My God, Rachel, do you know what you're doing?"

"I didn't say yes. I told him I would consider it."

"Oh, she knows what she's doing, all right," Joe said knowingly. "She knows exactly what she's doing."

"Will you stop talking nonsense, Joe Fineman!" Becky snapped. "This is my seventeen-year-old sister talking about getting married. And she doesn't even know what it costs to live!"

"I think she knows a lot more than you imagine, Becky," Joe answered quietly. "A lot more."

"Oh, is that so? Well, maybe she can tell me how they expect to be able to provide for a family of six."

Joe smiled, anticipating Rachel's reply. *She's got it all worked out,* he thought.

"Paul earns enough," Rachel began.

"Oh, yes, I'm sure!" Becky said scornfully. "How much does he earn, this Mr. Wonderful?"

Rachel's face grew red. She looked at Joe, silently asking him for support.

"Tell your sister, Rachel," he said. "It may help her to understand."

"Paul earns over thirty dollars a week," Rachel said reluctantly. "He also gets some kind of bonus."

Becky's mouth dropped open. "Thir—? My God, Joe, that's twice what you earn!"

"More than twice, Becky." Joe nodded.

"It's a fortune! What does he do that he can earn as much as my Joe and Lou together?"

"I told you. He supervises the entire night shift at Korman's. He's a very good manager."

"He must be," Becky said. "And he's agreed to take on the children?"

"No," Rachel corrected her sister. "He *insists* on it. He says it would be a mitzvah. He's a good man, Becky."

Becky and Joe looked at each other, each sensing the other's guilt. Paul Abrams must be a good man indeed if he, a complete stranger, considered it a blessing to provide a home for the children they had sent to Sachshaven.

"There's something else, Rachel," Joe said gently. "Something none of us has ever talked about to you." He looked at his wife and nodded, leaving it to her.

"Rachel, have you thought about the other responsibilities of being a wife?"

Rachel's cheeks grew even redder. She nodded as eyes darted from Becky to Joe and she struggled to reply.

"Paul said he would . . . wait. Until . . ." She tried to speak, but the words caught in her throat.

"Yes?"

"He says he'd wait."

Becky ran her fingertips across her forehead and closed her eyes in an effort to collect her thoughts. She looked just like

Momma then, Rachel thought, startled at the momentary resemblance.

"Have you decided when you would get married?" Becky asked.

"Right away."

"I can't believe it," Becky sighed.

"Why not?" Rachel asked.

"Things like this just don't happen, that's why not!" Becky flared. "A seventeen-year-old girl doesn't just go to work one night and come home and say, 'Oh, by the way, a man asked me to marry him tonight, and I said yes!'

"You don't love this man, Rachel!" Becky continued angrily. "And don't tell me you do, because I won't believe it!"

"I think he is a good man. I respect him. He wants to marry me and I am willing to marry him," Rachel shot back defiantly. "What's wrong with that?"

"Nothing, Rachel, nothing," Joe said soothingly. "Look, we're only interested in your welfare. That's why we're asking you all this. We know nothing about your Mr. Abrams. Where's he from?"

"The old country."

"Rachel, everyone in America is from the old country. Where exactly did he come from?"

Rachel's heart raced as she realized she didn't even know where the man she was talking about marrying had come from.

"I can't remember the name of the place," she lied. "But I know he and his family came here right after the war."

"Is it a big family?"

"He has two parents."

"How very unusual," Joe said with a grin. "Doesn't he have any brothers or sisters?"

Rachel shook her head impatiently. "Why are you asking me all these questions, Joe? I'm not marrying his family!"

"You haven't met them, have you?"

"No," Rachel admitted miserably.

"Oh, Rachel, Rachel!" Becky said. "You don't know what you're letting yourself in for!"

"Rachel, let me ask you something," Joe said. "Would you consider, even for a moment, marrying this Mr. Abrams if the children weren't at Sachshaven?"

Dead silence descended upon the room as Joe and Becky awaited her answer.

"No. Of course not," she finally replied.

"Then, don't do this to him, Rachel. He's too good a man to be hurt," Joe said.

"I wouldn't hurt him."

"Oh, yes, you will, Rachel. You won't intend to, but sooner or later he'll realize that you never married him for love. What you're thinking of doing is wrong."

"Letting the children go to Sachshaven was wrong, but we did it!" Rachel cried. "Letting them put the children into foster homes is wrong, but we're doing it! How can you tell me this is wrong when we have watched our family being destroyed and did nothing?"

"All these wrongs don't make a right," Joe replied, his voice subdued by the guilt he felt.

"My sister and brothers are not going to foster homes and they are not going to stay in that damned orphanage!" Rachel yelled as she stormed from the room, slamming the door behind her.

Chapter Twenty

Ivan Wollmack stopped by the New York office of the CGWA at eight o'clock Tuesday morning, letting himself in with the key that he had neglected to turn in when he moved to Washington. He picked up a few flies and his diploma from City College of New York, which still hung on the wall of his now-vacant office. As he left the union office, he stopped by the front desk to leave a friendly note for the receptionist who had been at the CGWA for the entire ten years Ivan had worked there.

It was only then that he noticed the message she had left at the desk as a reminder: *Urgent! If Ivan calls, tell him to call Rachel Appelavitch at the Baltimore office.*

Ivan's call to the CGWA office in Baltimore came only moments after Rachel had left. She had stopped by on her way to work as she had done the day before.

"Did she leave a message?" he asked the receptionist.

"No, Mr. Wollmack. No message, but it must be important. She was here yesterday morning and yesterday evening and then again this morning. She really wants to talk to you bad."

"Listen, tell her to leave her address with you if she stops by later in the day."

Rachel's heart sank when the CGWA receptionist gave her Ivan's message when she stopped by the office on Tuesday night. "That's all he said, for me to leave my address?"

"That's what he said, honey. I guess he's going to write to you as soon as he gets back to Washington."

Rachel left her address and thanked the receptionist for her help. She tied her scarf tightly around her neck and pulled open the heavy glass door. Outside, the frigid night air lashed at her and she pulled the collar of her coat up around her face for protection as she made her way to her second job.

Paul Abrams was not surprised when Rachel told him she needed more time to think about his proposal.

"Take all the time you need," he told her, thrilled that she hadn't said no. He had waited anxiously for her to arrive and was certain she was going to decline.

Rachel was not ready to say yes, but she wasn't ready to say no either. She had no doubt that given a choice of bringing her brothers and sister home by marrying Paul Abrams or losing them to foster homes, she would bring them home. Still, she had a few days, and if possible, she wanted to discuss her decision with Ivan Wollmack. Although she had just met him and spent only a little time with him, she realized there was something about him that drew her to him, made her want to seek his opinion.

It was nearly ten o'clock before she reached the apartment. Becky and Joe were relieved that she was finally home. They couldn't remember it ever being colder than it was that February evening.

Rachel sank into a chair without taking her coat off and held her hands over her icy ears. Her eyes were squeezed shut against the frigid pain that seared her skin.

"Did you talk to Paul Abrams?" Becky asked anxiously.

"Let her thaw out for Christ's sake," Joe said.

"Rachel, did you tell him yes?" Becky asked.

"No," Rachel said, taking her hands from her ears.

Becky closed her eyes in relief.

"I didn't tell him no either," Rachel went on. "I told him I need a little more time."

"What did he say? Joe asked.

"He told me to take all the time I needed."

"What are you going to do?"

"Bring the children home, Becky. That's what I'm going to do. One way or the other, they're coming home. I'm not going to let them be separated.

"Rachel—"

"Please not now, Becky. I want to soak in the tub and think. Is there any hot water left?"

"There should be. Why don't you do that. I'll fill the tub while you get out of your things. Rachel, I'm sorry. I didn't mean to badger you. You just don't know how worried we've been about you."

Rachel took off her coat and scarf and dropped her wool knit hat on the chair where she had been sitting. She walked from the room without another word.

"Oh, Joe, what are we going to do? She's going to marry that man. I know she is."

"He could do a lot worse," Joe said, trying to lighten his wife's mood.

"What kind of thing is that to say?" Becky replied angrily.

"Look, Becky, let's think about this from their point of view. Rachel couldn't give a damn about marriage. She has one goal in life right now, and she can accomplish it by marrying this Abrams fellow. Marital bliss is not high on her list these days, so she isn't going to miss not having it. As for Abrams, I wouldn't worry so much about him. He's probably lonely and without any prospects. Whoever winds up with Rachel winds up with a twenty-four carat diamond. She's priceless. She's one in a million. So Abrams wins, the kids win, and Rachel gets what she wants more than anything in the world."

"Rachel is entitled to marry someday the man of her choice. She deserves the best, Joe, the very best. She's going to sacrifice that because she can't see beyond the crisis we have now."

"Rachel is entitled to do whatever she pleases with her life, Becky," Joe said firmly. "And you might as well admit that neither you nor I are going to have a whole lot to say about it."

* * *

It was eleven o'clock by the time they finished their coffee that night. Rachel had not spoken at all during dinner, and Joe and Becky had given up trying to engage her in conversation. The silence was broken by the knock on the door.

"Who could that be?" Joe asked.

Becky shrugged as Rachel glanced at the door. Only then did Ivan's message make sense to her. Her heart pounded as she watched Joe walk to the door of the apartment. He turned and shrugged in bewilderment as he reached for the doorknob.

"Hello, I'm Ivan Wollmack," the tall bearded man said as Joe opened the door. "I'm sorry for coming so late, but I . . ."

"Ivan! Ivan, you came!" Rachel cried, running to him.

"Of course I came, didn't you get my message?" Ivan smiled broadly as she threw her arms around him.

"Will somebody tell me what is going on?" Becky asked, totally confused by the scene.

"I was in New York and received a message that Rachel was trying to reach me. I was going to head back to Washington tomorrow anyway, so I decided to return tonight and stop off in Baltimore on the way. Didn't you realize I was coming, Rachel?"

"They just said you wanted my address. The receptionist thought you were going to write to me."

He shook his head. "Probably my fault. I must not have made myself clear. Anyway, what can I do for you?"

"Ivan, the orphanage is going to send the children to foster homes next Sunday. But my boss asked me to marry him, and he wants to have the children come live with us.

"Jesus Christ," Ivan said under his breath as he sat down. "You mean you're going to marry your boss so the children can come live with you?"

"Do you think I'm too young to get married?" Rachel asked, ignoring Ivan's question and Becky's and Joe's stunned expressions.

"Rachel, it has nothing to do with your being too young."

"You do think I'm too young, don't you?"

"No," he said without hesitation. "But you don't get married to solve a problem."

"Ivan, I won't let those children go into foster homes. I just won't!"

"Neither will I, Rachel."

"What?" she asked, confused by his reply.

"I said, I won't let this happen to Anna Appelavitch's children either. I owe her that."

Becky and Joe had watched the exchange in shocked silence. Now Ivan turned to them. "I have plenty of money."

"We can't take your money," Becky answered.

"You can damn well borrow it then."

The four spent most of the night talking and planning. With the money Ivan would loan them, the family could afford to buy one of the new row houses on Collington Avenue. A larger one sold for thirty-five hundred dollars, and while the price was high, the house could comfortably accommodate the entire family.

"Look, we can't work out all the details tonight," Ivan finally said. "Just tell the people at Sachshaven the children are coming home. We'll figure everything else out during the week."

It was two o'clock before they finished talking. Becky made up the couch for Ivan before she and Joe retired. Rachel waited in the living room while Ivan prepared for bed.

She sat down on the floor and leaned against the front of a stuffed chair as he lay down on the cover and turned on his side to face her.

It was quiet in the apartment. Ivan concentrated all his attention on Rachel, suddenly balling his hand into a fist to keep from reaching out to her.

"I'll never forget what you've done to help us," she said softly, reaching up to touch his arm.

"Would you have married Abrams?"

She paused a moment and then nodded.

"Yes. I think I would have," she whispered.

He opened his hand and gently took hold of her shoulder. "I'm glad you called me," he said softly.

Rachel glanced down at his hand and then returned her gaze to his eyes. He squeezed her shoulder tenderly.

She just looked at him and smiled.

Ivan left early the following morning. They had all agreed that just Rachel and Becky would look at the new homes that were for sale on Collington Avenue, as well as several old but large homes on Mount Vernon Place. Ivan would return to Baltimore the following Sunday after meeting Rachel in Laurel.

Ivan let himself into his fashionable Columbia Road

apartment, throwing his coat on the couch. He headed for the kitchen to fix himself a drink with some Scotch he had brought down from New York. It was easy to buy liquor in New York, but he had no idea where to find it in Washington. Though Ivan was not much of a drinker, he assumed the four-year-old Volstead Act would be taken very seriously in the nation's capital.

He returned to the living room and sank into a dark leather couch, taking a long sip of Scotch and closing his eyes.

My God, he thought to himself, *seventeen years old!*

Ivan sat there for over an hour, letting his eyes slowly roam over the walls and ceilings, taking in all of the detail he had never before bothered to observe. The stillness, the loneliness, the isolation in which he now found himself, began to overwhelm him. He brought his hands up to his face as though to shield himself from the stark reality that now held him captive. He was alone and eager for the love and companionship that had, for so long, been absent from his life.

Rachel's face blossomed into a broad smile as she caught sight of the locomotive making its way into Laurel. The train appeared as a small dark speck, a smudge of smoke hovering above it against the white fields of snow that had blanketed the Maryland landscape the night before.

Ivan, searching for Rachel, clung to the stair railing and leaned from the train as it rolled into the station. She waved excitedly as soon as she spotted him, and as the train slowed, he jumped down to the platform and embraced her warmly. He held her slightly longer than was proper, delighted by the feel of her body pressed so closely to his.

"Oh, Ivan, you should have seen Mrs. Goldschmidt when I told her the children would be coming home next Sunday!" Rachel exclaimed, her face flushed as she finally pulled away from him. "She laughed and cried at the same time."

"Come on, let's board. We can talk over coffee in the dining car," he said, taking her arm to help her up the stairs.

It was only after they were seated that Rachel realized he had shaved his beard. He saw the shocked look on her face and laughed at her belated discovery.

"Your beard's gone!"

He nodded, smiling from ear to ear.

"But why?" she asked, laughing.

"I grew it over ten years ago to make me look older. Now I want to look a little younger."

She reached up and touched his clean-shaven cheek with her fingertips. "You do look younger," she said softly, almost mesmerized by the newly discovered handsomeness of the man sitting across from her.

"How's the week been, Rachel?" he asked, trying to ignore the effects of her touch.

"Like a dream. Wait until you see the houses we saw."

"What did Abrams say?"

Rachel grimaced. "He was a dear, but I think he was hurt too."

"Of course he was. He lost a treasure."

She sighed. "I was very selfish when I said I would consider marrying him. I never considered what saying no would mean to him once he really got his hopes up. I really feel terrible about that."

"Rachel, there's something I want to talk to you about."

"What is it?" she asked, concerned by Ivan's seriousness.

"Rachel, I'm not a very compulsive man. I really think things through very thoroughly before I make major decisions. I have to know I'm right."

She nodded. "I understand."

"I've made a big decision, Rachel. The biggest decision I think I have ever made in my life."

"What is it?" she said quietly.

He reached across the table and took her hands in his.

She squeezed his hands affectionately to show her support for whatever he was about to reveal.

He took a deep breath before he continued.

"Ivan, it will be all right. Whatever it is, it will be all right," she said soothingly, puzzled by his nervousness. She thought, here was a man who'd moved thousands to action with his speeches—yet now he seemed to struggle for words. "Ivan, what have you decided to do?"

"Ask you to marry me." He peered into her eyes intently.

Her mouth fell open and her eyes widened as his words sank in. Her grip tightened on his hands and he squeezed back, almost imperceptively.

He had rehearsed all the things he wanted to say, but decided, on the spot, to let her react first.

"I can't believe this is happening," she finally said.

"It's happening."

"Why are you doing this, Ivan?"

"Because I think it's the right thing to do. I haven't felt this way for a long time, Rachel. I love you, Rachel. I want to preserve that love and nurture it and savor it every day. I think marriage is the way to do that."

"I've thought about you so much since we met. Sometimes I felt foolish even thinking you could have any interest in me." She felt awkward about expressing what she'd thought so many times since meeting Ivan.

"You have rarely ever been out of my mind, Rachel."

"What do you think people will say?"

"It's of no importance whatsoever. I have absolutely no interest in what anyone other than you has to say. What do you have to say?"

"You're positive you know what you're doing?"

He nodded.

Rachel looked deeply into Ivan's eyes. He had undoubtedly become the most important man she had ever known, nearly the central focus of all her thoughts ever since she walked into the union hall two weeks earlier to hear him speak. Because of her mother's ties to Ivan, Rachel felt as though she had known him for years. But rapidly her feelings for him had evolved into an attraction that went beyond friendship. While she had been flustered by her new feelings, she knew, after all, there was no harm in fantasizing about someone such as Ivan Wollmack—as long as you didn't get carried away. She'd never dared to dream their meeting would lead to this.

"Rachel, would you like to be my wife?" Ivan asked, breaking into her thoughts.

"Oh, yes!" she cried. "Oh, yes!"

He leaned across the table and took her face in his hands and kissed her softly on the lips.

Becky and Joe greeted Ivan warmly as he and Rachel entered the apartment. Rachel, who had been ecstatic all week, appeared especially radiant as she rushed to hug her sister.

"It must have been a wonderful afternoon, Rachel," Becky said, lifting Aaron high up on her shoulder. "What did the children say?"

"I don't ever remember seeing them so happy!"

"And I don't ever remember seeing you so happy, Rachel," Joe commented.

"I've never been so happy."

"Joe, Becky, I have something important to discuss," Ivan said importantly. "Let's all sit down."

Becky saw that he was serious, and for a moment she feared that he wasn't going to be able to provide the help he had offered earlier in the week. "Is everything all right, Ivan?" she asked as they all found chairs in the living room.

Ivan slowly took a deep breath and leaned forward in his chair. "Becky, Joe, I have asked Rachel to marry me."

Silence, utter silence, greeted his pronouncement.

"Before you react or say anything, please listen to me carefully. I have not asked Rachel to be my wife for any reason other than the deep love I feel for her. I felt instantly attracted to her from the moment I saw her."

Joe glanced at Becky, who appeared to be stunned by what she was hearing.

"I knew immediately," continued Ivan, "that she was an Appelavitch, and I feel as though I have known her for a long, long time. Rachel hasn't been out of my mind since we met. I haven't given any woman a second thought since my wife was killed in New York six years ago. Not until I met Rachel, anyway."

"Rachel?" Becky asked.

"I think I'm the luckiest girl in the world," she answered without hesitation, beaming radiantly.

"Ivan, *mazel tov!*" Joe exclaimed as he got to his feet.

Ivan rose from his chair, relieved and happy with Joe's reaction.

"I think this is incredible. I also think it's wonderful." Joe walked over to Ivan and embraced him. "I don't have a shred of doubt about anything you've said. I think you're both very lucky."

As Becky and Rachel hugged one another, Rachel felt her sister's shoulders heave as she began to weep.

"Don't mind the tears. I am truly happy for both of you. I just can't believe this is happening to my kid sister."

"Ivan, Rachel, what about the children?" Joe asked.

"They'll come live with us in Washington," Ivan said. "I'll have to get a larger place, but that will be no problem."

Ivan and Rachel were married in Elkton, Maryland, the following Thursday morning just before noon in a private ceremony performed by a justice of the peace. Rachel wanted no festivity, as it had been less than a year since her mother's death. She would have loved having Becky and Joe at the wedding, but did not want Yakov to be there, knowing that her father's presence would simply disturb her. Becky understood and asked only that Rachel and Ivan stop by the apartment on their way to Washington so that they could all enjoy a toast together.

Ivan watched as Rachel hugged her sister and brother-in-law warmly and then turned her cheek to her father, whose kiss, he thought, seemed perfunctory.

"Please take good care of her," Becky said as she kissed Ivan good-bye.

"Are you worried?" he joked.

She shook her head. "Not for a minute. I'm thrilled for Rachel."

"Good-bye Joe," Ivan said. "We'll see you on Sunday."

"Lots of *naches,* Ivan," Joe said. "You deserve nothing but pleasure from one another. I really mean that."

"I know you do, Joe. Thanks. I really appreciate all of your support."

Ivan walked over to Yakov, who stood off to the side, more a spectator than a participant in the small celebration that was just concluding.

"Yakov, I'll take good care of your daughter." Ivan grasped his new father-in-law's hand.

"I hope everyone can be happy again," Yakov replied. "It's been too long."

Ivan reached over and took Rachel's hand as he headed the car toward Route One, which connected every East Coast State from Maine to Florida.

"Nervous?" he asked.

"No, I don't think I'm nervous—just excited. I don't think I've ever been so happy."

"Hungry?"

"I'm starved."

"That's what you said the first time we met." He laughed.

"Where are we going?"

"If you can hold out for a little while yet, we'll have dinner in Alexandria, Virginia. I know a very old restaurant there called the George Washington Club. You'll like it."

"I've never been to Virginia. How far is it?"

"Alexandria is just across the river from Washington."

"Isn't it a long way to go for dinner?"

"If you're too hungry, we can stop on the way. It's just that the restaurant is near the hotel where we're spending the night."

Rachel felt a tightening sensation in her chest. It happened every time she thought about what would be expected of her now that she was a married woman. "Where . . . where are we spending the night?"

"At the George Mason Hotel. It's in the heart of Alexandria."

"Oh," she answered softly.

"Please don't worry about tonight, Rachel. Trust me."

She nodded. "I trust you. I had just assumed we would be spending the night at your apartment in Washington."

"It's *our* apartment, Rachel. We'll spend hundreds of nights there. Tonight is special. It's our wedding night, our honeymoon."

"I've never been in a hotel room before."

"I think you'll be pleasantly surprised."

The drive from Baltimore took them by the University of Maryland and through the old towns of Hyattsville and Blandensburg, Maryland, and into Washington, D.C., by way of Rhode Island Avenue. Rachel seemed engrossed with the nation's capital and was surprised how different the city was from Baltimore. The streets seemed wider and the row houses appeared to be larger. "I've never been to Washington. I expected something different."

"You mean government buildings?"

"Yes, I suppose so. This isn't what I expected the nation's capital to look like at all."

"The federal part of the city is closer to the river. We'll go through the Federal Triangle on the way to Alexandria. It's quite beautiful, Rachel."

As they approached LeDroit Park, near Howard University, Ivan turned south down North Capitol Street and the beautiful domed Capitol Building came into full view.

"Oh, Ivan, it's beautiful," Rachel exclaimed. "It's the most beautiful building I've ever seen."

"It gets better," he said with a laugh.

Ivan continued down the street until the Capitol seemed to tower above them, and then he turned right along Pennsylvania Avenue.

He pointed out the various buildings along the way, including the CGWA headquarters. As he turned left onto

Fourteenth Street, he slowed down so she could take in the entire view of the mall that ran from the Capitol to the Washington Monument.

"It's magnificent."

"It's your town now, Rachel."

As they continued south along Fourteenth Street, they passed the Bureau of Engraving and the Department of Agriculture. Moments later he pointed out the Jefferson Memorial and the Tidal Basin, and they made their way across the Potomac over the Fourteenth Street Bridge. A half hour later he pulled up in front of the George Washington Club after driving through the center of Alexandria.

"I can't believe all this has happened," Rachel said as the maître d' showed them to their table and pulled out a chair for Rachel.

"Thank you."

"You're most welcome, Mrs. Wollmack," the man replied. Ivan smiled at the look of delight on her face.

"I really am Mrs. Wollmack, aren't I," she said with a laugh.

He nodded. "For the rest of your life."

"So much has happened so quickly. It takes your breath away."

"Any second thoughts?"

Rachel smiled and shook her head. "Ivan, my only fear is that I am going to wake up and find that this has all been a dream."

"You know it's like a dream for me too. For six years there has been nothing but emptiness in my life. And then suddenly you appeared and nothing has been the same since. I feel excitement and longing for the first time in ages, Rachel. I've found something so decent, so innocent, so incredibly bright and so damned beautiful. If that's not finding a dream, I don't know what is."

Rachel could feel the color rise in her cheeks. "Do you really mean all of that?" she whispered.

"Why do you think I asked you to marry me, Rachel? When I realized you were prepared to marry that Abrams fellow, I knew I had to do something."

"You know, I had to reach you. I don't know exactly why, but I was frantic to talk to you."

"I think you knew marrying Abrams would have been the wrong thing to do."

"No, I don't think that was it. I think I needed to know what your reaction was going to be. It's strange, because I really am not sure why that was so important to me."

"I think we both sensed something special between us. I can't tell exactly why I dropped what I was doing in New York and rushed to Baltimore when I heard you were trying to reach me. I just knew that, at that moment, nothing else was more important than getting to Baltimore."

"I guess that's what fate is all about," she said seriously.

"Rachel, are you happy?"

"Happier than I have ever been in my life."

"Are you confident about the future—our future?"

She flashed a smile. "Absolutely. I have a way of knowing when I've made a right decision."

"Tell me."

"I ask myself if Momma would be pleased. I know she would have been very distressed had I married Paul Abrams."

"How do you think she would feel about us?"

"I think she would be thrilled."

Ivan and Rachel dined on peanut soup, pheasant served with hush puppies and sweet potatoes, and for desert, bananas foster. But for the sweet potatoes, there was nothing served at dinner that night she had ever seen, tasted, or heard of.

"That was delicious," she said. "I didn't know there were so many new dishes."

"Actually they're all very old dishes. The peanut soup was a favorite of the colonists. There are very few places that serve it anymore."

"You know your new wife has led a very sheltered life."

"My new wife is going to lead a very exciting life."

"Tell me about it," Rachel said enthusiastically.

"The labor movement is in full blossom, Rachel, and I'm right in the middle of all the action. Our organization is in Washington because that's where the country makes policy and sets direction. The CGWA's business is the nation's business, and the issues we deal with evoke great passion from those who support us and those who oppose us. You'll be a part of everything I do."

"It's a far cry from cuffing trousers and sewing buttonholes," she said half-jokingly.

"Your family works hard, Rachel, and the work they do is honorable. My job is to see to it that people such as your father and Joe and Becky get their fair share of the pie."

"Why would anyone fight that?"

"Because no one wants to give up any of the pie on their particular plate."

"You must feel very proud to be on the side of the worker."

"I think it's the only work I could ever do. I really love it."

It had begun to snow while they were dining, and the streets had already become slippery. They slowly drove the few blocks north along Washington Street to the George Mason Hotel in silence.

Ivan brought the car to a stop in front of the towering red brick building. "Nervous?" he asked, turning to Rachel.

She nodded and managed a smile.

He reached over and kissed her lightly. "Rachel, I will not let tonight become anything other than a fond memory. Trust me."

"You know I trust you. I just don't want to disappoint you, Ivan."

"You are not capable of disappointing me, Rachel. What we are going to do tonight is enjoy one another."

"I hope I will know how to do that."

"I will help you, Rachel. And remember, I love you."

Ivan had arranged for a corner room on the top floor overlooking Alexandria's main intersection, King and Washington streets.

As they entered the dimly lit room, Ivan saw the nervousness on Rachel's face. The over-size four-poster with its blanket and top sheet already turned down dominated the room like a gigantic altar.

"Rachel, come to the window for a minute. I'll give you a bird's-eye tour of one of American's oldest cities," he said, anxious to divert her attention away from the imposing and intimidating bed that at that moment, seemed to her to stand at the center of the universe.

She followed him across the room to the window. Ivan pulled open the drape and put his arm around her waist as she stood in front of him.

"Mount Vernon is no more than ten miles to the south down that street, Rachel." He pointed to Washington Street. "The Potomac River is just three blocks to the east down King Street, and if you look to the north that way on Washington, you can see Christ Church. You can barely make out the steeple across the street there. That's where George

Washington went to church, and soldiers from the American Revolution are buried there."

She turned and smiled up at him. "Thank you," she whispered.

Ivan took her gently in his arms and kissed her on the lips, softly at first, and then more passionately as he felt her respond. It was totally quiet but for the sound of a solitary automobile driving south along Washington Street, its tires crunching through the snow.

He embraced her tightly for several moments and then pulled away to look at her. "You are incredibly beautiful, and I love you very much."

She smiled again, nervously. "I love you too, Ivan. You are the most wonderful thing that has ever happened to me."

He drew the drapes and then led her away from the window toward the bed. He pulled her closer to him and began to slowly unbutton the front of her dress.

Rachel reached up and gently brushed aside his hands. As he looked into her eyes, she moved her hands to the next button and slowly unfastened her dress, letting it slip to the floor. Without taking her eyes from his she continued undressing, until she stood before him in naked innocence.

Ivan was awestruck by her supple beauty and gathered her in his arms once again. "Rachel, Rachel," he whispered.

"It's going to be all right," she said softly.

He undressed without taking his eyes from her and then reached out for her and picked her up in his arms, holding her against his chest as he walked to the bed and lowered her onto the crisp white sheets.

Ivan took his time, spending most of their first hour in bed caressing her and introducing her to sensations she had never before imagined. As they progressed from one plateau of pleasure to the next, Rachel's nervousness gave way to desire, and by the time he entered her, whatever pain she felt was lost in the ecstasy of the moment and her desire and love for her husband.

Chapter Twenty-one

Rachel was delighted over Becky's first visit to Washington, though she was only in town for the day.

"How about treating your big sister to a cup of coffee?" Becky said after Rachel showed her the apartment.

"What's wrong?" Rachel asked with a frown. Since her arrival Becky had seemed edgy and nervous, not at all her usual levelheaded self.

"Something has to be wrong before I can have a cup of coffee? Where's Ivan?"

"He went out with the children. He likes to shop early on Sunday mornings."

Rachel went into the kitchen and put on some coffee while Becky took off her coat and made herself comfortable.

"So, nothing's wrong," Rachel said, returning to the living room. "You came to Washington for my special coffee?"

"Well, there is something I want to talk to you about."

"I thought so. What is it?"

"It's Poppa."

"Something's wrong with him?"

"Nothing's wrong. It's . . . Rachel, he's planning to get married again."

"He's *what*?"

"He told me yesterday."

"I don't believe it." Stunned, Rachel sank slowly into a chair opposite Becky. "He isn't through saying *Kaddish* for Momma!"

"Rachel, he's lonely. What do you want from him?"

"It's not even a year," Rachel snapped angrily. "Who is it he wants to marry in such a hurry?"

"Her name is Ida Spellman. She's a widow. Her husband died a couple of years ago."

"How long has Poppa known her?"

"About six months. Someone from work introduced them."

"Six months ago Momma was hardly even . . ." Color rose in Rachel's cheeks. "How long have you known about all this, Becky?"

"I told you, I only heard yesterday that they plan to get married. But I've known Poppa was seeing her right from the start."

"I'll get the coffee," Rachel said, looking for an excuse to leave the room and gather her thoughts. "When are they going to get married?" she called from the kitchen.

"Sunday. Next Sunday."

Rachel came to the door of the kitchen and stared at her sister. "So soon? Doesn't it bother you at all, Becky?"

"What difference would it make if it did? It's not my decision, it's his. There's no sense trying to make him feel bad about it."

Rachel put two cups on a tray and came in with the coffee. The sisters were silent as she poured it. It was an uncomfortable moment.

"Have you met her?"

"A couple of times. She owns a grocery store over on East Baltimore Street. Poppa says her husband left it to her."

"That's not a very nice area."

"We can't all live in Mount Pleasant," Becky said tartly.

"What am I suppose to tell the children?" Rachel asked, ignoring her sister's gibe.

"Tell them the truth. Tell them Poppa is lonesome and that he needs someone because he's lost without Momma. But Rachel—be careful how you tell them."

"What do you mean?"

"You wouldn't want to turn them against Poppa, would you?"

"I don't need to do that, Becky. He's done that himself. You think they don't know what happened? You think they've forgotten he never came to see them at Sachshaven? Or that he let them be sent there in the first place?"

"Is it they who haven't forgotten, Rachel? Or is it you who never let them forget?"

"What's that supposed to mean?" Rachel asked sharply.

"You've got to learn to forgive him," Becky pleaded. "He was all alone. He had nobody to turn to."

"Neither did the children."

"Give him a chance. Maybe he'll be different once he has a wife again."

"What difference would that make?"

"They're *his* children, Rachel," Becky reminded her. "What if Poppa felt he could give them a home now?"

"On East Baltimore Street, over a grocery store?" Rachel said scornfully. If Poppa cares anything at all for his children, he'll leave them alone.

"Ivan is still their brother-in-law, Rachel, not their father."

"Do you really think Poppa wants the children?"

"No, no, I don't think so. But you don't want the children growing up thinking their father never had any interest in their welfare, do you?"

"Why not?" Rachel said coldly. "It's true."

Becky shook her head. "No, it's not. He loves them just as much as you do. The fact that he failed them doesn't mean he loves them less. Someday they'll understand that. They're growing up, and sooner or later they will make their own decisions. And no matter how good Ivan has been to them, they know Poppa is their father and Ivan is not."

"I don't think so."

"We'll see."

In the short term Rachel was right. Yakov married Ida Spellman and moved into his new wife's second-floor apartment over the grocery store. He quit his tailoring job and began working at Ida's side. He gave no indication that he wished to reunite his family; even if he had, Ida would have discouraged him. While they made a decent living, they were in no position to care for four youngsters, and certainly not the way Ivan and Rachel could.

In time, however, Rachel would find that she was wrong, and it was her younger brother Sol who eventually forced her to admit it.

Ivan and Sol were very close and had been from the first day the children came home to Mount Pleasant from Sachshaven six months earlier. Ivan was good with the children, listening intently to all their questions, honest in his replies. He told Rachel children always knew when you lied to them, and these children would know it more quickly than most.

Sol always came to him first, for help with his schoolwork, for approval, for understanding. He was growing tall now, already up to Ivan's shoulder. He had a thick shock of black hair, deep-set, thoughtful eyes, the face of a dreamer. Rachel smiled as she listened to her husband taking turn

with Sol to chant the Torah portion that Sol would soon b
called on to read at his bar mitzvah on his thirteenth birthday
She felt a solid, warm thrill of accomplishment, and c
security. It made her deeply happy that Sol had someone a
close as Ivan with whom to prepare and practice.

As they ended their rehearsal, Rachel heard Sol say to Ivan
that he would like him to have the second aliyah, or honor, a
his bar mitzvah by reading the blessing that is recited befor
each verse is read. Rachel looked up sharply, startled by Sol'
request. Ivan's eyes met hers and she saw the message in
them—*wait*.

"And who will have the first aliyah?" Ivan asked, taking
great care to sound neither hurt nor surprised.

"Why, Poppa, of course," Sol answered, as if Ivan'
question need not have been asked.

"Of course." Ivan nodded, busying himself by putting
away the books. "That is as it should be."

He saw that Rachel was about to protest and raised a hand
to silence her. "Rachel, I think Sol and I could use some tea.
Our throats are dry from all that singing."

"But—"

"Some tea, Rachel, please," he said firmly, cutting her off.
Several more times in the course of the evening she tried to
open up the subject, but each time he stopped her, and Rachel
had to restrain her anger until the children were in bed and fast
asleep.

"Why didn't you say anything?" she finally asked when
they were alone. "You must have been terribly hurt!"

"I suppose I was for a moment." Ivan said mildly. "But
there was nothing to say. The boy was right."

"Right? How can you say that? What has Poppa done to
help him prepare for his bar mitzvah?"

"Is that how you see an aliyah, Rachel, payment for
helping?"

"It's supposed to be a way of saying thank you."

"It's no such thing, and you know it. An aliyah is an honor.
Sol is honoring his father. And he is right to do so."

Rachel looked away but did not speak.

"Rachel, be proud of the boy, not angry with him," Ivan
said softly. "Sol knows how humiliated his father would be if
he had his aliyah after mine. So he honors him, according to
the Torah."

"You think Poppa will even care?"

"Yes, I do. I think he will be very moved."

"I think it's a waste."

"What do you want, Rachel? Revenge? If you do, your brother's bar mitzvah isn't the place to find it. Sol is saying he wants to put the past behind him. Maybe it's time you did too."

"I don't know if I can forget so easily."

"Sol seems determined to. That's what all this is about. That's why it's good, Rachel. That's why I am not offended to receive the second aliyah—"

"While Poppa gets the first," she finished as though thinking aloud. "I'd love to be there when he finds out."

"You will be."

"What do you mean?"

"I want you to be the one who tells him."

"Me?"

"Sooner or later you're going to have to make peace with your father. Maybe this is the time."

Rachel was silent for several moments. "I don't know," she finally whispered. "I don't know if I can."

"Then it's time to find out."

Ida Spellman was filing her nails when Rachel came into the little store and walked up to the counter.

"Hello, Ida," Rachel said with forced politeness. "Is Poppa here?"

Ida hardly glanced at her, giving Rachel neither greeting nor smile. "Jake!" she yelled. "Rachel's here!"

Rachel did not like Ida Spellman at the best of times, and she hated it when Ida called her father Jake. Sometimes she wondered whether Ida did it because she knew how much it annoyed her. Ida, a capable-looking woman in her mid-forties, made no secret of her aversion to Rachel and what Ida called her "hoity-toity airs." She was genuninely fond of Yakov and hated to see him punishing himself because he had not been able to take care of his family.

"So, to what do we owe the honor of this visit?" Ida asked now, making no effort to hide her annoyance.

"There's something I have to talk to Poppa about."

"It must be important to bring you around here. You know, it wouldn't kill you to come by more often. After all, he is your father."

Rachel felt her face grow red. Before she could answer,

however, Yakov emerged from the storeroom at the rear, wiping his hands dry on the front of the white apron he wore.

"Rachel, what a surprise!" he exclaimed, smiling. "I was just washing my hands. Opening all those boxes is a messy business. So, how are you, how is everyone?"

"Fine, Poppa. You should see the children. They're all growing so fast."

"Yes, yes, of course." He glanced uneasily at Ida. "But you know, we're so busy here all the time, there's always something that needs doing, I never seem to get a spare moment, do I, Ida? I'll come to Washington soon, though, yes. Soon."

"We were talking about you last night, Poppa. That's really why I came to see you."

"You and Ivan?"

"And Sol too, Poppa. We had a long talk. We want you to have the first aliyah at Sol's bar mitzvah next month."

Yakov was silent as tears came to his eyes. His jaw trembled when he tried to speak. He looked at Ida, then at Rachel.

"Me?" he faltered. "Me?"

"Oh, Poppa!" Rachel cried, compassion sweeping through her as she hugged her father. Yakov looked disconcerted for a moment, then he smiled and embraced his daughter.

"I didn't think you'd even ask me to come," he said quietly. "I never expected this."

Rachel fought to keep her own composure, realizing that she had been wrong to condemn Yakov for his behavior after Anna's death, that perhaps the worst was behind them.

"Oh, Poppa, Poppa, can't we all be together again, a family?" she whispered, wiping the tears from her cheeks. "Can't we all stop living in the past?"

Yakov took a deep breath. "I don't know, Rachel," he said nervously. He took her shoulders in his hands and held her at arm's length, looking into her eyes. "We could try, though, couldn't we?"

"Yes, Poppa! Oh, yes, please!"

Yakov looked at Ida, who had calmly continued filing her nails, unmoved by the tearful reconciliation taking place in front of her.

"You hear that, Ida?" Yakov said. "We're going to be a family again. What do you say to that?"

Ida Spellman looked up. "It's about time."

PART II

Chapter Twenty-two

When Berl and Dvoyra returned to Oleck-Podlaska from Vilna at the end of the war in 1918, Poland lay in ruins.

Three of the most powerful war machines in the world—German, Russian, Austrian—had passed several times across Polish soil, leaving behind devastation and impoverishment. What was not destroyed by the military operations was pillaged, confiscated, or ruined by the enforced contributions, fines, and levies imposed upon the hapless population.

The occupying powers took everything that could be removed—cash, securities, cattle, farm implements, factory machinery. Two million head of cattle, a million horses, one and a half million sheep and goats. Austro-German armies destroyed more than two million buildings in cities, towns, and villages, as well as nine hundred and forty railroad stations, and more than seven thousand five hundred bridges. Eleven million acres of cultivated land and forest had been laid to waste. More than seven and a half thousand million square feet of timber had been removed.

To the people of Oleck-Podlaska, to every Pole, all this could be reduced to a simple inescapable fact: economic ruin. There was no food, no shelter, no clothing, no shoes, no livestock, no machinery, no anything. In addition, there was financial chaos, with five kinds of currency—the Austrian crown, the German mark, the Ost-rouble and the Ost-mark, and the new Polish mark—in circulation.

Amid this chaos Berl Hoffman was in many respects more fortunate than most of the men who returned to their homeland following the Great War. His talents as a craftsman were immediately in demand throughout the area: Jews and non-Jews alike were repairing their homes, rebuilding their farms, trying to put their lives back together again. And while only a few could afford to pay him with money, Berl was more than willing to give his services in return for food. If he brought home flour, Dvoyra could make bread. If he brought milk, she could make butter or cheese. These, in turn, could be traded for other staples. Once in a while he brought home a chicken. A chicken would get you enough food for a week. Dvoyra, Berl, and the three children would struggle like everyone else, but they wouldn't starve.

Unlike the rest of Europe, Poland remained uneasy. In the north, Poland was newly constituted. The angry state of Prussia was divided into two parts by the so-called Polish Corridor, and the ancient city of Gdansk became Danzig, a "free city" yearning to unite openly with Prussia. In the southwest, where Poland had acquired much of what had been Silesia, the citizens of that former province of Germany were also unhappy. To the south, the Poles were endeavoring to add the Czech province of Cieszyn to the new republic. Nationalism was rampant. All the world seemed in flux as it tested its new boundaries.

But the poor Jews from Poland's little towns and villages found themselves again thrust into an alien political environment with which they had neither sympathy nor affinity. The czars were gone and so was Russian rule over the new republic of Poland. The new government consisted mostly of aristocrats and militarists, and for their civil rights the Jews were dependent not upon liberal advocates in positions of authority, but upon a piece of paper—The Minorities Treaty—which was despised by those in power who were responsible for its enforcement. Failing to shout for Polish nationalism, Jews aroused the suspicions of the nationalists.

Eight months after the war had ended, it began again in Poland. Joining forces with Simon Petlyura hetman of the Ukrainians, the Polish semi-dictator Marshal Pilsudski launched a full-scale war against Russia. The armies marched forth, sweeping to tremendous victories, driving the Russians out of the Ukraine and establishing there a free government, the first in a thousand years. On May 8, 1920, Kiev fell to the victorious armies, throwing the communists out of Eastern Europe. Bells rang all over Poland in celebration of this great event, but they were premature. Down from the north drove the Russian army of General Mikhail Tukhachevsky, and the even more terrifying horde of General Semyon Budenny's First Cavalry, a wild-riding pack of horsemen as savage and ruthless as the cavalry of Genghis Khan. By August 2 the Russian armies were in sight of Warsaw, and Leon Trotsky issued his battle order to the communist troops: "Comrades, let us take Warsaw! Sixteen versts more, and we will have all Europe ablaze!"

But Tukhachevsky failed before Warsaw, and like the Swedes, the Turks, and the Ukrainians before him, Budenny was thrown back from the fortress town of Zamość.

Warsaw was saved—Poland was saved, perhaps Europe itself. But such issues mattered little to the poor. The poor knew the true cost of the "miracle"—four and a half million acres of land destroyed, seventy-five percent of their livestock lost, nine out of ten of their farms ruined, inflation rampant. Before the war the American dollar, by which the value of Polish currency was measured, had bought ninety Polish marks; at the end of it, a hundred and eighty-six. Before 1921 was out, the figure would slide to nearly four thousand marks to the dollar.

In times such as these the people of Oleck-Podlaska clung to the only certainties in their uncertain world: the land and their familes, the rising and setting of the sun, the miracle of birth, the bitter sorrow of death.

Not until the fall of 1921, six months after peace had been officially declared between Russia and Poland with the Treaty of Riga, did Berl Hoffman get the chance to earn a real wage. It had been seven years since he had worked for any reward other than food and shelter for his wife and children.

The man who came to the Hoffmans' door that September was a stranger. He wore fine clothes, a long cloak, and gleaming leather boots. He surveyed the little house with cold blue eyes that gave his thin face, with its long, aristocratic nose, a haughty look.

"Good day to you, sir," Berl said.

"I am Victor Mereck," the man announced arrogantly. "My employer, Prince Stefan Madgellon, wishes to employ an overseer to look after his property in this area."

"I see," Berl said, recognizing the prince's name as that of one of the major absentee landowners in the area. "And how can I help you?"

"The Prince has chosen you, Mr. Hoffman. I am authorized to offer you a wage of one hundred and sixty-five thousand marks a month."

Dvoyra, standing behind her husband, stifled her gasp of astonishment. She knew people in the village who were getting dollars from their American relatives. American dollars were worth about sixty-five hundred Polish marks. This stranger at their door was offering Berl a salary equivalent to twenty-five dollars a month!

"It is a generous offer," Berl said evenly. "But why is the prince making it to me?"

Mereck smiled disdainfully, his condescending expression unnerving Dvoyra. *He looks as if he is just playing with us,* she thought. *As if we don't really matter.*

"The prince directed me to make inquiries," Mereck explained. "You have a reputation as an excellent craftsman, a hard worker, and an intelligent and reliable man, the sort of man the prince is looking for."

"There are plenty of hardworking, reliable craftsmen in this area," Berl replied.

Mereck made an impatient gesture. "The prince wants you, Mr. Hoffman. What may I tell him?"

"What would the job entail?"

"Repairs, administration, routine matters," Mereck said casually.

"And rents," Berl finished sharply.

"But of course."

"And from time to time the rents would have to be increased?"

"From time to time."

"And when the harvests are poor and the peasants need money to get through the winter, the prince will doubtless also wish me to negotiate the terms of his loans with them?"

"The prince would advance money to you for this purpose, if it became necessary."

"I'm a craftsman, Mr. Mereck. I've no desire to become Prince Madgellon's usurer!"

"Come, man, don't be foolish! The prince is offering you the chance to be someone."

"Yes, someone despised."

"Mrs. Hoffman." Mereck turned to Dvoyra and spread his hands in appeal. "Perhaps you can persuade your husband to listen to reason?"

"My husband will make his own decisions, Mr. Mereck," Dvoyra answered quietly.

"You know what I'm saying is true," Berl told Mereck.

"The peasants still hate the overseers you aristocrats send to collect your rents and your loan interest."

Mereck was not surprised at Berl's lack of enthusiasm. The absentee aristocrats had employed Jewish overseers down through the centuries to look after their interests. The peasants viewed the overseer as a symbol of an oppressive system. Frequently their resentment toward the landowner was directed at the landowner's local representative—the Jew. There had been periodic uprisings from time to time, the most vicious of which was led by the peasant cossack Bogdon Chmielnicki in 1648. Over one hundred thousand Jews were slaughtered in that pogrom. It had happened a long time ago, but every Jew in Poland remembered it.

"The peasants!" Mereck scoffed with a thin laugh. "They are like children. They want to live on our land, but resent paying rent. They want help when times are bad, but don't like paying interest on the money they get."

"Most of them work themselves to death on your land, producing for your pockets."

"No one forces them to stay," Mereck said, an edge to his voice. "Come, Mr. Hoffman, what is it to be? If you're so concerned about the peasants, the prince if offering you a way to help them. And there's something else you should consider."

"I'm listening," Berl said. Dvoyra slipped her hand into his and squeezed hard. He knew she understood his hesitation. Here was someone offering him more money than he had ever earned in his whole life, but there was good reason for the attractive wage Mereck was dangling in front of Berl. Berl could find himself caught in any future crossfire between the landowners and the peasants. He knew the talk of land reform was widespread.

"The prince is the largest landowner in this area," Mereck said. "To manage his properties you'll need help. You'd be in a position to give jobs to six or seven of your fellow Jews, Hoffman. Think about that."

"The prince would provide the funds to pay these workers?"

Mereck smiled and nodded, detecting the immediate softening in Berl's attitude. "Of course."

"You say no one has been looking after the properties since the war?"

"That is correct."

"Then the peasants must owe a lot of rent."

"Most of the farms were ruined during the fighting. The harvests have been poor or nonexistent. But now we think proper quotas can be established, and the peasants can start paying rent again."

"And who will set the quotas?"

"All production surplus to a family's needs will be sold on the prince's behalf," Mereck said, avoiding the question. "We will provide you with detailed information on a farm-by-farm basis."

"One more question. Who decides what is enough for a family's needs and what is surplus?"

Mereck sighed but controlled his temper. He needed Hoffman now more than Hoffman needed him.

"Mr. Hoffman, there will be plenty of time to ask questions later. I am a busy man. The prince awaits your answer. What is it to be?"

"Do the peasants know you're hiring a overseer?"

Mereck shrugged. "They're expecting an announcement. We'll call them together and tell them. You will be introduced. I think they will be pleased with our choice."

Berl Hoffman looked at Dvoyra for a moment and then stared off into space, absently stroking his chin as he pondered Mereck's proposition.

Mereck waited, concealing his thoughts. He knew he had been considerably less than honest with Berl. Like the sixteen thousand other estate owners in Poland, Prince Madgellon knew the winds of land reform would soon be blowing across Poland. To two and a half million peasants, it was the most important issue in their lives. Most of the landowners realized that it was a matter of time before the large estates were broken up, either peacefully or through civil war, as it had happened in Russia. To stand between landowner and tenant a shield against the wrath of the peasant who better than a Jew? As in the past, so now—the Jew was the perfect middleman.

"I don't want trouble with the peasants," Berl said bluntly.

"Nobody does, Mr. Hoffman. That's why the prince wants the right person to represent his interests here."

"And he really believes I am that person?"

"He does."

"And if he is not satisfied with my work?"

"Then he'll dismiss you."

"It's that simple?"

Mereck nodded, smiling. "That simple, Hoffman."

Dvoyra listened carefully as Berl described his meeting with the peasants. Mereck had summoned them all to a large barn on the outskirts of town to announce Berl's appointment as the prince's overseer.

Afterward, as the peasants filed out of the barn, Berl had tried to shake hands with one or two of them as they left. Most of them avoided him and looked away. Others shook their heads and edged past him.

Only one man stayed behind after the meeting. He was the same age as Berl and of medium height, with powerful shoulders and the sturdy body of a peasant. He wore a heavy mustache and his eyebrows were black and bushy. He approached Berl, his expression hostile.

"It will take more than a handshake to win their trust," he said confidently. "We're not as stupid as Madgellon may have led you to believe."

"No one thinks you are stupid," Berl said hotly. "I'm just trying to establish a good relationship—"

"Don't give me that shit!" the man cut in. "Madgellon thinks he can start squeezing us again, and you've been picked to do the squeezing."

"You don't know anything about me, yet you know what I'm going to do, how I'm going to do it? You must have second sight!"

"I don't need second sight to know what Madgellon wants a Jew overseer for!"

"What do you hate me for? Being an overseer, or being a Jew?"

The man's dark eyes burned into Berl's. "I'll answer that by telling you my name. It is Zoclow. My first name is Bogdon. As in Chmielnicki!"

Berl's mouth opened in surprise. He watched speechlessly as the peasant gave him a contemptuous half-bow and walked away.

"That one is a troublemaker," Mereck said, coming across the empty barn toward Berl. "What did he say?"

"Nothing worth repeating."

"We know all about him," Mereck confided darkly. "He's involved with this new peasant party, the Piasts. Trying to stir up the peasants, get them to agitate for land reform."

"You can hardly blame them for that."

"It would mean the ruin of the nation," Mereck said sharply, fixing Berl with a baleful stare. "You're not one of these damned communists, are you, Hoffman?"

Berl smiled blandly, and said, "I keep well away from politics."

"Wise man. You just look after the prince's interests. And let us know it that agitator causes any trouble."

Later that evening Berl told Dvoyra about the meeting. "We've lived among them all these years," he said, "yet we hardly know the peasants at all."

"They could say the same thing about us."

"I've got to find a way to work with them. I've got to make them see I'm not their enemy."

"Do you have any ideas?"

He looked at her and smiled. "No," he said with a shrug. "I don't even know where to begin. But I suspect Bogdon Zoclow does."

Berl Hoffman stood on the road outside Bogdon Zoclow's house, still undecided whether to go through with his visit or not. He knew that Victor Mereck might violently disapprove of any attempt Berl might make to befriend Zoclow, but he still felt it was worth trying. If he could make Zoclow believe he wanted to help the peasants on Prince Madgellon's land, he believed he could accomplish far more than he could by being threatening or demanding. He walked to the house and knocked on the door.

It was opened by a strikingly beautiful dark-haired woman, her surprise evident as the lamplight spilled across her face. She regarded him with suspicion, as one might look at a landlord who appeared without notice.

"Bogdon," she called without taking her coal-black eyes off Berl, "someone to see you!"

"Well, if it isn't Mr. Hoffman!" Zoclow sneeringly emphasized the title. "What an honor! Maria, this is the man I told you about. The one Madgellon has sent to look after our *interests*."

He grinned at his own sarcasm, hands on his hips. *He's enjoying this,* Berl thought, noting that Maria Zoclow seemed slightly embarrassed by her husband's rudeness.

"Won't you let me come in?"

"We can hardly stop you," Zoclow replied. "After all, the place belongs to your employer."

"That confers no special privileges on me." Berl looked from Bogdon to his wife. "This is your home. No one has a right to enter except as your guest."

"Please," the woman finally said. "Come in."

Berl nodded his appreciation and entered the tiny, two-roomed house. Cramped as it was, it was spotlessly clean. A glass jar filled with wildflowers stood on the scrubbed table, and the primitive furniture was shiny with use. Above the mantelpiece was a framed reproduction of the Czestochowa Madonna, while a wood fire glowed warmly in the fireplace.

"All right, state your business," Zoclow said abruptly. Maria Zoclow sat down by the fire, bending over her sewing. Once again Berl sensed she was distressed by her husband's rudeness.

"I came to talk to you. To see if I could convince you that I want to work with you and help you."

"I need no help from the likes of you," Zoclow growled. "We don't need or want Madgellon money here!"

"Surely you wouldn't argue that these properties need money if they're to be repaired properly?"

"I'd argue simply because I know Madgellon is only anxious to put us deeper into his debt, and therefore less likely to make trouble when the time comes."

"When what time comes?"

"You know what I'm talking about, Hoffman. Land reform. It's coming, and sooner than any of you parasites think!"

"Let it come. I am not against it."

"Do you think I'm fool enough to believe that?" Zoclow asked scornfully. "The people you represent will fight it to the bitter end. They know that without their obscene land holdings and the peasants who work them, they'll be nothing. Well, their time is coming to an end, Hoffman. And yours with it!"

Stung by Zoclow's words, slightly unnerved by the intensity of his animosity, Berl struggled to find the right response.

"Look, Zoclow, I'm not your enemy, believe me. I want to earn your trust. The work to be done here is overwhelming. I can't do it without the cooperation of the peasants. What must I do to earn your confidence? Tell me."

"Do what the jackal has to do to earn the trust of the fawn," Zoclow replied contemptuously.

"Is that how you see me, as a jackal?"

"How else would I see you?"

"I'm not a landlord. I was born here. My parents and my grandparents were born here. What is best for the people of this area will be best for me. I know land reform is essential, and when the time comes, I will support it."

"What damned liars you Jews are!" Zoclow exclaimed. "Why didn't you go to America like all the rest, Hoffman?"

"I could have. My wife already had her passage and desperately wanted to do just that. But I said no. I told her this was my home, and that this was where we belonged. I am a Pole, damn it. I'm here for the same reason you are here."

For the first time a smile touched Zoclow's swarthy face. "You really believe that, don't you?"

"Of course I believe it."

"Then you're not only a liar, you're a fool," Zoclow sneered. "Your livelihood is dependent on something that cannot last. What use will your prince have for you when he no longer has any land?"

"No use at all, I suppose. But Poland will be stronger when the land belongs to the people, and what is good for Poland will be good for me. So it doesn't matter whether the prince has any use for me then."

"Oh, but it does, Hoffman."

"Why?"

"Because we will have no use for you either."

Berl did not see Zoclow again for almost six months. He knew what was happening of course. Zoclow was telling the peasants not to trust him or accept him; telling them that the winter of 1922 would be the last one through which they would labor for the landowners. There was no way Berl could stop Zoclow, even if he had wanted to. All he could do was to work hard, to restore the estate to its prewar condition, and by his work prove to the peasants that he was on their side.

He spent every minute of each day, from sunrise to sunset, working on the prince's properties. He was now employing six Jewish workers from Oleck-Podlaska and an equal number of peasants as laborers. Within six months virtually all the fencing on the estate had been repaired, and even the most run-down of the peasants' houses had been restored to habitable condition.

He expected no thanks from the peasants, which was just as

well, for none was forthcoming. At best they tolerated him, and certainly trusted him no more now than they had when he first began to work for the prince. As he moved through the fields in his wagon, they would stop work for a moment and watch him expressionlessly. No one ever smiled or waved. They looked at him as if he were from a alien land.

One evening as he was coming home after a day in the fields, assessing the work that would have to be done in the few remaining weeks before winter's freezing hand closed upon the countryside, he saw a disabled wagon at the side of the road ahead. Although it was almost dark, he could see from the wagon's angle that one of the wheels was broken.

"Need any help?" he shouted as he drew near.

"I could use a lift," a voice replied. Berl could not quite identify the stooped figure on the far side of the hitch, but he knew the voice at once. The man came around the wagon and looked up at him. It was Bogdon Zoclow. Berl was tempted to crack his whip over the horse's back and speed on his way, leaving Zoclow to his own devices, but something stilled his arm.

"I hit a rock," Zoclow said finally. "Damned wheel is ruined."

"I'll give you a hand." Berl realized this could be the breakthrough he'd been looking for. "We'll put the wheel in the back of my wagon. You unhitch your horse and tie it to the rear. I'll give you a ride home."

Zoclow wordlessly followed Berl's directions. Then he clambered aboard the wagon and sat up front next to Berl.

"How are the repairs going?" Zoclow asked casually, shoving his hands into his coat pockets and hunching his shoulders against the evening's chill.

"I think all the fencing is intact for the first time in ten years."

"Yes, I noticed. I'm impressed."

"Thank you. What about your work?"

"You talking farms or politics, Hoffman?"

Berl grinned. "Your real work."

"Ah, politics. It goes well. Pretty much everyone around here is a member of the Piast party."

"Do I congratulate you?"

"My success has been achieved at your expense."

"I'd have to be deaf and blind not to know that."

"Don't say I didn't warn you."

"You warned me."

"Well, Pilsudski will be elected next week," Zoclow said. "And that will be the beginning of the end for Madgellon and his kind."

"What if Pilsudski doesn't become president?"

"What if the sun doesn't rise in the morning?"

"Did God give you a guarantee?" Berl asked quietly.

"Who could possibly beat Marshal Pilsudski?" Zoclow questioned, a frown of uncertainty on his brow.

"No one. If he runs."

Zoclow laughed out loud, then spat into the road. "You had me fooled for a moment, Hoffman. I thought you knew something I didn't know. Why on earth wouldn't Pilsudski run?"

"Because he has nothing but contempt for what Parliament has made of the presidency. He's honest enough to turn his back on the whole thing."

"You do know something."

"I hear there's been a great deal of speculation that he may not run," Berl admitted, not revealing that Mereck was the source of that bit of information.

"Nonsense! Absurd!"

Berl did not reply. They were silent for several moments, only the creak of the wagon wheels and the soft fall of the horses' hoofs on the dusty road disturbing the stillness of the night.

"If you're right, who would be left to run for president?" Zoclow said querulously, as if Berl's remarks had put him out of humor.

"I'm told the strongest candidate would be Count Maurycz Zamojski."

"Zamojski! He's the richest of the rich, the largest land-owner in Poland!"

Berl again said nothing.

"Zamojski, president? It's obscene!"

"This is a parliamentary system we have here now. If Pilsudski doesn't run, the strongest parties will decide who will be president. The strongest party is the Rightists."

"They don't control the parliament."

"They control a lot more of it than the Piasts do!"

"Pilsudski will run. He wouldn't allow the country to fall to the Rightists."

Again Berl remained silent.

"You'd love to see Zamojski win, wouldn't you?" Zoclow sneered. "That would suit you perfectly."

"What do you know about a man named Gabriel Naruto-wicz?" Berl asked, refusing to rise to Zoclow's jibe.

"He is a radical who supports the Populist Peasant Party."

"I hear that if Zamojski appears to be the only other candidate, Narutowicz will run."

"He'd never attract enough votes!" Zoclow scoffed. "The Populists are too radical. I'm not even sure the Piasts would support him."

"Then we'd all better pray Pilsudski runs," Berl said grimly.

When next he saw Zoclow, the peasant was leading his wagon along the road not far from where it had broken down a few days earlier. Since then, the newspapers had confirmed the news that Marshal Pilsudski would remain as chairman of the Inner War Council, the highest military position in the country, but would not run for the presidency. He considered the presidency too weak an office; "a bird in a gilded cage" he had called it.

"I see you had to replace the wheel," Berl commented. "I'm sorry. It must be expensive."

"Only a few months' earnings," Zoclow said bitterly. "I see you bastards have got your way in Warsaw."

"It looks as if Zamojski will be elected."

"Those whores will destroy this country!" Zoclow growled. "The man who butters your bread must be delighted."

"What will the Piasts do? Team up with the Populists?" Berl asked, ignoring Zoclow's insult.

"They won't support Zamojski, I can tell you that."

"Why don't you demand that your party fight him?"

Zoclow raised his eyebrows. "You surprise me, Hoffman. You surprise me all the time. As a matter of fact, I'm going to urge the Piasts to support Gabriel Narutowicz."

"Do you think they'll pay attention to you?"

"Who the hell knows?" Zoclow said with a shrug. "I've been one of their most successful organizers. If they don't listen to me now, I've been wasting my time."

"I wish you luck, Bogdon. I mean it. I hope you're successful."

"There you go again. You really mean it, don't you?"

"Yes, I do."

"Then why don't you help us?"

"I have no party, Bogdan. You're the politician."

"You Jews vote as a bloc."

"No one listens to the Jews."

"The Minorities bloc could be crucial in this election. If the Leftists, the Piasts, and the Minorities withheld their support, Zamojski would be lucky to get two hundred and thirty votes. Nothing close enough to win the election."

"And how to you propose to bring that little miracle to pass?"

"I'm not going to. You are, Berl!"

Berl was speechless. Zoclow had never called him by his first name before. The peasant reached up and took hold of his arm.

"Listen to me, Berl. You work for the biggest landowner in this area. You would have a lot more influence than you think."

"Bogdon, I'm no politician. I wouldn't know where to start!"

"I can tell you that!" Zoclow slapped his thigh emphatically. "You must talk to Yitzhak Gruenbaum. He's probably the most influential Jew in Parliament. You must go to Warsaw, Berl, and persuade him to get the Minorities to vote for Narutowicz!"

"It's preposterous. He'd laugh at me!"

"I don't think so. I think he'd be impressed."

"How do you know he would even see me?"

"The Piasts can arrange it."

"It could cost me my position," Berl said quietly.

Zoclow nodded without taking his eyes off Berl. "I thought so," he said contemptuously. "All your talk about wanting to earn our trust, believing in land reform—that's all it was, talk?"

"No!" Berl said vehemently.

"Then you have no choice."

It was more than three hundred versts, two hundred miles, from Suwalki to Warsaw, a journey of over twelve hours by rail. Berl hardly took his eyes from the window as the clanking train sped through the darkening day at over twenty miles an hour. He was fascinated by the ever-changing scenery, the great tracts of forest, grim and featureless beneath the covering snow.

They passed through Augustów and Grodno and were approaching Bialystok as night fell. Pulling his cap forward over his eyes and turning up the collar of his overcoat, Berl huddled into the corner of the compartment, sleeping fitfully as the train clattered through the silent night. He awoke, stiff and dry-mouthed. The windows were fogged with condensation. He wiped a clear patch with his sleeve and looked out at the gray, snow-covered countryside. They were passing through a tiny village, and he caught the name on a signboard in the station—Treblinka. He heard someone say they would be in Warsaw in two hours.

The train stopped long enough at Tluscz for passengers to buy hot, strong tea from the station vendors. An hour later they were trundling through the suburbs of Praga and across the great bridge spanning the Vistula River. Berl felt his pulse quicken as the buildings of the old town began to pass by his window. The train made a long looping curve to the left around the northern edge of the city, entering the echoing Central Station from the west.

On Jerozolimski Street people were hurrying to work in the thin, freezing drizzle blowing up from the river. Pulling his overcoat tighter around his body, Berl began walking toward the center of town, following the directions Bogdon Zoclow had given him. Yitzhak Gruenbaum had offices in the town hall. Berl looked up at the great clock in the tower above the station. Plenty of time. Gruenbaum was not expecting him until ten.

He felt exhilarated and apprehensive when he thought of his imminent meeting with the politician. While he had serious reservations about Gruenbaum's Zionism, he could not help but admire what Gruenbaum had achieved. Here was a Jew who, more then ten years earlier, had thrust himself into Polish politics on behalf of the unrepresented and often vilified national minorities of Poland, and fought to ensure their rightful representation in Parliament.

Berl hurried along the avenue, stopping now and again to look at the fine clothes in the windows of the grand shops and stores. He wandered through Saxon Square, staring in wonder at the great cathedral with its five gilded domes and soaring belfry. He followed a street into an open square with small gardens shaded by trees. Two hundred feet above it soared the tower of the Ratusz, the town hall. He looked up at the clock. Ten minutes to ten.

Only now did Berl fully realize what he was about to do. In just a few minutes he would urge a prominent Jewish politician to take a position strongly contrary to his employer's interests. Berl had no doubt that the position he was about to advocate was good for Poland, but he did not want a confrontation with a powerful landowner. Yet Berl knew land reform was coming, and he had resolved not to serve as a lightning rod for Madgellon once the real storm began.

Ten minutes later he was ushered into Yitzhak Gruenbaum's office by a young assistant. Gruenbaum was tall, spare, and dignified, and Berl gussed his age to be about forty.

"Ah," Gruenbaum said, rising to shake Berl's hand. "So you are Hoffman, the Jewish Piast!"

"Jewish, certainly," Berl said with a smile. "But I'm no Piast."

"You're certainly the first Jew the Piasts ever arranged a meeting for," Gruenbaum observed with interest. "The Jews and I are usually involved with very different issues. There aren't very many Jews in the world of the peasant. The peasants have only one issue."

"Land reform?"

"And nothing else." Gruenbaum motioned Berl to sit down. "They must think highly of you to go to so much trouble. Is that what you've come to see me about—land reform?"

"No. The presidential election."

"Go on," Gruenbaum said with a slight lift of the eyebrows.

"I understand that Marshal Pilsudski will not be a candidate."

Gruenbaum nodded. "He wants nothing to do with the presidency. He says Parliament has rendered the office powerless."

"People say that if the Marshal does not run, Count Maurycz Zamojski will probably become president."

"It seems extremely likely."

"How much do you know about me, Mr. Gruenbaum?"

"You work as an overseer for Prince Stefan Madgellon in Oleck-Podlaska, do you not?"

"That's correct."

"Then I would have thought the prospect of Zamojski as president would be to your liking."

"I'm Madgellon's overseer, yes. But I spend a lot of my

time among the peasants. I hear what they say. They believe it would be a calamity if Zamojski were elected—the death of land reform in Poland."

Gruenbaum nodded. "Very probably. Which should be even better news for you and your employer."

"I, too, believe the election of Zamojski would be a tragedy for this country."

Gruenbaum allowed his surprise to show. "I wondered why the Piasts were so interested in you. Now I see. Tell me, Mr. Hoffman, why do you espouse the cause of the peasants? It scarcely coincides with the interests of your employer."

"Mr. Gruenbaum, I've never even seen my employer. But I live and work among the peasants. I know what they think and what they say. And what they are saying now is that they want land reform. If it does not come—"

"You think the peasants will revolt?" Gruenbaum allowed himself a small smile. "No, no, Mr. Hoffman. They won't revolt. They are much too, what shall we say, conservative for that."

"They revolted against absentee landlordism once before."

"That was three hundred years ago, Mr. Hoffman. Bogdon Chmielnicki has been dead a long time."

"I know. The point I'm making is that he's still a hero among the peasants. But it was not the landlords who suffered. It was the Jews. How do you think we Jews would fare if it happened again?"

"And that's why you came to see me?"

"That's why I'm asking you to vote against Zamojski."

"And while I am at it, to deliver the Minorities bloc to Zamojski's opponent, is that it?"

"Exactly."

Yitzhak Gruenbaum leaned back in his chair. He regarded Berl judiciously, as if trying to gauge his sincerity.

"Suppose I were to support Narutowicz, Mr. Hoffman. Do you have any idea what that would mean to the Jews?"

"No. I know nothing about politics."

"You will by the time you have left this office," Gruenbaum said grimly. "Gabriel Narutowicz is a Leftist, Mr. Hoffman. Some people think he is much too cozy with the radicals. He has plenty of experience. Do you know anything at all about him?"

"No."

"He was a minister of Public Works for a while. More

recently he served as Foreign Affairs minister in the Sliwinski and Nowak administrations."

Berl shrugged. He knew nothing at all about the governments Gruenbaum was talking about.

"If I were to cast the support of the Minorities behind Narutowicz, Mr. Hoffman, and he were to defeat Zamojski, do you know what would happen? You shake your head. Very well, I will tell you. The Jews will get the blame. I know. I campaigned for a seat for Jagiello in the fourth Parliament ten years ago. He was running against an anti-Semite. When he ran, you'd have thought he'd been elected by the Jews alone."

"Nineteen-twelve. I remember that."

"All we were doing at that time was electing someone to a seat in Parliament. This election is for the presidency of Poland. Anti-Semites, such as that priest Lutoslawski and the rest of them, will rant and rave that the Jews have put Narutowicz in power for their own ends."

"So what you're telling me is, if you don't support Narutowicz it will be bad for the Jews, and if you do, it will be equally bad for the Jews."

"You understand, Hoffman," Gruenbaum said with a wry smile. "I told you you'd know something about Polish politics before you left this room."

"May I ask if you have decided what you will do?"

"I have not yet made up my mind. I'll have to give it a lot of thought. It could be the worst possible issue for the Minorities bloc to cut its teeth on."

"I'm sorry to hear that," Berl said grimly.

"You have gone to a great deal of trouble to come and tell me your views. I wish more people would do that. I am impressed with what you have done. I will try to do the right thing, my friend. I will try. I hope you will be glad you came," Gruenbaum said sincerely.

"Thank you for listening."

Gruenbaum stood up and reached across the desk to shake Berl's hand. The door opened, and the assistant who had brought Berl up to the office conducted him down to the ground floor. When he went out into the street, the icy drizzle had stopped, but now a bitter east wind moaned around the corners of the buildings. Despite Gruenbaum's position, Berl was glad he had come. He knew he had done the right thing. Now he walked aimlessly through the city, killing time and thinking. The train for Suwalki would not leave for another two hours.

Again and again he went over his conversation with Yitzhak Gruenbaum, wishing he had put his argument better, but knowing he had said all he had to say. He found himself in front of the huge, imposing Royal Palace, where kings had onced lived, and followed a wide street called Zjazd down to the bridge across the Vistula. To the north he could see the Citadel, the railway bridge he had crossed on his way into the city, and the buildings of the old and new sections of the city converging and extending down to the edge of the river. On the hill above him the Royal Palace with its terraced gardens stood solid against the slate-colored sky. On the bridge itself was a sign which bore one word: Vistula.

His thoughts returned to his conversation with Yitzhak Gruenbaum about the elections a decade ago, when Wladyslaw Jagiello had defeated Kucharzewski, the anti-Semite. What a miserable time that was, Berl thought, remembering the anti-Semitic graffiti that had appeared on walls all over Poland: *Only one nation along the banks of the Vistula!* He had just met the man who had unleashed that violent wave of hatred and, in effect, asked him to do the same thing again.

How would the members of Parliament vote? Could his visit have possibly made a difference? Was land reform really coming to Poland? What would be the relationship between the Jews and the peasants of Poland? What would happen when his employer learned of his own political boldness? The questions swirled in his mind like the wind howling through the streets.

He turned away from the river and hurried back to the railway station and the train that would take him home.

October 28, 1923

Dear Tante Dvoyra,

So much has happened since we last wrote you. Poppa has remarried. His wife's name is Ida. She has not only changed Poppa's life but ours too. She owned a grocery store in East Baltimore when she married Poppa. Her brother was also in the grocery business in a city called Alexandria. It's in Virginia right across the Potomac River from Washington, D.C., the capital of America. Well, she and Poppa moved to Alexandria when her brother told her about a very good store that was for sale. Shortly after they moved there, they wrote to tell us about another corner grocery store that was for sale. They even lent us and Sheara and Lou the money to buy the small store, so we all live in Alexandria near Rachel and Ivan. We live above our store. Colored people live all around us and are mostly very nice, although they are also very different. They talk different and have different customs, but they work hard and are good customers for our business.

The children are happy and they really love Ivan. What Rachel and Ivan have done for those children is a real mitzvah, a blessing for all of us. The biggest blessing of all is that we are all together again as a family.

Life has gotten easier in America. The entire country seems happy since the war ended, and everyone is busy trying to have a good time.

How are things there? Is all the fighting and arguing between Poland and Russia finally over? We don't think there will be any more great wars like the last one. Everyone here is too busy enjoying themselves to go off and fight a war. Besides, America has been destroying its warships and so is Japan. Can you imagine two nations destroying their navies so that they can't fight! Well, we know America and Japan won't go to war anyway.

We have all contributed to help make things easier for you and your family. We hope the ten dollars buys some of the things you need.

Please let us hear from you soon.

> Love from all of us,
> Rebecca

Berl and Dvoyra had just finished eating when they heard someone pounding on the door, shouting Berl's name. Berl ran to the door and threw it open. Bogdon Zoclow stood panting on the threshold, his eyes bright with triumph.

"We've done it, Hoffman!" he yelled, grabbing Berl's hand and pumping it up and down madly. "We've done it! Narutowicz is President!"

"Is it true?" Berl asked, astonished.

"I'm telling you! Narutowicz is President!"

"You'd better come in."

Zoclow nodded and entered the tiny living room. His excitement seemed to fill the whole house.

"How did it happen?" Berl asked as they sat down at the table with Dvoyra.

"It took five ballots of Parliament, but Gruenbaum finally did it. He delivered the Minorities bloc to Narutowicz."

"My God," Berl whispered. "I can't believe it."

"You realize what this means, Hoffman? It means the peasants and the Jews determined the outcome of the election!"

"No," Berl said, still stunned at the news.

"It's true, I tell you!"

"If it is, it will be the Jews the Rightists remember," he said grimly.

"Ach, don't talk such nonsense. Narutowicz won by two hundred and eighty-nine votes to two hundred and twenty-seven. They can't blame that on a handful of Jews."

"They can," Berl said, "and they will. Gruenbaum said the same thing happened in 1912 when Jagiello defeated Kucharzewski with the help of the Jewish vote."

"Well, let's not worry about that now!" Bogdon exclaimed. "We've won, we've won! You know what this means, don't you?"

Berl nodded, but did not say anything. Maybe the anti-Semites would accept what has happened, he thought. *Maybe they won't make our lives miserable.*

"I'll never forget what you did, Berl."

"You can't imagine anything I said influenced Gruenbaum!" Berl scoffed. "It took five ballots, didn't it? Five ballots before he delivered the Minorities bloc. It had nothing to do with my going to see him."

"But you went. That's what I'll never forget."

"Let's hope there's no repeat of 1912."

"You worry too much, Berl," Zoclow said with a laugh. "Well, I'd better be going." He got up. "I have some things to do. Berl, I want to thank you again for what you did. I mean what I said—I'll never forget it."

"Good night, Bogdon. Next time you come, bring your wife to visit us."

"All right. I might, at that."

When Zoclow was gone, Berl sat down at the table once more and cradled his head in his hands.

Dvoyra, sensing his mood, touched his shoulder. "What is it, Berl?"

"I didn't want to say anything while Bogdon was here. He isn't concerned about what may happen to Jews."

"You think something will?"

"I hope I'm wrong," he said, worry evident in his tone. "I'll go to Suwalki tomorrow and see what I can learn."

Next day he drove his wagon over to Suwalki. He hitched the horse to a fence near the railway station and walked across to the kiosk facing the platform. There, among the many newspapers on display, he saw the sickening headline:

Narutowicz—The President of the Jews!

With a shaking hand Berl picked up the paper and skimmed through the story below the provocative headline. A sentence leapt out at him: "'How do the Jews dare to impose their president upon us?' asked Father Kazimierz Lutoslawski." Berl recalled Yitzhak Gruenbaum's words. The notoriously anti-Semitic priest was the very person Gruenbaum had predicted would malign the Jews if Narutowicz won the election. Berl felt an all-too-familiar sensation of sick dread sweeping through him. He remembered experiencing the same icy contraction in his belly when he read the archduke's deposition order during the war and again when the czar's government began the prosecution of Mendel Beilis for ritual murder.

"*Will it never end?*" he whispered to himself. "*Dear God, will it never end?*"

When Berl got back to Oleck-Podlaska, he found Victor Mereck waiting for him as he entered the house. Mereck's eyes betrayed his displeasure as his gaze flicked toward the newspaper in Berl's hand. He did not rise to greet Berl.

"So," Mereck began softly, "you're pleased about the election results?" Berl knew Mereck's visit could only mean trouble, as Victor Mereck had not been to Oleck-Podlaska for weeks.

"Have you come all the way here to discuss politics?" Berl asked with a nervous smile.

"In a way. Is it true you went to Warsaw to visit Yitzhak Gruenbaum?"

Berl felt his mouth turn dry. Mereck had not wasted any time. "Yes, it's true."

"What for?"

"It was a private matter," Berl responded firmly.

"It wasn't because the Piasts arranged it for you?"

"It was my decision. No one else was involved."

"It was an act of enormous stupidity!" Mereck snapped. "Don't you realize these people were using you, Hoffman?"

"Yitzhak Gruenbaum is not influenced by the likes of me," Berl protested. "My conversation with him could have had no effect on the election."

"It never occurred to me that it had," Mereck said coldly. "I didn't say you'd done something of consequence, Hoffman, I said you'd done something enormously stupid."

"I think you'd better get out of my house!" Berl said, his own anger flaring.

"Gladly." Mereck got up. "But let me ask you one last question, Hoffman. How do you propose to support yourself and your family after I leave?"

"How will you manage the land in this area after you leave?"

"A minor problem," Mereck said offhandedly. "We'll manage, I'm sure. But you, Hoffman."

"We'll manage too."

"And the Jews you employ?"

"They serve you and the prince faithfully and well." Berl realized with dismay what Mereck was threatening to do. "There is no need to punish them because of what I have done."

"As I said a few moments ago, Hoffman, yours was an act of enormous stupidity," Mereck said, contempt in his every movement. "I will leave you to reflect upon it. Good day."

He went out of the house, not bothering to shut the door behind him.

Almost a week passed before Berl saw Victor Mereck again. He met him on his way out of Oleck–Podlaska to fix some fencing that had been torn down by vandals. Why anyone would want to tear down fencing was beyond Berl's understanding, but it had been done, and his automatic response was to get his tools and some lumber, put them into the back of his wagon, and go repair the damage.

"Well, Hoffman!" Mereck exclaimed, pulling his horse to a halt and jumping from his carriage to approach Berl. "What are you up to?"

"Some fencing has been torn down. I'm on my way to mend it."

"Torn down, you say? By whom?"

"I have no idea. Vandals probably. They're always up to some mischief or other."

Mereck went around behind the wagon and lifted up the tarpaulin Berl had thrown over the timber in the wagon bed.

"You really are on your way to repair the fence, aren't you?" Mereck shook his head. "Why would you bother when you don't even work for the prince anymore?"

"Let me explain something to you, Mr. Mereck," Berl said evenly. "I'm a craftsman. I take pride in my work. I've spent six months of my life getting this property back in decent shape, and I'm not going to sit still and see someone tear it down again, whether I'm working for Prince Madgellon or not."

"Let me tell you something, then, Hoffman. You don't have nearly enough wood."

"There wasn't that much damage."

"When did you inspect it?"

"Yesterday afternoon. Why?"

"You don't know, do you?"

"Look," Berl said impatiently. "I've got work to do. Could you get to the point, please?"

"There's at least a third of a kilometer down now."

"What?"

"It's the peasants, Hoffman. The peasants. Your friends the Piasts are tearing down your fences."

"That's insane!"

"I quite agree," Mereck said coolly. "But it's no less true for that. Here." He took a piece of paper from his pocket, and Berl read it with disbelief: "You will not have the product of Hoffman's labor without Hoffman."

"Who wrote this?" he said angrily, handing the note back to Mereck.

"I don't know. It was delivered to me late last night."

"It's coercion!" Berl snapped. "And I'm damned if I'll be a party to it!"

"Listen," Mereck said with sudden urgency. "I was on my way to see you. I thought over my actions, and I decided I was hasty in dismissing you. I have spoken with the prince. He wishes you to remain in his employ. With no loss of pay."

"I see," Berl said slowly. "In other words, you're letting them coerce you."

"Forget that! I'm offering you your job back. Do you want

me to say I'm sorry. I'll say it—I'm sorry. But let's end thi foolishness now! We do not want strife here on the prince land."

Everything was clear to Berl now. Only a few days earlie he had talked to Bogdon Zoclow, who had been incensed when Berl told him he had been dismissed by Mereck fo going to see Yitzhak Gruenbaum. Zoclow considered Berl comrade in the struggle for land reform. Berl had put his ow welfare on the line to help the peasants, and Zoclow wa determined to stand by Berl if the aristocracy tried to punis him.

"That bastard," Zoclow swore. "He won't get away with this!"

"Of course he will," Berl said. "What can you do to him?"

"I'm not sure yet. But I'll think of something."

"Don't you do anything of the kind, Bogdon!" Berl warned his friend. "Mereck already has you down as a troublemaker. He can be vicious if he wants to."

"So can we. So can we."

"You can't force them to retain me. Mereck dismissed me, and that's the end of that."

"Is it? We'll see," Bogdon had said ominously.

Berl turned his attention back to Mereck, who was waiting for Berl's response. Mereck was offering more than was necessary to win Berl's agreement, Berl thought, but he and Dvoyra were in no position to lose the wages the prince paid.

"Hoffman, listen to me. I shouldn't have dismissed you as I did. I want you to come back. You can take on a couple more Jews to help you. How's that?"

Berl could not believe his ears when Mereck authorized the hiring of two additional workers. He looked at Mereck and nodded.

"You'll come back?" Mereck asked with relief. "Good, good, it's all settled! I'll go into town, spread the word you're working for us again."

"Fine," Berl said flatly as Mereck climbed up on his carriage and picked up the reins.

"It all turned out to be much ado about nothing anyway, didn't it?" Mereck said cheerfully.

"What do you mean?"

"Haven't you heard about Narutowicz?"

"What about him?"

"He was assassinated yesterday at the art museum in Warsaw. I thought you knew."

Berl stared at him dumbfounded.

"As I said, Hoffman"—Mereck released the brake and slapped the reins on the horse's rump to start it forward—"Much ado about nothing."

December 14, 1923

Dear Rebecca,

We pray this letter finds you and the rest of the family in America well and happy. In spite of the political situation here, we are all well. Berl's work ensures that we will not starve, and there are many in Poland today who would wish to be as fortunate. Very few have steady work; conditions throughout the country are quite bad. Many of the peasants who work on the land here pay Berl with food for the extra work he does. Food means more than money where we live. It is hard to believe, but our money is worthless. Two years ago we were able to exchange the American dollars that you sent us for one hundred and twenty Polish marks each. Last week I was told that one dollar was worth six million marks. And even if you have the marks, you cannot buy anything.

We don't know what will happen here. Everything is in turmoil. Berl says we will have anarchy if the government does not do something soon. Everything has been in a mess since our president, Gabriel Naruto-wicz, was murdered by a madman named Eliguisz Niewiadomski. He said he did it because Narutowicz was "president of the Jews." Can you imagine such madness? Anti-Semites here in Poland acted as though the murderer was a national hero. We read in the papers that in Warsaw hundreds of newborn babies were named Eliguisz after this assassin. And this is the country in which we must live and raise our children!

Give thanks to God that your parents took you to America. It was the greatest blessing they could have bestowed on you. I know I have said this before. It is truer now than ever. I wish we could have done the same thing for our children.

Well, enough of my complaining. Maybe things will change here someday. What everyone prays for is that someone strong will become president, perhaps Marshal Pilsudski. Then sanity may return to Poland.

Kiss and hug everyone for us, and tell them all how much we think of them. May God bless you all.

Love,
Tante Dvoyra

Chapter Twenty-three

Dvoyra and Peninah went together to Suwalki to exchange the ten dollars Rebecca had enclosed with her letter. It was the first real money they had possessed for some time. In the wake of Narutowicz's assassination, the value of the Polish mark had plunged from about fifty thousand to the dollar to more than six million. The vicious cycle of prices, wages, and foreign exchange rates whirled at a delirious pace. Wages brought home at the beginning of the month had depreciated by more than half a fortnight later. In the fall of 1923 a wave of strikes swept the country, and a general strike was proclaimed on November third. There were riots in Tarnow and Boryslaw, and most spectacularly in Cracow on November fifth, when the workers took control of the town, disarmed an entire infantry battalion, captured five thousand rifles, machine guns, and armored cars in day-long fighting during which thirty-two men were killed.

A new cabinet was installed, and the new Central Bank Polski introduced a new currency, the zloty, which was valued at one gold franc, or five dollars and eighteen cents. Old marks were to be converted at the rate of one million eight hundred thousand to the zloty. Dvoyra learned all of this when she arrived at the currency exchange.

"But only last week an American dollar was worth six million marks!" she protested.

"There are no more marks," she was told. "The new zloty replaces all old currency. One new zloty is now worth nearly two million old marks."

"And will the merchants accept these new zloty?"

The bearded old money changer shrugged. "They haven't any choice. There are no more marks. Next, please."

Dvoyra left the currency exchange counting the zloty she had been given, then put them carefully away in the old leather purse that had once belonged to Chaya Sara Engle. It was all very confusing. You never knew from one week to the next what things were going to cost. But there was no use complaining—to whom would one complain?

As Dvoyra and Peninah walked through the Jewish quarter, they passed a handsome young man standing on the sidewalk handing out pamphlets. His wire-rimmed glasses made Peninah think he was from the university. Dvoyra hardly noticed him, so preoccupied was she with thinking about the new currency. Peninah, however, took one of the leaflets he held out toward her and read the crudely printed slogan.

> By Blood and Fire Judea Fell;
> By Blood and Fire Judea Shall Rise.

"Momma, what does this mean?" Peninah passed the leaflet to Dvoyra.

"Zionist nonsense!" Dvoyra said sharply, glancing at the boy who had given Peninah the paper. "Zionist literature is being distributed by these dreamers all over Poland."

"But what does it mean?"

"There are some people who believe we Jews should all go to Palestine and build a new country there. They are called Zionists."

"I've heard of them," Peninah said as they crossed the street. "Why do you say it's nonsense?"

"Because what they advocate is a dream, Peninah. People can't just get up and leave their homes and start a new life half a world away."

"But isn't that just what Tante Anna did?"

"That was different. There was already a country. There is nothing in Palestine but some Arabs, some Jews and some Englishmen who run the place."

"But if Jews can't go to America anymore because of the new immigration laws Rebecca wrote about, maybe it's not such a bad idea to start a new country just for Jews."

Dvoyra listened to her daughter's words and realized, with a start, that Peninah was nearly twelve, the threshold of adulthood. The child in her seemed to be fading. Instead, here was a young person with ideas and ambitions and dreams of her own, Dvoyra thought.

"It's a bad idea, and I'll tell you why, Peninah. The people who say we should all go there don't tell anyone how hard it would be. Harder than you can imagine."

"Harder than it is here, Momma?"

Dvoyra thought for a moment. "No, I can't say that. I don't think life could be more difficult anywhere else than it is here in Poland."

"Then—"

"Not everyone believes we should all leave our homes and go somewhere else. Your father for one. He believes it is better if we stay here and try to make Poland a better place to live."

Peninah looked at the pamphlet again, frowning. "What do they mean when they say 'By blood and fire Judea fell, by blood and fire Judea shall rise'?"

"Those who go to Palestine will have to fight for whatever land they get. There are thousands of Arabs there already. And the land is controlled by the British."

"Have the British always been there?"

"No. They took the land from the Turks in the Great War."

"And who owned the land before the Turks?"

Dvoyra shook her head. "I'm not sure. I'm not an expert on Palestinian history. Maybe you should ask Poppa."

"Please, Momma," Peninah begged. "I really want to know. Who was there before the Turks?"

"I know that hundreds of years ago Christian crusaders were there. Fighting the Turks."

"And before that?"

"The Greeks, I suppose. And the Romans. The Romans conquered Palestine long, long ago. Although it was called something else then."

"Who did they conquer?"

"The Jews."

"The Jews ruled the land?" Peninah asked, astonished. "It was Jewish land?"

"Yes, but that was nearly two thousand years ago."

"Now I understand. Now I see why the Zionists want to go there. It is the ancient land of Israel!"

"That's what they say. But it doesn't mean we all have to go there."

"But Momma!" Peniah said impatiently. "Where else could we go?"

"We don't have to go anywhere," Dvoyra answered firmly. "Now, come. We must buy some food. And Poppa needs a pair of work gloves."

But Peninah was reluctant to drop the subject. She found the whole thought of a new land, a place for Jews and only Jews, exciting. She silently vowed to find out all she could about these Zionists and their movement.

From that day forward Peninah dreamed of Eretz Israel, the land of Israel, reading everything she could find on that ancient land, about Jewish kings and folk heroes.

By the time she reached her fifteenth birthday, the plight of the Jews in Poland had become her single greatest interest. Rather than spending time playing with Yitzhak or her sister, or with friends her own age, Peninah preferred to listen to her father and the older men talking about politics.

Ever since Berl's brief involvement with Yitzhak Gruenbaum and the ill-fated election of Narutowicz, Polish politics had become a passion with him. He measured most political developments by the impact he believed they would have on Poland's Jews. The more Peninah listened to the men, the more she realized what confusion there was among the Jews as to the right course to follow.

There were those who called themselves assimilationists. They argued that Jews should be Poles first and Jews second. Then there were the secularists. They said it was time the Jews concerned themselves with the issues of the day, rather than dwelling on the teachings of the Torah. The Bundists called for equality of the worker through socialism. The traditionalists insisted that the only true course for Jews to follow was that of the Torah. And the Zionists took issue with all of the others, arguing that there would never be a place for Jews in Poland.

"Not as long as you radicals urge Jews to turn their backs on the fatherland," the assimilationists would say.

"Among Jews you cannot get lost," the traditionalists would nod.

"You Zionists, you're troublemakers," they all said. "The hooligans in the streets shout at us, 'Zhid, go to Palestine!' Whoever heard such things being said before you people started poisoning the air?"

Peninah listened, and learned, and waited. "There comes a time, a precise moment," she would say, many years later, "when you stop wondering and start believing." For her, that moment came on a balmy, spring day in 1928. She was strolling home from school with her one good, close friend of her own age. Tsipa Tannenbaum was the daughter of Aaron and Ida Tannenbaum, who owned a clothing and fabric store, and were considered to be one of the more comfortably placed families in Oleck-Podlaska. Tsipa was a very bright girl and the only young person Peninah knew whose interests paralleled hers.

"What did you think about the lecture?" Peninah asked Tsipa. She could still feel the chill that had coursed through her as the teacher praised the Facist National Party—the Endecja—and said that they would be the salvation of Poland. How could anyone praise a political party that preached hatred of the Jews as the Endeks did?

"I hate being Jewish!" Tsipa blurted. Shocked, Peninah stared at her friend. Tsipa was such a kind, gentle girl. To hear her say "I hate being Jewish" was like blasphemy.

"How can you say such a thing, Tsipa?" Peninah whispered.

"It's true!" Tsipa cried. "I hate it, I hate it. Being Jewish is a curse!"

"No, Tsipa, no!" Peninah protested.

"Yes! You tell me something, Peninah. Are you happy? Are you? Go on, tell me."

"I . . . never thought about it," Peninah said, groping for an answer.

"You're nearly sixteen, Peninah. You're bright, you're pretty. You should be happy. But are you?"

"What does that have to do with being Jewish?"

"It has a lot to do with being Jewish. Because you're *not* happy. None of us is. We can't be happy. We're Jewish!"

"Tsipa, this is silly! What is this, happy, unhappy?"

"Normal people are happy. People are supposed to be happy."

"And we will be, one day. It's just that times have been hard."

"Times are always hard for Jews!" Tsipa said, tears in her eyes. "The Endeks campaign to boycott Jewish businesses. There are classroom ghettos in the universities where Jews must *sit* by themselves in the back of the class. There are anti-Semitic slogans painted on the walls. The goyim thugs taunt the young Hasidim and pull their earlocks. They hate us, Peninah. They hate us. And it's never going to change. Every day for the rest of my life I am going to dread waking up and knowing I am a Jew!"

Peninah was speechless. The intensity of her friend's outburst left her breathless.

"It's not true," Peninah said softly. "Being Jewish is not a curse."

"It is in Poland. It is, Peninah. I've never done anything to make people hate me, but they do. I don't want to be afraid for no reason, but I am. I don't want my children to be despised, as I am, but they will be."

"No one despises you, Tsipa."

"Are you blind?" Tsipa shouted angrily. "Of course they do! And they hate you too! They hate your mother and your father and Annette and Yitzhak. They hate us all. They hate every one of us!"

With that final outburst Tsipa turned and ran home, leaving a dazed Peninah standing alone in the middle of the dusty street. She turned and made her way homeward, walking very slowly. Her throat felt tight, and every moment or so she found herself swallowing to keep from vomiting. When she got home, she went straight into the bedroom and sat down on the edge of the bed. After a while the nausea ebbed. She took a deep breath, closed her eyes, and lay down on the bed, Tsipa Tannenbaum's words ringing in her ears.

My God, she thought, *it's true. We've become so accustomed to being despised that we accept it as the natural order of things.*

"Why?" she asked aloud.

Chapter Twenty-four

Rachel enjoyed driving with Ivan to Alexandria on Sunday mornings to visit her sisters. The drive was beautiful and she always found the brief excursion through Washington to be exhilarating. Today, the Sunday before May Day, was not the first time she had seen pickets in Lafayette Park opposite the White House. They were part of the landscape, and the causes they championed often found expression nowhere else in the nation's capital. Rachel would try to read the signs the picketers carried, and while they frequently addressed issues that were totally alien to her or advocated views with which she disagreed, she liked knowing that in America anyone could say whatever they pleased without fear of recrimination, even in front of the White House itself.

The picketers in Lafayette Park were a welcome sight to Rachel, until that Sunday in April 1924. That's when she saw the sign carried by the tall man cloaked in what looked like a white sheet. He wore a hood that covered his entire face except where holes were cut out for his eyes, nose, and mouth. He looked hideous, she thought, and the sign he held sickened her.

> Bolshevik Jews
> Infest
> Labor
> Movement
> In New York

"Ivan, did you see that?" she asked urgently as they passed by the park.

Ivan nodded. "Yes, I saw it."

"It's horrible."

"Yes, it is. Unfortunately it's also true." He turned south on Seventeenth Street.

Rachel looked at her husband, not believing what she had just heard. "What do you mean?"

"I mean the Communists are slowly but surely taking over the labor movement, in New York anyway."

"The entire labor movement?"

"No, damn it, just the Jewish labor movement. We Jews dominate the garment trades, Rachel. You know that. What was once a movement founded by ethical, idealistic, and principled men and women is now being taken over by some of the most brutal, arrogant, and politically motivated people imaginable. They are bright, vicious, and incredibly well disciplined, and they are going to destroy a quarter century of achievement."

"Ivan, are you saying the CGWA is being taken over by the Communists?" she asked with alarm.

"No, but that's no victory. We've grown weak in New

York. Our people have gone over to the more militant unions. Whatever strength we have is in other cities, such as Baltimore and Philadelphia. But the heart of the garment industry is in New York, and right now Moscow's influence in New York is greater than ours. That is why the CGWA moved its executive offices to Washington."

"Isn't there anything that can be done?"

"The leadership of the ILGWU is fighting to keep the Communists from taking control of the locals, but I think it's a losing battle because the Communists have only one objective, and they can concentrate all of their energy, which is considerable, on winning over the rank and file. They keep whittling away at the memberships, and when the time is ripe, they'll find some issue over which to have a showdown with the leadership."

"I'm glad the CGWA isn't mixed up with the Communists."

"They'll make life miserable for us too, Rachel. Our ability to represent labor will be compromised in this town if Congress views us as a Communist-infested labor movement," he replied as they crossed into Alexandria. "See that house there?" He pointed to a large white frame house on the southeast corner of Washington and Oronoca Streets.

"Yes, it's beautiful."

"That's where John L. Lewis lives. He is one of the most powerful men in the American labor movement. He represents the coal miners, and because of him, they have tremendous influence in Washington. Some people think that's the second White House."

"Do you want to become another John L. Lewis?" she asked, smiling at him.

"No. All I want to do is help people such as your father get a fair shake. We'll never have the clout Lewis has."

"Why not? You can call a strike just as he can."

"True. But when we strike, people are merely inconvenienced. They may have to wait awhile to buy a new suit. When he calls a strike, the whole damn country closes down. That's clout."

"Would you want that kind of clout?"

"Not really. Sometimes you can wind up with more power than it takes to represent your members. That's when the people will turn against the labor unions."

"Do you think that will happen here?"

"Ten years ago I would have answered no to that question. Now, I'm not so sure. Some of the unions seem to have lost their sense of mission. They've become big businesses themselves. Others have become terribly political. They want to make war against the employers, and they see unions as armies with which to fight."

"Like the Communists?"

"Exactly. They're using the unions to wage a far broader battle. Sooner or later the people in this country are going to get fed up, and the entire union movement will suffer as a result."

It did not take long for events to make a prophet of Ivan. A long and ill-advised strike that gripped the New York garment industry the following year spread to other cities, and Ivan was urged to call his members out of work in sympathy with the larger and more powerful New York unions. Ivan believed the strike was motivated primarily by the Communists' desire for a showdown with the old-line leadership of the needle-trade unions. At first he had little sympathy for a strike that was little more than a naked power play, and he refused to call his members out in support of their New York brethren. As the accolades from the manufacturers grew in response to Ivan's resolve to keep his people working, so did the contempt with which he was held by the New York trade unionists.

None of the harsh criticism from New York bothered him, nor did any of the Communists' appeals for solidarity. The visit from Rudy Meinholtz, however, was another matter.

Meinholtz showed up at the CGWA office late in the afternoon one Monday in July. He had no appointment, but because he said he was from Local 610, Ivan agreed to see him. Local 610 was one of the New York left-wing locals, and Ivan was curious to see what they wanted.

Rudy Meinholtz was a menacing figure. A swarthy, well-built man and a flashy dresser, he appeared incapable of earning an honest living. He had an olive complexion, thick, black wavy hair, dark piercing eyes, and a generous nose that gave him a distinctly Semitic appearance.

Rudy Meinholtz was a killer, or at least he used to be. Now he was an employer of hired assassins who, for a fee, would either maim or murder as their clients wished.

Ivan knew Meinholtz was a thug the minute Meinholtz entered his office. Meinholtz continuously studied his newly manicured fingernails as he spoke, as if to signal his contempt for Ivan.

"The local asked me to come offer my services," Meinholtz said casually.

"And just what are your services?" Ivan leaned back in his chair, but kept a careful eye on his visitor.

"My client is worried that so many people are upset with you for turning your back on the New York locals that someone may, you know, come after you or your family. My job is to protect you and yours."

"We don't need protection," Ivan said firmly, glaring at the New York mobster.

"Sure you do, Mr. Wollmack. That young wife of yours alone all day in that apartment on Columbia Road, and her old man and her sisters in those rinky-dink grocery stores in Alexandria. They're all real vulnerable if you get my drift."

Ivan tried to control the sick feeling that radiated through his body as Rudy Meinholtz divulged how much he knew about him and his family.

"Lot of nasty people upset with you, Mr. Wollmack, but you got friends in New York. They don't want nothing to happen to you. They want me to look out for you. Meantime, you'll make my job a whole lot easier if you try not to antagonize those guys that are fighting for the working man."

"You mean, if I pull my people off the job in sympathy with the striking locals."

"All they want is a little sympathy from the CGWA."

"You tell those Bolsheviks you work for that I'm not going to pull their nuts out of the fire by sending my people to the poorhouse."

"Now, you don't want me to tell them that, Mr. Wollmack. Why don't you sleep on it for a while."

"Why don't you go to hell!" Ivan snapped.

"Don't be a schmuck." Meinholtz rose to his feet. "The world don't need no more schmucks, Mr. Wollmack."

Ivan decided not to tell Rachel about his encounter with Rudy Meinholtz. He intended to ignore the matter and saw no point in alarming anyone. At first he briefly considered calling the president of Local 610, a furriers union firmly in the grasp of the Communists. But he realized, however, that they expected him to call following Meinholtz's visit. Silence, he decided, would be his only response.

Ivan knew that both sides in the New York labor wars had resorted to strong-arm tactics and that they routinely used underworld thugs to harass one another. There had been reports that when management hired the Legs Diamond gang to intimidate pickets, the left-wingers fought back by paying mobster Jake "Little Augie" Orgen to strike back at the manufacturers. Several locals were even rumored to be controlled by the same thugs that ran the notorious Murder Inc.

While Ivan read all of the New York papers that covered the growing violence within the labor movement, an item in *The Times Herald* the Saturday following the Meinholtz visit jumped out at him. A plant that was being picketed by Local 610 of the furriers union had been vandalized and the management was blaming the local for the damage. According to the story in the paper, someone had broken into a storage warehouse and poured red paint on nearly one hundred expensive fur coats. The company, which faced ruin, called the attack a new low in the three-month-old dispute. Local 610, of course, denied any knowledge of the incident.

Ivan's first impulse was to refuse the call from Rudy Meinholtz the following Monday. Then he thought perhaps it would be better to know what the thug wanted.

"Hello, Mr. Wollmack, I hope you had a nice weekend," Meinholtz said as soon as Ivan picked up the receiver.

"Mr. Meinholtz, I've very busy. What do you want?"

"Well, I was hoping I could tell the local that they could count on the CGWA for support—you know, that your people hadn't turned their backs on the working man."

"And what will they pay you to deliver the CGWA?" Ivan asked contemptuously.

"Ah, Mr. Wollmack, you shouldn't talk like that," Meinholtz answered, nonplussed by Ivan's rebuke. "We're just fighting for the working man, that's all."

"I read how you fight for the working man in *The Times Herald* Saturday. You make me sick."

"Oh, you mean that incident with the paint? Didn't you read we didn't know nothin' about that? You must have seen that in the story, Mr. Wollmack."

"Yes, I read the denial."

"Well, then, you shouldn't go around saying things like that, Mr. Wollmack. You could hurt somebody's reputation that way."

"I have to go, Mr. Meinholtz. Tell your people the CGWA wants no part of their misguided strike."

"I'll tell them you're thinking about it, Mr. Wollmack. There's too many hotheads up there to tell them you've turned your back on the working man."

"Now you listen to me, you no good—" Ivan heard the insulting sound of Rudy Meinholtz hanging up on him. He now understood that the matter wasn't closed; it had just begun. There seemed to be nothing to do but wait to see what the local would do next. The ball was in Meinholtz's court, and the thought sickened Ivan.

That night Rachel knew Ivan was upset, but he insisted that it was nothing when she asked if anything was wrong. Reluctantly she dropped the matter. Later, however, after she settled into bed next to him, she asked if she had upset him.

"No, of course not." He pulled her close. "Why do you ask?"

"You're not yourself. Something has upset you."

"It's just something at work, Rachel. I shouldn't have brought it home with me. I'm sorry I worried you."

"If you worry, I worry."

"Please don't worry. It's nothing."

"Ivan, the night we were married you said I would be a part of everything you do. Do you remember saying that?"

He smiled at her and pulled her even closer. "God, I love you," he whispered.

"You're changing the subject," she said, smiling.

"Which would you really have me talk about, my love for you, or the office," he teased.

"That's not fair." She took a mock slap at his shoulder.

"The choice is yours." He dropped a kiss on her lips.

"You're terrible, Ivan Wollmack," she said softly, nuzzling his shoulder.

For the moment Ivan's concern over Rudy Meinholtz and the veiled threat from Local 610 waned, and he surrendered to the passion that Rachel stirred within him.

When Ivan arrived at work the following morning, he was greeted by his secretary, who told him Rachel had phoned and wanted him to call home as soon as he got in.

"Anything wrong?" he asked the secretary as he sat down behind his desk.

"Mrs. Wollmack sounded upset. She really wanted you to call first thing."

"Rachel, what is it?" Ivan asked as soon as she answered their newly installed telephone.

"Oh, Ivan, something terrible has happened."

"What is it?"

"Someone broke into Joe and Becky's store last night. Fortunately they didn't try to enter their apartment, but they could have easily done that if they had wanted to."

"Calm down, Rachel," he said evenly, sensing from her voice that she was very upset. "What did they take?"

"They didn't take anything. They just vandalized the store."

"What do you mean they just vandalized the place?" Ivan asked, though he had a sickening premonition of what was coming next.

"They poured red paint over all of the meat in the display case. They ruined it all," Rachel replied frantically.

Ivan closed his eyes and his shoulders sagged as her words sank in.

"Why would anyone do such a thing?"

"Have they called the police?" he said, evading her question.

"Yes. They arrived while Becky was talking to me. Oh, Ivan, she's terribly upset. They had over one hundred dollars' worth of meat in the display case and it's all ruined."

"Probably just some neighborhood pranksters," he lied. "Don't worry about it. I doubt that it will ever happen again."

Ivan leaned back in his chair and tried to concentrate. Meinholtz had sent a message. He had left his calling card, and he did it in a way that told Ivan it could have been a lot worse.

Rachel was still upset when Ivan returned home that evening. She said the police thought the vandalism was the work of someone who had a grudge to settle with Joe and Becky and that they could probably expect more trouble.

"Ivan, who could have a grudge against Joe and Becky? They haven't an enemy in the world."

"No one has a grudge against them," Ivan said as he dropped onto the couch.

"The police said maybe some of the colored don't like the idea of whites in their neighborhood."

"They didn't do it, Rachel."

"It doesn't make any sense to me either, but who else would do such a thing?"

"It has nothing to do with Joe and Becky."

"What are you talking about?"

Ivan reached into the inside pocket of his suit jacket. "Rachel, this is what it's all about." He handed her the news clipping from Saturday's *Times Herald*.

Rachel sat down opposite him and began to read the story about the furriers' strike in New York and the pelts that were ruined with red paint.

"Oh, my God," she murmured. "Do you think someone got the idea to do this because they read about the vandalism in New York?"

Ivan smiled grimly. "No, Rachel. This is not the work of someone copying something they read in the paper. It's not that at all."

"Ivan, what does this article have to do with Becky and Joe?"

"The man who ruined the furs in New York is also the man who ruined the meat in their store."

"What!"

"Insane, isn't it?"

"Ivan, you can't be serious."

"I'm afraid I am serious," he said grimly, and quickly explained his theory.

"What are you going to do?" Rachel asked, shocked at his explantion.

"If we weren't married, I know exactly what I would do, but there's no way I'm going to subject you to any danger."

"Ivan, you can't let this Meinholtz animal get away with this. Besides, I think we will be in greater danger if you do nothing."

He smiled fondly at her. "Any ideas?" he asked, his frustration at the situation evident in his tone.

"You could go to the police."

"No, I've thought of that. It would not accomplish anything."

"Why?" she asked, perplexed.

"First of all, I can't prove anything. Meinholtz and the local would deny everything and accuse me of being a trouble-maker. Secondly, the police would consider this a feud between unions. They wouldn't care a whole lot and they wouldn't do much. Besides, if the first card I played was ineffective, it could only make them more brazen."

"Then what can you do?"

"I have to convince them quickly and decisively that they are barking up the wrong tree."

"Can you do that?"

He thought for a moment and then nodded. "Yes, I think I can."

Ivan arrived at the Seventh Avenue offices of Local 610 just before noon the following day. He spent the entire five-hour train ride thinking through what he was doing to say when he confronted Seymore Beckerman, the Communist president of the striking furriers' local. There was a lot of activity at Local 610. Union offices were always busy during a strike. Ivan knew he could be walking into a hornets' nest if things didn't go well. He also knew he had a very weak hand to play and that bluffing against these people could be dangerous.

"Seymore Beckerman, please," he said as he approached the secretary whose desk blocked the entrance to the president's office.

"Is he expecting you?" the woman asked.

"You bet he is." Ivan brushed past her to throw open the door to Beckerman's office.

"Hey, you can't go in there!" she yelled, jumping to her feet to follow him.

Beckerman was startled by the intrusion, as was the man sitting opposite him with his back to the door.

Ivan recognized Beckerman's visitor as he stood and turned to face him. "Well, Mr. Meinholtz."

"Mr. Wollmack!" Meinholtz exclaimed.

"Planning your next paint job, Mr. Beckerman?" Ivan asked sarcastically.

"Ivan Wollmack, it's a pleasure to have you here," Beckerman said, struggling to regain his composure. With a wave of his hand he dismissed the secretary, who had followed Ivan into the office.

"What the hell are you doing here?" Meinholtz asked angrily as the office door closed.

"Nice company you keep, Beckerman," Ivan observed, ignoring Meinholtz's question.

"Rudy, why don't you leave Mr. Wollmack and me alone so we can talk."

"Rudy," said Ivan, sarcastically lingering on the name. "Before you leave, I was wondering, I need a hundred dollars. Seems my brother-in-law's store was broken into and there was some damage—about a hundred dollars' worth. I want to help him out," Ivan said, taking Meinholtz completely by surprise.

"You can go to—"

"Rudy!" Seymore Beckerman yelled, cutting him off.

Meinholtz turned to Beckerman, confused.

"Surely you can help Mr. Wollmack," Beckerman said.

"What?"

"A hundred dollars, Rudy. You heard Mr. Wollmack. He needs a hundred dollars."

"Oh, yeah, sure." Meinholtz still wasn't sure what was going on. "Here, here," he said, peeling off two fifty-dollar bills from the wad he pulled from his pocket.

"Nice seeing you, *Rudy*." Ivan made a sweeping gesture toward the door with his hand.

As Meinholtz left the office Beckerman said, "Well, Mr. Wollmack. I can't tell you how pleased I am to meet you."

"I'm here to help you, Mr. Beckerman."

A smile erupted on Beckerman's well-fed face. "I knew we could count on you, Wollmack. I knew it! You're going to pull your people out!" Beckerman said excitedly. "I couldn't be more happy."

"And you couldn't be more wrong."

The smile quickly faded. "I thought you said you were going to help."

"I am."

"How you going to help?"

"I can keep you out of jail."

"What? What did you say?"

"I can keep you out of jail."

"I didn't know I was going to jail," Beckerman answered impatiently.

Ivan grew very serious and locked his gaze on Beckerman. "You are going to jail, Beckerman, and I'm the only person who can prevent it."

"What the hell are you talking about?" Beckerman demanded, his temper quickly rising to the boiling point.

"Red paint. That idiot you have working for you used paint

in Alexandria from the same can that he used here in New York last week."

It was an enormous gamble, but Ivan was certain the paint would match.

A smile broke out across Seymore Beckerman's face. "I see. You're going to complain to the industrial squad of the New York Police Department and they're going to lock me up. Is that it?"

Ivan returned the smile. "No, that's not it. I wouldn't waste my time with the New York police on this."

"Oh, you're going to have the Alexandria police come get me," Beckerman said with a small laugh.

"Wouldn't waste my time with them either, Beckerman. Why bother with breaking, entering, and vandalism when I have you nailed on crossing state lines to commit extortion. That's federal, Beckerman. That's serious. That's big trouble."

"You can't prove nothing, Wollmack," Beckerman said, beads of perspiration suddenly visible on his forehead.

"Want to bet?"

"You gonna tell that cockamamy story to the government?"

"I will or my lawyer will. He has it all in writing," Ivan bluffed.

"Who's your lawyer?"

Ivan grinned but didn't speak.

"So what do you want from me, Wollmack?"

"I would have gone to the government before now, Beckerman, but I am not anxious to see the entire labor movement maligned in Washington because of a few bad apples such as you. But if you or any of your goons so much as breathe near anyone in my family, I'll have your head."

"You wrote all this and gave it to some goddamned lawyer?"

"And he knows what to do with it if anything happens to me," Ivan said smoothly.

Ivan and Beckerman stood staring into one another's eyes for several moments before Beckerman's face broke into a smile.

"Hey, ain't nothing going to happen to you, Wollmack," Beckerman said with his patronizing grin.

"Keep out of my way, Beckerman," Ivan warned. "I know

how to put you away for a long time, and I'd love an excuse to do it."

Without saying another word Ivan turned his back on Seymore Beckerman and walked from his office.

Chapter Twenty-five

March 7, 1930

Dear Tante Dvoyra,

I am sorry it has been such a long time since I wrote, but the days seem to just fly past. Hard times have returned to America, and we are working even longer hours than ever. It all began last October, when there was a panic on the stock market. Millions of people lost all their savings, and since then many banks have closed their doors, unable to pay their depositors. According to the papers, five million people are out of work. I have read that things are bad in Poland too. Joe says this depression, as they are calling it, will get a lot worse before it gets better.

Last time I wrote you, Lou and Sheara had just had their second son. Now I have more good news for you. Our baby sister Esther is to be married next month. Her husband is a fine young man named Chaim Wysocki, whose family came over from Minsk ten years before we came with Momma. He is a trainee accountant and works in an office in Washington. We were amazed to learn that he was born on the very same day we arrived in America in 1911.

Ivan and Rachel are fine, although Ivan has had a lot of difficulty at the union. The children are all well, and Rachel's little daughter Anna is now a beauty.

Although times are hard, business in the store is good. Alexandria is becoming a very popular place to live, and many well-to-do families are moving here. All of us are well. Sheara's boy Mark will begin school this fall. He is a fine boy, very bright, quite different in personality from his brother Bernard. Joe and I are fine. Sonia is tall and slender, and everyone says she is the image of Joe's mother when she was a child. Aaron is already up to all the mischief you would expect from a seven-year-old. Poppa is keeping well, although from time to time he complains about not being as young as he used to be. Ida makes fun of him and says creaking doors always swing the longest.

We look forward to having another letter from you soon. Don't worry if you don't have anything special to write about. Just because life in the countryside is uneventful, as you say, doesn't mean we don't want to hear from you and know you are all well and happy. Everyone here looks forward so much to your letters. We hope the enclosed ten dollars will be enough to buy whatever you might need.

By the way, Sol has become very interested in photography and has bought a Brownie camera. Next time I write I will send photographs of Esther's wedding.

Love,
Becky

The bonus marchers, camped along the banks of the Anacostia River while they carried their crusade to Washington, seemed incongruous to Rachel. They were reminiscent of a time and a threat she had come to believe were forever gone from the fabric of American life. But now those bad times were back, with their ugly manifestations erupting everywhere.

The marchers were petitioning Congress to speed up payment of a bonus they were to receive in 1945 for their participation in World War One. The bonus was awarded to them by a grateful nation; now its payment was being denied them by a mean and isolated administration.

Washington, D.C., had been relatively free of the more harsh visitations of the economic crash that had crippled the nation. Government was the largest employer in Washington, and it didn't go out of business, even in a panic, or in a depression as it was now called. But the bonus marchers brought with them to the nation's capital a living portrait of the misery that had gripped the rest of the country.

"What do you think the government should do, Ivan?" Rachel asked as they drove through the city on the way to Alexandria.

"You mean for the bonus marchers? Well, they deserve the five hundred dollars they're asking for. They're clearly entitled to it, but the government can't very well pass legislation in response to a demonstration. The city would become one huge fortress under siege as one group after another came to present their demands."

"Well, they have to do something. They can't just let millions of people starve."

"We need massive reform in this country, Rachel, but it isn't going to happen as long as the Hoover administration is in office."

"Don't they care?"

"It's not that the administration doesn't care. It simply believes this depression is just a phase that will pass, and that government should let events take their course."

"The depression will pass, won't it?"

"That's not the question. The real question is, what kind of country will we have when the depression finally ends? That's the real question, Rachel."

"I suppose we'll have the same kind of country we had before it began."

"I wouldn't bet on it."

"Go on," Rachel urged, anxious to hear what he was getting at.

"I don't know where we'll wind up politically, but I do know there will be a response in reaction to this damned mess we're in."

"You don't mean revolution, do you?"

"I wouldn't rule it out. Those bonus marchers are reminiscent of the birth of more than one of history's revolutions."

"That's a frightening thought."

"Frightening, yes; farfetched, no. Do you think those men are vastly different than the men who stormed the Bastille in France or who finally rebelled in Russia fifteen years ago?"

"I don't think that's a fair comparison, Ivan."

"Why not?"

"Because the government attacked the workers in France and in Russia. That could never happen here. These people are not here to fight. They're here to plead with their government for help."

"The only way they are going to leave Washington, Rachel, is if Congress capitulates or if the government orders MacArthur to run them out."

"I can't believe the government of the United States would ever 'run them out,' as you say. These men are all former soldiers who fought for their country. The government would never attack them the way the czar sent troops against the demonstrators in Russia."

"Want to bet?" he replied tartly.

"It will never happen, Ivan."

He reached over and squeezed her leg affectionately. "I hope you're right, Rachel."

"There was a terrible panic in the United States shortly after we arrived. Momma said it was terrible, but it passed."

"This one is different, Rachel. Too many people have been ruined. In the past people lived off their savings until times got better. This time the panic came when millions of people were in debt. The banks that lent them money closed because people couldn't pay their debts. Those same banks were where other people had deposited their savings. When the goddamned stock market crashed, people lost all they had ever invested. Nobody will buy anything, so nobody is producing anything, so more people lose their jobs, and they in turn stop buying things and then still more people lose their jobs. We've never been in such a vicious cycle before."

"It's so frightening."

"It's killing the CGWA, Rachel. It's absolutely killing us."

"I know how worried you've been, Ivan. I didn't realize it was that bad, though."

"You can't get blood from a turnip, and you can't get union dues from an unemployed worker."

"How badly has the membership fallen?"

"We've lost half our members, and the rolls keep dwindling every month. Oh, we'll get most of them back when things improve, but right now it's very rough."

"Ivan, what is going to happen? I mean, what do you think will happen?"

"The country is going to come out of this mess with the scales tipped heavily in favor of the employer or heavily in favor of the worker. What we'll lose is any semblance of balance."

"Well, I think the scales have been tipped in favor of the employer long enough."

"I agree, but I also know that either extreme can be dangerous."

"That's a strange thing for a union leader to say."

"It's probably treason," he said with a laugh. "But I've seen abuses on both sides, and they produce equally ugly results."

"What would you like to see happen?"

"I'm not smart enough to know everything that should be done. But I do think workers should have the basic right to organize if a majority chooses to. Now, you have to bring the employer to his knees in order to organize. Strikes are the only effective organizing tool we have. We have to make a lot of people miserable in order to organize. It shouldn't be that way."

"Do you think labor will ever win the legal right to organize, Ivan?"

"I don't know, but the right to organize will certainly be a big issue in the next election."

"Maybe something good can come out of this horrible panic."

"Rachel! It passed!" Ivan cried as he burst into the apartment. "The NIRA is the law of the land! Roosevelt signed the bill!"

Rachel ran to him and hugged him tightly as he swept her off her feet.

"Federally enforced work standards and the right to organize! Can you believe it? Only a year ago the bonus marchers were here, and now we have the right to organize!"

"Oh, Ivan, it's wonderful," she said excitedly.

"And it couldn't have happened too soon. Our membership has been decimated by the depression."

They talked about nothing else at dinner.

"It's going to take a ton of work, Rachel, but I can rebuild the CGWA within a year because of the National Industrial Recovery Act," he said.

"Is it really that wonderful?"

"No. It's a terrible piece of legislation, and our attorneys think it's probably unconstitutional, but section seven A gives us what we need right now. Frankly I don't care if it's found to be unconstitutional later on."

"What will you do?"

"Work my ass off for the next year. Rachel, I'm going to have to travel a great deal. The NIRA gives us the right to organize, to campaign for the union in one city after another, in one plant after another. I'm the organizer in the CGWA."

Rachel's excitement quickly faded as he continued.

"I don't know how long we'll have this opportunity, so we have to accomplish everything while we can. I will have to campaign in every local election, and the employers will be there campaigning against me every time."

"Then what has the NIRA changed?"

"This time there will be a federally supervised election in every case. Majority rules, Rachel. We'll win those elections if the campaign is run well. I know we will. I'll beat those bastards every time."

Rachel was heartsick at the thought of Ivan's being away for most of the coming year, but she understood the importance of his new mission and she was fully supportive of the work he had to do.

The NIRA was passed on June sixteenth of President Roosevelt's first year in office. By the first of July Ivan was on the road, on his way to factories that he considered ripe for organizing.

He didn't return to Washington until the third week in August. He'd gone from plant to plant, first in Philadelphia and then in Baltimore, where he'd concentrated on relatively small producers at first, easily winning out over the confused and disorganized employers. He returned home physically exhausted but clearly exhilarated. In one month the CGWA membership rolls, after three years of decline, had increased by fifteen thousand new members. However, the next round of elections was not to go as easily as the initial organizing efforts. The employers would be ready for Ivan this time.

Ivan stepped from the railroad terminal in Trenton, New Jersey, and quickly surveyed the area as he stood waiting for a taxi. It was a late September Sunday afternoon and the streets were nearly deserted. The mood of the city seemed somber and humorless, he thought.

Ivan asked the cabdriver to take him to the Titusville factory, which stood on the east bank of the Delaware River, halfway between Washington Crossing and Pennington. *Trenton, the cradle of democracy*, he mused silently as he studied the old red brick edifice. *Well, we'll see just how democratic they really are here.*

The driver took him to his motel just outside Princeton, not fifteen miles away. Ivan paid the driver and checked into the small roadside establishment that had obviously fallen upon hard times. He dropped his valise on the floor of his room and studied the dingy, sparse surroundings that would be his home for the next week. Then Ivan took off his jacket and tie and stretched out on the bed to wait for his visitors.

Roy Plunkett, whose father had come to America from Ireland at the turn of the century, and Issac Goldman, a German immigrant, came to Ivan's room just after dark. Plunkett seemed an intense and humorless fellow, but Goldman welcomed Ivan with a warm handshake.

Ivan judged both men to be in their mid-thirties. They had jointly signed the letter urging Ivan to come to Titusville to help unionize the twenty-two-hundred-man work force there. Both men were married with children.

"It won't be easy," Roy said. "The owners of the Titusville plant say the blue eagle flag of the National Recovery Administration will never fly at their plant. They hate the NRA, Roosevelt and the whole new deal, and they say unions are communist and un-American."

"They can't stop an election," Ivan replied. "If a majority votes union, that's the end of it."

"They say they'll close the plant first," Issac said.

"They all say that," Ivan said with a smile. "They never do though."

"Gallanger—he's the supervisor over at Titusville—says there are thousands of workers in Camden who will take our jobs in a minute if we go off the job."

"Issac, no one is going off the job. We have the right to hold an election. If we win, Titusville is going to be a union shop whether the owners like it or not. We're going to follow the law to the letter. No one is going to lose their jobs."

"We've arranged a rally tomorrow at the Zeiss farm over near Harbourton," Roy said. "We're meeting at the factory next Friday, the evening before the election. The men don't want to meet at the plant a whole week before the election. They're afraid they'll get too much pressure from the bosses there."

Roy agreed to pick up Ivan at the motel at seven-thirty the next morning. They would meet Issac at the front gate of the plant and hand out notices of the rally to the workers as they arrived.

It was an uneventful morning. No one tried to interfere

with the distribution of notices, although Ivan was sure he had spotted more than one member of management among those who walked up to him to receive the literature he was handing out. He made it a point to smile and to appear as relaxed as possible, but no one returned the smile and the apprehension of the workers was evident by the solemnity of their expressions as they filed past him.

Mick Gallanger, the Titusville supervisor, stood at a third-floor window looking down at the Jew from Washington handing out literature to his workers. He glanced at the notice one of his foremen had handed him only moments before.

"Communist bastard," he whispered.

The next day Ivan borrowed Roy's battered old truck, and using a map Roy had drawn for him, he drove out to the Zeiss farm, hoping to get a feel for the outdoor surroundings that would become his makeshift assembly hall. Ivan didn't like the feel of the Zeiss farm. It consisted of an apple orchard and a clearing, sufficient for several hundred people to gather, but far from ideal. The space was too open and it would be difficult to develop any real rapport with his audience.

Ivan returned to the Zeiss farm around six-thirty. Two loudspeakers were set up on either side of a crudely made platform that would serve as a stage for Ivan. Light bulbs had been strung around the perimeter of the clearing and tables with beer, soft drinks, and pretzels stood at the edge of the area. A steady stream of cars and trucks made their way up the dirt road that led to the farm, and by seven o'clock at least two hundred men had arrived.

Ivan climbed up onto the platform and surveyed the farm and the gathering crowd of workers. The wind had picked up, and Ivan knew the gusts would blunt the extent to which his voice would carry over the inadequate loudspeakers. Dark clouds that had begun to gather on the horizon only a short time ago were now rushing toward them, and nightfall seemed to be descending upon the entire Delaware Valley earlier than usual that night. As he looked beyond the clearing, he saw the apple trees extending their branches in his direction as though they were turning away from the ever-increasing force of the wind. *I don't like this at all,* he thought.

"We'd better begin before she really starts to blow," Roy yelled up to him.

Ivan nodded and walked to the solitary microphone that stood at the center of the platform. He looked down at the crowd, which had swelled to about four hundred. His hair blowing wildly in the brisk wind, he raised his arms and yelled into the microphone.

"Do we need union at Titusville?"

"Yes!" the crowd replied in unison.

"What did you say?" he yelled, pretending he hadn't heard them.

"Yes!" came the roar of the crowd, much louder than before.

"In one week you will decide the future at Titusville," he said as the crowd grew silent and attentive.

"In one week you will decide how high you will hold your heads. In one week you will decide whether you will speak as *one* when you talk to management.

"You no longer have to fight for a union. You only have to vote for a union." Ivan paused momentarily for effect. "Do you want it?" he yelled.

"Yes!"

"I can't hear you!"

"Yes!"

Ivan continued, emphasizing the history of the union movement in America. The crowd was hungry for the message Ivan had to deliver. He reviewed for them the new NIRA legislation and the procedure that would be followed for one of the first federally supervised union elections ever held on the east bank of the Delaware.

"So how do we vote next Saturday?" he asked the crowd, concluding his speech.

"Union!" the workers shouted.

"How?" Ivan yelled down to them.

"Union!"

"How?"

"Union!" they yelled. "Union! Union! Union!"

Ivan glanced up over the crowd and saw the headlights of a caravan in the distance. He knew it meant trouble. A long line of vehicles seemed to be heading their way along the narrow highway that passed the Zeiss farm, and Ivan assumed that the police were coming to investigate the large gathering. Ivan wanted to quickly change the tone of the meeting from an emotionally charged rally to a more festive event that would seem less threatening to the police.

"Happy days are here again!" he yelled to the cheers of the crowd. Then he began to sing. Immediately the crowd joined in. "Again!" he yelled. And as they began to repeat the chorus, Ivan saw that it was not a caravan of police cars, but of open-bodied trucks with men hanging off the sides. They were approaching from the rear of the clearing, so that at that moment only Ivan saw them, and the singing of the crowd drowned out the sound of the trucks.

It began to rain as the workers laughed and sang in the dusk of the evening.

"Run!" Ivan shouted futilely. "Run for the trees," he yelled as he saw that the trucks were heading directly for the crowd.

It all happened so quickly. There was pandemonium as the trucks drove through the crowd. The chain-wielding goons twirled their weapons like lariats, striking the workers as they tried to run for the cover of the trees. Within five minutes it was over. The trucks sped off, leaving behind a bruised and bleeding crowd. They were dazed and confused, many of them yelling in outrage or weeping in pain. Ivan had caught a chain across his face as he jumped from the platform and tried to run alongside one of the trucks in an effort to pull the driver from the vehicle. As he struggled to his feet, he saw that circulars had been thrown from the trucks and now littered the ground. They all said the same thing.

Let the ruling classes tremble at a communist revolution. The proletarians have nothing to lose but their chains. They have a world to win. Working men of all countries, unite!

"What is it?" Roy asked.

"Roy! Are you all right?" Ivan asked, seeing the red welts on the side of his neck and cheek.

"No worse than you, Ivan. What do you have there?"

"The grounds are strewn with circulars quoting Marx. They want to make this look like a communist rally."

The crowd was rapidly dissipating, and the state police arrived a few moments later, calling for Ivan Wollmack. As soon as Ivan stepped forward, he was placed under arrest for inciting a riot.

Ivan knew it would serve no purpose to argue with the state troopers who had come to arrest him. He, Roy, and many of the others had no doubt that Mick Gallanger had orchestrated the attack. He assured the men who had gathered around him to protest his arrest that he would be all right. He was less restrained, however, when he was led into the office of Captain Len Socorski of the New Jersey State Police, Princeton Barracks.

"I wanted to see you before you were booked and fingerprinted," said the thick-necked Socorski.

"Good, I wanted to see you before you were charged too," Ivan replied.

Socorski smiled. "You're skating on thin ice opening your mouth to me like that. I don't have to take that from a commie agitator like you."

"I am president of the Confederated Garment Workers of America. I was addressing a meeting of workers from the Titusville clothing factory as part of a federally sanctioned labor election. You're violating the law by interfering with that election."

"You were trespassing on private property, Mr. Wollmack. There was a riot, and communist propaganda was all over the place. I don't think the new federal National Industrial Recovery Act sanctions those activities."

"Now you listen to me," Ivan said, his temper rising. "We were holding a peaceful rally at the Zeiss farm with the permission of the owner. The only riot, as you call it, occurred when goons from Titusville stormed the rally in trucks. They were swinging chains and it's an absolute miracle that no one was killed. They were the ones who littered the farm with communist propaganda."

Socorski smiled patronizingly. "Can I see your authorization from Mr. Zeiss?"

"I don't have it, but I am sure I can get it."

Socorski nodded, his pursed lips suggesting a measure of disbelief.

"You say the trouble was caused by people from Titusville. Name them, Mr. Wollmack."

"I can't. We didn't see any of them, but we suspect Mick Gallanger, the supervisor at Titusville, is largely involved."

"You say they drove all through the crowd, but you didn't see any of them?"

"It was dark and there was total chaos."

"And I guess you didn't see this either." Socorski handed Ivan the communist literature.

"I saw this a minute before your people came. Gallanger's thugs from Titusville were the only troublemakers there tonight."

"Mr. Wollmack, if you're not careful, you're going to wind up being charged with slander, too, before this is all over. You can't prove a single thing you've said about Mick Gallanger and the people over at Titusville."

Ivan remained silent. He knew Socorski was right. He couldn't prove a thing.

"Mr. Wollmack, you should know that Elmer Zeiss has filed trespassing charges against the CGWA."

"What!"

"You've got a shit pot full of trouble on your hands, Mr. Wollmack."

"I'm being set up," Ivan said angrily. "You know damn well I'm being set up."

"I suspect you're right, but the facts as we know them now leave us no choice but to book you for trespassing and inciting to riot."

"I've done nothing, absolutely nothing, wrong," Ivan argued.

"Well, you'll have a chance to prove your innocence, Mr. Wollmack. But meantime you'll have to post a bond for your bail and you'll not be allowed to leave this county until your hearing."

"When will that be?"

"Hard to say. Probably sixty to ninety days."

"You expect me to stay here for sixty to ninety days?" Ivan asked disbelievingly.

"You bet your ass we do. You might be here for Christmas."

"It's impossible. I can't do that."

"Mr. Wollmack, you let anyone hear you talk like that and you'll be held without bail. As it is, I would guess bail is going to be set pretty high."

"What do you mean?"

"I'd guess fifty thousand dollars," Socorski replied blandly.

"Listen, I have business next week and the week after and every week. I can't sit around here for three months."

"Mr. Wollmack, you don't seem to understand. You're in trouble. Sitting around here for ninety days is the least of your problems. If the trial doesn't go your way, we're talking prison—maybe three years. People hate communists around here."

"I'm no communist!" Ivan exclaimed angrily.

"You'd be smart to play ball, Mr. Wollmack."

This is a cat-and-mouse game, Ivan thought. "Play ball? What do you mean, 'play ball'?"

"This is a peaceful community, Mr. Wollmack. I think I can help you out if you promise not to cause any more trouble."

Ivan looked at Socorski suspiciously. "Go on."

"Well, you agree not to speak at that rally next Friday over at Titusville, and I think I can arrange to have all the charges against you dropped."

"Do you realize that innocent people were beaten tonight? Beaten with chains? That only a miracle prevented someone from being killed?"

"None of them were here complaining, Mr. Wollmack."

"They must be too scared."

"Mr. Wollmack, you come from a trade that's riddled with communists and gangsters. Believe me, you don't want to stand trial. You know, it's only been six years since Sacco and Vanzetti were hung."

"That's obscene," Ivan said acidly.

"But it's true. Why don't you just agree not to speak at that rally on Friday, and I think we can forget the whole thing."

Rachel was dumbfounded by what Ivan was telling her. He had called from a pay phone at the railroad terminal in Trenton. The telephone at his motel had a party line and Ivan wanted privacy.

"What did you do?" she asked anxiously.

"Rachel, I had no choice. I agreed not to speak."

"Ivan!"

"Rachel, I couldn't afford to sit here until Christmas. I can sign up fifty thousand workers between now and then."

"But the people at Titusville are counting on you."

"Right now the only thing they're counting are welts and bruises," he said sarcastically.

"Oh, Ivan, you can't let those people down."

"Rachel, they can still vote for the union Saturday."

"But they won't. They'll feel abandoned. If the CGWA isn't standing there giving them support they'll never take on their employers."

Ivan was silent.

"You have to do something, Ivan."

"I can't, Rachel. They'll throw the book at me. I think we're going to have to write this one off," he said grimly.

"What are you going to do between now and the election?"

"I'll help Roy Plunkett and Issac Goldman organize a union campaign," he answered without enthusiasm. "Curiously, my agreement with the authorities only prohibits my speaking at the rally. They won't interfere with our organizing efforts. They're too smart for that, but they claim I could incite another riot if I speak at the rally."

Ivan spent each evening that week with Roy and Issac. They reviewed the situation each night and tried to determine where the union stood. Things did not look encouraging. The workers did feel abandoned, and they showed little enthusiasm for Saturday's election.

Ivan arrived at the plant at six-thirty Friday evening, the rally was to be held on the floor of the warehouse. From seven to seven-thirty management would review the compensation and benefits program at Titusville. At seven-thirty, the time when Ivan had been scheduled to speak, they decided to have an open forum so that any of the workers could take the floor. That way, Roy and Issac reasoned, it would not appear as though anyone was there as a mere substitute for Ivan Wollmack.

The warehouse was mobbed, and it appeared as though the entire work force was there. The crowd was orderly, almost subdued, Ivan thought.

Management's message was simply for everyone to stick together, that they were a family and the outside agitators would only lead to their ruin.

When the floor was turned over to labor, Issac Goldman walked to the platform that had been placed at the wall opposite the entrance and stood before the microphone. He tried hard to convince the workers that they were entitled to be represented by a union. But Gallanger's attack had sapped their resolve and frightened them into passivity. Issac could tell they weren't buying his message. Ivan could also see that Titusville would not go union. Not that night, he thought.

"Who else would like to speak?" Issac asked. There was silence.

"It's an open mike," Issac said. "Surely someone else wishes to speak." Ivan saw several members of management smile as the silence grew deafening. He saw Captain Socorski standing off to the side of the room watching him intently. His expression seemed to say, *Don't do it, Wollmack.*

Then, when it appeared Issac Goldman was about to give up and adjourn the meeting, a woman's voice called out from the rear of the warehouse.

"I would like to speak!"

Ivan's heart raced as he heard Rachel's voice. Everyone turned to see the attractive woman walking down the aisle toward the front of the room. Ivan was on the opposite side of the warehouse, and he knew he could not reach her before she got to the platform.

Rachel looked frightened but determined, her face flushed with the excitement of the moment. Ivan was startled once again by her resemblance to her mother Anna. He moved to the front of the room and reached the center aisle as his wife reached the microphone. There was a murmur moving through the room as everyone tried to determine the identity of the young, beautiful woman who now commanded center stage.

"My name is Rachel Wollmack," she began. "I am the wife of Ivan Wollmack."

"Jesus Christ," he whispered as she spotted him in the crowd for the first time. Ivan could see that she was petrified and he gave her a reassuring smile.

"I am twenty-six years old," she continued. "I came to America with my mother over twenty years ago. She came to join her husband, who was a tailor in the garment trade in Baltimore. She came to work, she came to be free, and she came to free her children. I think that's why you are all here too." The room broke into applause.

"My husband was going to speak tonight, but to do so would have cost him his freedom for the next ninety days and maybe for longer. He was accused of being an outside agitator, like the ones described earlier tonight."

"No!" someone shouted.

"He was accused of inciting a riot last Friday night."

"No!" came the spontaneous eruption throughout the room.

"He was accused of distributing communist literature to you last Friday night."

"No!" they yelled in unison, more thunderously than before.

"He was accused of trespassing."

"No! No! No!" they yelled.

"Why would people do such a thing?" she asked rhetorically as the room fell silent.

"Because someone is afraid of his message. Ivan Wollmack is a good man. He has devoted his entire working life to helping people like you free themselves from the chains of tyranny and oppression. He has fought unscrupulous employers, he has fought the communists, he has fought the gangsters, and he has fought to give you the right to decide your own destiny. Tomorrow you can do that with a ballot. That's a newfound right that you have. It's a right many people tried to deny you, and it's a right many people are still trying to deny you. Last Friday they tried to deny you that right with trucks and chains. Tomorrow, you will decide whether chains or ballots will determine your future.

"My mother came to America to be free, just as you and your parents came to America to be free. But my mother was enslaved by a sewing machine the third day she was here. She never stopped working. Never!"

Ivan saw that the audience seemed mesmerized by Rachel's speech, and that some people were nodding their heads in sympathy.

"Once my mother even worked for the CGWA," Rachel continued. "They had to fight to organize a union back then, just as you had to fight last Friday night. But you have a right Momma and Poppa never had. *You* can call an election. *You* only need the courage to use the right that a generation of struggle has won for you.

"The CGWA is no threat to your employers here. It can never ask for anything you don't feel is fair. The CGWA believes you have a right to work in a safe and clean place. Don't you believe that too?"

"Yes!" they shouted.

"The CGWA believes in the dignity of the worker. Don't you believe in that too?"

"Yes!" they yelled.

"The CGWA believes that every man's wage should reflect the value it represents. Don't you believe that?"

"Yes!" they cried.

"The CGWA believes you should be able to unite for one another. Don't you believe that?"

"Yes!"

"Are you going to vote CGWA tomorrow?"

"Yes! Yes! Yes!" they chanted in cadence. "Yes! Yes! Yes!" The chanting continued as Rachel walked from the stage.

"Yes! Yes! Yes!"

Ivan embraced her as soon as she reached him in the center aisle.

"I didn't come here to speak," she yelled above the din. "I came to be with you. I was in the back of the room watching the meeting. I couldn't find you in the crowd. When no one got up to speak, I nearly died. I knew how agonizing it had to be for you. I had to do something."

"You sure did," he said happily, hugging her.

"Will you get in trouble for what I did?"

"No, I don't think so." He laughed and hugged her even tighter as singing and clapping filled the room.

> *Happy days are here again!*
> *The skies above are clear again!*
> *Let's all sing a song of cheer again!*
> *Happy days are here again!*

The following day the union won by a landslide. Eighteen hundred of the twenty-two hundred employees at Titusville voted to affiliate with the union.

It was a victory for the CGWA and Ivan.

It was a victory for Rachel. And Anna's memory.

Chapter Twenty-six

It did not take Peninah long to discover Ha-Shomer ha-Zair, which had evolved from a merger between Ha-Shomer, a youth organization, and Zeirei Zion, a cultural group. Ha-Shomer ha-Zair openly and aggressively espoused settlement in Eretz Israel. Peninah joined the Zafim, the scout group, and became active as a *magshimim*, or organizer.

The organization occupied all of Peninah's spare time. As required, she studied Hebrew, Jewish culture, and the history and geography of Palestine. She became totally dedicated to the movement and its goal of creating a Jewish nationalism. Peninah and thousands of other young Jews derived satisfaction and stimulation from the discipline Ha-Shomer ha-Zair imposed upon its members. Everyone had a part to play in the redemption of Eretz Israel, the land of Israel.

To these young Jews the miracles being accomplished in Poland in the thirties—the uniting of the provinces, the reconciliation of the judicial, educational, and administrative systems, land reform, social security, health care, the growth of industry, the abolition of titles, the nationalization of the railroads—meant little. They were turning their heads toward Eretz Israel, consumed by their desperate need for an identity. In Poland they were treated as aliens. For Peninah and hundreds of thousands like her, second-class status was intolerable. She was determined to belong somewhere.

"Zionism, Zionism, Zionism!" Annette shouted angrily. "Can't we ever talk about something else in this house?"

"Annette, stop that!" Dvoyra said. "Don't we have enough problems without fighting among ourselves?"

"Well, she's crazy!" Annette said. "And she's making Yitzhak crazy too!"

"We want to train to live in Eretz Israel," Peninah said calmly. "What's so crazy about that?"

"Hah!" Annette replied scornfully. "You hear what she asks, Momma? 'What's so crazy about that?' You need to ask? You want to go and live in some godforsaken desert land where Arabs will kill you just because you're a Jew, and you ask what's so crazy?"

Dvoyra shook her head; it was almost as if her daughters could not be in a room together without the same argument breaking out again and again. There were times when she wished she had never heard of Palestine.

Peninah's talk of leaving Poland and settling in Palestine unnerved her younger sister and had become the source of constant friction between them. Annette at twenty looked more Polish than Jewish with her long, red, wavy hair and her pale green eyes and freckled face. She saw the Zionists, with their outspoken contempt for Poland, as a thorn in the side of those who still believed assimilation was both possible and desirable. Annette, like her father, saw Poland as her country and considered the Zionists foolish and hopeless dreamers who would only make life difficult for those Jews who were trying to make their way in Poland as Poles.

"Girls, girls,' Dvoyra murmured.

"It's all right, Momma," Peninah said. "She doesn't understand. But you will, Annette. One day you'll see the only hope for the Jews of Poland is in Eretz Israel."

"Oh, Momma, how can she possibly believe such rubbish?" Annette said, turning to Dvoyra. Dvoyra shook her head, unwilling to come between them.

"Peninah is right, Annette," Yitzhak said. "Our only hope is to leave Poland."

"Why?" Annette said. "We have always lived here. Momma and Poppa and their parents and their parents before them lived here. Our roots are here, our traditions are here. Here! Not in some barren, hostile country thousands of miles away!"

"Don't you see what is happening, Annette?" Peninah cried impatiently. "Don't you read the papers? In Germany the Nazis have made laws against the Jews. They tell their people Jews are parasites, that they have alien blood. They make hating Jews something to be proud of. Can't you see—"

"What's happening in Germany won't happen here!" Annette broke in. "The Polish people are not like the Nazis. The Poles see us as different from them, set apart by a different culture and heritage. But that's all."

"They hate us, Annette!" Yitzhak said. "Even you cannot be so blind that you don't see that. Isn't our own government advocating emigration? Didn't our own Minister of Foreign Affairs, Josef Beck, openly call for colonies where Poland could send her Jews?"

"Jews have lived here for centuries," Annette maintained, unwilling to give an inch. "If Jews run away and abandon Poland to start a new country, how can you expect the government to react any other way?"

"The government!" Yitzhak said bitterly. "If the Endeks, the fascists, had their way, they'd treat us like the Nazis are treating the Jews of Germany! They don't care whether we perish or survive!"

"And do you think you'll survive in Palestine?" asked Annette.

Peninah looked from Annette to Dvoyra and sighed. She stood up to leave the room, and Yitzhak rose to follow her. As Peninah reached the door, she turned and looked at her sister.

"We will survive in Palestine, Annette," she said, fire in her eyes. "I wish I was sure the same will be true of those who stay in Poland."

When she was gone, Annette turned to Dvoyra, vexation still evident on her face, hands planted on her hips in a way that reminded Dvoyra of her sister Esther, long, long ago.

"Momma, are you going to let them go off hundreds of miles with that Ha-Shomer ha-Zair crowd to Lublin and pretend they're living in Palestine?"

"They're not children, Annette. If they are determined to go to a Zionist camp, there is nothing I can do to stop them. And I'm not sure that what Peninah says is wrong."

"You don't believe any of that Zionist rubbish, do you?"

Dvoyra shook her graying head. "It's all too complicated for me. But Peninah believes it, Yitzhak believes it, thousands of other people believe it too. I don't know if they will ever see their dream of Eretz Israel come true, but if such a miracle can be made to happen, it will be because there are people such as Peninah and Yitzhak who believe it can."

"I thought you would be sick with worry at the thought of Peninah's going to train to be a pioneer in Palestine."

"It may be good for her," Dvoyra said. "She may find that living the life of a pioneer is very difficult, perhaps a lot more difficult than she expects. Better she should find out now than find out when she is in Palestine. At least she will have a better understanding of what is involved in making aliyah. After all, resettling in a strange land is not going to be easy, not even in Eretz Israel."

"If you let her go to Lublin, she will make aliyah, Momma," Annette prophesied.

"If that is what she wants."

"You'll let her go to train for aliyah?"

Dvoyra nodded.

"What does Poppa think?"

"Your Poppa sees both sides of the argument. He can understand why Peninah and Yitzhak feel the way they do. He says there is a lot to be said in favor of making aliyah, and a lot against it. He says, after all, that we are Poles and that gives us a right to be here, just like anyone else. He says what he always says, Annette. It takes time for things to change."

"They will, Momma! I know they will."

"I wonder."

* * *

In the summer of 1936 Peninah traveled the two-hundred-odd miles from Oleck-Podlaska to Lublin to attend the training camp there for young Zionists. It was the longest journey she had ever made in her life, nineteen and a half hours in all, but it seemed to be over in no time. She spent the whole journey glued to the window, fascinated by the changing landscape, the spires and fortifications of the cities. She could not believe she was so far from home.

The camp was run by Ha-Shomer ha-Zair to give their members an opportunity to live for six weeks during the summer as they would live in Eretz Israel. The camp was organized as a communal settlement called a kibbutz. Already Ha-Shomer ha-Zair owned land in Eretz Israel, near a place called Ashkelon, where they would etablish a kibbutz for their Polish members.

Peninah loved the camp right from the start. Working outdoors in the bright, strong summer sunshine, eating simple food, joining in the intense evening discussion meetings and mixing with people who believed as she believed, felt as she felt, gave her a feeling of enormous satisfaction.

By the end of her second week Peninah met a young man named Tsvi Aronovitch. Although Tsvi had never been to Eretz Israel, he led a daily discussion about what life would be like on a kibbutz. Life would be hard and the dangers great, he said, but if they succeeded, they would live in total freedom in a world where everyone—politicians, farmers, mechanics, cooks, dishwashers, watchmen, physicians, managers—was Jewish. In return, the young members of Ha-Shomer ha-Zair were expected to commit the rest of their lives to the kibbutz. He made it all sound like paradise. Peninah, who, at twenty-four, had never been physically attracted to anyone, was at once drawn to the brash young socialist.

She learned from the others that he was originally from Lvov, where his parents had been killed following the Great War during a pogrom. Tsvi was tall and thin, and while he spoke very softly, he was the most intense man she had ever met. Peninah could not tear her gaze away from his piercing blue eyes as he spoke fervently about the rising tide of Polish anti-Semitism.

"It got vicious when Marshal Pilsudski died last May," he said, pacing back and forth, banging his right fist into the palm of his left hand to emphasize his words. "Our own government is adopting the same anti-Semitic policies that are rampant in Germany. Mark my words, the Jewish community is finished in Poland. No one speaks out against the fascists. You wait, and you will see!"

As they worked in the fields and took their meals together, Peninah gradually became friends with Tsvi. She learned that he desperately wanted to leave Poland for Eretz Israel, but that Ha-Shomer ha-Zair wanted him to stay, at least for the time being. They believed, as he believed, that the increasingly hostile atmosphere being propagated and even encouraged by the government would soon erupt into violence. The leaders of Ha-Shomer ha-Zair judged Tsvi Aronovitch to be a born leader, one of a handful they felt they could rely on to prepare thousands of emigrants when the time came.

Tsvi was the most interesting person Peninah had ever known. Everything he said fascinated and excited her, and she admired his strength and honesty. After the third week they were rarely apart for more than a few hours at a time. They worked, they ate, they attended meetings, together. By the end of the summer they were in love.

Instead of Yiddish they spoke Hebrew, the sacred tongue only Zionists used outside the synagogue and the yeshiva. And always—always—they spoke of the immortal return, the return to Zion, the Promised Land, Eretz Israel.

On their last night together in Lublin, Tsvi took Peninah into the forest and made love to her in a field under a clear sky and a bright August moon. And afterward as they lay together, the oppressive ugliness of their world was briefly overshadowed by the power of the dreams they shared with one another. Tsvi proposed marriage by simply asking Peninah to accompany him to Eretz Israel when he was ready to go. She kissed him again and agreed.

That autumn they corresponded regularly and saw each other a few times during the winter and the following spring. In the summer of '37 they returned to the camp at Lublin, this time to train other young Jews for aliyah. Tsvi's Zionist convictions had grown even stronger during the past year.

"We must work hard. We must be ready!" he exhorted the new arrivals. "There's already war in Spain and in the Far East. Soon there will be war in Europe. And when it comes, God help all Jews!"

He was tireless. He was ruthless with weak minds, scornful of bleeding hearts. He urged the young Zionists to be proud of being Jewish, taught them the watchword of Ha-Shomer ha-Zair: *"Chazak v'amotz!"*—be strong and courageous!

"You have heard the fascist Falanga Party preach that Jews should be deprived of their political rights, eliminated from all social associations, and denied the right to serve in the armed forces. You have heard them say no Jew should be permitted to participate in Polish business, to employ any Pole or to work for one. Oh, yes, they have a new slogan now, my friends! Have you heard it? A radical elimination of the Jews from Poland, they say, is the ultimate solution of the Jewish problem! Our own people want to expel us from our own country! They mean to deprive us of the right to live! Well, we will deprive them of the right to exploit us!"

When they were alone, Peninah and Tsvi discussed their own plans. Next year perhaps, or 1939 at the latest, they would leave for Palestine.

"But what about Momma and Poppa? And Annette?" Peninah asked.

"You'll have to convince them that their only chance is to come with us."

"It won't be easy."

"You must try."

"I will. It's not really Momma and Poppa I worry about. It's Annette. She simply refuses to discuss the subject."

He shrugged. "There are some people you can't argue with. Annette is one of them."

"Yes, but don't you see, Tsvi? As long as Annette remains determined to stay in Poland, Momma and Poppa will feel they can't leave either."

"There must be a way to persuade her," he said softly. "There must."

"I wish I knew what it was."

Peninah knew her mother would be taken with Tsvi when he came to visit in the spring of 1938. He saw the world so clearly and Dvoyra would like that. It was her father's reaction to Tsvi that surprised her. Maybe it was the clarity with which Tsvi presented Eretz Israel that subdued the anger the Zionists usually aroused in Berl. Berl did not debate with Tsvi. He simply listened. Even Annette reluctantly found herself drawn into the discussion.

"Look what's happening, Annette," Tsvi said in his soft, convincing voice. "Austria belongs to Germany now. That German madman will not stop there. Next it will be Czechoslovakia. Or Poland. Or both.

"And did you hear what our noble government did in

response to the Nazi attack on Zionist headquarters in Vienna? They enacted a law depriving Polish Jews in Austria of their citizenship, in case Hitler decided to repatriate them."

"What next, Annette?" Peninah asked urgently.

"I don't know!" Annette said angrily. "I wish you wouldn't keep on at me all the time about what is happening to Jews in Austria and Germany. What's that got to do with me?"

"Annette!" Yitzhak said, leaning across the table. "Don't you understand? Anything that can happen to a Jew in Germany or a Jew in Austria today can happen to a Jew in Poland tomorrow. That's what it's got to do with you!"

"Oh, leave me alone!" Annette shouted, jumping up abruptly. "Leave me alone, all of you!" She grabbed her coat and rushed out of the house, slamming the door behind her.

"Let her go, Berl," Dvoyra said with a sigh as her husband got to his feet. "She'll be all right. I think she is just frightened by all this talk about Nazis."

"I'll just see where she's going," Berl said, following his younger daughter out the door.

"Momma, why is she so stubborn about this?" Peninah asked. "What do we have to do to convince her that what we say is true?"

Dvoyra shrugged. "It's not that she doesn't believe what you say, Peninah. It's that perhaps you're pushing her too hard. Maybe she'd react better if instead of trying to drag her through the door, you just left it standing open."

"Of course, that's what's wrong!" Tsvi said. "We're trying too hard. You're right, Mrs. Hoffman."

"You needn't sound quite so surprised, Tsvi," Dvoyra said with a smile. "We parents have been known to get things right once in a while."

"Is that so?" Tsvi said. "And have you got it right, Mrs. Hoffman?"

"Oh, don't you start on me!" Dvoyra shook a warning finger at him. "You talk to my husband. He's heard all the arguments, and I've heard them all from him."

"Have you talked about it, Momma?" Peninah asked. "About all of us going to Palestine?"

"Often. It always ends up the same way. Poppa says 'We don't have to decide tonight, do we?' or 'There's plenty of time.'"

"I'm not so sure there is time, Mrs. Hoffman," Tsvi said grimly.

"Well, I'll give you something to be sure of." Dvoyra got up from her chair. "And that is, if you don't clear the table and let Peninah and me wash the dishes, there'll be no tea and cake. Tsvi, put on the kettle. Yitzhak, some plates and cups."

Dvoyra had deftly evaded their questions yet again, thought Tsvi. Peninah had told him that her mother would gladly emigrate, but until Berl decided to do so, Dvoyra would remain loyal to him.

Chapter Twenty-seven

Annette Hoffman was twenty-three that summer. Like her older sister, she was slender and fair; but unlike Peninah, who took life so seriously, Annette was vivacious and friendly, with a cheerful word for everyone. People smiled when they saw her. "She's just like Esther," Dvoyra always said.

Annette wasted little time on the admiring young men of Oleck-Podlaska. She knew there was a lot more to life than the dusty streets of her hometown and the clumsy gallantries of farm boys. She had seen pictures in magazines of women in fine clothes who lived in houses that looked like palaces. They were rich. That was the world Annette Hoffman wanted to see. Desert communes might be fine for the Zionists, but they were simply not for her.

Her friends at the Suwalki furniture factory where she worked indulged her flights of fancy and called her The Dreamer. Annette took no notice, knowing that one day she would show them all. Her confidante was a girl named Lyova Jacobovitch, who lived on the other side of Oleck-Podlaska. They sat next to each other every day on the bus to Suwalki and came back together each evening.

Every Wednesday after work Annette would visit Lyova's house, or Lyova would come over to hers. They often joked about the fantasy they shared: One day they would go together to Paris and walk down the famous boulevard called the Champs-Élysées. They would meet two fabulously handsome millionaires who would marry them and take them to live in one of those great houses they had seen in the magazines, and in films at the Suwalki cinema. Sometimes in summer the women would visit until late in the evening before saying their good-byes.

The two Polish soldiers—deserters from the Second Army Corps stationed in Grodno—were drunk. They had broken into a barn looking for food and found some bottles of homemade vodka. They were settling down to the second bottle when the farmer heard them and came after them with dogs and a shotgun. They fled across the fields clutching the bottle and managed to elude the pursuit. They came to an unfamiliar road, but they could see the lights of a small village about half a kilometer away.

"Giz a drink," the taller of the two said, snatching the bottle from his companion's hand. He sat down on the grass at the side of the road and tilted the bottle, his Adam's apple bobbing as the vodka gurgled down his throat.

"Hey!" the other man said. "Leave some for me!" He grabbed the bottle back and took a healthy swallow, wiping his mouth with the back of his hand. Aram Bojak was quite young, and beneath the grime was a not a bad-looking boy.

The bigger man—about thirty, with the battered face of a brawler—was named Janko Barski. "Well, Bojak, what we goin' t'do, eh?" he said, banging the younger man on the back. "Got any bright ideas, eh?"

"Find some food. In the village maybe."

"Full of fucking Jews, I 'spect." Barski spat into a ditch. "Most of these fucking villages are."

"Jews eat too. Might as well go and see."

"Hello!" Barski said, looking up. "What's this?"

They saw a young woman walking toward them from the direction of town. She was dark and slender and pretty, in her mid-twenties, Bojak judged. Barski was aroused almost immediately by the power he felt over the frightened girl standing in the road. It had been so long since he had even touched a woman.

"Hello, darlin'," Barski slurred, scrambling to his feet and reeling out into the center of the road. Lyova looked about desperately to see if anyone was nearby. It was almost dark. There were lights in the windows of houses across the fields.

"Goin' far, darlin'?" Barski leered, barring the girl's way.

"I'm going home."

"Far to go, have you?"

"Just . . . a little way. Down there." She made a gesture to a lane leading off the road.

"Tell you what," Barski said with a heavy wink to Bojak. "We'll see you home. Make sure you don't come to any harm. Eh?"

"No, thank you. It's all right."

"Be safe with us, darlin'," Barski said grinning. "Never know who you'll bump into on a dark night like this."

"Come on, Janko," Bojak said nervously. "Leave her alone."

"Don't you worry, darlin'." Barski put his arm around the girl's shoulder and glared at Bojak. "We'll look after you. Won't we, Bojak?"

"Right," Bojak said unwillingly.

"Please!" Lyova said, trying to escape the dirty hand now clamped around her shoulder. "Leave me alone!"

"Aha!" Barski said. "You don't want our company, eh? Too good for the likes of us, that it?"

"No, please! Leave me alone! Just leave me alone." She could not break away from the big man's grip despite her efforts. "Let go of me, do you hear? Let go of me or I'll—"

"Scream, darlin'?" Barski snapped. "Goin' to scream, eh? We can't have that, can we?" He let go of her face, clamping his meaty hand over the girl's mouth. She bucked against his grip and kicked out wildly. Her foot connected solidly with Barski's shin, and he cursed violently.

"Little bitch!" he shouted. "Here, Bojak, hold her!"

Bojak reached out to grab the struggling girl, and as his hand closed on the neck of her cotton dress, she jerked away from him. The material tore apart like paper, revealing her firm white breasts.

"Well, well, well," Barski said. "Nice, eh, Bojak?"

"Yeah," Bojak breathed, his eyes riveted to the naked flesh. The girl tried to kick out at him, but he evaded her flying foot, then grabbed her leg.

"Get her down!" Bojak hissed, his reluctance finally giving way to lust. "Come on!"

She fought strongly, silently, angrily, while they pinioned her arms and feet and dragged her to the ground. The moment the big man removed his hand from her face, she screamed as loudly as she could. Barski hit her repeatedly in the face until she lapsed into moaning semiconsciousness. Then they did what they wanted to her.

Panting, scratched, the drunkenness partially dissipated by what they had done, the two men lurched to their feet, fastening their trousers. They looked down at the sprawled, half-naked figure of the once-pretty Lyova Jacobovitch.

"Here," Bojak whispered. "Not dead, is she?"

Barski bent over and laid a hand on the bruised and naked breast. "Nah."

"What we goin' to do, Janko?"

"Get the hell out of here as fast as possible."

"What about her?" Bojak jerked his chin at the girl. "We can't just leave her there."

"Why not?"

When Peninah came back from the camp at Lublin in September, she learned about the brutal rape of Annette's friend.

Annette told her that the girl was still under medical care. "They say she may never be normal again, Peninah! She's afraid of strangers and can't stand to be alone. What kind of animals could do a thing like that?"

"Have the police—"

"They said they would make inquiries. Inquiries! They aren't concerned about what happens to a Jew. Nobody is!"

"That's what we've been telling you all this time, Annette," Peninah said quietly. "That's why we want to go to Palestine."

"I want to come too."

"Have you told Momma?" Peninah asked, pleased at Annette's decision, though saddened that it had been brought about by such a tragic event.

"Yes. She says if I want to go, then I must go."

It was as if the rape of Lyova Jacobovitch was an omen. A new wave of pogroms swept through Poland. In October, Hitler browbeat the leaders of Britain, France, and Italy into supporting his demand that Czechoslovakia turn the Sudetenland over to Germany. And on November 9, 1938, the Nazi terror was openly unleashed throughout Germany—in retaliation for the murder of a German diplomat by a young Polish Jew whose parents, along with seventeen thousand other Poles living in Germany, had been forceably deported to

Poland. Two hundred and sixty-seven synagogues were plundered on that night, over eight hundred Jewish shops wrecked, twenty thousand Jews arrested, and thirty-six killed.

Peninah, Yitzhak, and Annette read the news of these events with the mounting certainly that the winter of 1938–39 would be the last they would spend in Poland. In December, Peninah received a single-sentence letter from Tsvi. It read, "Next year in Jerusalem."

"Momma, we have to talk," Peninah said one evening after returning from a political meeting.

"Go ahead, talk," Dvoyra replied as she polished the household utensils.

"No, Momma, come and sit down. This is serious. Tonight one of our most active leaders spoke to us in Suwalki. His name is Mordechai Anielewitz. He has been traveling all over the country during the last month. He says the German demand that Poland surrender Danzig is just an excuse. He told us there will be war in six months."

"All this war talk!" Dvoyra said wearily. She put down the kettle she had been polishing and sat down at the table facing Peninah, Yitzhak, and Annette. "Germany wants Danzig now? A year ago it was Czechoslovakia. "What will they ask for next?"

"Mordechai Anielewitz says Poland will be next, Momma," Yitzhak said. "But that's not the important thing. Tell Momma about Palestine, Peninah."

"The British have issued something called a White Paper. They say they are going to establish a unified, independent Palestine. They will restrict Jewish immigration to seventy-five thousand a year for the next five years, and after that none, unless the Arabs agree. And when Britain leaves, they say they will turn Palestine over to the Arabs."

Dvoyra nodded as the import of what Peninah was saying became clear. If what Mordechai Anielewitz said was right, very few Polish Jews were going to get to Eretz Israel. The Germans had already stopped the emigration of German Jews.

"Momma, we are all going to Palestine. Tsvi and I, Yitzhak, Annette. We're leaving with the next group that goes, this coming summer."

Dvoyra sighed. She looked around the room and then back at Peninah. "Maybe you're right," she said very softly.

"Maybe it is time we all leave this place. But, to run away from war here only to fight a war with Arabs in Palestine? How can that be better?"

"Do you think we will be allowed to fight against the Germans if there is war here? It won't be a fight. It will be a bloodbath, the pogrom to end all pogroms. At least in Palestine we will have a chance."

"It's like a dream," Dvoyra said. "All of it."

"So, we're dreamers," Yitzhak said. "Is that so bad? Haven't we all been dreamers every time we ended the Passover seders with 'Next year in Jereusalem'? Well, Momma, 'next year' is here, now. And our generation has been chosen to make it happen."

"Your father says—"

"That's what we want to talk to you about," Annette broke in. "We talked about it, all of us. We want to leave together. Us, you, Poppa. As a family."

Dvoyra did not reply.

"Momma," Peninah said, mistaking Dvoyra's silence for disapproval. "Didn't your own sister leave to find a better life? Well, that was nearly thirty years ago, Momma, and things are worse now than they ever were then. What in the name of God is so special about Oleck-Podlaska that we can't all leave it behind and go find a better life for ourselves too?"

Still Dvoyra did not reply, her eyes moving from object to familiar object around the room. Then she sighed. "I'll talk to Poppa tonight when he comes home from work."

Peninah rushed to Dvoyra and embraced her. "Oh, Momma, you won't be sorry! We'll have a wonderful life, you'll see!"

"You have to promise me one thing, Peninah," Dvoyra said, her arms on her daughter's shoulders, looking her directly in the eye. "All of you, listen now. You must promise me that you will respect Poppa's decision, no matter what it is."

"He'll say yes, Momma," Annette said. "I know he will."

"He is not a Zionist, Annette," Dvoyra said. "And he won't let you turn him into one."

"Then show him this!" Yitzhak said. "This is what Hitler said." He took a piece of paper from his pocket and put it on the table. Dvoyra's eyes picked out the two paragraphs that had been underscored:

And one more thing I would like now to state on this day, memorable, perhaps, not only for Germans. I have often been a prophet in my life and was generally laughed at. During my struggle for power, the Jews primarily received, with laughter, my prophecies that I would someday assume the leadership of the State and thereby of the entire Volk and then, among many other things, achieve a solution of the Jewish problem. I suppose that meanwhile, the then-resounding laughter of Jewry in Germany is now choking in their throats.

Today I will be a prophet again: If international finance Jewry within Europe and abroad should succeed once more in plunging the peoples into a world war, then the consequence will not be the Bolshevization of the world and therewith a victory of Jewry, but on the contrary, the destruction of the Jewish race in Europe.

Dvoyra looked up from the paper, her face ashen. "The destruction of the Jewish race?" she whispered.

"Yes, Momma," Yitzhak said, his expression grim. "That is Hitler's plan. He is going to destroy the Jews."

"Hey, hey!" Berl said, holding up his hands as if to ward them all off. "Give me a chance to speak!"

They were all seated around the table, and the talk, again, was of Palestine. Berl had listened to Dvoyra's pleas, to Peninah's persuasion, to Yitzhak's arguments, to Annette's enthusiasm. He was still not sure that to leave was the right decision. It was not, after all, the first time Poland had faced a crisis. Poland wouldn't give in the way the Czechs had.

"But if Hitler means to destroy the Jewish race, what other decision is there?" Peninah asked.

"Hitler cannot destroy the Jewish race," Berl said. "Nobody can. It is just the ravings of a madman. There are more than three million Jews in Poland alone!"

"And how will they live if the Nazis come, Poppa?" Yitzhak said. "Like the German Jews—who are deprived of all means of livelihood and all state benefits, whose children may not attend school, who are forced to clean streets and public lavatories?"

"I don't like running away," Berl said doggedly. "Palestine is not my country. This is my country."

"No, it was never your country," Yitzhak said quietly. "A Pole does not have to beg to be recognized as the equal of another Pole. A Pole does not have to spend his life wondering whether his children will have a future. A Pole does not fear that his house will be burned to the ground in a pogrom. A Pole is not hated and spat upon simply because he is a Pole. You are not a Pole, Poppa. You are a Jew."

Berl shook his head. In one short minute Yitzhak, whom he loved as his own son, had demolished every argument Berl had to offer against leaving Oleck-Podlaska. *It has been inevitable all along,* he thought. *I have wasted thirty years failing to understand what my children knew in their teens.*

He looked at Dvoyra, and then at each of his children in turn. They were all he had: there was nothing else. After a lifetime of work he had little more than he had begun with. To stay in Poland was to condemn them to the same fate, or worse.

He took Dvoyra's hand, smiling. "And you? What about you, Dvoyra?"

"Whither thou goest," Dvoyra whispered.

Berl nodded, feeling a swell of love and pride in his heart for all of them.

"Poppa?" Peninah said.

"We will go."

"You mean it?" Peninah breathed, almost unable to contain her excitement.

"We will leave together," Berl said. "As a family."

Dvoyra closed her eyes and wept as Peninah rushed into her father's arms. *Anna,* she thought, *at last.*

Word arrived from Tsvi in May that passage had been arranged for all of them on board the ship *Colorado,* sailing from Danzig. There were to be ready to leave by June fifteenth. They would celebrate Rosh Hashanah and Yom Kippur in Eretz Israel, Tsvi wrote.

There was no longer any doubt in their minds that they had made the right decision. It was clear that war was almost inevitable. Conditions were deteriorating daily.

Sitting at the table, Dvoyra set out all the photographs from America in front of her. There was Rebecca with Joe and the children in the yard of their new house; Sheara and Lou standing in front of their store; Rachel and Ivan smiling at the camera; Chaim and Esther on their wedding day. For the very first time in her life, Dvoyra had hope that she might, at last, see them all. Somehow she felt that going to Palestine would be only a stop for her and Berl on a journey that would end in America.

She picked up the pen and started to write her last letter from Oleck-Podlaska to Rebecca. The house was silent except for the scratching of the pen and the occasional rustle as Berl turned the pages of his newspaper. Dvoyra glanced across at Berl as he sucked in a deep, noisy breath. He looked tired, she thought, and his face was pale.

"Berl, are you all right?"

"I don't know. I feel as though I have to take a deep breath every few seconds."

"Maybe it's indigestion."

He shook his head, and then again drew in a short, sharp breath. "Dvoyra, come feel my heart." He unbuttoned his shirt.

Frowning, Dvoyra crossed to where he sat and slipped her hand into his shirt. His skin felt clammy to the touch. There were beads of perspiration on his forehead, and his heartbeat was irregular and very rapid.

"Dvoyra, I . . . I can't . . . catch my breath."

"Don't move! I'll send Peninah for a doctor!"

As Dvoyra ran from the room, Berl felt pain pulsate from his right shoulder down his arm toward his elbow. He tried to take another deep breath, but it was as if his lungs would not expand. *My God, it's a heart attack,* he thought. His chest muscles felt as though they were tightening. *Better lie down,* he thought. He rose from the chair, but he had taken only a few steps when everything began to whirl around him. Dvoyra ran back into the room just as he crashed to the floor.

Dvoyra came out of the bedroom and leaned against the doorframe, her hands covering her face. Peninah, Yitzhak, and Annette watched her anxiously. It had been well over half an hour since the doctor arrived. He was still in the bedroom with Berl.

"What is it, Momma?" Peninah asked.

"A heart attack." Dvoyra lowered her hands and looked at them. "The doctor says it is a serious one."

The door opened again, and the doctor came out, his

expression grave. He put his hand on Dvoyra's shoulder and led her toward the door.

"Complete rest," Dr. Lipinski said very quietly. "You understand? Absolute quiet, Mrs. Hoffman. I'll come back in the morning. If there's any change, send for me."

Dvoyra slowly closed the door, then turned to face her children.

"What did he say, Momma?"

"He says Poppa is in God's hands."

"He'll make it," Yitzhak said, placing his arm around Dvoyra's shoulders. Peninah covered her eyes with her hand.

"We'll just have to delay our departure," Annette said. "The *Colorado* won't be the last boat to sail from Danzig."

"Listen to me very carefully, all of you," Dvoyra said. "You will not postpone your departure by so much as a single day. You will sail on the *Colorado* as planned."

Peninah took her hand away from her eyes. She looked first at Yitzhak and then at Annette, but she did not speak.

"We can't leave the two of you here!" Yitzhak protested. "Peninah, tell Momma we'll wait till Poppa is fit to travel!"

Peninah was about to reply when Dvoyra raised her hand to silence her. "Don't argue with me, Peninah. You will all go, as planned. Poppa and I will follow as soon as we can."

"But Momma, what if . . . ?"

"If Poppa should die? Then he will at least die knowing you are all safe. Do not take that away from him."

"But I'm afraid you'll be trapped here," Peninah said.

"I know, Peninah. But there is no choice. If Poppa gets well, all five of us will be in Eretz Israel. If he doesn't, I'll join you there as soon as I can. But I will not let you stay. Nothing means more to me than knowing the three of you are safe. Nothing. Twenty-eight years ago I condemned you to living here by choosing to stay in Poland myself. Your opportunity to escape this nightmare is here now. You will not let the opportunity pass. You must leave. You must!"

And so, on June 20, 1939, Peninah, Yitzhak, and Annette joined Tsvi Aronovitch and sailed from Danzig on the *Colorado*. They were among the last Jews to be spirited out of Poland. On August 31, only hours before the German battleship *Schleswig-Holstein* began firing at Polish bunkers on a speck of land in Danzig harbor called the Westerplatte, Berl Hoffman died quietly in his bed in Oleck-Podlaska.

The following morning, Germany launched it blitzkrieg.

World War II had begun, trapping some thirty million Poles, among them Dvoyra Engle Hoffman.

August 31, 1939

Dear Tante Dvoyra,

I hope this letter reaches you without difficulty and finds you and the rest of the family in good health. Our postman was concerned that the trouble with Germany might interfere with mail deliveries. Maybe by the time this letter travels all the way to Europe, Hitler will have stopped threatening other countries.

I know you must be very worried about the future, but I am sure events will not be as bad as they threaten to be today. After all, Poland is a big country with over thirty million people, and surely the Germans do not think they can fight all of Poland. They must also know that America, Britain, and France will not stand by and allow Poland to be attacked. Perhaps by the time you read this letter things will be better. Please, please try not to worry. I know everything will be all right and that God will watch over you.

Have you heard from Peninah? Have they reached Palestine yet? I read in the newspaper that over one-half million Jews have now settled in Palestine. Just think, your family will be part of a new Jewish nation someday, and their children will be born there. While I know how much you must miss them, I also know how happy you must be with the knowledge that they will be part of a new land, a new country, and a new life.

Everyone is well here. It still thrills me to see how a whole new family has developed here in America. Every time I read of a new pogrom in the old country, I thank God for bringing us here, where such insults are unheard of.

Before ending this letter, I must tell you of a dream I had last night. Remember this dream, Tante Dvoyra. I know it means something and that it will give you encouragement about the future just as it lifted my spirits. I dreamt that all of us came together for a family reunion in Eretz Israel. The whole world was at peace. All of us from America came with our children, and Peninah and Tsvi were there with Annette and Yitzhak too. We all came together from three different directions and formed a circle in a meadow full of spring flowers, each of us putting our arms around the shoulders of a loved one on either side. We swayed back and forth and then we raised our faces to the sky and began to dance under the warm sun.

I will think of my dream every day until I know that everyone is at last safe and at peace.

May God protect you and your dear family.

Love,
Rebecca

PART III

Chapter Twenty-eight

The Germans arrived just after dawn on November 29, 1939. It was a bitterly cold morning, with flurries of snow whirling out of a flat gray sky.

In her empty house Dvoyra Hoffman heard the convoy slow down and stop. The sound of metal grinding on metal pierced the stillness of the morning as the tailgates of the German trucks in the town square were lowered. Angry, guttural voices shouted orders. The sound of men running through the town echoed off the walls of the buildings. Keep calm, Dvoyra told herself as she dressed quickly and went to look out the window.

A gray-painted truck with a mounted loudspeaker turned into the street. As it rolled down the road, a voice screamed instructions that would be heard in every village and city in Poland during the months and years ahead.

"*Achtung! Achtung!* Attention! Attention! All Jews in the Oleck-Podlaska area are to assemble . . ."

Stunned, Dvoyra sat beside the window as the sound truck drove past and disappeared down another of the dirt streets of the village. She looked about her, unable for a moment to comprehend the enormity of what she had just heard.

Dvoyra felt a shiver run through her body as she recalled the deportation of Jews during the last war. Then, it was the Russians who were their tormentors. They thought the Jews were sympathetic to the Kaiser because of the similarity of Yiddish and German.

"*Achtung! Achtung!*" the loudspeakers blared again.

"God in heaven, will it ever end?" she whispered.

Dvoyra gathered up her most precious possessions, the family photographs and picked up her purse. She looked around and tried to think what else to take. Soap, some towels. Clean clothing. A piece of black bread. She crammed everything into a valise, threw on her coat, and wrapped a shawl around her shoulders. Then she walked out of the house, heading toward the square. From every direction she saw frightened men, women, and children making their way toward the center of the village. Everyone was silent, except for one or two small children who were crying, frightened by the fear they sensed in their parents, and by the hostile men in green-gray uniforms lining the streets, rifles pointing at the villagers.

Dvoyra saw the Jacobovitch family huddled in the middle of the street with other neighbors. Lyova's face was buried in her mother's shoulder, and her brothers stood with their father, staring defiantly at the menacing troops as they moved through the growing crowd. She started to make her way across the street to join them when several soldiers formed a barricade with their rifles and began pushing a group of several dozen townspeople, Dvoyra among them, back toward one of the trucks. Another group, including the Jacobovitches, were being pushed by other soldiers toward another truck.

Dvoyra found herself with a group that soon swelled to about three hundred people. In front of them stood a frail-looking, bespectacled man of about fifty, wearing the black uniform of the SS. He was no more than twenty feet away from Dvoyra and she studied his appearance carefully. If this was the Master Race, he was a pretty poor specimen, she thought. His complexion was horrible, and his teeth were widely spaced and stained. She wondered what he had been before he became a soldier. He looked like a grocery clerk. She was not afraid. If anything, she was angry at these men for frightening the children.

"Listen carefully!" the man shouted, his thin voice whipped away by the wind. "These instructions will not be repeated. Anyone who disobeys them will be shot!"

A murmur of astonishment escaped the assembled villagers. The German ignored it.

"All Jews have been declared enemies of the Third Reich, which now includes the territory of Poland, stolen illegally from Germany by the international Jewish conspiracy at Versailles!" he shouted. "All Jews in these territories are to be resettled at points of concentration determined by the General Government of the Reich! Everyone assembled here is to be immediately transported to Baila-Podlaska to await resettlement!"

As he spoke, a caravan of fifteen trucks rumbled into the square, encircling the Jews.

"These trucks have been generously provided for your transportation!" the German shouted. "Boarding will commence immediately!"

"When will we be allowed to return to our homes?" someone called out. The Nazi's eyes narrowed to slits.

"Who asked that question?" he snapped. When there was no reply, he allowed himself a small smile. He turned away and walked toward the staff car that stood waiting. As he turned his back, two or three voices pleaded simultaneously.

"Tell us when we will be coming back home."

"Yes, when can we come back?"

"When can we return to our homes?"

The officer half-turned, one jackbooted foot resting on the running board of the Opel. The same thin, cruel smile creased his face again.

"Never. Jews!" he shouted. "Never!"

He entered the car and waved an imperious hand at the driver. The car sped away, leaving the shocked, silent Jews of Oleck-Podlaska staring after it in disbelief.

Now the troops in their green-gray uniforms surrounded the crowd, motioning with their rifles for the Jews to board the trucks. The Jews stood immobile, not in defiance, but each reluctant to be the first to move. A German lieutenant stalked across to the front row of assembled townspeople. He pointed at the trucks.

"*Einsteigen!*" he shouted. "*Schnell, schnell!*"

No one moved.

The officer shook his head, muttering disgustedly under his breath. He walked across to a young woman holding a crying child in her arms. Again he pointed at the trucks. She clutched the child tighter, but still did not move. The officer took out his pistol and put the barrel against the child's forehead.

"*Gnädige Frau,* please be so kind as to board the truck," he said softly, as though inviting her to share a taxi after an evening at the theater. The girl stared at him for a moment, stunned by the obscenity of his invitation. Then she walked slowly to the rear of the nearest truck and, tears streaming down her face, climbed into the truck with her young son.

Now the others began to move forward and took their

places in the waiting vehicles. The soldiers held their weapons level at chest height, herding the Jews, shoving them forward.

"Rein, schnell, rein!" they shouted. *"Rein! Schnell!"*

When everyone was on board, the tailgates were slammed shut and fastened with metal pins. Whistles shrilled, commands were shouted. Guards armed with machine pistols took up positions at the rear of each truck. Then four-man squads began a house-to-house search of the town. The shivering prisoners heard them kicking open doors and smashing windows as the Nazis searched for anyone attempting to evade the deportation. The sound of a woman's terrified scream sent chills through the waiting crowd.

Soon the soldiers returned to the square, dragging with them a dozen men and four women. Several of the men were bleeding from cuts on their faces. One woman clutched the front of her dress where it had been torn open by her captors.

On the far side of the square was a two-hundred-year-old wall in front of the village blacksmith's shop. The sixteen Jews were herded over to the wall and lined up in front of it. The officer shouted an order and the soldiers backed away, leveling their machine pistols at the petrified cluster of men and women.

"Feuer!"

In full view of the entire caravan the German soldiers fired a burst of several hundred shots at the defenseless men and women. Dvoyra watched in horror as they held out their hands as though to shield themselves from the bullets. Chunks of stone were blasted out of the wall. The wind whipped away the smoke to reveal the dead Jews lying motionless on the freezing ground. A command was shouted. The soldiers ran for their trucks and piled aboard, and the fifteen-truck convoy started south on its two-hundred-mile journey to Biala-Podlaska. The eyes of the prisoners remained fixed on the bullet-riddled bodies in the square until they could be seen no more.

Dvoyra learned a great deal on the journey to Biala-Podlaska. She learned that not one person in the crowded truck rattling south had any idea why the man in the black uniform had called them enemies of the Reich; no idea why they were being uprooted forever from their homes; no conception of what would happen to them when they arrived in Biala-Podlaska. Most embittering of all, she learned that no one was going to lift a finger to help them.

Dvoyra crossed her arms in front of her and squeezed her shoulders as though to ward off the biting cold. *I've never been so alone in my life,* she thought, closing her eyes. Then she remembered Peninah and Tsvi and Annette and Yitzhak and she thought, *They're free, they're free!* "Thank God they're free," she cried softly. And then, for only a moment, she let her attention turn to memories of Berl, and tears ran down her face. "They're all free," she whispered.

It was late morning as they passed through Augustów, about twenty-five miles south of Oleck-Podlaska. People on the sidewalks stopped to watch impassively as the caravan passed through. Looking at them, Dvoyra saw that their expressions were neither angry nor concerned, as if they were watching an anonymous funeral cortege go by. *My God,* Dvoyra thought, *they don't care what happens to us! Nobody will help us! The Nazis can do whatever they want with us!*

The caravan continued south, through Lomza and Sokalow and on to Biala-Podlaska, a small town on the River Krzna. There were nearly seven thousand Jews in Biala-Podlaska, more than half its total population.

From the German point of view Biala-Podlaska was an ideal point at which to concentrate Jews. There was already a large Jewish quarter with its own Jewish infrastructure; the crowding of more Jews into a ghetto would arouse little opposition among the non-Jewish population. More importantly, the town was situated on the main Warsaw–Moscow railway line. Access to rail transportation was to become a fundamental requisite for all such concentration points. Finally, Biala-Podlaska was located almost exactly halfway between two places marked by circles drawn on a secret planning map posted in a location far to the west, in the Berlin office of Reichsfuhrer-SS Heinrich Himmler.

On this map a circle was drawn around the hamlet of Treblinka, approximately one hundred miles northwest of Biala-Podlaska. Another appeared about two hundred miles southeast of the city, around Sobibor. There were four other circles on the map: at Majdynak, just south of Lublin; another still further south at Belzec; a third nearly three hundred miles to the southwest at Oswiecim; and the last far to the west of Warsaw, at Chelmno.

After driving all day the convoy finally reached Biala-Podlaska late in the afternoon. When the trucks came to a stop, the passengers were ordered to disembark and line up in the street facing an abandoned apartment building. In addition to the German guards, who continued to watch the Jews closely, some civilians stood nearby, all of them wearing white armbands bearing a blue Star of David. *They look like zombies,* she thought. The men with the armbands surveyed the new arrivals from Oleck-Podlaska with indifference. Dvoyra found them to be as frightening as the men with armbands bearing the dreaded swastika. The soldiers stared stolidly ahead, as if the Jews of Oleck-Podlaska were not there. No one spoke. No one came forward.

They stood silently in line for nearly forty minutes. By the time a military staff car sped into the street and pulled up in front of them, they were numb with cold and many of the children were crying with hunger and fear. There were four men in the Mercedes, with its two red swastika flags flying from the front fenders. The two men in front jumped out quickly and opened the rear doors. Two SS officers got out of the car and walked across the street to confer with the army officer in charge of the troops assembled to guard the new arrivals. After several minutes one of the two SS officers turned and stood in front of the frightened prisoners. He stared at them with unconcealed contempt.

"Listen to me, Jews!" he shouted. "I am SS-Untersturmfuhrer Karl Deitcher. I am in charge of your resettlement. Cause no trouble, do as you are told, and we will get along fine. I believe you have already seen a demonstration of how we deal with troublemakers. Do not forget it. There are no second chances here!" He stalked along in front of them, then turned and walked back again, glaring at the Jews as if to be sure they were as terrified as they looked.

"First, you will be assigned living quarters in the building you see before you. These Jews"—he made a disdainful gesture toward the civilians wearing the white armbands—"will record the names of everyone, by family, and then direct you to your quarters. That is all," he concluded before getting into the Mercedes and driving off.

It was a simple enough procedure. One of the Jews with the armbands would approach a prisoner, jot down the relevant information, and accompany the prisoner and his family into the building. After a few minutes he would return to repeat the process with the next family waiting in one of several lines in the street. After about half an hour, a tall, thin man with gray hair and red-rimmed eyes approached Dvoyra. He wore wire-rimmed glasses, a dirty old dark suit, and a black sweater. There were no buttons on his jacket. As he prepared to write, Dvoyra saw that the skin on his hands was badly chapped and that his fingernails were bitten to the quick, the cuticles torn and marked with dried blood. His right hand shook slightly as he put pencil to paper.

"Your name, please?"

"Dvoyra Hoffman."

"How many in your family are here with you?"

"I am alone."

"I'll put down three," the man said in a low voice, looking around conspiratorially and consulting his list. "They won't give a whole apartment to a single person."

"Why are they putting us in an abandoned building? This place doesn't look as if anyone has lived in it for years."

"There was some kind of epidemic a few years ago. A lot of the people who lived here died. The others all moved out. Then it just . . ." He shrugged, still intent on his list. "I'd say eight B would be the best one for you. It's in the basement, which means there won't be any windows. But it won't be drafty in the winter either. Incidentally, don't tell anyone you are living alone."

"Why?"

"Take my word for it." He tapped the side of his nose with the pencil.

"Are you from Biala-Podlaska?"

"Yes. My name is Perchik Feldman. I am, or rather I was, a tailor. A good one too. But I have had no work, not since the war started. So I work as a volunteer for the Jewish Self-Help. That way my wife and children are at least assured of food every day at the Self-Help kitchen."

He picked up her valise and signaled Dvoyra to follow him. Apprehensively she walked through the doorway and into the dilapidated building. Dirt crunched underfoot, and the dark, musty hallway smelled of the excrement of stray animals. A staircase led up to two additional floors, and another down to the basement level.

Perchik Feldman pushed her gently forward, nodding to indicate that she should lead the way down. Dvoyra suppressed a shudder and started gingerly down the stairs. At the bottom was a long dark corridor. It was very narrow, with unpainted plaster walls broken only by a line of old wooden doors, each marking the entrance to an apartment. Every forty feet or so a bare light bulb hung from the flaking ceiling, half the bulbs burned out or smashed. They walked down the long corridor, past apartment after apartment. From behind the closed doors Dvoyra heard the muffled sound of people crying.

"This is it, eight B," Perchik Feldman said, fumbling for the key. Dvoyra looked at the paint peeling off the door and the water stain that ran down the wall alongside it. As her eyes traced the water stain up to the ceiling, she saw several roaches run along the junction where wall and ceiling met. Dvoyra pressed the back of her hand to her mouth to suppress a gasp. Perchik Feldman did not seem to notice the vermin.

He opened the door and, turning on the light, motioned her to go in. Dvoyra stared in shock at the scene before her. The walls of the apartment were covered with paint peeling as badly as that on the door. There were holes in the walls where pictures had once hung. There were no windows. The only source of light was the solitary light bulb hanging from the center of the filthy, damp-stained ceiling. In the center of the room was a wooden table and four wooden chairs. At one end of the room was a doorway leading into a kitchen, another to a bedroom. Broken remnants of mildewed linoleum covered parts of the floor.

"There is a public kitchen at the end of the next block to the right, as you leave the building," Perchik Feldman was saying. "You'll be able to get some hot soup and meet other Jews there."

Dvoyra hardly heard him leave. She looked at the filthy ruin that was to be her home, and her eyes filled with tears. She went into the kitchen. In one corner stood a battered old icebox. It was a mockery, she thought bitterly. Where would a Jew get ice in Biala-Podlaska? She took hold of the lever and jerked it upward to open the door. As it opened, she saw scores of roaches scurrying to escape the light. She slammed it shut hastily, shuddering with disgust.

In the bedroom there were four mattresses thrown on the floor. They were stained with urine, or semen, and what appeared to be blood. The ticking covers were torn, the cheap stuffing gray with damp. Although they were obviously old and unfit for human use, there was nothing else in the room at all. She stood for a long time, staring at the filthy room, her shoulders slumped in despair. *They are going to treat us like animals,* she thought. Worse than animals. She turned to leave the room, then froze. On the wall facing her was a message smeared in black paint.

Welcome Zhid

The Jewish Self-Help kitchen was crowded, and to Dvoyra it seemed that most of the Jews from Oleck-Podlaska were there. She saw the Jacobovitches, the Tannenbaums, and several other families she knew. There was a great deal of noise in the huge room as friends and families greeted each other, crying, shouting, embracing.

The kitchen was set up in an old abandoned warehouse, large enough to accommodate hundreds of people and serve as an assembly hall as well as a dining room. Around the exterior walls were tables from which hot soup and salt crackers were being dispensed. For most of them, it was the first food they had eaten for nearly twenty-four hours.

A series of announcements interrupted the excited discussions going on all around the hall. The first was that there was a Jewish clinic operating in the ghetto, and anyone seeking treatment would find assistance there. Next, the hours of the soup kitchen were announced. Dvoyra strained to hear what the anonymous voice was saying above the concentrated volume of the voices all around her.

"You are reminded that under the General Government decree of November twenty-third, 1939, all Jews and Jewesses over the age of twelve are required to wear a white armband with a blue Jewish star. No exceptions are permitted."

There was another announcement, something about sleeping in the soup kitchen that night if the accommodation they had been assigned was uninhabitable. Dvoyra only half-listened as she hungrily ate the soup and crackers she had been given. She looked around the great building, packed with men, women, and children of every age violently uprooted, forced to witness the murder of their neighbors, delivered to this godforsaken place, all in the space of one day. And she thanked God again that her children were far away in Palestine.

"May I have your attention, please?"

At the end of the warehouse was an old loading platform,

and on it, speaking into a microphone, was a tall man who appeared to be in his fifties, with black hair beginning to gray at the temples. Well-dressed and striking in appearance, he spoke with authority.

"My name is David Berg," the man was saying. "I owned a textile factory near here that was confiscated by the Nazis a month ago. I have been active in the affairs of the Jewish community in Biala–Podlaska for many years, and I have been asked by the Jewish Community Council to act, for the time being, as liaison with the German command. I will do the best I can to represent the interests of all the Jewish citizens. I want to assure you that we will do everything in our power to make your life here bearable."

Dvoyra studied David Berg as he spoke. Obviously, she thought, a decent, good man, a leader imbued with the tradition of service to the community. A few weeks ago he had been a prosperous businessman. Today he was just another Jew.

"First I will explain about the council. The governor-general of occupied Poland, Hans Frank, has issued a decree requiring us to establish councils of Jews called *Judenrat* all over Poland. Communities of up to ten thousand inhabitants will have a twelve-man council, larger ones twenty-four. The German command will communicate with you through our *Judenrat*. You will be fully responsible to the council, which in turn will be responsible for you to the Germans. As I told you, I have been chosen to act as liaison. We must now begin to address certain realities of our situation."

The room grew very quiet. Every face was turned toward David Berg.

"Survival, with as much dignity as possible, will be our primary objective. I will be honest with you. All of us are going to have to work very, very hard together if we are to survive as a community. Soon it will be winter. We must plan for all our needs. We must assure there will be adequate food, shelter, and fuel to see us through until spring."

His words fell like blows on the listening audience. Dvoyra felt nausea rise in her throat as each sentence Berg uttered drove home the realization that her life, and the lives of every man, woman, and child standing around her, had been redefined. From now on, life would have to be lived on a day-to-day basis.

"I have been instructed to tell you that no Jews will be

allowed to leave the ghetto without the specific authority of the German command," he said gravely. "This is a matter of the utmost importance. Do not attempt to leave the ghetto area without authorization. Any Jew who attempts to do so will be executed."

Dvoyra shuddered and looked around as several of the women near her began to cry. Every face she saw wore the same shocked expression. Parents instinctively reached out for their children and gathered them into their arms as the agonizing reality of their helplessness and the fragility of their existence came home to them.

"I have been told," Berg continued, "that the Biala-Podlaska ghetto will receive an adequate ration of food. I have not, however, been able to establish with the German command what they consider adequate. I am making the assumption that little or no effort has been made to plan for our food supply. We will of course make further representation to the German command."

"What do they want to do, starve us to death?" someone shouted from the floor.

"They will do no more for us than they must," David Berg said chillingly. "We are not their first priority. Their terms are not negotiable, as you will see. I have one further item that I must discuss with you."

Again, the audience fell silent.

"On October twenty-sixth the governor-general issued a decree dealing with the question of Jewish labor. I do not know any way to make what I have to tell you pleasant. So I will simply read you what the decree says."

He reached into his pocket and brought out a sheet of printed paper. He cleared his throat and began to read.

Pursuant to section five, paragraph one, of the Decree of the Fuhrer and Reich Chancellor on the Administration of the Occupied Polish Territories of October 1, 1939, I issue this Ordinance:

Effective immediately forced labor is instituted for Jews aged fourteen to sixty resident in the General Government. For this purpose Jews will be concentrated in forced-labor teams.

Directives required for the execution of this Ordinance will be issued by the Higher SS-and-Police Leader. He may designate areas east of the Vistula in which he execution of the Ordinance is suspended.

"They can't do that!" some shouted. "It's slavery!"

David Berg nodded. "Yes. It is. That decree permits the Germans to march into our community and form labor teams whenever they choose."

"No!" he heard several men shout. "No!"

Berg held up his hands. "Listen to me! It will do us no good to antagonize them. These are vicious men who would love an excuse to brutalize this community. We have no rights, no resources, and no means to resist. We must make them feel that we are willing to cooperate if their demands are reasonable. Here is what I plan to do: I will propose they give us a schedule of their labor requirements each week. We will guarantee to make available the laborers they need, providing they guarantee that all laborers will be allowed to return home each night, and that they either be paid for their labor, or that the ghetto will receive a credit for the labor provided, which can be used to buy vital goods, food, medicine."

"We're not animals, Berg! You can't hire us out like mules! They can't make us work for them!"

Berg held up his hands again for silence. The clamor of voices below faded.

"Listen to me!" Berg said, his voice now cold and unfriendly. "We are not a political party. We are prisoners of war, without any of the rights to which prisoners of war are usually entitled. The only way we can deal with these people is to barter with them. What we cannot and must not do is to give them an excuse to make an example of any of us. I assure you they would like nothing better than an organized protest by Jews."

"We could all refuse to work!" a man called out. "They couldn't do anything if we all acted together!" A rumble of approval greeted his words.

Berg shook his head sadly. "What do you think would happen if you did that, my friend?" he asked softly. "Do you think they would negotiate with you, these people? Make no mistake. If you defy them, they will kill you. If you defy them, you will be risking much more than just your own safety. They have been known on more than one occasion to kill ten people for the offense of one."

Dvoyra scanned the room. Dozens of separate arguments

and heated conversations were going on all around her. Berg saw that he was losing control of the meeting and raised his arms to call for attention.

"We will post notices in this room!" he shouted. "Meanwhile, remain calm and try to get as much rest as you can. We hope to have a food distribution plan worked out within the next twenty-four hours. If you have any other questions, there will be someone here at all times to answer them."

As he completed his remarks, the doors in the rear of the warehouse burst open, and a dozen armed German soldiers marched into the room and took up positions around the perimeter of the great hall. An SS officer walked in behind them and stood with his hands on his hips, surveying the assembled crowd. The din that had preceded his arrival ceased as abruptly as if it had been cut off with a knife.

The SS officer walked slowly through the crowd, which parted ahead of him as the Jews shrank out of his way. He stared very deliberately at each face, his composure and contempt utterly intimidating. Without speaking a single word he established his incontrovertible authority.

He climbed onto the dais and stood staring down at the people below for a moment. "Here is another announcement, Jews. Listen carefully.

"I am SS-Standartenfuhrer Hans Botchermann. Think of me as God and we will get along fine." He paused, smiling menacingly.

"A nine P.M. curfew is hereby imposed upon the Jewish ghetto. As of this moment I never again want to see a Jew face on the street after nine o'clock!" He glared at the upturned faces, hatred coming off him like heat off a stove. Then he turned to David Berg, who was standing to one side. "You! Tomorrow morning I want forty volunteers for road repair work between here and the Bug River. Have them assembled in front of this building at six A.M. *Verstanden?*"

Berg nodded, and the SS officer shouted a command to his soldiers, who snapped into formation and followed him out of the warehouse. Dvoyra felt relief flood through her as the doors slammed shut behind the Nazis, and she heard the rising babble of voices all around as the tension that had enveloped the building dissipated.

She heard Berg urging everyone to go to their quarters and get some sleep. She saw some of the men with white armbands working their way through the crowd, signing up "volunteers" for the morning. As she was about to leave, someone handed her a paper bag filled with biscuits to tide her over until more suitable food was available, and she followed the shuffling crowd out of the kitchen and down the dark, narrow street toward the apartment building that was her new home.

Dvoyra did not dress for bed. She tried to wash herself as best she could with cold water; there had been no hot water in this building for many years, she decided with a grimace. She spread some old newspapers over one of the dirty mattresses, and then covered the makeshift bed with the towels she had brought with her from Oleck-Podlaska. She put out the light and lay deep in thought.

Her first thoughts were of her children, and again she thanked God that they had escaped. She tried to imagine where they might be and what it was like for them in Eretz Israel. Tel Aviv—the Hill of Spring. She wondered if it was as pretty as it sounded. Her thoughts drifted into the past. She remembered her sister Anna and her three children on the eve of their departure for America. It seemed only a little while ago she had kissed Anna and begged her to write often. *She was better off dying in America than I am living in Poland,* she thought, and felt the tears streaming down her face in the darkness. Last, she thought of Berl. *Why did you have to die?* she sobbed. *My God, we came so close, so close. Why did you have to die?*

Dvoyra slept the sleep of total exhaustion. When she awoke, she was still lying in the same position. It was dark in the room, but noise from the first-floor corridor told her it was morning. Her first thought was of the "volunteer" work detail. It must be those men whose shuffling feet she could hear overhead. She got up and turned on the light. The stark, filthy room mocked all she had left behind. Instinctively straightening her hair and rearranging her clothes, Dvoyra went upstairs to the street entrance.

It was still dark outside, but there were streaks of lighter gray in the sky that would soon give way to dawn. There were several dozen men standing in front of the apartment building, talking in low-pitched voices. Dvoyra wondered why the work party was assembling here instead of at the warehouse as they had been ordered.

Before she could ask any of the other observers, four trucks rumbled down the street from the direction of the meeting hall, headlights glaring. The first truck carried a squad of soldiers; the two behind it were empty. The fourth, trailing behind the others, was a tow truck. A Jew wearing a white armband ran frantically alongside the trucks. As the convoy drew to a halt in front of the apartment building, he dashed forward, his expression one of uncontrolled alarm.

He stopped in front of the forty volunteers who stood defiantly, waiting for the Nazis. Panic distorted the Jew's face.

"You were told to assemble at the meeting hall!" he panted. "Why didn't you do as you were told?"

"A good question," observed an SS lieutenant standing at the rear of the first truck, his hands clasped behind his back. "Answer it."

No one spoke for a moment. Then at last a young pale, thin man stepped forward.

"We want to ask you something before we report for work," he said with the half arrogant air of a schoolboy challenging a teacher. The lieutenant did not reply, but signaled by slightly lifting his head and raising his eyebrows that he was listening.

"We want to know how much we are going to be paid and what time we will be allowed to come home."

The officer stared at him in disbelief. Then he walked forward till his face was only inches away from the boy's.

"Get into the truck," he said between clenched teeth.

The young Jew swallowed nervously. "Not till you answer our questions."

"Last chance, Jew!"

The young man merely shook his head, his mouth too dry to speak. With that simple gesture he sealed his fate. The SS officer lifted his arm and waved the tow truck forward. As it pulled in front of the other vehicles and came to a stop, everyone stared in horror: a hangman's noose dangled from the crane on the back of the truck.

"Take him!" the officer shouted. *"Los!"*

Two of the soldiers ran forward and grabbed the young man by the arms. They dragged him to the tow truck, tied his hands behind his back, and put the noose around his neck, pulling it tight. As they did, the other Jews in the working party surged toward the empty trucks.

"No!" they shouted. "No!"

"We'll work, we'll work!"

"Let the boy be!"

The SS squad held their Schmeisser rifles at chest level, blocking the workers from boarding the trucks, herding them back several yards where they would be forced to watch what happened next.

The defiant young Jew was not allowed another word. The officer shouted an abrupt order and the crane was activated. In full view of everyone in the street, including Dvoyra, who was still standing in the doorway of the apartment building, the boy was yanked off his feet and hoisted into the air.

His body jerked like a marionette, his face contorted and his eyes bulging as he fought for life. It seemed to take an eternity. The men in the street watched in horror as the boy's face turned blue, and his swollen tongue burst from his gaping mouth. All at once there was a sharp crack as his neck broke. The obscene contortions of the body ceased; it hung limply on the rope, turning slowly.

Dvoyra stood speechless as the workers, tears streaming down their faces, boarded the trucks. The SS squad climbed into their vehicle, and the four trucks drove off with the tow truck, the boy's body swinging grotesquely from its crane, bringing up the rear.

Later Dvoyra would have no memory of running down the long narrow street to the Jewish Self-Help Center, blinded by her tears; no recollection of asking the men in white armbands where she could find David Berg. She found herself running from office to office on the second floor of the building, pounding her fists on one door after another until she came to one with a frosted-glass panel.

As she reached for the doorknob, the door flew open, and she found herself face-to-face with the same SS officer who had addressed the Oleck-Podlaska arrivals the night before. They stared at each other for a moment, the pudgy, cold-eyed Nazi and the slender Jewish woman.

"Get out of the way!" he snapped, sweeping her aside with a powerful hand as his surprise turned to anger. He stormed past her out of the office and down the stairs to the street.

David Berg was standing in front of her, behind a wooden desk. He looked strained and tired, as if he had not slept all night.

He looked up as Dvoyra came in. "Yes?" he said wearily. "What is it now?"

"My name is Dvoyra Hoffman." She struggled to catch her breath. "I wanted to tell you—they killed him. . . . They put a rope around his neck. . . . It was . . . !" She could not go on and began to sob uncontrollably. David Berg walked around his desk and pushed the door shut, gently putting his arms around her. Frightened and distraught, she buried her face in his chest and cried. He said nothing, waiting until she regained her composure.

Finally she lifted her eyes to his. "They just killed him. Like an insect."

"Yes," Berg said softly. "I know."

"Why?"

"Any reason will do."

"But it was murder!"

"Yes. I know that too."

She stepped back, embarrassed that she was still in his arms. "Then what are you going to do about it?"

"I am going to beg people to believe me when I tell them that the Nazis will not hesitate to kill anyone who defies them."

"That's no answer!" she shouted. "You must do something!"

"Would you like to tell me what?" he answered angrily. "You saw the Nazi who just left. Do you know who that was?"

Dvoyra shook her head. "He spoke to us yesterday. When we got here from Oleck-Podlaska."

"His name is Botchermann. SS-Standartenfuhrer Hans Botchermann, SS and Police Leader in charge of security in this area. Do you know what the SS is?"

Again Dvoyra shook her head. "Are they the ones in the black uniforms?"

"That's right. The ordinary soldiers wear the green-gray uniforms and the SS the black ones. The SS control all police functions and all matters pertaining to us Jews. They have divided the country into sectors that they call *Abschnitte*. This is one of them, and Botchermann is in charge of it."

"What did he want?"

"He came here to tell me Daniel Dienavitch had been executed. He came here with his mother from Lukowiska, a few miles west of here, about two weeks ago. He was twenty. A promising violinist. He had been accepted at the Sorbonne in Paris and even had a scholarship. Instead of being a student in Paris, he became a victim in Biala–Podlaska."

"Can't anything be done?" Dvoyra asked in a whisper.

He shook his head. "Botchermann came here to warn me that the insubordination of workers will not be tolerated anymore."

"Tolerated?" Dvoyra gasped. "They murdered that boy for asking a question!"

"And next time they will murder ten for the same reason!" he said, his voice like iron. Then he gently touched her shoulder. "Sit down, please. A moment." He gestured toward an old stuffed sofa that rested against the wall.

Dvoyra sat down and watched as he poured her a cup of tea from a pot sitting on a small hot plate behind his desk. She nodded her thanks as she took the tea, looking around the room as she sipped it. On one wall was a large-scale map of the city, the borders of the ghetto marked off with a heavy black line. His desk was littered with papers, and an ashtray full of cigarette butts testified to the pressured hours he had spent there.

"I can't believe all this is happening to us," she said. "Where is it all going to end?"

"Are you looking for reassurance, Dvoyra? Or my honest opinion?"

She noticed that he had called her by her first name, and she raised her eyes to meet his. She sensed strength and honesty in his gaze and felt as though she had known him much longer than just these few minutes.

"I would like reassurance," she answered after a moment. "But I would prefer the truth."

He nodded approvingly, as if the question had been some kind of test and she had passed it.

"Have you read *Mein Kampf*, Dvoyra?"

"No. I have never heard of it."

"It is Adolf Hitler's autobiography. The title means 'my struggle.' Mostly it is a lot of nonsense, ravings about Hitler's early life and his view of Germany and its problems. But one message shines from it like a beacon, Dvoyra. The man has a pathological hatred of Jews—all Jews."

"But that's impossible! Insane! How could anyone hate what he does not know?"

"Let me answer your question with a question, Dvoyra. How do you feel about rats?"

She frowned. "What kind of question is that?"

"Just answer it. What do you think of rats?"

"I loathe them."

"Which ones?"

She stared at him. "Are you saying . . . ?"

"Yes. Hitler loathes Jews as you loathe rats. All Jews."

"But we are not vermin!"

He held up a hand to stop a further outburst. "Hitler boasts he will establish a new German Reich that will last a thousand years, Dvoyra. That is what this war is all about. But whether he wins or loses, one thing is certain. He wants a Europe that is free of vermin. They have a word for it—*Judenrein,* cleansed of Jews."

"Is that why we have been brought here? They said we were to be resettled. Will we be sent somewhere else?"

"Perhaps," he said, as though his thoughts were far away. "That would be one solution."

"What other could there be?"

He looked at her, a flicker of pity in his eyes. "Dvoyra, I want to show you something."

He led her out of the office and up the stairs at the end of the corridor. They made their way up four flights of stairs to the top floor, and then up a metal ladder built into the wall. He pushed open a trapdoor in the ceiling and helped her out onto the roof of the old building.

From the top they could see out across the rooftops of the city to the surrounding countryside beyond. He pointed out the boundaries of the ghetto, tracing the continuous line of barbed wire and barricades zigzagging across the city.

"It's like a prison," she said with a slight shudder.

"It *is* a prison, Dvoyra." He took in a deep breath and let it out very slowly. "What you see down there is being repeated all over Poland. Within a year or two every Jew left alive in Poland will have been herded into one or another of them."

He was standing behind her, and she felt him place his hands on her shoulders. She was shivering, but not from the cold.

"And what then, David?" she whispered.

He did not answer.

Dvoyra spent the rest of the day trying to clean her filthy apartment. With a bucket of lukewarm water and the battered remnant of what had once been a yard broom, she scrubbed the walls and floor as best she could, sweeping pools of muddy filth out of the room and through the door into the corridor outside the apartment.

She traded half of her bar of soap for a tin of roach powder and sprinkled it liberally everywhere. She killed all the roaches in the icebox by setting fire to a piece of newspaper and putting it inside. All her efforts had only a limited effect on the appearance of the place, but it made her feel better and took her mind off the nightmare she had witnessed at dawn and the recurrent pangs of hunger gnawing at her stomach.

As darkness fell in the late afternoon she left the apartment to return the bucket and broom to the Self-Help kitchen. As she left her building, three trucks squealed to a halt in front of her, the same three trucks that had transported the work party. The SS squad emerged and shouted at the laborers to get out of the trucks. Dvoyra watched in horror as the Jews half-climbed, half-fell out of the vehicles. Their clothes were white with dust, their hair matted with dirt and sweat. Many of them looked dazed and confused; and one or two were openly weeping.

My God, thought Dvoyra, *they look like whipped animals.* She ran across to one of the laborers, a strongly built, older man, and asked him what had happened. He stared at her dumbly.

"Madness," he finally said. His eyes were glazed and red-rimmed. "Madness. Look at them. Look at those boys!"

One of the younger men was sitting on the curb, his head between his hands, utterly exhausted. All of them looked cold, drawn, defeated.

"They mean to work us to death," the big man said, grabbing her shoulder. "Do you understand? Without mercy! Like animals!"

"They made us break rocks all day," another muttered. "All day, hour after hour. They let us stop for fifteen minutes. They gave us some soup. Dishwater. 'That's all,' they said. 'Back to work. Time you Jews did some honest work.'"

The SS soldiers in the lead truck hollered as the convoy drove off. *"Arbeit macht frei, Juden!"* one jeered. "Don't forget, Yids! Work sets you free!" They roared with laughter as the trucks rumbled down the cobblestoned street.

One by one the laborers dispersed, some into the apartment building, others in the direction of the Self-Help kitchen. One day, Dvoyra thought, that was all it took. Their spirits have been completely broken. She sensed someone standing behind her and turned. It was David Berg, his face grim.

"Come," he said, "I need to talk to you." Somewhat mystified, Dvoyra followed him the two blocks to his office in silence. He led the way up the stairs to the second floor and unlocked the door. The building seemed even dingier at night. Sitting on his desk was a tray with a pot of soup, a bowl with a few pieces of cheese, and a loaf of freshly baked bread.

"The privileges of rank," he said sarcastically. "Please, join me."

She heard the plea in his voice and sensed he needed someone to talk to, but he did not speak as they ate the food. Finally she asked him if he had a family.

"My wife died about five years ago." He was silent for several moments. "Cancer. It was mercifully quick."

"You have no children?"

"We had a little boy. He died in a playground accident when he was four."

"I'm sorry."

He nodded and then took a deep breath, as if making a decision. "My parents were both killed in the Great War. I have a brother, Stephan, who went to America in 1929. The last time I heard from him, he was living in Chicago."

"I had a sister who emigrated. In 1911. Her family lives in Alexandria, near Washington."

They fell silent again, but this time there was a closeness in the silence that had not been there before.

"We should have gone too," he said with a wry grin. "It's better than here, that's for sure."

"Is this how it's' going to be from now on, David?"

"Maybe. I don't really know. Maybe it will get worse."

"How can it get worse? They kill our people if they will not work, and if they do work, they kill them that way."

"Before I met you in the street I went to see Botchermann," he said slowly. "To ask permission for a burial service for Daniel Dienavitch. He refused."

"Why?"

"Mass meetings of Jews are prohibited. Funerals are no exception. And anyway, according to Botchermann, Daniel is not entitled to the honor of a proper burial because he was a criminal."

"A criminal? What did he do?"

"He defied an order. That makes him an insurrectionist. The punishment for insurrection is death."

"But if they will not allow a burial service . . . ?"

"Botchermann says arrangements will be made to dispose of the body."

"He can't stop us from burying—" Dvoyra stopped in mid-sentence, and David Berg nodded.

"You're beginning to understand. He can. They can do anything they want."

"Is that why you were looking so grim when I met you in the street?"

"Partly. You see, I talked to Botchermann about the way our people had been mistreated. I offered him a deal."

"A deal with that animal?" Dvoyra said, her voice full of contempt. "I'd rather die!"

"Would you, Dvoyra?" he said softly.

She did not reply, but instead looked away in anger.

A small, sad smile touched his lips. "Listen to me. Have you any conception of what life would be like here in the ghetto with every man walking around in fear of instant conscription into a labor gang? It would be unbearable! No man would feel safe on the street. No, what I proposed to Botchermann might just save us from that. It might even mean that those who do work get some compensation for their labor."

"From whom?"

"From Jews. There are already over seven thousand Jews here in the ghetto. At the rate the Germans are resettling them, it could be well over eight thousand by the end of the year. Many of the Jews who have been brought here are relatively wealthy. Some are frail, others sick or not capable of strenuous labor. Others will simply not wish to work for the Germans."

"Are you suggesting that they be allowed to buy their way out of it?"

"Exactly."

"That's despicable."

"No, it's rational," he retorted. "Money is a rare and valuable resource. Those who have it can use it to avoid being conscripted. If they use the money to bribe a Nazi, no one benefits except the two parties involved. If, however, they pay an exemption fee to the Jewish Council, or *Judenrat* as they call it, the money can be used to pay those who actually work. If I were a teacher and this an economics class, I would call that the redistribution of wealth."

"This is not a schoolroom, David. This is the ghetto of Biala–Podlaska."

"The rules are the same," he said with a tired smile. "Out there or in here. Money makes the world go round. And make no mistake, Dvoyra, we will need money desperately."

"Do you think Botchermann will agree?"

He shrugged. "He said he would think about it."

"And what about our people?"

"If this was last night, I would say they would react badly. After what happened today, I suspect their reaction will be quite different."

She thought of the shivering, wretched men she had seen standing in the street just a while ago and thought again of those awful moments when Daniel Dienavich's body had jerked at the end of the rope.

She did not doubt that David Berg was right.

Chapter Twenty-nine

SS-Standartenfuhrer Hans Botchermann leaned back in his chair, folded his hands across his belly, and hooked his thumbs over the top of his black leather belt. The Nazi was warmly dressed in his black wool uniform with its silver insignia, the red armband bearing its black swastika and the collar patches the *sigrunen* of the SS, like twin strokes of lightning. He regarded David Berg impassively with his cold blue-gray eyes.

David was dressed in the same black suit he had been wearing when the Nazis first came for him ninety days ago. While the jacket and trousers had long since lost their shape and hung on him loosely, the wool fabric still helped insulate him from the cold winter air.

"I am trying to be helpful, Berg," Botchermann said. "But you are not making it easy for me with your excessive demands for more food."

"Excessive!" David said with a hollow laugh. "Our people are starving, Colonel!"

Botchermann leaned forward, the flesh of his thick neck bulging over his neat white shirt collar. "Look here." He jabbed a pudgy finger at the food request David Berg had laid on his desk. "You're getting nine thousand eggs next month. Nearly forty tons of potatoes, thirty-five tons of vegetables. And you talk starvation! There are plenty worse off than you!"

Herr Standartenfuhrer, there are nearly eight thousand people in the ghetto. You are allocating barely one egg per month to each of them, and ten pounds of potatoes. Five ounces a day! Four and a half ounces of vegetables!"

"I know exactly what you are receiving. You Jews will just have to plan more carefully. There is nothing I can do. I have my orders, and I must carry them out."

"Please, Colonel, listen to me. We have less than half an ounce of milk per person per day. There are children, babies—"

"Enough of this!" Botchermann snapped, banging his hand flat on the desk. "You can't expect us to provide enough food for you Jews to sit down to a feast three times a day! We have good Germans to feed. Be thankful we're looking after you as well as we are!"

David knew Botchermann was toying with him. He suspected, correctly, that Hans Botchermann enjoyed these sessions and considered David's periodic pleas to be proof that the rations were being properly administered.

"You want me to be thankful when our people have frostbite because they don't have enough coal to keep warm?"

"I see." Botchermann leaned back. "Now it's coal, eh? Don't you Jews ever stop whining?"

"I'm not whining, Colonel." Anger flashed in David's eyes. "We receive only five pounds of coal per day for each household, if and when it arrives. Our water pipes are frozen. The sewage drains too. People are freezing in their own homes. It's minus fifteen degrees out there!"

"There is no additional coal available," Botchermann said with finality. "Even we are rationed."

"But—"

"Hear me, Berg," Botchermann said loudly. "You are being given food. It may not be as much as you would like, but that is of no importance to me. You are being given what we have decided can be spared."

"Yes," David said, unable to conceal his anger any longer. "Spoiled vegetables, tainted meat, flour with weevils in it. Half of what you allocate to us is unusable!"

"Then you will have to learn to be inventive!" Botchermann said sharply. "Save your milk for the children. Put one day aside for a communal casserole by sharing what you have with your neighbors. Burn coal only when absolutely necessary. You'll manage!"

"There's snow a foot deep out there!" David shouted, pointing at the snow-covered roofs outside the window of Botchermann's warm office.

"Tell your people to put more clothes on!" Botchermann impatiently swept the food request aside. "Now, let us get to why I sent for you."

David drew in a deep breath, resigned to the futility of arguing with Botchermann, but vowing he would continue to do so. He regarded the man opposite him as if seeing him for the first time.

"That insurrectionist." Botchermann snapped his fingers to prompt his memory. "What was his name?"

"You mean the gifted young violinist your men murdered two months ago, Colonel? His name was Daniel Dienavitch."

"I mean the insurrectionist, Berg," Botchermann said icily. "I am not interested in whatever gifts you Jews claim you have. This Dienavitch acted contrary to the maintenance of good order and delivered himself up to summary justice."

"You call that justice? To hang a twenty-year-old boy from the back of a tow truck?"

Botchermann looked at David for a long moment, as if he were considering whether to talk to him or strike him in the face. David grew more tense, but Botchermann smiled coldly and shook his head.

"Let me tell you something about justice, Berg. When the Fuhrer proclaimed himself the supreme judge, there were fifteen thousand judges in Germany. Did they rise up as one man and say, 'No!'? There weren't more than a thousand SS then in the whole of Germany, remember. They could have crushed us. But you know what they did? Nothing! It was those spineless, whey-faced guardians of the law, those thousands of judges, who allowed us to disregard it. They made *us* the legal system of the Reich. *This* is justice wherever we go, Berg." He pointed to the swastika on his armband. "That is the new justice. What the Fuhrer says is right. What is good for the Reich is justice, Berg. That's why the insurrectionist's execution was just. Remember that. What is good for the Reich is justice."

His voice had risen as he spoke, his eyes flashing with pride and self-certainty. His face was flushed, the veins on his neck standing out like cords. The light of fanaticism illuminated his staring eyes. Then, as if he had turned off a switch, it went out and he blinked.

David understood the implications of Botchermann's words. To the Nazis there was no question of legality or accountability with respect to their treatment of the Jews. If their actions or policies were deemed to be good for the Reich, they were deemed to also be legal.

"So," Botchermann went on, exhaling noisily, "Dienavitch. His death raises an important issue."

"What is that, Colonel?"

"From time to time there may be other . . . deaths in the ghetto."

"Yes?" David did not miss the momentary hesitation. *Executions, you mean,* he thought.

"Funerals, all mass meetings, are forbidden on pain of death. However, we must have a system. Therefore I want a six-man burial unit organized, to be responsible for collecting the body of any Jew on the day the death occurs. You will see to it that they take the bodies to the Jewish cemetery in Biala-Podlaska for burial."

"You'll provide transportation to the cemetery?"

"Transportation?"

"Yes, for the deceased, for the family."

"Are you crazy? You expect us to provide transportation? There's a war going on, you fool!"

"What does the colonel suggest? How does the colonel expect the bodies to get to the cemetery?"

"Your people can construct wagons of some kind. They can push them to the cemetery."

"Push them?"

"Yes. You Jews are used to pushcarts, aren't you?"

"But that's barbaric! You can't—"

Botchermann jumped to his feet and banged his fist on the desk. "Can't?" he roared. *"Can't? I can do whatever I want. I will* do whatever I want! And you will obey me! Do you hear me, Jew? You will obey!"

David stared at the Nazi, but did not reply right away. He knew Botchermann could snap his fingers and have him dragged out of the office and shot like a dog in the street.

"I'll look into it, Colonel," he said, managing to control his shock and anger. "The question of lumber—"

"Out!" Botchermann yelled, waving at the door. "Out, out, out!"

David hurried across the square toward the ghetto. The tiny park was bordered on all four sides by empty shops, many of which had been owned by Jews. They were mostly boarded up now, except for those the Nazis had converted into offices for their own use. As he walked away from Botchermann's office, David pondered the options available to the Jews of Biala-Podlaska. They were precious few, he knew. Resistance was out of the question. They had no weapons and consequently no power. Anything the Germans wanted they could simply confiscate. All he could do was to try to make sure that his people's resources were carefully managed, and that the hopelessness of their situation would not crush their spirits entirely.

The SS-Schütze guarding the entrance to the ghetto checked David's papers carefully, then swung back the barrier to let him pass.

"In you go, you Zhid bastard." He grinned at another guard.

As David crossed the road, he noticed a young woman pacing back and forth on the other side of the street in front of the food distribution center. Since there had been no food to distribute for two days, the center was closed. He watched her for several moments and then realized she was cradling a baby in her arms. *Don't let it be,* David said to himself as he started across the snow-covered street.

"Madam, I'm David Berg." He placed his hand on her arm. She stared at him blankly.

"You shouldn't be walking the streets with a baby in weather like this. Come, I'll walk back with you to where you live."

"The baby needs milk," the woman said tonelessly.

"Then I'll take you to the Self-Help kitchen. They'll give you milk there."

She continued to stare at him dumbly, and he saw that her skin was flushed, her empty eyes glazed.

"Are you sick?"

"I'm dead," she whispered in a daze.

"No, no. Don't say that. You are alive. What can I do for you?"

"The baby needs milk," she repeated mechanically. David reached down and lifted the blanket so he could see the child.

"My God!" he whispered as he looked at the baby. Its skin was mottled and shiny, its tiny lips parched and parted in a feeble cry that was barely audible. "How long is it since your baby was fed?"

"I don't know," the woman said absently. "Two days? Three?"

"Have you eaten anything?"

"No. I was given bread yesterday, but someone grabbed it from me on the street and ran away."

"Then come with me." David took the child from her arms and hurried toward the Jewish clinic, the woman following. Another day without food and this child would be dead, he knew, cargo for Botchermann's pushcarts.

"The baby is starving and dehydrated," the nurse explained. "Leave her here for a day or two. I think she will be all right, but if you'd delayed any longer . . ." She shook her head.

"Come, let's have a look at you," the nurse said as she led the mother behind a curtain that separated the reception room from the treatment area.

David sat down and covered his face with his hands. It had actually begun to happen—the starvation that would lead to the destruction of an entire people.

He walked back to his office and slumped into his chair. He could not even raise a smile for Dvoyra, who had been waiting for him. They'd become close friends since the evening when they shared their family histories.

"What did he say?" she asked.

"That bastard!" he muttered. He threw the food request onto his desk, angrily shaking his head.

Dvoyra pushed a cup of tea in front of him. There was no point in asking any more questions, she thought. The two words he had spoken said it all.

After a while David shook his head once more, as if to throw off the dark thoughts plaguing him, and sipped the tea.

"Was it bad, David?"

"It was bad. Botchermann will do nothing for us. Correction—there is one thing he is going to do for certain. He is going to turn the ghetto into a living hell for all of us!"

She picked up the food request and looked down the long list of supplies approved for delivery in January. "It looks like a lot."

He shook his head. "Get a piece of paper, Dvoyra. Multiply five tons by two thousand two hundred and forty, and then again by sixteen. No, don't bother, I'll tell you—the answer is one hundred seventy-nine thousand two hundred ounces. Now, divide that by thirty-one, and then again by eight thousand, and you'll find that the meat ration per day, for every person in the ghetto, is slightly less than three quarters of an ounce. Add to that five ounces of potatoes, four of vegetables, and a sip of milk—less than a pint a week. No fats, no fruit. That's if the system works. When it breaks down—and it will, Dvoyra—there will be days, perhaps three or four in a row, when there is no food at all. Some people will hoard. Others will pay extra to get more. There will be black marketeering, and maybe worse."

Dvoyra said nothing as she thought of the smuggling in Vilna so many years ago. "My God," she had screamed at Berl. "What is happening to our people?"

"Isn't there anything you can do, David?" she whispered. "Nothing at all?"

"Dvoyra, the more miserable we are, the more pleased the Nazis are. Botchermann gauges his success by the misery in the streets."

"Doesn't he realize people are starving? Is that what he wants—dead people in the streets?"

David started to tell her about Botchermann's order to organize burial details, to build pushcarts for the dead, but the thought sickened him.

Dvoyra looked at David and understood the meaning of his silence. "We're going to die here, aren't we?" she asked quietly.

He looked away and closed his eyes tightly, and Dvoyra watched as he fought to control the frustration that ate at him. She rose and walked over to him. Leaning down, she softly kissed his closed eyes. It had been meant as a gesture of consolation, but as her lips touched his flesh, Dvoyra, for the first time since Berl's death, sensed the rekindling of desire. For an instant Berl's face emerged from the shadows of her mind, more a farewell than a threatening intrusion, and at that moment of Dvoyra's final passage into the harsh reality of the present, she felt her fingers dig into David's shoulders. He reached up blindly and took her in his arms and without opening his eyes, buried his face in her bosom.

"I can't fight them, Dvoyra. I have nothing to fight them with."

"You have, David." Dvoyra rocked him gently in her arms. "You have strength. And we're going to need it now more than ever."

She felt his grip tighten around her waist. Dvoyra pulled back just enough to look into his eyes. She took his face into her hands and brought her lips down to his, her touch searing his senses. David reached up and, taking her by her arms, pulled Dvoyra down until she was on her knees in front of him. They gazed at one another for a moment, overwhelmed by the raw emotion that was consuming them both. Her eyes were soft and damp and spoke silently of the admiration and after embracing for a moment, desire she felt for him. Then he pulled her into his arms, and they undressed hurriedly, their kisses deep and urgent. There was a desperation to their lovemaking that first time. Surrounded by death and suffering, they lost themselves in a frenzied passion they could not control.

As winter laid its iron hand on the Jewish ghetto, David Berg turned for help to an old acquaintance. Years earlier he had worked as a liaison between the Jewish and Catholic communities in Biala-Podlaska. His contact was a young priest named Stanislaw Kollonawicz, who nicknamed David his "stray parishioner." He decided to write to the priest.

The letter, requesting an urgent appointment, was forwarded through a Catholic intermediary. David wondered if Father Kollonawicz would remember him. The last time they had met was in 1936, shortly after an anti-Jewish pastoral letter, written by Cardinal Hlond, the Primate of Poland, had been read from pulpits all over the country. David remembered that Kollonawicz had been especially friendly, as if to prove that not all Catholics subscribed to such anti-Semitic feelings. Well, it didn't matter whether the priest remembered him or not, David thought. He was willing to try anything.

Father Kollonawicz replied immediately. His letter was

unusually formal and perfunctory, suggesting that David present himself at the Catholic church in Biala-Podlaska to discuss Jewish support of Catholic charities. David knew its purpose was to enable him to leave the ghetto. He presented himself at Botchermann's office and was given the necessary exit permit, good until curfew. He was also reminded that if he did not return, ten Jews would be immediately executed for his transgression. David did not doubt for a minute that Botchermann would act on his threat.

He hurried through the snow-covered streets to the Catholic church in the center of the old town. When he arrived, he was ushered into a small vestry in the basement. Father Kollonawicz sat at a large, heavy oak table in the center of the room.

David was shocked by the priest's appearance. Although younger than David, he now looked ten years his senior.

He stood as David approached and embraced him. "How are you?"

David shook his head and spoke at once of his concerns. "You know what is happening to our people."

Father Kollonawicz sighed and sat down at the table, gesturing for David to take a chair. "There is nothing we can do, David. Nothing. The Germans will not tolerate interference from the Church. Our parishioners are terrified of them. Even if they understood what the Nazis are doing to your people, the teachings of our Church have done little to engender sympathy for the Jews."

"Father, I—"

"Let me finish, David. There aren't many people I can speak openly to these days. I am in disfavor here. I am no longer allowed to hear confessions or offer communion."

"But why?"

"Because what I am saying to you, I have said to others. I believe, and have said publicly, that our relationship with Christ demands that we, too, wear the Star of David on our clothing, and even on our vestments."

"Very brave, Father," David said softly. "But very foolish."

"You think so? Tell me, where do you think the idea of making Jews wear special identification came from?"

"The Nazis, of course."

"No, David. The idea came from the Church Council of Gnessen, the oldest diocese in Poland. Originally canonical law required Jews to wear specially shaped hats, but that was considered insufficient. So in 1279 it was decreed that all Jews must sew a red cloth on the left side of their garments."

"Father, that's ancient history. What's the point?"

Father Kollonawicz leaned forward. "What's the point? I'll tell you what the point is. Almost all the anti-Jewish laws that the Germans have passed during the last five years have their models in canonical law. All I am trying to say to you, David, is that what we are witnessing today is the result of a climate that has been developing for centuries. And if the Church— my Church—did not actively foster that climate, it certainly did very little to prevent it."

He looked up at a large bronze crucifix hanging on the wall of the vestry.

"I love my Church, David, and I love my Christ. But I believe the Church has failed."

"If you believe that," David said urgently, "then do something about it. Help me, Stanislaw!"

Father Kollonawicz looked up.

"What can I do?" he asked doubtfully.

"We need food," David said. "At least thirty thousand quarts of milk a month—a cup of milk per person per day. We need meat, tons of it. Flour. Clothing. Coal—fifteen hundred tons a month, for the rest of the winter."

The priest shook his head, his eyes stricken. "Impossible!" he whispered. "There is nowhere I, or anyone else, could get such quantities. We are turning away our own parishioners, David. The Germans confiscate everything. It's all sent west, to Germany. They give us hardly enough to keep body and soul together. Can't you ask the authorities—"

"The authorities!" David laughed mirthlessly. "You think the Germans would lift a finger to help a Jew? I believe they are actually manufacturing the shortages so that more of our men will sign on for their labor camps, hoping there'll be more food available there."

Father Kollonawicz's eyes widened. "What do you know about these labor camps?" he whispered.

"I heard the Germans talking about using Jewish labor to build an enormous network of antitank ditches in a place they call the Bug-San Gap. It's in the south somewhere, between the Bug and San Rivers. They told me they will be recruiting soon for laborers to work at camps near the Russian frontier. Have you heard anything?"

"It's never specific. Just that something is going on and no one will talk about what it is. I asked one of my parishioners, a man who had been working in the south, at a place called Belzec. I said, 'What are they building there?' And you know what he replied?"

"Tell me."

"He said, 'Hell, Father. They are building Hell.'"

The two men stared at each other for several moments.

"What do you think is going on?" David asked quietly. "The area between the Bug and San is mostly marsh and forest, and Belzec is little more than a railway stop. What could they possibly be building?"

"I don't know. I don't know if I want to know either."

"I must go," David said with a sigh. Father Kollonawicz held out his arms, and they embraced each other.

"Go with God, my son," the priest said.

"You'll try to help us, Stanislaw?" David pleaded. "My people are desperate."

"I'll try. I'll beg the authorities for additional supplies for the ghetto. I'll tell them their treatment of the Jews is having a bad effect on the attitudes of our parishioners toward the Germans. I don't know if it will do any good, David, but I'll try. I'll try."

Two weeks after David's visit word spread through the ghetto that Father Stanislaw Kollonawicz had been killed by a German staff car while returning to the church following a meeting with Botchermann. "A most unfortunate accident," the Nazi wrote in a note to the cardinal.

Chapter Thirty

Conditions in the ghetto deteriorated daily. Though the cooperatives that David had organized did help to even out the distribution of food and fuel, the death rate was increasing at an alarming rate. The sight of old men and women collapsing in the street from malnutrition and exposure became commonplace. With no ambulance service, and no room in the already overcrowded apartments for them to be taken to, they were often left where they fell, their bodies covered with old newspapers. Each day the burial units made their rounds, picking up the dead from the streets. Locked in the bitter grip of winter, the starving, demoralized Jews of Biala-Podlaska waited and hoped for an early spring.

David had asked Dvoyra to organize a day school for the children in the ghetto. He believed the children needed some day-to-day structure, and a ghetto school, no matter how primitive, would improve the morale of both children and parents. The school was allocated eight empty rooms in the basement of an abandoned building. By providing one day of instruction to every child in one of the eight makeshift classrooms, Dvoyra reasoned that approximately twelve hundred children would, each week, be able to enjoy some classroom experience. Desks and chairs were spirited into the eight rooms from a nearby school, which, while deserted, was off limits to the Jews. Within a week of the time David had asked her to take on the school project, Dvoyra had the Biala-Podlaska Jewish School in full operation.

Word of the project spread rapidly through the ghetto, and youngsters and volunteer instructors alike soon crowded into the basement of the abandoned building. The school had been in operation for about three weeks, and, as was becoming part of her daily routine, Dvoyra hurried to David's office to meet him before dinner.

At dusk that night David Berg watched Dvoyra as she sat staring at the pathetic little fire that burned in the old coal stove in the corner of his office. She seemed mesmerized by the dancing flames and oblivious to his presence. Her dark brown eyes relected the light of the fire, and as he watched her, David thought she was the most beautiful woman he had ever known. For a long while he was silent, not wishing to break the spell of the moment.

He was pleased she came to the office most days now. Her presence gave him a sense of security and permanence he badly needed.

"Dvoyra?" he said softly.

Her eyes answered but she did not speak. His body tingled with desire as her soft gaze conveyed the emotion that neither of them had spoken of.

"I love you, Dvoyra."

She turned her eyes to the fire, still not answering. He moved from his desk to where she sat and knelt on one knee in front of her. Slowly he reached out and softly touched her chin with the tips of his fingers, gently turning her face to his so that she was once again looking into his eyes.

"Did you hear what I said?"

"Yes," she answered finally, her voice so low that he hardly heard the word.

He saw tears in her eyes and smiled. "It's all right, Dvoyra. It's all right."

She shook her head, the tears coming now without restraint.

"You don't . . . feel the same way?"

"David, how can I tell you what you want to hear?" she whispered. "How can we talk of love when there are people dying in the streets?"

"Dvoyra." He took her by the shoulders. "What is out there is our world, as it exists for us, whether we like it or not. But it hasn't destroyed my ability to feel love, Dvoyra. And it mustn't destroy yours!"

"David, listen to me. I want to tell you something that happened to me. On my way here I passed one of the old apartment buildings and saw two children sitting on the stoop in front of the entrance. They stared at me without expression. I stopped and felt a chill run through my body, and my knees started shaking. Yet still they just stared.

"There was no hint of childhood on their faces, David," Dvoyra whispered. "Just a profound sadness. Perhaps even disgust, I don't know. I went over to them. I knelt down so my face was level with theirs. And I said, 'Hello, my name is Dvoyra Hoffman, what's yours?' They stared at me. The little girl gnawed at a piece of stale bread. Their expressions did not change. I looked at her hand, David. Such a little hand. Tiny fingers . . . tiny . . . fingernails . . . such tiny . . ." She broke off, unable to control her tears.

"Dvoyra, Dvoyra," David said gently. "It's not your fault. You've got to face it and be strong. That's how things are now."

"Yes, yes, I know." She dashed away the tears with her hand. "I understand, David. And so must you."

"Dvoyra, listen to me. Our ability to feel compassion, as you did with those children, and our ability to love, as I love you, those are the only things they can't take away from us. If you let them stop you from loving, Dvoyra, the Nazis have won the most important victory of all. Don't let them, Dvoyra! Don't be afraid to feel love!"

"I am. I'm afraid to love anyone anymore, in case they die."

"Dvoyra, that's all the more reason to love." He took her into his arms.

"I wish we had more time, David. More time for us to know each other better."

"We know all we need to know." He stroked her hair, sadly admitting to himself that they were, in fact, running out of time.

"I do love you, David Berg," she whispered as he embraced her.

"And I you, Dvoyra," he murmured into her hair.

The intruding sound of a passing police siren pierced the cold evening air as Dvoyra's dress slid from her shoulders.

Dvoyra longed for the winter to end, but with spring came devastating news from the war front. The Third Reich seemed to be invincible. On April ninth Denmark fell and Norway was invaded. On May tenth Germany invaded the Low Countries. Word spread that the British had been driven right out of the European continent, and that it was only a matter of time before the Nazis took France and Norway surrendered.

The faint hope that free Europe, enraged by what had happened in Poland, would rise up and rescue the enslaved peoples of Eastern Europe evaporated like morning mist. Now the Jews knew they were truly alone. And what was worse, the Nazis knew it too.

The German demand for Jewish labor increased as they stepped up their public works activities such as road and bridge repair. David Berg's voluntary labor registry worked reasonably well. Notices to report for work were delivered to Jewish volunteers between the ages of eighteen and fifty-five. Whenever possible, David rotated the names on the lists so that no one would have to work more than seven days without a day of rest.

He also established a work-exemption fee of fifty zloty, excusing an individual from one day's work. Each paid exemption made it possible for him to pay ten workers five zloty for a day's work. The Nazis were satisfied with the system. The Jews reported for duty on time, worked hard all day, rarely complained, and provided free labor.

Though the system was working well, David was not

surprised when he was summoned to Botchermann's office. He predicted that, as usual, the Nazi officer would complain groundlessly about the quality of the workers as a prelude to further demands for Jewish labor.

The walk from the ghetto to Botchermann's office took about twenty minutes and provided perverse but welcome relief from the dismal cityscape of the ghetto. The sky was clear and the breezy warmth of the sun was soothing and welcome. It was the kind of day that stirred memories of other springs, happier times, thought David. Once spring had been a time for young people, a time for falling in love, a time for celebration. Now, spring was a time to thank God you had lived through the winter.

An SS guard led him into Botchermann's office. Botchermann, seated behind a massive wooden desk, dismissed the guard and gestured for David to sit.

"You sent for me?" David asked.

Botchermann's eyes narrowed as he regarded David coldly. "I want two hundred men, a week from today, for a project of great importance to the Reich!" he snapped. "See to it!"

"Very well, Colonel." David met Botchermann's glare with a boldness that he knew infuriated the Nazi even more. "What time are they to be ready each morning, and where do you want them to assemble?"

"In front of your office, six A.M. And Berg—heads of families only."

David frowned. Botchermann had never asked that laborers be heads of families before.

"Two hundred men, one week from today, in front of my office at six A.M. Very good, Colonel. May I ask when they will return?"

Botchermann lifted his head slightly, his cold eyes full of malice. "Perhaps at the end of October," he said with a cruel smile. "If, and I say *if*, we have no further use for them when the project is completed."

David stared at Botchermann incredulously. "You're asking me to recruit two hundred men, heads of families, to let you take them away from their wives and children, with no certainty that they will even be back at the end of October?"

"No, Berg, I'm not asking you," Botchermann said, raising his voice. "I'm telling you!"

"But, Colonel, I don't understand. Why can't we supply the men you need on a daily basis, the way we have been doing up to now?"

Botchermann stared at him for a moment, tapping a pen against his desk, as if deciding whether or not to explain.

"I am not at liberty to discuss the work they will be doing," he said at last. "But I can tell you this—it's not patching holes in the roads. This much I will tell you, but no more: They will be relocated at a camp near Belzec to complete the work."

David was stunned. He heard the voice of Father Kollonawicz repeating what the parishioner had told him. *Hell, Father. They are building Hell.*

"One more question, Colonel, please! Why are you taking only heads of families?"

"It is our belief that such men will have a . . . shall we say, better attitude," Botchermann said sarcastically, "knowing we are taking care of their families while they are working at the camp."

"You mean you are going to hold their families hostage to keep them in line!"

"Something like that."

David thought for a moment. "I want to see the camp. I want to go to Belzec."

"Out of the question!" Botchermann said impatiently. "This is *Geheime Reichssache*. Do you know what that means?"

"Something very secret. But Colonel, listen to me. If I can tell the men and their families that I've seen the camp, won't that allay their fears?"

Botchermann smiled cunningly, and too late David saw the pit into which he had stumbled.

"Of course," Botchermann said slyly. "You can tell them what a nice, healthy place it is. Yes, a very good idea, Berg. You will accompany me to Belzec tomorrow." He leaned back in his chair and smiled expansively. "I didn't expect you to be this helpful, Berg. Maybe I've misjudged you."

"I don't think so, Colonel," David said stiffly. "On second thought I would prefer not to go to Belzec."

"You'll go, Jew. And when you come back, you'll tell your people what I tell you to tell them!"

David shook his head. "I won't lie. I won't tell them something that isn't true."

"Yes, you will, Jew," Botcherman said, taunting him now. "You'll tell them what a wonderful place Belzec is. And if you don't, and we don't get our two hundred workers, we'll come and take four hundred. Four hundred and one, actually. Because we'll take that Jewess of yours too!"

David's hands clenched into fists, and he fought the urge to lunge at his tormentor.

"Touch me, Berg, and your Dvoyra is dead!" Botchermann hissed.

David froze, pulling in a deep breath and forcing himself to open his clenched hands.

Botchermann smiled triumphantly. "Oh, yes, Berg, we know all about your Jewess. We make it a point to know such things. All I have to do is snap my fingers. That's all, Jew. One snap of the fingers. Remember that!"

David nodded dumbly. Hatred seethed inside him. He had never in his whole life felt anything like the anger that he felt now. And there was nothing he could do about it.

"So!" Botchermann said. "Tomorrow we will go to Belzec! Be here at ten. Wear your best suit, eh?"

The black Mercedes staff car made good time on the country roads between Biala-Podlaska and Lublin, arriving at the old city in just over an hour. No one spoke the whole way, and David concentrated on seeing as much as he could through the windows of the car.

It was a beautiful spring day. After the prison conditions of the ghetto, it was strange to see open countryside, people working in the fields, fruit trees in blossom. The world went on, David thought. The only difference was that you were no longer part of it.

It saddened him to see Lublin—so long a center of Polish economic and cultural life—festooned with swastika banners and crowded with German troops. On the Crakowskie Przedmiescie, the city's principal thoroughfare, military-gray BMW motorcycles with blunt-nosed sidecars buzzed in and out of the traffic. Lines of army trucks were parked in the side streets. They passed the famous Crakow Gate and rumbled down the cobbled slope of Grodska Street past the forbidding walls of the old Jagello castle. Botchermann remarked to a staff member that it was being converted back into a prison, which it had been before the Great War.

They threaded their way through the southeastern outskirts of the city and into the little town of Majdynak. To David's surprise it too was crowded with German soldiers. He asked one of Botchermann's aides if a new army installation was being developed in the area. The German stared ahead in stony silence.

Outside Majdynak the driver picked up speed, sounding his horn to overtake the occasional army truck or plodding farm cart. The bright red fender flags and blaring horn ensured their swift passage through crossings and traffic lights as they sped through Krasnystow, with its three-hundred-year-old baroque Jesuit monastery, and on to Zamosc.

The city held a special place in the hearts of all Poles; it had been here, in 1920, that the Russian armies were thrown back, saving Poland from utter defeat in the war between the two countries.

As the Mercedes passed the great Zamosc library, a convoy of Nazi trucks lumbered past in the opposite direction, several of the vehicles towing field guns. Again David wondered what reason there could be for such a concentration of troops so far from the real war, which was going on in the West.

Once outside Zamosc the big car ate up the miles, covering the distance between Zamosc and Tomaszow-Lubelski in about half an hour. In another fifteen minutes they were at Belzec.

David noticed even more troops here than in the other cities they had passed through. There were large numbers of SS here, many of them wearing the skull-and-crossbones insignia the Nazis called *Totenkopf*.

It was almost two by the time they arrived at the campsite. Botchermann got out and stretched, pushing his hands into the small of his back and bending backward. Then he pulled his uniform jacket into place, settled his cap firmly on his head, and turned to face David.

"Well," he said. "This is it."

The camp was smaller than David had expected, consisting of a few shoddy hutlike barracks buildings, and a ten-foot-high barbed-wire fence around the perimeter, with guard towers at about fifty-yard intervals. Even empty, an air of menace seemed to hang over the camp. The presence of power-line construction equipment told David that the fences were to be electrified. The ground inside the perimeter was trampled and devoid of grass. In rainy weather, he thought, it would turn to mud.

Botchermann looked at David expectantly. *As if he wishes me to approve,* David thought, amazed.

"Well?" Botchermann said.

"It's not very big. How many men is it supposed to hold?"

"I've no idea," Botchermann said, but from his tone David suspected that he knew but had no intention of telling.

They walked across to the barracks and went inside. The place still smelled of sawdust and cut timber. The huts were long and rectangular, with no furniture other than a row of bunks, three tiers high, down each side of the room. There were three small windows on each side, each covered with bars, and a single exposed toilet.

As they exited, David looked up at the guard towers.

"Come!" Botchermann snapped, leading the way at a rapid pace, as if he were anxious to be about other business. He pointed out where the SS barracks would be built, bathhouses, machinery sheds, and so on.

"Have you seen enough?" he asked abruptly.

"Yes, more than enough." David recalled his meeting with Father Kollonawicz. *Hell, Father. They are building Hell.*

They reboarded the Mercedes and soon they were bumping down the narrow road, away from the camp. As they sped through Belzec, David noticed surveyors working on the site adjacent to the railroad station, which was little more than a signal box and two platforms. Alongside these, it looked as if roads were being crudely staked out. What really caught David's attention, however, was the presence on the platform of an SS-Sturmbannfuhrer overseeing the work of the survey team.

"It looks as if they plan to enlarge the station considerably," David ventured. "Are they expecting heavy traffic in this area?"

"My job is to supply two hundred men for the labor camp," Botchermann said tonelessly. "Nothing else that is going on here concerns me. Or you either."

Not another word was spoken on the journey back to Biala-Podlaska.

That night David sat in his office looking over a register of all the families living in the ghetto, sifting through page after page of names. Some of them were unfamiliar to him, but many were names with which he could associate faces.

To his horror he found himself mentally crossing off certain names. He could not bring himself to select men he knew for the labor gang. He was deliberately picking strangers.

"My God!" he said aloud. His hands began to tremble. The names on the pages blurred before his eyes. Every selection he made would devastate a family. He could not even be sure the men would ever come back. He saw again in his mind's eye the fences and watchtowers of Belzec and shivered.

David sat for a long time with his eyes closed, rubbing his forehead with his fingertips, trying to come up with some alternatives. Only Dvoyra knew of his journey to Belzec. Despite Botchermann's orders, he did not yet know if he could tell others. If he said nothing, there would be no questions. And right now he was not sure he could answer questions honestly.

What, then? Tell the men to refuse to go?

The Nazis would love that. They would hang the resisters, as they had hung Daniel Dienavitch, or shoot them on the spot. Then they would double the number of men specified, dragging them from their homes and killing them if they put up a fight. Would they harm Dvoyra? What could he do?

Ask for volunteers?

If he did that, he would have to report on his trip to the camp. Botchermann would permit nothing but an announcement that there was nothing to fear at Belzec, and David had no intention of lying.

That left only one course. The selection of the two hundred men would have to be done by lottery. He would write down all the names of those eligible on separate pieces of paper, and then draw them from a box. David sighed, thinking of the ancient story of Passover, which the ghetto Jews had only recently observed. *And which doors will the Angel of Death pass over now?* he wondered.

He began, carefully folding and tearing sheets of paper into small squares. When he had prepared two thousand such slips, he wrote on each the name and address of the head of one ghetto family. He then folded the makeshift ballot and dropped it into a box that had once been used to store old prayer books. He worked steadily, stopping only to sip some lukewarm tea. When he finished, he looked at the clock on the wall. It was five A.M.—he had been working for ten hours.

Emotionally and physically exhausted, David fell onto the battered old sofa in his office and went to sleep almost instantly. He dreamed it was snowing, but the snowflakes were ballots. On each fluttering piece of paper was the face of a man. He saw children running to catch their fathers, and women their husbands. He ran out into the snow, but when he got outside, it disappeared. The street was empty except for two raggedly dressed children, a small boy and girl, their dark eyes huge. They did not speak, but the little girl lifted her hand and pointed at him. David tried to tell her that she did not understand, but he could not speak. The two children came toward him, fingers accusing. David ran away from them, weeping.

At nine o'clock that morning Dvoyra let herself into David's office and found him sleeping on the couch. She carefully removed his shoes and was about to cover him with her coat when she heard him moan, as if he had been dreaming. She leaned down and kissed him, letting him sleep for two more hours.

David opened his eyes slowly, as if unsure of his surroundings. Then he saw Dvoyra standing by the window, smiling at him, and thought she looked like an angel. She went to him and touched his cheek with her fingertips.

"I love you, David," she whispered.

He closed his eyes and sighed, thinking how much he had wanted to hear her say those words, how he had begged her not to let the misery that surrounded them prevent her from loving. But loving him had put Dvoyra in mortal danger, he thought. If he ever defied Botchermann, Dvoyra would suffer. *All I have to do is snap my fingers.* David put his arms around Dvoyra and held her close, drawing strength from her nearness and warmth.

"What's wrong?" she asked, her cheek against his.

He sat up and released her. "Nothing's wrong," he said, but as his eyes strayed to the coardboard box filled with names, a shiver ran through his body.

"You were moaning. In your sleep."

"Just a dream."

"Was it the camp? Belzec?"

"That's part of it. It's everything. That place, Botchermann. He's ordered me to select two hundred men to go to Belzec."

"Two hundred?"

"Two hundred, all of them to be heads of families. And if I don't, he will take twice that many. And some of the women too." Once more he thought of the grave danger Dvoyra herself was in.

"How will you select them?"

He gestured to the cardboard box on the floor beside his desk. Dvoyra frowned, then went to the box and lifted the lid. Slowly she reached into the box and took out one of the folded pieces of paper, opening it slowly. She picked up another, then another, opening and reading them.

"A lottery?" she whispered.

"It's the only thing I can think of. The only fair way."

"But David, some of these are men with large families! Some of them have sick wives or children, or elderly parents. You can't do this. The Germans can't ask you to do it!"

"They didn't ask me," he said bitterly. "They don't ask. They just said to have the men ready. Or else."

Dvoyra was silent for a long time, staring intently at the folded ballots before she put them back into the box and closed it.

"Will you tell the men you went to Belzec?"

"I'll say I've been there, and that it's impossible to tell what conditions will be like, because no one knows how many men will be sent there. I'll tell them the Nazis say they will be there for six months."

"The Nazis say!" she said with a hollow laugh. "Do you think these men will be back in six months?"

"No."

"What, then? Nine months, a year? Never?"

"Maybe never, Dvoyra."

"Then why are you doing this?"

"I have no choice. I told you, if I don't produce the two hundred men, Botchermann will take twice that many. Not to mention the reprisals."

"You know what will happen, don't you, David?" Dvoyra said quietly. "Everyone in the ghetto will hate you. The families of those men you select will hold you responsible for all their misery. They will die cursing you."

"I know," he said quietly. "But I have no choice."

"And what will you do next time, when they want another two hundred? Or five hundred? And what will you do the time after that?"

David put his head in his hands, unable to answer. Everything she said was true. Those who went to Belzec would curse his name to their dying day, and those who did not would loathe and fear him, lest they be the next ones he chose.

"David, answer me. Would you sacrifice half of this community in order to save the other half?"

He lifted his head from his hands and stared at her. She stared back, both of them realizing at the same moment that she had stumbled on the ultimate issue confronting the Jews of Biala-Podlaska.

"Why are you asking me these questions, Dvoyra? They are questions which have no answer."

"David, my dear, dear David." Dvoyra put her arms around him, rocking him against her bosom as if he were a child. "Listen to me, my darling. You must decide what you are going to do. Not for the people of this ghetto, but for you, for us. There are ghettos like ours all over Poland. They are all facing the same kind of decisions—you told me yourself that the Nazis are taking Jews from many communities for Belzec. And God knows how many labor camps like Belzec there are. If we just hand our people over to them in order to save the others, we will begin a process that cannot be reversed. Two hundred today, two hundred next week. Half of those remaining and then half of those, and so on until there is no one left!"

"What shall I do, Dvoyra? What shall I do?"

"Tell the truth. Tell them that the men may never return, that you are trying to protect nearly eight thousand of our people by giving the Nazis two hundred. Tell them that you cannot guarantee there will not be more demands. Tell them you know there will be terrible reprisals if we resist. Tell them it is their decision, David, not yours. Because it is. You cannot take the responsibility for every man, woman, and child in the ghetto!"

He held her tightly and drew in a deep breath, experiencing the first peace of mind he had felt since his meeting with Botchermann two days ago.

Chapter Thirty-one

David told them the truth.

The Nazis had constructed a labor camp at Belzec, and he had been there. He told them about the barracks and the electrified fence. He told them that several thousand workers, including two hundred men from Biala–Podlaska, were to be sent there.

What would conditions there be like?

Primitive at best.

For how long would they be gone?

He told them that while Botchermann had said the work might be finished in October, there was a possibility that they might be assigned to another project elsewhere without returning to Biała–Podlaska first.

Was there any guarantee the Nazis would not demand further labor gangs from the ghetto in the months to come?

No, there was not.

Was there any way they could keep in touch with their families?

He did not know if the Nazis would permit that.

Did he have any idea what they would be working on?

Only rumors: that they were to create a huge antitank ditch in the Bug–San Gap, that there were many other work projects including road and bridge construction.

How was the selection of the first two hundred men to be made?

He told them his plan for a lottery. And he told them that if he did not produce two hundred men, the Nazis would simply come and take twice that many. It was not what he would have chosen to do, but it was the only system that seemed fair.

They agreed it was preferable to being dragged away at the point of a gun.

Now it was time to make the selection, and David's heart sank as he pulled the box of ballots onto his desk.

He stared at the box for a long time before he reached down and began stirring the pieces of paper around. Two thousand men. Doctors, farmers, electricians, carpenters. What were they doing at this moment? Holding children in their arms? Embracing their wives? Were they on their knees, praying not to be selected? Were they afraid?

He picked up one of the folded ballots. *Whose name is this?* he thought. *How old is this man? What will happen to his family if I send him to Belzec?*

He unfolded the paper and laid it flat. He picked up a pencil and wrote the name, Yitzhak Brodsky, on the top line of a ruled pad. Beneath the name he wrote Brodsky's address.

"Who are you, Yitzhak Brodsky?" David whispered. "What is your wife's name? How many children do you have? What are you dreams and hopes, Yitzhak Brodsky?"

One by one, name after name was added to the list until an entire page was filled. By ten–thirty the list was complete. Out of the two hundred names on it, there were only a dozen or so with which David could associate faces. The rest were strangers.

For that, at least, he thanked God.

The street was packed with women and children who had gathered to say good-bye to the two hundred men already lining up to be marched to the station. From his office window David looked down at the emotion-charged scene. As he turned away, unable to watch any longer, Dvoyra entered the office, her face white and taut with tension.

At that moment three German trucks swept into the street. SS soldiers emerged and took up positions all around the crowd. A rough German voice boomed out over a loudspeaker.

"Achtung! Achtung! Attention! Attention! The men who have been selected for temporary resettlement at Belzec will form a line four abreast. We will proceed on foot from here to the railroad station in the Aryan section. All others will remain here. No Jew other than those destined for Belzec is to leave the ghetto. There will be a roll call at the station. Anyone not present will be considered a fugitive. His family, along with the heads of ten other families, will be taken into custody until the criminal fugitive surrenders himself. We will depart for the station in precisely two minutes!"

The harsh announcement gave way to an enormous eruption of emotion, and the street filled with the agonized weeping of nearly a thousand men, women, and children.

Dvoyra stood at the window with David, looking down upon the tragedy unfolding on the street below. She saw dozens of her students, dazed and saddened by chaos they did not understand.

Suddenly a blast of rifle fire filled the air. The rough voice on the loudspeaker called for silence, and an eerie stillness descended upon the mass of people jammed into the narrow street. The loudspeaker crackled again.

"March!" the voice snapped.

With that command the men began to march toward the train station, flanked by SS guards. At first their wives and children kept pace alongside them, but when they reached the end of the street, the troops turned and formed a barrier to block them from going any farther. They watched in silent agony as the men disappeared into the distance, leaving their wives and children alone and helpless on the street in the heart of the ghetto.

★ ★ ★

David Berg was permitted to join the march to the station. He wanted to be there in case there was any trouble between the workers and the authorities. When they arrived, the Germans lined the men up on the street opposite the station entrance for the roll call. The workers were instructed to step forward and cross the street as their names were called.

David watched as the line on the station side of the street grew; each time a name was called, he felt a stab of guilt and shame.

They all came, he thought sadly. *Nobody dared refuse.*

The soldiers marched the column into the station to await the train, which arrived fifteen minutes later. As it slowly steamed into the station, swastika flags fluttering, David's heart sank. Down the dirty metal sides of the locomotive, in runny white paint, someone had daubed anti-Jewish caricatures and the words "We're going to Poland to thrash the Jews!"

The train clattered into the station, and as it drew level, David stared along its length in disbelief. There were no passenger cars, and as the engines ground to a halt, it became clear that this was a freight train. The men were going to travel to Belzec in cattle cars.

An SS sergeant shouted orders at the lines of Jewish men, who shuffled down the platform to board the last two cars. David wondered what cargo the train was carrying to Belzec, and he peered closely at the cars. Through the slats of the battered old freight cars he could see the outlines of faces, bodies. Here and there fingertips protruded through the slats. He stared at the boxcars in horror. They were jammed full of men.

He turned around, searching the platform for Botchermann, who was standing with a group of SS officers, nodding and smiling. David approached him quickly.

"You've done well, Berg," Botchermann said before David could speak. "You can go back to the ghetto now."

"Herr Standartenfuhrer, please, why are these men being transported in freight cars?"

"I'm afraid the first-class coaches are already filled," Botchermann said, the SS officers snickering at his witticism.

"Then who are the men in the other cars? Where are they from? How long have they been penned up like that?"

Botchermann made a clucking sound, like a good-natured teacher dealing with a particularly trying child.

"They are Jews," he said very slowly, as if to an idiot. "They are from Torun. They left there at nine o'clock last night. Anything else, *Herr* Berg?"

David was so shocked he did not even hear the Nazi's sarcastic use of the formal address. He turned away just as the last man from Biala-Podlaska climbed into the boxcar at the end of the platform. The man turned to stare at David, who was standing with Botchermann and the other SS officers. Their eyes locked until the door was slammed shut and locked, sealing the men into the boxcar. David turned back to Botchermann.

"For God's sake!" he shouted. "Those are men in there, not animals!"

Botchermann stared at him for a moment, his eyes unreadable.

"That, Jew, is entirely a matter of opinion," he snapped. He turned on his heel and stalked away with the other officers, leaving David standing alone on the platform. The locomotive belched steam and the train slowly began to move. Long after it had disappeared, David Berg stood staring down the tracks toward the south, asking himself the same question over and over.

What have I done? My God, what have I done?

David headed back toward the ghetto, still trying to come to terms with what he had seen in the railroad station. He felt disoriented, feverish. From time to time he stopped to lean against the wall of a building until his head cleared. As he approached the ghetto, he paused again, leaning against a fence. He looked up at the cloudless sky and thought of the train moving south across the green fields, and the men packed inside the cattle cars, the stinking, half-lit, rattling cattle cars on their way to Belzec, and to what?

Oh, God, he prayed silently, *let them be safe.* His head spun as the words went around in his head, and he heard his own ragged breathing and the sudden pumping of his heart. He slid to the sidewalk, his senses reeling.

When he came to, he found a young German soldier trying to help him to his feet.

"Are you all right?" the soldier said. He was young, not more than twenty-five, with blond hair and blue eyes. The perfect Aryan, David thought, contempt and anger surging through him.

"Better let me help you. You could get in trouble. A Jew lying on the street in the Aryan section—they could arrest you. Look, I'll give you a hand, lean on me—"

"I don't need help from your kind!" David said angrily, yanking his arm from the German's grip. The young soldier released his hold, and David saw the hurt in the boy's eyes. *Good,* he thought, somehow pleased to have hurt one of *them.* He shook his head as if to clear it and started walking in the direction of the ghetto.

"Sir!" the soldier called after him. So surprised was David by the polite address that he stopped and turned to face the German. The boy was looking at him anxiously.

"We're not all madmen, you know." His voice was almost a plea. "There are still decent Germans."

"Yes," David said bitterly. "And they guard the gates of ghettos!"

As David entered the ghetto and walked to his office, he sensed the hostility of the people he passed on the street. They did not speak to him or even look at him. When he reached the doorway of the building in which he had his office, a group of men standing outside talking parted in silence so that he could pass. He felt their cold stares on his back as he climbed the stairs.

He turned the corner at the top of the stairs and found Dvoyra on her knees, weeping as she tried to scrub his office door clean.

Someone had painted a swastika on it.

All David's requests to secure information about the men at Belzec were rebuffed. Botchermann told him bluntly that he was not to bring up the subject again, and that the Jews should consider themselves fortunate indeed that, so far, no further demands had been made upon them.

Word circulated quickly that the likelihood of the men's returning was small. Rumors drifted into the ghetto to form a picture that was all to clear. Someone had said there were over a hundred forced labor camps in Poland just for Jews, where terror, violence, and sadism ruled. The men worked from dawn till dusk, driven to the point of collapse clearing forests, draining marshes, digging ditches, quarrying and hauling stone until they were sick, prematurely aged, and wasted.

Someone else said that camps with only four hundred to five hundred laborers experienced ten to fifteen deaths a day.

In October 1940 Botchermann curtly informed David that the labor camp at Belzec had been dismantled after the completion of the Himmler Line, the huge complex of anti-tank ditches between the rivers Bug and San. The surviving Jews—David did not miss the ominous use of the word "surviving"—had been immediately reassigned to camps in Hrubieschow and Radom, to replace laborers who had died there.

Few people in the ghetto were surprised by the news. They had hoped but had never truly believed that the men would come back. The news of their reassignment, the use of the word "surviving," all confirmed what everyone had suspected. The men who had gone to Belzec were dead, or as good as dead. They were spoken of in hushed tones, and conversations about them ended with a shake of the head.

As a chill in the autumn air sharpened, and the sky grew progressively grayer with the approach of winter, the Jews of Biala-Podlaska no longer thought about the future. Parents no longer pictured their children growing into adulthood, continuing their education, marrying, having children of their own. No longer did they dream of what their children might accomplish or what career they might choose. Now they prayed only that their children would survive the coming winter and the illnesses for which there would be no treatment.

The Jews lived on snatches of rumor, strands of hearsay, mostly uttered by Poles who worked for the Germans. Sooner or later the news traveled from ghetto to ghetto—the compound at Lodz two hundred and fifty kilometers away, with over 150,000 Jews in it; another at Kielce two hundred and twenty-five kilometers away; another at Radom only one hundred and fifty kilometers away. In Warsaw they were building a wall all around the biggest ghetto in Poland, with half a million Jews locked within its walls and guarded gates. At Cracow Jewish tombstones were used in the construction of the ghetto walls.

The Jewish ghettos of Europe had many things in common: they were always located in the oldest, poorest parts of town, often without sanitation, proper lighting, or paved streets. People lived in crowded conditions so that even a minimal level of privacy was impossible. The wind carried the stench of latrines and broken sewers.

And there was the hunger.

Hans Botchermann didn't have to tell David that German policy was to starve the Jews. Starvation stalked the streets with disease and frostbite as its allies. Beggars lined the streets, their pleas for help filling the air. Most were children, but sometimes whole families begged, huddled together in their rags, crying for bread, for potatoes, for money that no one had to give.

Every day the death toll rose.

"How long can this go on, David?" Dvoyra asked him as he sat at his desk studying the mortality reports. "This misery?"

He sighed. "I don't know, Dvoyra. I just don't know. The secret radio reports from Berlin say the Germans have made an alliance with Japan and Italy. All of Europe is in their grasp. France, Norway, Holland, Denmark, Poland, Czechoslovakia. They're bombing British cities to rubble. Their troops have entered Rumania. They seem invincible. Who can stop them from doing whatever they wish to do?"

"You mean to us, to the Jews? What else could they do to us?"

"My instincts . . ." He hesitated, not sure whether to go on. Dvoyra looked at him expectantly.

"My instincts tell me that the treatment we are receiving is not the solution to the Jewish problem that Hitler talks about. I can't believe that they merely wish to contain us. I suspect there is another stage. But what it will be . . . ?"

Dvoyra was silent. Like all Jews, she believed in their ultimate survival and the preservation of the Jewish people. Individuals of course would die, but not the community. And yet she was haunted by the feeling that the people of the Biala-Podlaska ghetto were like tinder being piled on the ground but not yet lit. As enraged as they were, they could not drown the flame that would eventually consume them.

That conflagration eventually was nearer than she dreamed. A few days later, on December 18, 1940, Adolf Hitler signed Directive No. 231, Case Barbarossa, the plan for the invasion of Russia. At the same time Reichsfuhrer-SS Heinrich Himmler was initiating an even more sinister undertaking—the extermination of the Jewish people.

Chapter Thirty-two

"Rachel, there's terrible news in the *Forward* this morning!" Ivan called as he rushed into the apartment with the paper.

Rachel hurried from the kitchen to meet him, his face as white as the shirt he wore.

"Ivan, what is it?"

"Come, let's sit." He took her by the arm and led her into the dining room. They sat at the round wooden table as he spread out the pages of the *Daily Forward*.

The headline under Ivan's trembling finger screamed its one word message—"MASSACRE"

Together they read the dreadful account of the slaughter of Jewish civilians by Nazi soldiers in Minsk, Brest-Litovsk, Lvov, and so many other places.

"My Aunt Dvoyra lives in that area," Rachel said. "Thank God her children got out of Poland in time to make their way to Eretz Israel."

"Thank God, indeed, Rachel. My whole family is in Minsk."

"Do you think it's true?" she asked, the horror evident in her voice.

"They quote eyewitness accounts. They say it's happening wherever the Nazis go."

That evening Rachel and Ivan joined Sheara and Lou at Becky and Joe's for dinner. The conversation remained centered on the disturbing news in that morning's *Forward*.

"If the Nazis are killing Jews, how come there is nothing about it in *The Washington Post*," Joe asked. "Lou, Ivan, did either of you read as much as a word about this?"

Lou shook his head.

"No," Ivan said. "There was nothing."

"You think it's not true?" Sheara asked.

"If something like this happened, how could it not be in the *Post*?" Joe asked impatiently.

"But it's in the *Forward*. You read it," Becky said.

"How could the *Forward* have a story like this and the *Post* miss it completely?" Joe persisted. "I'm telling you, it's impossible."

"Joe, the *Forward* didn't make it up," Rachel said. "It's right there on the front page."

"Did anyone read all of the *Post* today?" Becky asked.

"I just read the front section," Joe said. "What about you, Ivan?"

"Just the front today."

"I just skimmed the sports pages," Lou said.

"Well, if the *Forward* had a story like this on the front page, it would have been front page in the *Post* too," Joe said.

"Not necessarily," Ivan replied.

"Jews are being massacred and that's not important?" Joe asked.

"Millions of people are being massacred over there, Joe. Do you think the *Post* worries about the killing of Jews the way we do?"

"But the *Forward* says the Nazis are rounding up Jewish men, women, and children and shooting them in cold blood. It's not just a story about people getting killed in the war."

"So?"

"So, you think the *Post* hasn't heard about these massacres?"

"If there have been massacres that the *Forward* has heard about, then I think the *Post* has heard about them too," Ivan replied.

"Then why isn't it in the paper?"

"I don't know, Joe. You tell me," Ivan answered.

"Let's just pray it's not true," Rachel said quietly.

Ivan waited eagerly for the *Forward* to arrive each day, searching for news about the fate of the Jews who had fallen into Nazi hands. As reports of the slaughter began to appear more frequently in the Yiddish press throughout the remainder of 1941 and on into 1942, Ivan became more and more somber.

Each day he would search *The Washington Post* or *The Evening Star* or *The Times Herald* for confirmation of what he read in the *Forward*.

"Ivan," Rachel called, walking into the dining room where he stood over the table. As she approached him, she saw the pain in his eyes, his normally relaxed expression was replaced by a twisted grimace. "Ivan, what is it?"

"Rachel, it says the Germans are sending all of Europe's Jews to Poland for extermination. There is a killing center in Chelmno where they are gassing Jews. It says they believe there are other killing centers in Poland. Rachel, over seven hundred thousand Jews have been murdered already and it goes on every day."

"Is it in the *Forward*?" she asked, shocked at the news.

"Yes, it's in the *Forward* on page one, but look here." He grabbed up another paper and hurriedly flipped through the pages. "I was given a June twenty-sixth copy of *The Boston Globe* by the accountant at the office. It's on page twelve, but look what it says." He jabbed his finger at the three-column headline: "Mass Murders of Jews in Poland Pass 700,000 Mark."

"Ivan"—she gently tugged at his arm—"please try to calm down. I've never seen you this way," she pleaded.

"Rachel! They're killing all of our people in Europe!" he cried.

"Ivan, you'll make yourself sick. Please—"

"It's not even in *The Washington Post*, Rachel." He slammed his fist down on the table. "It's so unimportant to the rest of the world that they don't even report it."

He disappeared into the darkness of their bedroom while she turned the *Globe* back to the front page and scanned the war news that dominated it. Then slowly she turned page after page to see for herself what filled the eleven pages of more important news and advertisements. "Mass murder of seven hundred thousand Jews . . . just another item on page twelve," she whispered.

Rachel continued turning the pages of the *Globe*, looking for nothing in particular, skimming the stories until she spotted a small article with a headline that caught her eye:

Committee for a Jewish Army to Take Case to Washington

The Committee for a Jewish Army, which advocates the formation of a separate Jewish army comprised of Palestinian Jews and Jews from Nazi-occupied countries, will present to members of Congress on the steps of the

Capitol at noon on Sunday a petition calling for U.S. support of such an effort, signed by thousands of victims of Nazi oppression who have volunteered for service in a Jewish army to be stationed in Palestine.

Rachel left the apartment at ten forty-five to attend the meeting of the Committee for a Jewish Army that Sunday morning. When she'd told Ivan about the meeting, he had wanted to accompany her, but a previously scheduled appointment prevented him from doing so.

While the temperature was expected to climb into the low nineties, it was still cool as Rachel waited for the streetcar that would take her to the Capitol.

Rachel wasn't sure exactly what she expected to witness that morning, but there was no crowd at the Capitol when she arrived. In fact, but for the steady stream of Sunday tourists moving in and out of the building, there seemed to be no one gathering there at all. Then at noon a group of four men appeared at the very top of the stairs, along with a photographer. They posed for the photographer as two of the men made a great show of handing a stack of papers to the two other men. Rachel asked a passing policeman if he knew who the people were.

"Sure, that's Congressmen Celler and Dickstein," the officer replied. "Those young fellows are a couple of Jews who want to start a Jewish army. Everybody has something to say about how this damned war should be fought," he muttered.

A minute later the congressmen dissappeared back inside the Capitol, and the two young Jews strode down the steps, nearing Rachel.

"Good morning," she called, "and good luck."

They stopped for a moment and smiled.

Rachel put out her hand to introduce herself. "I'm Rachel Wollmack. I came to see you present your petition. You're from Palestine?"

"From Eretz Israel," one replied, correcting her.

"I wanted to wish you well."

"Thank you for coming. I am Ari Mazeloff and this is my colleague Reuben Topaz." Ari was tall and striking, with reddish-blond, wiry hair and pale blue eyes. He was, Rachel thought, about Ivan's height of six feet, but broad-shouldered and heavy set, whereas Ivan had always been trim. Ari's face had been tanned from the summer's sun, and she could see the faint scars from an earlier youthful bout with acne. It left his face with a toughened, but nonetheless handsome, quality.

Reuben was not as tall as Ari and had dark curly hair and greenish-brown eyes. His wire-rimmed glasses made him look more like a lawyer or a doctor than a warrior in search of an army.

"Are there no other members of your organization here with you?"

"No, just us," Ari Mazeloff told her.

"Not exactly an army," Rachel observed.

His smile disappeared.

"I meant no offense," she said quickly. "Do you work full time trying to build your army?"

He paused for a moment before answering her. "No, I don't spend all my time trying to build an army. I spend my time trying to wake up a nation."

"Do you think America is in danger?"

"America will survive."

"Then what concerns you?"

"The nine million Jews of Europe. They are being systematically slaughtered."

"We have read the reports. It's terrible."

"It is the worst crime in the history of the world."

"No one seems to be able to do anything," Rachel replied.

"No one wants to do anything. That's even worse."

"You can't mean that."

"I can and I do. Do you think *they* care?" He tossed his head toward the Capitol, which towered over them.

"What can they do?" Rachel asked. "You don't really think they can save Jews in Europe while they sit playing politics in there, do you?"

"Yes, I do. Right now those bastards are the only people who can save Jews."

"How? How in the world can they save Jews in Europe?"

"By providing refuge for them before they fall into Nazi hands. For a year now Jews have been fleeing all over Europe, but they keep getting boxed in as one nation after another falls to the Nazis. This country, this citadel of freedom you call home, hasn't done a damn thing to help."

"I know, and they've instituted those terrible quotas."

"Quotas! Mrs. Wollmack, the United States isn't even filling its quotas from Europe. That man who sits at the other end of Pennsylvania Avenue hasn't lifted a finger to help the Jews."

"Are you crazy? Franklin Delano Roosevelt is leading the world in its struggle against the Nazis. He is the greatest president in this century."

"And therefore he has been in a position to show real statesmanship, Mrs. Wollmack. He could walk through those doors and tell Congress that those who bar Jews from the West are as guilty as those who are sending the Jews to the East. I am telling you, America's silence is what is killing Jews by the tens of thousands."

"I think you are interpreting the President's silence incorrectly.

"Am I? I think he doesn't want to deal with the Jewish issue. That's my interpretation. And I'll tell you something, that's Hitler's interpretation too."

Rachel was stunned by the anger in his voice and didn't speak for a moment. She noticed that people were turning to look at them as they walked by.

"You shouldn't talk that way, not here, not in these times."

"Help us, Mrs. Wollmack."

"Me? What can I do?"

"More than you think."

"Oh, I don't know."

"Yes, of course," he said hastily. "Everyone is busy."

"No, I don't mean that I am too busy."

"Yes?" he asked, staring at her.

She stared back, speechless for a moment. "What can I do?" she asked softly.

"Help us tell the world what is happening, Mrs. Wollmack."

"How can we do that?"

Ari smiled. "By getting people's attention."

Rachel wanted to ask, *And how do we do that?* Instead she just nodded. "Oh, I see," she finally answered, seeing nothing at all of what Ari Mazeloff had in mind.

"Why don't we all have something to eat?" Reuben Topaz broke in. "I'm starved."

"I shouldn't. I really must get back home."

"On an empty stomach? Never!" Ari said with a laugh. "Come on. There's a cafeteria below the Senate Office Building." Taking Rachel by the elbow, Ari turned and started up the stairs. "It's too hot to walk. We'll take the subway over."

"You certainly know your way around," Rachel said as they negotiated the narrow corridors under the building to the subway used to whisk senators and staff members back and forth between their offices and the Capitol.

"I feel as if I've lived here for the past week," Ari said.

Rachel listened to the two Palestinian Jews as they talked over lunch.

Their conversation fascinated Rachel. Not once was the subject of a Jewish army even raised. Instead they spoke of advertising, debating whether a new advertisement should run in both *The Washington Post* and *The Evening Star* or just in The *Post*.

"We don't have money for two papers," Reuben said.

"So what! We don't have money for one paper either," Ari replied. "The ad will raise the necessary money."

"If they let us run it at all," Reuben reminded him.

"Why would either paper accept an ad from us?"

"We'll cross the bridge when we come to it," Ari said.

"You two sound like a couple of retailers. What in the world does all this talk of advertising have to do with a Jewish army?"

"Mrs. Wollmack, the worse crime in history is taking place in Europe and it barely produces a yawn in Congress," Ari replied.

"What do you want Congress to do? Demand that the Nazis behave themselves?"

"We want them to open the door," Reuben answered. "An entire people is banging on your door, begging for sanctuary."

"It doesn't seem Congress will lift the quotas, does it?" she asked.

"Lift the quotas! The State Department isn't filling the quotas as it is!"

"I know. I just don't understand it."

"Nobody wants immigrants coming here. They're afraid jobs will be lost to foreigners," Ari said.

"The Depression is still fresh in everyone's minds," she reminded them.

"Rachel, we're talking murder! What kind of people bar their doors to someone about to be murdered?" Ari asked angrily.

"People here don't understand what is happening to the Jews. My husband, Ivan, is making himself sick with anger over the war. He's furious that American newspapers don't consider the murder of the Jews a major news story.

"Newspapers write what they think their readers are interested in reading." Ari answered. "Because the press doesn't give a damn, the government doesn't give a damn. And because the people that work in this building don't care, the people at your State Department don't care either."

"Which is why your President is willing to ignore the murder too," Reuben added.

"Don't say President Roosevelt is ignoring murder," she said defensively.

Ari looked at Reuben and sighed. "Is it any wonder?" he asked.

Reuben reached inside his suit jacket pocket and withdrew a folded piece of paper. Without speaking, he laid it down on the table and unfolded the over-size document. Rachel could see that it was an advertisement reproduced on a large sheet of paper, but could not make out the the copy as it lay facing the two men. Then, watching Rachel carefully, Reuben slowly turned the page around until it faced her.

The bold-type message jolted her.

> For Sale
>   70,000 Romanian Jews
> Guaranteed Human Beings
> $125 each

"Oh, that's horrible," she said. "Who would print such a thing?"

"It's an advertisement that's going to run in *The Washington Post*," Ari said.

"Who is doing this?" she asked.

"We are."

"You can't do this. It will offend people terribly."

"What do you suggest we do then?" he asked. "Romania has offered to let seventy thousand Jews leave—buy their own way out of the country. If those Jews fall into Nazi hands they will be murdered. The Romanians want one hundred and twenty-five dollars for each Jew they transport to a safe border, and time is running out. Few Romanian Jews have any money with which to redeem themselves. How would you raise ten million dollars?"

"I would go to our government," she replied quickly.

"To the government? Who would you go to, the Secretary of Human Procurement?"

"This is not a joking matter!" Rachel exclaimed, pointing to the advertisement.

"We don't intend the ad as a joke. We want to run this ad in order to either bring Jews out of Romania or wake up people in this country to what is happening. Seventy thousand Jews will die in Romania. As I've explained, the Romanians will guarantee them safe passage for one hundred and twenty-five dollars a Jew. We don't have a year for the United States Department of State to decide how to respond to the Romanian offer. Now, you tell me, Mrs. Wollmack, what would you do?" Ari demanded.

She stared into his piercing blue eyes, their gentleness replaced by a questioning glare. Rachel glanced back down at the advertisement and slowly read the rest of the message. They were serious. They wanted to rescue the Jews of Romania by buying their freedom.

"Do you really think this will work?" she asked.

"No," Reuben said. "We'll be lucky to raise enough to pay for the advertisement."

"Then what will you accomplish?"

"We believe the ad may cause people to think. If people don't begin to get angry here in this country, your government won't lift a finger to rescue Jews. We want to make people angry. The Jews of Europe need for someone to care. You understand that, don't you?"

Rachel nodded. "Yes, of course I understand."

"Will you help?"

"What can I do?"

"The committee is sponsoring a pageant called We Shall Never Die. It will appear in six cities throughout the country. Edward G. Robinson and Paul Muni have agreed to appear in the performance as well as many other Jewish entertainers and a large number of refugees. Ben Hecht, a famous movie producer, has been a huge help to us."

"You want me to sell tickets?"

"No." Ari laughed. "We don't want you to sell tickets. We want you to call on high-ranking public officials to see if you can get them to attend the Washington performance of the pageant. Their presence would emphasize the importance of rescue and help wake up the press to the size of the calamity."

"High-ranking officials! They wouldn't see me and I wouldn't have the slightest idea what to say to them."

"They probably won't see you, but their staffs will. We need someone to go back day after day after day." Ari pounded his fist on the table for emphasis.

"And what am I to say?"

"You tell them millions of lives have been lost and that millions more are at stake. Tell them the pageant will be covered by the press and an absence of government officials will be interpreted by the rest of the world as a sign that the United States of America doesn't care what happens to the Jews. Tell them that if it appears that the powerful won't bother to support the performance, then the world will think they won't bother to help the Jews of Europe either," Reuben answered.

"It will look as though we are trying to blackmail them into coming," Rachel said.

Ari's gaze softened. "We are." He smiled grimly.

No one in the family, except for Ivan, was very happy about Rachel's involvement with the Committee for a Jewish Army, but they all knew better than to interfere. They saw virtually no value in the pageant and everyone seemed to find the advertisement which Rachel had a copy of, terribly offensive.

Rachel never asked their opinion about the committee or about the work they had asked her to do. She merely announced that she had volunteered to work for the rescue of European Jewry.

Not since Rachel's obsession with the reunion of her own siblings from Sachshaven, nearly twenty years earlier, had she thrown herself into anything with such zeal. Ari and Reuben provided no direction to Rachel other than handing her a list of dignitaries whose attendance at the pageant, they said, was her responsibility.

Rachel scanned the list. "You must be joking," she said to them, reading the list out loud.

"President Franklin Roosevelt, Secretary of State Cordell Hull, Assistant Secretary of State Breckinridge Long . . ." Rachel stopped and looked up at Ari and Reuben, expecting that they would be apologetic at the impossible task they had given her. Instead she saw that they were serious.

She scrutinized the list thoughtfully before looking up a second time. "What matters is that the people on this list learn of the committee. I will force them to think about the murder of the Jews. If nothing else, they will be uncomfortable every time I show up."

Rachel returned home elated from her first day's calls.

"Oh, Ivan, I'm sorry to be so late." She brushed his cheek with a kiss and kissed each of the children.

"Well, my beloved diplomat, did you see anybody today?" he asked affectionately.

She thought for a moment and shrugged. "Yes and no."

"Yes and no? What kind of answer is 'yes and no'?"

"You asked if I saw anybody. I did. That's the 'yes' part."

"And the 'no' part?"

"I didn't see anybody who was anybody."

"From the look you had on your face when you came through the door, I thought you had seen the President himself."

"Not quite. I got as far as the gate on Pennsylvania Avenue. I told the guard I wanted to deliver an invitation to the President. I don't think he believed me at first. You should have seen the look on his face when I told him I represented the Committee for a Jewish Army."

Ivan laughed and shook his head in disbelief. "What did the guard say?"

"He smiled at me as though I were a child. I thought he was going to pat me on the head or something."

"So?" Ivan asked in anticipation.

"So I told him I was a volunteer for the Committee for a Jewish Army and that we are trying to save millions of Jews before they are murdered by the Nazis. I said I have to deliver to the President an invitation to the pageant. When he heard that Edward G. Robinson was going to star in the pageant, he suddenly got very serious.

"He called someone on the staff at the White House and said there was a visitor at the gate they should probably see."

"So?" Ivan asked excitedly.

"So, tomorrow I have an appointment with Russel Forester."

"Who?"

Rachel smiled and shrugged her shoulders. "He works in

the State Department, in the huge ugly building next to the White House. He's on the White House staff."

Now it was Ivan's turn to smile. "It's a beginning, Rachel." He put his hands around his wife's waist and pulled her into his arms.

Chapter Thirty-three

One important development of that sad and bitter winter of 1940–41 was the establishment of a secret Jewish archive in Biala-Podlaska. The idea originated in Warsaw, where a Jewish historian, Dr. Emmanuel Ringelblum, conceived the practice of recording daily events of the ghetto. Volunteers were assigned the task of recording all rumors, prevalent debates, even the jokes making the rounds. Underground newspapers, diaries, Nazi orders and directives, and news reports were preserved. Anything that might give future generations insight into the life of the Jews in the ghettos was kept and buried in sealed containers. The name of the clandestine archive was Oneg Shabbat, the Pleasures of the Sabbath. It spread rapidly to other ghettos in Poland.

Dvoyra first heard about it from a young member of Ha-Shomer ha-Zair who had stolen into Biala-Podlaska on his way to the Russian frontier.

"Maybe through Oneg Shabbat the world will one day learn what they did to us," the young man said. "And maybe one day they will have to answer to someone for it."

To whom, Jew? The jeering voice of Botchermann taunted David as the young man told them about Oneg Shabbat. Dvoyra immediately argued that such an archive should be established in Biala-Podlaska. "It is one way we can fight back, David. Maybe, just maybe, we can make them answer for what they have done." David agreed.

They decided that the man best qualified for the task was Dr. Leonard Hoffmeister, a former professor of European history at the University of Cracow. Hoffmeister had been in the ghetto for a year, having been dragged out of the ancient Jagellion Library at the university when the Germans rounded up the first Cracow Jews. Twelve hours later he and hundreds of other Jews from that city were incarcerated at Biala-Podlaska.

Hoffmeister was a tall, thin man in his mid-fifties with hair that was now completely white. He wore battered bifocal glasses perched on the end of his nose, giving him a perpetually quizzical and sometimes mischievous look. When he was excited, he had a habit of vigorously rubbing his hands together, as if he were warming them before a roaring fire. He did so now, as David told him about Ringelblum's Oneg Shabbat.

"Yes, yes." His eyes glowed with enthusiasm. "The perfect activity for an unemployed history professor!"

"Dangerous activity, Leonard," David said. "We are talking about subversion. If you are caught, they will kill you."

"Let's not play games with one another, my friend," Hoffmeister said. "Sooner or later they are going to kill me anyway. Oneg Shabbat will enable me to do something worthwhile with the time left to me and perhaps cause them some grief after I am gone."

"When will you begin?"

"What's wrong with now?"

"Nothing," David said. "But Leonard—don't tell too many people. The fewer the better. No one can be forced to tell something he doesn't know."

"Give me a few days," Hoffmeister said. "I'll talk to one or two people. Then I'll come and see you."

"I'll bring you some of the work the children have done!" Dvoyra said after Hoffmeister had left. "Some of it is beautiful, David. Essays, poems, pictures—they would be ideal for Oneg Shabbat!"

"I don't want you to bring anything that could be traced back to you, Dvoyra," David said. "You know what the Nazis will do if they catch—"

"I already save most of it. I wouldn't dream of throwing it away. So why not turn some of it over to Professor Hoffmeister? Shouldn't there be some record of how the children felt, too?"

"Just be careful. Bring whatever you select to me. I'll see that it is properly concealed."

She reached out and touched David's hand, her smile radiant and warm. He returned her smile, gazing into her eyes. Without speaking, they expressed their love for one another.

"Dvoyra?" he finally whispered.

Dvoyra smiled and rose from her chair. She put out the light and took his hand. "The answer is yes," she told him in the darkness as his familiar embrace enveloped her.

While David, Dvoyra, and Professor Hoffmeister finalized plans for the Oneg Shabbat in Biala-Podlaska, another group of planners was convening several hundred kilometers to the southwest, at a labor camp in the heart of the Silesian coal-mining region.

On March 1, 1941, Reichsfuhrer Heinrich Himmler, head of the SS and chief of the German police, arrived by train at the little Polish town of Oswiecim, now rechristened with a German name: Auschwitz. With Himmler was a substantial entourage, consisting of Gauleiter Bracht, the administrative presidents, the SS and police leaders of Silesia, several high executives of I.G. Farben Industries, and SS-Gruppenfuhrer Richard Glucks, Inspector of Concentration Camps.

A convoy of staff cars took the party a mile south of the station to the labor camp, an unremarkable facility located in the center of a network of stagnant fish ponds, presently used as quarters for a company of German construction troops.

It was an unimpressive place, damp, misty, and muddy, flanked on the west by the River Sola, a tributary of the Vistula, which it joined a couple of miles to the north of the town. However, there was one aspect of Auschwitz that made it worth the Reichsfuhrer's time and trouble. Auschwitz sat on a junction of three railway lines, connecting it easily with Berlin and Katowice to the northwest; Radom, Lublin, and Warsaw to the northeast; Cracow to the east; Czechoslovakia and Vienna to the south.

This facility, according to the report made by the Inspectorate for Concentration Camps, made the site an ideal location for a quarantine center. All that was needed to make the place functional was certain building and sanitation work.

Himmler and his party briefly surveyed the area and hurried back to the office of the camp's commandant, SS-Hauptsturmfuhrer Rudolf Hoess, recently arrived from duties at Oranienburg concentration camp in the village of Sachsenhausen, north of Berlin.

Himmler told him that he was to commence work immediately: to drain the surrounding swamps, and to enlarge the camp to hold thirty thousand peacetime prisoners, ten thousand of whom would be put to work in a synthetic rubber factory to be built by I.G. Farben on the west side of the complex, south of town. Simultaneously, a new camp was to be established at nearby Birkenau, to take an expected hundred thousand prisoners of war.

Hoess protested that the buildings, although orginally well constructed, had been allowed to fall into disrepair and were swarming with vermin. Glucks glared at Hoess, whom he had earlier warned against reporting anything disagreeable to the Reichsfuhrer-SS, of whom Glucks lived in mortal fear.

Himmler dismissed his objection with a smile. "Gentlemen," he said to the entourage, "the camp will be built. My reasons for it are far more important than your objections. Problems of water supply and drainage are purely technical matters, which the specialists have to work out, but they cannot be raised as objections. Every means will have to be taken to accelerate the construction work. You must improvise as much as possible, and any outbreak of disease will have to be checked and ruthlessly stamped out!"

He paused for breath. The thin winter sunlight glinted on his gold-rimmed glasses. He regarded them humorlessly for a moment, then went on.

"The delivery of drafts to the camp, however, cannot, on principle, be halted. The actions that I have ordered my security police to undertake must go on. I do not appreciate any difficulties in Auschwitz."

He turned to Hoess. "It is up to you to manage somehow, Hoess. I want to hear no more about difficulties."

"Yes, Reichsfuhrer!" Hoess blurted. "Of course!"

"Good," Himmler said.

Dvoyra sat at her desk in the makeshift classroom and watched her class, thinking of her own children whom she hadn't heard from since they escaped Poland, while the ten- and eleven-year-old students composed poems about Eretz Israel. It was so quiet in the room she could hear the sound of the children breathing, and their all-too-frequent coughing. Her attention was caught by an attractive girl with long curls and large dark-brown eyes, staring at the ceiling as she concentrated on composing her verse, her lips moving silently as she thought it through.

Dvoyra's heart ached as she looked at them all, their pale faces, the dark shadows beneath their eyes. How could such young children become the mortal enemies of Hitler's Reich? What kind of madness made it possible for one nation to starve the children of another to death?

She shook her head to banish the depressing thoughts. "All right, children, lay downy your pencils. Now, who is going to be first to read a poem to the class? Yosselle?"

The youngster at the back of the room grimaced. As Yosselle Abramowitz stood up, the other children turned to face him, some giggling at his shyness. He swallowed hard to bolster his courage and held his paper in front of him. He looked over the top of it into Dvoyra's eyes.

"Go ahead, Yosselle," she said encouragingly.

Yosselle Abramowitz wet his lips and took a deep breath. "'I Am Israel,' by Yosselle Abramowitz," he began.

> I am Israel, the home of Abraham, Isaac, and Jacob;
> I am the home of the children of Jacob;
> I am Israel, waiting for my children to return from Egypt;
> I am the Israel of Saul and David and Solomon;
> I am Israel, and I withstood the wrath of the Babylonians;
> In Babylonia my children dreamed of Israel and their dream still lives;
> I am Israel, and I heard Cyrus sound the first return to Zion;
> I am Israel, and I withstood the pillage of the Romans, and I cried at the sacrifice of Masada;
> I am Israel, and I saw them send my children away;
> I am Israel, and I wait to embrace my children once again;
> I am Israel, and I see the storm raging on the horizon and I see my children in the yoke of the oppressor as in the days of old;
> I am Israel, and I want my children, and when they are with me again, I will take them to my bosom, and they will be forever free;
> For I am Israel.

The room was utterly silent. Stunned, Dvoyra stared at Yosselle Abramowitz, biting her lip so that she would not shed the tears that had filled her eyes. "Oh, my child," she whispered. "That was beautiful."

When the class came to an end, Dvoyra called to the boy before he left the classroom. "Yosselle, may I keep your poem?"

He shrugged his shoulders. "Why not? Nobody is ever going to read it anyway."

"Maybe they will. Maybe one day somebody will."

After the children were gone, she sat alone for a while in the empty classroom. The deserted desks, no longer filled with beautiful boys and girls, seemed like an ominous warning. She walked to the back of the room and sat at Yosselle Abramowitz's desk. *He is only two or three years away from becoming a bar mitzvah,* she thought. When she thought of the odds against the boy's ever being called to the Torah as a bar mitzvah, the tears she had been holding back fell unchecked.

"Have you read any of this?" David asked Professor Hoffmeister as they sorted out the children's poetry.

"Only a little," Hoffmeister said quietly. "It is heartbreaking."

"Listen to this." David picked up a sheet of paper. He smiled at Dvoyra, who was watching him intently.

> "We are going home to Israel
>   to the land of our fathers;
> They cannot keep us from going home;
> Their armies and their bombs
>   cannot stop us;
> Death will only speed our journey;
> When we arrive in Israel
>   we will have won our freedom;
> We are going home to Israel
>   and when we arrive, we have won."

David laid down the poem with a sigh. "This is not the poetry of youth."

"No," Hoffmeister replied, "it's the poetry of the Diaspora, David. The poetry of the martyrs of the last two thousand years."

He laid the poem gently on the stack of papers in front of him and put that pile onto a large sheet of waxed paper, making a small parcel, which he tied with string.

"Have you decided where the archive will be concealed,

Professor?" Dvoyra asked, leaning forward with her arms around her legs, her chin resting on her knees.

"The cemetery," Hoffmeister said.

"The cemetery?" Dvoyra repeated, surprised.

"It's the best place," Hoffmeister said. "Where else would digging attract less attention? We'll put everything we wish to preserve into supply canisters or leather trunks, seal them tightly with tape. The burial detail can bury them. When all this is over, whoever comes next will know where we buried our people. They will look there first for any message from us."

"I just hate to think of the children's poems being buried in a cemetery." Dvoyra shuddered.

"The cemetery is the safest place, Dvoyra," David said. "The Nazis never even go near it."

"You think anyone will ever find it?"

"Someday," Hoffmeister said confidently. "One day, maybe all we save now will be in a real archive somewhere."

"Whom can we trust to bury it, Leonard?" David asked.

"Why, me, of course," Hoffmeister said. "You will obtain credentials for me to serve on the burial detail, David. Every week or ten days I will join them in burying our dead. Except I will be burying a little something extra."

David nodded. "I want to be there when you bury these papers."

Hoffmeister looked up in surprise. "That would be unnecessarily foolhardy. Your presence on the burial detail would unquestionably arouse suspicion."

"I wasn't thinking of joining the burial detail."

"What, then?"

"I was thinking that you and I could take the Oneg Shabbat material to the cemetery tonight and bury it together."

"David!" Dvoyra said. "It's too dangerous!"

"She's right, David," Hoffmeister agreed. "Why take such a risk?"

"You're a historian, Leonard," David said. "You figure it out."

'Ah," Hoffmeister said. "The first Oneg Shabbat burial. You want to be a small part of history, is that it?"

"No, Leonard, I want to preserve a small part of history."

Reichsfuhrer-SS Heinrich Himmler's Berlin office was on the second floor of Gestapo headquarters on the Prinz Albrechtstrasse. It was an undistinguished building in the shape of an H, with high, vaulted ceilings, thick walls, and

portes-fenêtres that rose from the floor to twice the height of a
tall man. Himmler's office was like the man himself, cold,
precise, unemotional. A portrait of the Fuhrer dominated the
wall behind his antique desk. Beneath it hung the Imperial
banner Himmler had carried during the putsch in 1923.

It was to this office that the commandant of Auschwitz, SS-
Hauptsturmfuhrer Rudolf Hoess, presented himself in
Himmler's anteroom after a sleepless journey from Katowice.

Himmler summoned him right away, wasting no time
getting to the reason he had sent for Hoess.

"What I am going to say to you must remain utterly
confidential, Hoess," he said in his thin, schoolteacherish
voice. "Utterly confidential!"

"Of course, Reichsfuhrer!" Hoess said emphatically.

"You're a lucky man, Hoess. There are times when being in
the right place can do more for a man's career than a dozen
battle citations. And this is one of them. I have selected your
camp to carry out one of the Reich's most sacred missions."

"It will be my honor to serve the Reichsfuhrer in any and
every way, as I have endeavored to do ever since the Reichsfuhrer invited me to join the active SS seventeen years ago."

"It will not be I you will be serving, Hoess," Himmler said
with a smile. "You will be acting on the direct orders of the
Fuhrer himself, for it is he who has ordained our actions."

Hoess leaned forward in his chair, his sallow, high-
cheekboned face alight with interest. If the orders came direct
from the Fuhrer, there might well be a promotion in this.

"The Fuhrer's sacred mission is to render all of Europe
Judenrein," Himmler droned. "I have selected several camps to
administer what will be a final solution to the Jewish problem.
Auschwitz, by virtue of its isolation and rail facilities, will
become the largest and most important installation executing
that program. Orders are already being transmitted to the
Eastern front to send Jews from all the occupied territories to
Auschwitz for processing."

"But surely the Reichsfuhrer knows that Auschwitz will
hold no more than a hundred and fifty thousand prisoners!"
Hoess protested. "How . . . ?"

Himmler leaned back in his chair and smiled primly at
Hoess's dismay. "You can accept only one hundred and fifty
thousand Jews *at one time*. Do you understand me, Hoess?"

Hoess stared at Himmler, his startled expression giving
way to a knowing smile. This was even bigger than he had

expected. His self-confidence flooded back. It would be hell's own work, but he could handle it.

"We will ship a hundred and fifty thousand Jews to Auschwitz, Hoess. When you have processed them, another one hundred and fifty thousand will be sent, and then another, and so on, until we have completed the task set for us by the Fuhrer."

"I will return to Auschwitz immediately and begin preparations."

"Good. Remember what I said, Hoess. Although the Fuhrer has given us his confidence, and we are about to write one of the most glorious pages in the history of the Reich, it is to remain now and forever a secret Reich matter. Understood?"

"Of course, Reichsfuhrer!"

"Very well. I will send SS-Sturmbannfuhrer Adolf Eichmann, head of the Department for Jewish Affairs in the Reich Security head office, to see you. Together you will work out the methods by which the Fuhrer's will is carried out. And Hoess—we must not fail! We must once and for all remove this cancer from the body of Europe!"

Chapter Thirty-four

Russel Forester was a thin gray-haired bureaucrat whose wired-rimmed glasses gave him an owlish look. He wore a bow tie and his hair was parted in the middle, which, Rachel thought, looked almost silly. His eyes were light blue and soft and seemed reassuring.

"I am Russel Forester," he said in a soft Southern accent as he rose from behind his cluttered desk to greet her. His tiny office confirmed his junior rank.

"My name is Rachel Wollmack." She took his hand.

He moved to a corner of his office behind his desk and picked up a chair for Rachel. As he moved to the front of his desk, she saw he was dragging one foot as he maneuvered the chair.

"Let me help you."

"Oh, I can manage fine. It's not as difficult as it looks."

He held the chair for her, and after she was seated, he moved back behind his desk and sat down himself.

"Now, do I understand correctly that you were sent here by Edward G. Robinson?" he asked skeptically.

Rachel laughed. "No, I have not been sent by Edward G. Robinson. I have been sent here by the Committee for a Jewish Army."

"The Committee for a Jewish Army?" he drawled slowly. "You represent the Committee for a Jewish Army?"

Rachel nodded.

"Are you here to declare war, or to ally yourself with the United States and Great Britain?" he asked with a smile.

Rachel failed to return it.

"You're serious, aren't you?"

"Very serious," she replied somberly.

Russel Forester leaned back in his chair. "Mrs. Wollmack, just what is the Committee for a Jewish Army?"

"Originally the committee wanted to raise an army of Jewish refugees from the occupied countries who would join with Jews from Palestine to fight the Nazis. Now the committee devotes all of its efforts to the rescue of Jews who have fallen into Nazi hands."

"Many victims of this war have fallen into Nazi hands, Mrs. Wollmack. Why do you only want to rescue Jews?"

"The others have a chance of surviving. The Jews are being murdered."

"Mrs. Wollmack, what do you think the White House could possible do to help those Jews?"

"Show that you care," Rachel answered without hesitation. "Men, women, and children are being slaughtered, murdered simply because they are Jews, and our government does and says nothing."

"How can you say we are doing nothing? We are fighting a war, and winning that war is the only thing that can save lives over there."

"Mr. Forester, do you know what the first thing the Nazis do when they invade a village in Poland or Russia? They round up the Jews—children, women, old people—and have them dig a large pit. Then they shoot them. This is happening every day. It's happening now as we sit here talking."

He sat in silence. Then he slowly removed his glasses, and

squeezing his eyes shut, he rubbed the bridge of his nose as though to relieve the tension there. He finally opened his eyes and looked at Rachel as he carefully replaced his glasses.

"Tell me, Mrs. Wollmack, what has all of this to do with Edward G. Robinson?"

"He and Paul Muni are starring in a pageant that will play here in Washington and in several other theaters around the country. It's called We Shall Never Die, and we want the President to come. We want to influence the Americans who see it or who hear about it or read about it. Then maybe the press will begin writing the truth about what is happening to the Jews. If enough people get upset, maybe the murder will stop."

"It will stop when the war ends, Mrs. Wollmack, not before. There is nothing we can do here that will help the Jews in Europe."

"We could admit those that are fleeing into the United States."

"You make it sound as though the United States doesn't care what happens to the Jews."

"How much have *you* cared, Mr. Forester?" she asked, an edge to her voice.

He stared back at Rachel, stung by her question and unable to respond.

"What is your job here, Mr. Forester?" she asked, finally breaking the silence.

"I shag fly balls," he admitted, his embarrassment obvious. "I'm one of several aides to the White House appointments secretary. We screen requests for appointments from people or groups no one has ever heard of and recommend which should get appointments and with whom."

"I'm a fly ball?"

"You and thousand of others."

"Am I wasting my time, Mr. Forester?" Rachel asked bluntly.

Forester paused before answering her question. "Mrs. Wollmack, I really don't know. I hope not," he finally said.

"You will help us?" she asked excitedly.

He hesitated again before replying. "I'll try, Mrs. Wollmack, but I don't want you to get your hopes up too high. I am not exactly a tower of influence here. I'm just an associate political science professor from Vanderbilt. I wound up here after I was injured in North Africa. I'm here because my uncle is a congressman and a friend of the President's. But I'll do what I can."

Rachel could tell that Ari and Reuben were disappointed. They were meeting over coffee at People's Drug Store on Pennsylvania Avenue, several blocks east of the Capitol. They had come to Washington to attend hearings on the refugee problem.

"He's really a very nice man and I think he wants to help," Rachel explained.

"I'm sure he does want to help, Rachel. We just don't know if he is in a position to help. We've never heard of a Russel Forester, and he's not on any of our White House staff lists," Ari replied.

"He is the only person I have been able to make an appointment with. Everyone else has had some clerk see me. They're very polite, but I can tell they are not really very interested."

"Rachel, maybe there is something Mr. Forester can do for us," Reuben said.

"What's that?" Rachel asked with interest.

"I think we should run an advertisement that directly attacks America's refugee policy."

"I don't like the thought of doing anything that attacks America," Rachel objected.

"So far all we've done is run ads that talk about death and suffering. People are numb when it comes to death and suffering. War does that to people," Reuben said. "We need to make the Roosevelt administration squirm a little."

"We're at war," she reminded him.

"No one wants to see the Allies win more than we do," Reuben argued. "But this government is pursuing a deliberate policy that is resulting in the unnecessary deaths of hundreds of thousands—maybe millions—of innocent people. Our people, Rachel."

Rachel's eyes closed as she thought of her Aunt Dvoyra and wondered if she was still alive or how long ago she may have died.

"What Reuben says is true," said Ari. "You should have heard your Assistant Secretary of State this morning. Listening to Mr. Long, you would think the United States had really opened its doors to the victims of Nazism."

"Are you sure we're not doing all that we can? I mean, there is a war going on. Maybe we just can't do any more," Rachel said, her frustration evident.

"From all the reports we get, it's practically impossible for refugees who have so far eluded the Nazis to get entry visas from the United States. Instead of expediting the process, your government is deliberately slowing it down."

"Well, I still don't understand how Russel Forester can help."

"We need information," Reuben said.

"What kind of information?"

"I have a hunch that the actual statistics on immigration would shock the hell out of decent men and women throughout the country. Everyone is being fed inflated answers that go down well. But we must tell them how many people are being murdered every day because of the immigration policies of your government."

"I don't know," Rachel answered. "Asking people to support the pageant is one thing. Criticizing America in advertisements is another. This is no time to be fighting with the government."

"It isn't?" Reuben snapped. "Then you tell me when we should fight with the government over this immigration business?"

Rachel was silent.

"So when do we fight, Rachel?" he went on. "After the war is over? After every Jewish man, woman, and child lies dead in the streets and fields of Europe? You're like all the rest! It's all statistics to you. These are lives that are being destroyed over there, and soon it will all become just one colossal statistic, all because no one wants to criticize America during the war. Well, then don't criticize America. Criticize those who are betraying what the world thought she stood for."

"What do you want me to do?" she asked softly, worn down by his outburst and ashamed at her hesitation.

Reuben's eyes darted to Ari for a moment. "See if your Mr. Forester can find out precisely how many refugees we are admitting each month," Reuben said.

"That's all?"

"It won't be as easy as it sounds. The State Department's public pronouncements make it sound as if the government is moving heaven and earth to rescue war victims. If the actual numbers being admitted are as low as we think they are, the government will find itself in a very embarrassing position.

"How low do you think the numbers are?"

"My guess is that the government is not even filling the quotas."

Rachel nodded. "I'll see what I can do."

The three of them walked out into the warm spring air to wait for the westbound trolley on Pennsylvania Avenue. Ari and Reuben disembarked at the Capitol. Rachel stayed on until she reached the White House at the other end of Pennsylvania Avenue.

Forester was surprised when a guard phoned down to tell him that Mrs. Wollmack was there to see him.

"Mrs. Wollmack," he said with a smile as he rose to meet her.

"I thought I would stop by to see if you had any news for me, Mr. Forester."

"Please, sit down. I didn't contact you because I didn't have very much to tell you."

"It's been a week since I was here."

"Yes, yes, I know," he said quickly, as if he was nervous. "Is anything wrong?"

"No, it's just that I had hoped I would be able to tell you more."

"Have you discussed the situation we talked about with others in the government?"

"Yes."

"And they'll help?" she asked intently.

He avoided her anxious stare. "It's not that simple."

"It seems very simple. Innocent people are being murdered and America can save many of them. Why is that not simple?"

"Because our government does not believe it can help very much in any way other than by winning the war as quickly as possible."

"But while we're busy winning the war, we could let in as many Jews as possible."

"The State Department says we are doing all we can."

"Do you believe that?"

Russel Forester rose from his chair and went to the window of his office. He stood with his back to Rachel and did not speak.

"Do you?" she asked again.

"No," he finally said.

"How many are they letting in?" she pressed.

"I don't know." He turned to face her.

"There must be someone who could tell us."

He nodded his agreement.

"Do you know whom we could ask?"

He nodded again. "Yes, I know."

"Would you?"

"I have."

"And?"

"They said we are doing all that we can."

She stared at him. "They won't tell you?"

He looked away, as if he was ashamed.

"But why?" she continued. "Surely they would tell us if we are filling the quotas."

"The people at State are very sensitive about the refugee problem."

"I would think the country would be proud of what it is doing to save lives."

He was silent for a moment while he considered his reply. "Maybe . . ." he murmured, his eyes still closed. Rachel strained to hear him.

"Maybe what we are doing is nothing to be proud of," he finally said.

"You think we are not filling the quotas?"

"Mrs. Wollmack, I really don't know. Not for sure. But I think very few refugees are being admitted."

"That's murder!" she cried.

He returned to his desk and sat down once more. "I don't have to tell you that there is still a lot of anti-Semitism in this country, Mrs. Wollmack. There is concern in this administration that a flood of refugees could cause a backlash in this country that could get very ugly. You know it wasn't so long ago that people were calling the President's New Deal the Jew Deal."

"Mr. Forester—"

"Please call me Russel."

"Russel, do these people in the administration understand that the Jews who are not admitted will probably be killed?"

He thought for a moment. "May I call you Rachel?"

"Please."

"These people are senior officials at State. They have no illusions about what is happening to the Jews who fall into Nazi hands."

"What are you saying?"

"What I'm saying could cost me my job. What I'm saying is that the Jewish refugees are seen as a big political liability to the President."

She was stunned. "I don't understand," she finally said, afraid of the direction the conversation was taking.

"I think you do."

"Do you think the President understands?"

"Rachel, I don't know what you intend to do with what I am telling you, but this discussion could be my ruin."

"Or your salvation," she replied with a touch of anger in her voice.

He smiled. "The road to salvation might be more treacherous than you imagine."

"Russel, do you think the President understands?" she asked again.

"Yes, I do."

Rachel lowered her eyes to her lap. "I feel sick," she whispered.

"I'm a historian, Rachel. The President's advisers are politicians. Politicians never see beyond the next election. Their advice is predicated on doing nothing that could hurt the President in an election. From that point of view, avoiding the Jewish issue may be good advice. As a historian I know their advice is horrible and will eventually stain this administration for all of time."

"The President must be made to understand what you have just said."

"He and I don't exactly chat every day," he replied sarcastically.

"You could write to him."

"The letter would never reach his desk. I'd tell him if I could. God knows I would."

"There is a way," Rachel persisted.

"I'm listening."

"The committee wants to run an advertisement in the newspapers. If we knew the actual number of refugees being admitted into the United States, we could run ads that would be certain to get his attention."

"They would consider that treason around here," he said, shaking his head.

"Since when has telling the truth been treason?"

"Rachel, we're not talking about some minor difference of

opinion here. We're talking about a scandal of major historical proportions. We're talking about a volcano of protest, about the biggest and maybe the ugliest controversy ever visited upon this administration. We're talking about injuring, maybe mortally injuring, this President's credibility with Congress. That means the President's ability to pursue the war effort could also be compromised. Whoever conveys the information you're looking for will become a pariah."

"Will you try?"

"Ruin is forever, Rachel."

"So is death."

He closed his eyes momentarily and then looked at her again.

"Russel, please," she pleaded. "Will you help?"

"I'll be in touch." His eyes searched hers for understanding.

She was silent for a moment, hesitant to pursue the matter any further. Then without another word she stood and left his office.

Within two weeks after Russel Forester had passed the refugee information he had wrangled from the State Department on to Rachel, newspapers across the country were carrying this message to the nation:

90% Condemned—America's Gift to Hitler
When judgment day comes, America will share the responsibility with Germany for the destruction of the Jewish people in Europe. For surely he who refuses shelter to the hunted must share the guilt of the hunter.

America is slamming shut the gates of life to nine out of ten refugees eligible to enter the United States under current immigration quotas. While hundreds of thousands of Jews are being led to slaughter, America is admitting less than twenty refugees a day. For every one Jew allowed in, America turns her back on nine others.

These victims are America's gift to the Nazis. The enemy feasts on the blood of those turned away.

Committee for a Jewish Army

Rachel called Russel the day after the ads ran in selected Sunday editions. "Russel, it's wonderful! The truth is finally out and no one will ever be able to sweep it under the rug again."

"Yes, yes, I know," Forester answered.

"Someone is going to have to answer for leaking that information," Rachel warned.

"I don't think so. It seems the information got out while Assistant Secretary of State Long was away. No one is taking responsibility over at State, and no one will want to get blamed for conducting a purge."

"There will be a national debate over this insane policy, Russel. It's just beginning."

"Let's hope so. Let's hope so."

Chapter Thirty-five

In the ghetto all the talk was of the new war, the war in the East between Germany and Russia. There were those who fervently believed that, at last, Hitler had bitten off more than he could chew. The Russian streamroller would flatten him, they said. There were others who believed the opposite, who pointed to the incredible speed with which the German Panzers were penetrating into the heart of Russia. According to rumor, German tanks were already on the outskirts of Kiev. One way or the other, the ghetto dwellers agreed that with the new war, the Germans were going to be too busy to torment the Jews.

Then the other rumors began to trickle in. Atrocities, torture, mass killings. The Germans denied the rumors of course. The people of the ghettos, not knowing whom to believe, could only pray the stories were untrue.

"I can't believe it," David said to Dvoyra as they walked together to the Self-Help kitchen. "And I think we ought to stop all this speculation. Things are bad enough here as it is."

Dvoyra smiled and squeezed his hand. "People are strange. It's almost as if by telling such horror stories, believing that somewhere out there mass killing is going on, the ghetto becomes more bearable."

The long line of people waiting patiently in the broiling sun for soup had become a permanent feature. David and Dvoyra were about to go into the kitchen when a young volunteer who worked in the clinic, Arthur Zygelbaum, came running after them. He took David to one side and spoke to him in an urgent undertone. Dvoyra saw David frown, then nod.

"We have to go back to my office," he said to her.

"What is it?"

"There's been a massacre. A survivor has been brought here." They hurried off with Zygelbaum, to the office, where two men were waiting. On the old sofa by the wall lay a young woman in torn, bloodstained clothing. She was sleeping, one arm hanging down toward the floor.

"David Berg?" one of the men said anxiously. "I'm Nathan Celemensky. This is Chaim Meltzer. We are members of Ha-Shomer ha-Zair. We were making our way north to Bialystok when we found her." He gestured toward the sleeping woman. "Her name is Chana Piorsky. She was wandering about on the road to Blazawa. We were coming this way and thought she would be safer here."

"Where is she from?" David asked.

"South of here. Przemysl, I think," Nathan Celemensky said. "We don't know exactly. She's been incoherent, but something pretty terrible must have happened to her. She's exhausted. She needs food and a place where she can rest."

"We'll look after her," David promised. "What about you?"

"If you can spare us a little food to take with us, we'll be grateful. But only if you can spare it."

The men left soon afterward, while Chana Piorsky was sleeping. David asked Dvoyra to sit with her until she awoke to reassure Chana that she was among friends. He returned to the office in the evening to find Chana devouring some food that Dvoyra had brought her. Dvoyra's face was white with shock.

"Dvoyra! What is it?"

"Call the people together, David," she said in a low voice. "Bring them all together at the Self-Help kitchen."

"Why?"

"So that they can hear what Chana Piorsky has to tell them."

The basement of the Self-Help kitchen was used mostly for storage. It was dark and dirty, with only a single light bulb hanging in the center of the room. The place was packed with people when David and Dvoyra brought Chana Piorsky down the stairs and sat her on an old trunk beneath the light. She was still wearing the soiled, ragged dress, and she looked dazed, as if her eyes were focused on something other than the people around her. She clasped her hands together and held them between her thighs.

The silence in the room was immense. Dvoyra knelt in front of the woman and touched her arm. "Chana," she said softly. "Chana?"

The woman's eyes lost their unfocused look as she stared at Dvoyra without speaking. She was clearly in great distress.

"Tell us where you are from, Chana."

"South of Przemysl, near the border with Czechoslovakia," Chana Piorsky whispered.

"Do you have a family? A husband? Children?"

The woman looked directly into Dvoyra's eyes and shook her head. "Not anymore. They shot them. All of them."

"Your whole family?"

"My family, all the families," Chana said without emotion. "Hundreds of them."

"Tell these people what you told me, Chana," Dvoyra urged. "Tell them what happened."

"The Germans came. In their trucks." She spoke slowly, lurchingly, as though her mind was a great distance away. "They ordered us—all of us Jews—from our homes. We were told to bring nothing. Only the children." She looked at the faces of the Jews who had come to hear her story, then closed her eyes for a moment. She sighed and went on.

"They told us to get into the trucks. There were not enough trucks for all the people. They said those who could not get into the trucks would have to run along behind. Everyone tried to climb into the trucks, but there was no more room. I had my little girl, Raizel, with me. Some of the women were carrying two or three children. They drove away and we tried to keep up. We tried, but some of the women tripped and fell. Some just couldn't run anymore. They . . . they just . . ."

She closed her eyes again, as if to block out the horrible vision.

"What happened then, Chana?"

"They shot them," she whispered. "They shot them, right where they fell. In the street."

David held up a hand to still the group's angry, fearful reaction. "Go on, Chana," he said.

"They took us outside the town, a wooded spot near a ravine. They lined us all up at the side of the road and told us to take off all our clothes. They took all the clothes away—men, women, even the children. Then they . . ."

Again she stopped, her breathing labored. She sighed deeply and lifted her head, staring at the ceiling for a moment.

"They took about fifteen of the people out of the line and marched them away, behind a hill. We heard shots, screams. Then the soldiers came back. They took away another group. There were more shots. More screams."

The room was as silent as a tomb now as the dozens listening hung on every word.

"I lost count of how many they took before it was my turn," Chana said, still speaking in the same unemotional monotone. "They took my Raizel away from me, just carried her off with the group before mine. I never even saw . . . They shot her among strangers."

She put her face in her hands and at last, wept. Her sobs sounded unnaturally loud in the silence. Again Chana Piorsky struggled to regain some kind of composure.

"Then it was our turn. They took us up the road and behind the hill, then up the hill. I was standing with my sister and a friend. We were crying, holding on to one another. A German pushed us forward, and we saw a pit. I looked down and I could see bodies. Dozens of them. Some of them were still alive. Squirming, twitching, moaning and crying. And blood. Everywhere, blood. A stink of blood and . . . oh, God, it was awful, it was awful!"

She swallowed hard and nodded when Dvoyra took her hand and held it tightly to comfort her.

"I heard the soldier loading his machine gun behind us. I knew I was going to die. There was death all around me. I got dizzy, and I thought I was going to vomit. I think I heard the machine gun firing, but I must have fainted just as he started shooting. I don't know how long I was unconscious. When I came to, there were bodies all around me and on top of me. Here and there someone moved, and I could hear moaning. Then I passed out again. When I awoke the second time, it was quiet. There were more bodies on top of me. They must have saved my life. I don't know how I did it, but I climbed out of the pit. Everyone was dead. Everyone. They killed my whole family before my eyes. My mother, my grandmother, my sister, Raizel . . ."

"How did you get away?" someone whispered.

"There were clothes scattered all around the area. I found this dress hanging on the branches of some bushes nearby." Every eye in the room was on the bloodstained rags she was wearing. "I escaped through the woods, running until I was exhausted. Then I slept in a ditch. The next day I was found, and my rescuers brought me here."

"Did the Germans tell you why they were executing the people?" someone asked. "Was the town being punished?"

"They are doing the same thing everywhere. I heard the soldiers talking. They were part of a special military unit, an *Einsatzgruppe*."

"A special task force?" someone translated. "What is their function?"

"They kill Jews," Chana said flatly. "They were talking about the places it was happening. They had been shooting Jews by the thousands. In Lvov, in Stanislawów, Tarnopol, Zloczow, Brezezany. God alone knows how many other places they have been or are going to. But that's all they do. They kill Jews."

"Impossible," someone whispered.

"Special army units that do nothing but kill Jews?" a man said. "She's mad!"

"No, she is not mad!"

Every head in the room turned toward the speaker. It was Professor Hoffmeister. Everyone knew him, and his words carried more weight than those of most men, for everyone respected his intellect.

"She is not mad," Hoffmeister said again. "They are mad perhaps. But not this good woman. I think we are seeing the first evidence of what Hitler meant when he boasted that war would mean the destruction of the Jewish people in Europe. This is his solution to what he calls the Jewish problem."

"Solution?"

"You think they intend to kill us all?"

"All of us?"

"Yes," he said. "All of us. The ghettos are temporary. They have something else in mind."

"You can't be serious!" a man burst out. "You can't expect us to believe they are going to take more then three million men, women, and children out into the countryside and shoot them!"

"Of course not," Hoffmeister said. "That would be too noisy. Too visible. And it would take too long. Our Nazi friends are much more efficient than that."

"Then how, Professor? How will they do it?" Dvoyra asked.

Hoffmeister shook his head, indicating he had no answer. "They will find a way."

The two visitors from Warsaw were both young men, still in their early twenties, but their faces looked older and their eyes were like those of hunted animals. Mordechai Anielewitz and Maurice Asher were on their way to a secret meeting with partisan leaders who were camped near Brest, and they had snuck into the ghetto of Biala-Podlaska for the night.

David was eager to hear news of the Warsaw ghetto and was impressed by their account of the efforts being made there to maintain as many normal activities as possible. He was particularly interested in what they told him about the establishment of a vigorous underground press. David, in turn, told them about the Oneg Shabbat archive, and they promised to pass the news to Dr. Ringelblum, who would be gratified to know his movement had spread this far. David then asked the two young men why they were making their dangerous journey.

"To discuss the future," Maurice replied.

"The future?" David said.

"You said you were impressed by our efforts to preserve some kind of cultural stability," Mordechai told him. "Some of us wonder whether we have not perhaps been wasting valuable time. Time that might have been spent preparing for what the Nazis have in store for us."

"I'm not sure I follow you." David frowned.

Maurice and Mordechai exchanged glances. "The Nazis have gone mad," Maurice said. "They have swept through the occupied territories like a cyclone. In Lvov the Ukrainians joined the Germans in house-to-house searches for Jews, shooting them on the spot when they found them. And then there was a pogrom to avenge the fifteen-year-old death of

Simon Petlyura, the self-styled leader of the Ukraine. Can you believe that? A Jew killed that anti-Semitic butcher in 1926, and in 1941 they avenge him by slaughtering thousands of our people!"

"We heard about the *Einsatzgruppen* from a woman who came here." David described Chana Piorsky's account of the butchery in her village. The two young men said nothing during David's recounting of the awful story. It was clear that it was one they had heard, with variations, many times before.

"What do you think will happen to those of us who are locked in the ghettos?" David asked.

"The same," Maurice said.

"The Nazis have committed themselves," Mordechai explained. "Once they finish with the Jews of the Eastern territories, they will turn their attention to the Jews of Poland."

"Then it really is true?" David asked quietly. "They plan to kill every Jew in Europe?"

"Unquestionably," Maurice said.

"We believe the time has come for us to organize ourselves," Mordechai announced. "Prepare to resist the Germans."

"You want to organize *zelbshuts*?" David said with a scornful laugh. "Self-defense against the SS? How do you propose to do that?"

"Very simple," Maurice said abruptly. "You teach everyone capable of firing a gun how to kill a Nazi."

"Are you insane?" David cried. "These aren't drunken peasants you're talking about, or even a company of cossacks. This is the SS! If we lift a finger against any one of them, they will kill a hundred of our people!"

"And if we do not lift a finger, they will kill them anyway," Mordechai said. "And a hundred more, and then more, until all are dead."

"No," David said firmly. "I think you are wrong. I would never condone such thinking here in Biala-Podlaska. It would be suicide."

A slight cynical smile touched Mordechai Anielewitz's face, his expression suggesting that he had heard all this before too. "You'd rather allow your people to be led like sheep to the slaughter."

"There are millions of Jews left in Poland!" David exclaimed. "If we negotiate these troubled waters carefully, hundreds of thousands, maybe millions of Jews can survive the war."

"Mr. Berg, you are not going to *negotiate* these troubled waters of yours, or any other," Mordechai said angrily. "You are talking about survival as if that is the only issue."

"And what is more important than how best to survive?"

Mordechai stared at David before he replied, "How best to die, Mr. Berg."

David said nothing, so moved was he by the young man's simple words. *They are not talking about self-defense anymore,* he thought. *They are talking about defiance in the face of death, honor in the place of passivity.*

"We do not want our people to be remembered as one that dug its own grave and stood silently on the brink of that grave while its executioners took aim, Mr. Berg," Mordechai went on. "I, for one, will not dig my own grave and wait for them to shoot me. And I cannot understand why you, or anyone else, would do so!"

"You make it sound simple. But of course it is not."

"It is, Mr. Berg," Maurice said. "You can either die fighting, or you can die like an animal in a trap."

"That's why we're going to Brest," Mordechai said. "Our people, the Ha-Shomer ha-Zair, representatives of the other youth movements will be there. We will find out more about what the Nazis have been doing in Russia. We also hope to meet someone from the partisans to see if they can supply us with weapons."

"Do you have any yet?"

"Two revolvers," Maurice said.

"Nothing else? You're talking about fighting the Nazis, and you have two pistols?"

"We will use them to teach others to shoot. We will buy guns on the Aryan side. Maybe the partisans will help us."

"We can't fight them," David whispered. "We can't."

"You're wrong, Mr. Berg," Maurice Asher said. "We must!"

Dvoyra was excited when David told her about his meeting with the two young men from Warsaw. Her reaction to the name of Mordechai Anielewitz surprised him.

"You know him?"

"No, I never met him. But Peninah went to a lecture he gave in Suwalki in the spring before the war started. David, he saved Peninah's life! It was he who convinced her to emigrate to Eretz Israel!"

She gazed into space, and David knew she was thinking of her children, as she was apt to do so often these days. He said nothing, not wishing to interrupt her reverie. Later he promised her that if the two men stopped at Biala–Podlaska on their way back to Warsaw, he would arrange for her to meet them.

The opportunity came sooner than she expected, for they stopped overnight in the ghetto a week later. Their mission had been partially, but not completely, successful. There, as elsewhere, opinion was divided on the wisdom of confronting the Nazis. Two points of view had emerged: one, that honor and vengeance demanded resistance; and the other, that the ghetto was no place for guerrilla warfare, and that resistance would be more successful if they joined up with the partisans in the Russian forests.

Dvoyra was startled when she saw the two men for the first time. *They are so young!* she thought as they rose to greet her.

"I have heard about you," she said to Mordechai Anielewitz. "I can't tell you how much it means to me to finally have the chance to meet you."

She stared into his eyes, desperately wishing she knew more about him. He was Peninah's age, and like Peninah he had understood what was happening long before most of Poland's Jews. For a moment neither of them spoke. Finally, not knowing what to say, he smiled awkwardly.

"I'm sorry I was staring." Dvoyra smiled. "We have never met, but my daughter met you. Well, actually, I'm not even sure she did. She attended a lecture you gave in Suwalki in the spring of 1939."

"Suwalki." He looked away as if he was trying to recall something from the past. "Suwalki. That was a bad time. Frustrating. We knew what was going to happen, and we knew there wasn't a thing we could do to stop it."

"My daughter told me, the morning after your talk, that you had said there would be war, and that it would be very bad for the Jews. You were quite a prophet, Mr. Anielewitz."

"It gives me no pleasure to know it, Mrs. Hoffman. Is your daughter well?"

Dvoyra smiled at the tactfulness of his question, the ghetto euphemism for *Is your daughter alive?* "She is in Eretz Israel, thanks to you. She made up her mind to go after hearing you speak. My younger daughter and a nephew went with them. You saved their lives, Mr. Anielewitz. I thank you."

Too moved to speak, Mordechai Anielewitz looked down at the floor.

"I didn't mean to embarrass you," Dvoyra apologized.

"You didn't. It was joy, not embarrassment, Mrs. Hoffman. It thrills me to know that there are Jews living free in Eretz Israel."

"Living free because of you."

"I only wish there could have been more."

"And what will become of you and Mr. Asher now?" Dvoyra asked. "Where will you go from here?"

"Back to the Warsaw ghetto," Maurice said, as if the question had surprised him.

"Back to the ghetto? Why?"

"I am needed there. We both are."

Dvoyra reached up and kissed Mordechai Anielewitz on the cheek. Taking his hands into hers, she looked into his eyes again. "God bless you, Mordechai Anielewitz. I will be thankful all my days that you and my Peninah crossed paths." She released his hands and stepped back.

"We have to go," Asher said.

"Will we ever see you again?" Dvoyra asked.

Mordechai Anielewitz shrugged. "God knows."

Chapter Thirty-six

By the end of 1941 the accounts of atrocities committed by the Nazis in Russia had become so frequent, and so appalling, that the ghetto dwellers no longer questioned their authenticity. The only question now remaining was: What did the Nazis intend to do with the Jews of Poland?

"If they wanted to kill us, they would have killed us already," said one faction.

"If they want to kill us, they can do so whenever they choose," argued another.

"Don't worry," said a third group. "We'll probably all be dead before the winter's over anyway."

The icy winds that had howled around the walls of the ghetto throughout November gave way to snow, thick, relentless, swirling snow that blanketed Biala-Podlaska two feet deep. As a Christmas gift to the starving Jews, the Nazis delivered a consignment of stale bread to the Self-Help kitchen.

From the warm comfort of his office, SS and Police Leader Hans Botchermann looked down at the icy streets below. He unlocked his briefcase and placed inside it the dispatches and memoranda that had arrived that morning. Hardenberg, his aide, had sorted them into three piles as usual: urgent, requiring attention, and routine. The routine stuff he could read later. He shuffled through the second batch, which would require some sort of action or decision from him.

At the top of the urgent pile he saw a memorandum with the familiar Berlin heading of Reichsfuhrer Heinrich Himmler's office:

To all SS and Police Leaders in the General Government

A new quarantine center is nearing completion in the town of Auschwitz, near Katowice. During the initial period of operations, when special procedures are being refined, it will be desirable for limited numbers of Jewish criminals whose conduct requires their quarantine from the population at large to be sent there.

SS-Hauptsturmfurhrer Rudolf Hoess is to be notified of all shipments to be effected, together with the names, ages, and sex of those being transported to Auschwitz. This matter is to be given your highest priority.

Heil Hitler!

It was signed with Himmler's jagged double initials. Botchermann stared at the document. This was no routine directive. If he acted wisely, this could be his passport to much bigger things. If he was among the first to send "criminals" to Auschwitz, odds were that Hoess would mention him by name in his reports to Himmler. He curled the documents into a cylinder and shouted to Hardenberg to bring his car around. He was going to the ghetto.

"Look at those poor men," Elena Hoffmeister said, peering through the window of the Self-Help kitchen. "They look half-dead!"

Huddled together in the snow-covered Platz Volnustike were about a hundred Russian prisoners of war. They had been marched mercilessly for two hundred miles on their way to internment at a camp somewhere in the west. They were weak with starvation and severe exposure and were only allowed to drop to the ground so that their guards could rest.

"Can't we take some food to them?" Dvoyra said. "Some of the stale bread that was delivered?"

"We can't just walk among them handing out bread," Else Kramerman said. "The guards would stop us in a minute."

"There aren't that many of them," Elena said. "I can only see about ten."

"Suppose we just walked along the sidewalk, near where the men are lying?" Dvoyra said. "We could put down the bread in baskets, and they could pass them to the other prisoners."

"What about the guards, Dvoyra?" Else said.

"They look pretty tired. They probably won't even notice us."

"Even if they do, what's the worst that can happen?" Elena said. "They'll take the bread and eat it themselves."

Dvoyra, Elena, Else, and three other women packed the stale loaves into baskets and set out walking in single file toward the square. When they reached it, they stopped for a moment. They did not notice the young German guard on the opposite side of the square who watched them intently as they decided what to do.

As they moved toward the far side of the square where the prisoners were lying, the guard crossed to the rear of the prisoners and turned onto the sidewalk thirty yards behind the women. He quickened his pace as they began walking faster. He saw several of them dart to the edge of the street and lay down their baskets next to the Russians.

"Halt!" he yelled. "Halt, or I fire!"

The women froze in their tracks. Four of them had already set down their baskets. Dvoyra and Elena still carried theirs.

"It's all right," Dvoyra whispered as the other guards,

attracted by shouts, moved slowly toward them. "Stay calm."

As the Germans drew nearer, Paula Mielewitz, who was farthest from Dvoyra, turned as if to run.

"Paula, stop!" Dvoyra screamed, as one of the guards jerked his machine pistol into firing position. The frightened woman stopped, trembling and began to cry.

"It's just bread," one of the guards said, poking the barrel of his rifle into the baskets on the ground.

Some of the Russians were holding out their hands, begging for the food.

"Please, we meant no harm," Dvoyra said to a young lieutenant who had now appeared on the scene. "We only wanted to give them some bread."

"You were very foolish!" he snapped. "You could have been shot! How was anyone to know it was only bread you had in the baskets?"

"Will you let us go now?"

"That is up to the police. It is out of my hands." The young soldier turned away as two SS officers crossed the square toward him and explained to them what had happened.

"Leave this to us," one of the officers said. "We'll take care of these Jewish swine."

At that moment they saw the low-slung black Mercedes staff car turn into the square. Botchermann's driver jumped out and yanked open the door. Botchermann emerged, clutching a rolled-up bundle of papers in his hand. "What is going on here?"

The two SS officers snapped to attention and saluted. "Smugglers, Herr Standartenfuhrer! These Jewish swine were smuggling bread to the Russian prisoners!"

"No, we—"

"Where did you obtain this bread?" Botchermann shouted, snatching a loaf of the stale bread out of the basket on Dvoyra's arm.

"From the Self-Help kitchen," she stammered.

"You took bread? Scarce bread given you by the Reich? You tried to give rationed food to these—subhumans?" he screamed at her.

"They are men!" she cried. "They were starv—"

"Be silent, bitch!" he yelled, slapping her across the face with the rolled-up papers he held in his fist. She lifted a hand to touch the place where he had hit her, already marked with an ugly red welt. Botchermann stared at the papers in his hand. *Jewish criminals,* he thought. Himmler's directive had stipulated that Jewish criminals be sent to Auschwitz. He smiled.

"Please," Elena Hoffmeister begged. "Let us go. We're sorry for what we did. We won't—"

"Silence!" one of the SS officers shouted.

"Take them away!" Botchermann said, turning his back on the women. "Hold them under guard until arrangements can be made to transport them to Auschwitz!"

"Right away, Colonel! How soon do you want transportation to be available?"

"Immediately! Tell Hardenberg to get right on it."

"Jawohl, Herr Standartenführer!"

Botchermann got into his car as the SS officer ordered some soldiers to escort the women to SS headquarters. He directed his driver to take him straight back to his office, where he instructed his aide to contact Hoess at Auschwitz to make sure they were ready to receive criminal Jews pursuant to Himmler's directive. Then he dictated a report for the Higher SS and Police Leader in Lublin:

SS and Polizei Fuhrer
XXV Abschnitte, Biala-Podlaska
December 30, 1941

Subject: Criminal acts of the following Jewesses:

1. Eva Ullerman
2. Else Kramerman
3. Paula Mielewitz
4. Dvoyra Hoffman
5. Elena Hoffmeister
6. Hannah Rappaport

The above-named subjects were apprehended while attempting to smuggle bread to Russian prisoners of war. Further inquiries established that the bread had been stolen from the Jewish food distribution center in Biala-Podlaska, to which it had been supplied by the SSPF.

The above-named subjects have been found guilty of theft, smuggling, and attempting to establish contact with the enemy, and resisting arrest. The prisoners have been transported to the criminal quarantine center at Auschwitz.

Heil Hitler!

Botchermann looked up as Hardenberg came into the room.

"We got through to Auschwitz," the aide said.

"And?"

"Affirmative. They are receiving criminal elements as directed by the Reichsfuhrer's memorandum."

Botchermann picked up his pen and scribbled his signature at the bottom of the transportation order.

"You have arranged for a vehicle to take these women to Auschwitz?"

"It will be ready within the hour."

"Excellent." Botchermann leaned back and slowly rubbed his hands together. "Excellent!"

The six women sat shivering in the basement of SS headquarters for nearly an hour. No one spoke to them or came near their cell.

"What are they going to do with us?" Hannah Rappaport asked fearfully.

"That man said something about transport to Auschwitz. Where is Auschwitz?"

"It's near Katowice, to the south," Elena Hoffmeister said. "It's the German name for Oswiecim."

"They won't send us all the way to Katowice just for trying to give bread to the Russians," Dvoyra said, trying to hide her doubts. "Don't worry, Hannah."

Dvoyra knew something terrible was happening, but she was not afraid—only heartsick at the realization that she would not see David again. More than anything, she wanted to hold him one last time.

"It's just that if I'm not home by sundown, my husband will be worried sick."

"It's all right, Hannah." Eva Ullerman put her arm around the young woman's shoulders. "They'll let us go soon, you'll see."

They heard the heavy footsteps on the stone floor outside the cell. Keys jangled, and then the door flew open. An SS guard entered, his expression threatening. He smiled constantly and his cold blue eyes seemed to dance with delight as they drank in the fear and misery the women tried to conceal.

He looked at the prisoners one at a time. "You will come with me!"

"What are you going to do with us?" Paula Mielewitz asked. The guard looked at her, and his smile widened. Paula was a pretty girl, dark and petite.

"What would you like me to do to you?" Approaching her, he grabbed her chin.

Paula tried to turn her face away, but the guard held her tightly, leering at her until she began to cry.

"Ach!" he said impatiently, and let her go. "Get up, all of you. Come on, come on! *Schnell! Schnell!*"

The six women were taken from the cell out into a cobbled courtyard at the rear of the building. A canvas-covered Opel truck was waiting, its motor running. The two guards at the rear of the vehicle motioned for the women to climb inside the truck, which had been fitted on either side with rough bench seats. The two guards followed them in, taking the seats at the open end, their guns on their knees and pointed at the terrified women.

It was just after eleven as the truck pulled out of the courtyard and headed southwest on the Radom road.

News of the arrests did not reach David Berg until two that afternoon, when he returned from his daily inspection tour of the ghetto. Arthur Zygelbaum told him what had happened and gave him the names of the six women arrested.

"Dvoyra?" David felt as if someone were tightening bands of steel around his chest. "They took Dvoyra?"

"No one could do anything, Mr. Berg," Arthur said. "It was Botchermann himself who had them arrested."

David ran all the way to SS headquarters and presented himself to an aide, requesting an urgent interview with Botchermann.

"Wait there," the aide said coldly. "I'll see if the Colonel is free."

Hurry up, damn you! David thought, gritting his teeth as the minutes ticked away. He still could not believe that the women had been detained for more than five hours for something as simple and harmless as giving bread to hungry prisoners of war.

The aide returned to escort David to Botchermann's office, closing the door as he went out.

Botchermann was studying some papers. He did not look up. "What is it, Berg? I'm busy."

"You arrested six Jewish women this morning. I understand they are here. I have come to take them back to the ghetto."

Botchermann looked up, a look of puzzlement on his face. "Are you serious? You expect me to release them?"

"You have had them in confinement for nearly six hours. Surely you've frightened them enough. They won't do anything inappropriate again."

"Inappropriate? What they did was not inappropriate, Berg. What they did was criminal. And they are to be treated like criminals!"

"Colonel, please! Don't torment these people or their families. You surely don't intend to keep them in prison just for giving bread to starving men?"

"In that, at least, you are correct. I don't intend to keep them in prison. They are already on their way to a new quarantine center for criminals near Katowice."

"They're *what*?" David shouted, his anger so fierce that Botchermann flinched.

"My orders are to send criminals to the new quarantine center at Auschwitz. That is what I have done. Now, get out."

David heard the guards enter behind him and struggled to control his fury. He turned and exited without another word.

Dvoyra and her five companions arrived at Auschwitz at noon on December 31, 1941. It was immediately apparent to them that the camp was being readied to accommodate an enormous number of people. Construction work was going on everywhere. Rows of barracks were already built, and the sound of sawing and hammering indicated that even more were being readied. Most sinister of all to Dvoyra's eyes was the frightening number of SS stationed in such a remote place.

The Opel truck pulled into a vast open area, which was cut in two by a rail line. The tracks entered the perimeter through an opening in a long, single-story building, an observation tower built over its entrance.

"Everyone out!" a voice shouted from the rear of the truck. "Out! out! *Raus, raus!*"

Shaking with fear, the six women climbed down from the truck and looked about them.

"God in heaven, what an awful place," Elena Hoffmeister whispered.

"What's going to happen to us?" Paula whimpered. The other women did not answer her. No one knew.

A gang of construction laborers, working on a massive rail platform alongside the railroad tracks, stopped what they were doing to stare at the six women standing in the center of the receiving area. The SS guard strode among them, shouting, and the men hastily resumed work.

"This is not a camp," Eva Ullerman whispered. "It is a prison. Look at the fence—it's electrified."

"If it's a prison, it must be the biggest one in the world," Elena Hoffmeister observed. "That fence runs as far as you can see."

"Look how long the railroad platform is," Hannah said. "You think they are going to bring people here by rail, like the men they took to Belzec?"

"Why have they brought us here?"

Dvoyra shook her head. "I don't know, Paula."

"You think they are going to keep us here until the war ends, Dvoyra?"

"No," Dvoyra said gently, tears blurring her vision. "I don't." Elena Hoffmeister looked at her, understanding the meaning of Dvoyra's words.

"No talking!" a guard shouted. "You will follow me to that building over there!"

He led them to the tall tower with the observation deck. Once inside, the women were taken to a large room furnished with a desk, a table, and swivel chairs. They stood waiting for several minutes until the door opened and an SS second lieutenant entered the room. The guard who had brought them from Biala–Podlaska snapped to attention and handed the officer an envelope that contained Botchermann's report. As the officer read it, another man entered the room. He carried an instrument that looked like a large pen, with an electrical cord extending from the end opposite the point. He sat down at the table.

Putting the report down on the desk, the officer looked up at the women, his expression one of acute boredom. "You were apprehended smuggling bread to enemy prisoners. You have been sent here for disposition by the SS and Police Leader of Biala–Podlaska. You will—"

"We meant no harm!" Dvoyra spoke up. "We only wanted to—"

"Silence!" the officer shouted. "You are guilty of grave offenses."

"We've done nothing!" Elena Hoffmeister protested.

The SS officer looked up, his eyes now angry. He snapped his fingers and one of the guards moved forward, grabbing Elena Hoffmeister by the hair and dragging her from the room. The officer got up from behind the desk and moved to stand directly in front of the remaining women.

"Let what you have just seen be a lesson to you Jews!" he said in a low tone, his voice even more menacing because it was so quiet. "You will learn there is only one road to freedom here—obedience! From now on, life will be a day-to-day achievement. Never again make the mistake of expecting to be treated like anything other than the Jew vermin you are!"

Dvoyra hardly heard him.

"It will only be a matter of time until every Jew in Europe is resettled in a camp such as this. You are among the first to sample its pleasures. Later, thousands will come. Perhaps millions."

"This camp will hold millions?" Else Kramerman asked in horror.

"I said millions will come here." The SS officer let his words hang there until the women grasped their meaning. "How long they are allowed to live will be up to them. Now," the officer continued, "get undressed!"

The women stared at him in disbelief. Paula Mielewitz instinctively wrapped her arms around her shoulders.

"Are you deaf? Take off your clothes. Disrobe, *this instant!*"

Dvoyra saw the anger in the man's eyes and watched as he drew in his breath. Before he could shout out the next command, she swallowed hard and began to unbutton her dress. The other women looked at her, dumbfounded. Dvoyra let her dress fall to the floor, then removed her shoes. Blinded by tears of shame, she removed her undergarments. The other women followed suit. Dvoyra folded one arm across her breasts, moving her free hand down in a pathetic gesture of modesty.

"You are learning," the officer said with an obscene smile of appreciation. When all of them were undressed, one of the guards gathered up their clothes and dropped in front of each of them a striped prison dress. The man with the strange electrical instrument called out the name of Paula Mielewitz.

"Yes?" she whispered.

"Over here," the man said.

She walked to him, staring wide-eyed at the instrument he held in his hand. He grabbed her wrist tightly, and as he began tattooing on her right arm the number she would carry for the rest of her brief life, Paula Mielewitz cried out in pain. Impassively the Nazi repeated the procedure with each of the prisoners.

Dvoyra and her companions were assigned to work gangs, clearing construction debris. They were routed from their squalid bunks in the barracks before dawn and marched to one or another of the various construction sites at the new camp called Birkenau. There, Dvoyra and the others loaded broken bricks, spare lumber, and chunks of concrete into waiting trucks. Dvoyra weakened rapidly as the daily ration of one slice of bread, one bowl of soup, and one small piece of bacon took its toll.

Even though the January weather was bitterly cold, the swampy terrain around Auschwitz was not yet frozen. They marched along roads sticky with clay, out into the empty, deserted landscape, where the outlines of the new camp disappeared far beyond the dark line of the forest in the early morning mist. They were pale and gaunt with hunger and exhaustion, infested with lice; no longer alive, yet still not dead.

The camp had several off limits areas. In one of these some large buildings were being erected; one of them had five separate smokestacks. Dvoyra also observed two construction projects taking place inside several large peasant houses she passed each day on her way to Birkenau. These, too, were off limits to all prisoners. She tried to find out why the windows of the houses were sealed off, but no one seemed to know.

As the weeks passed, the number of Jews arriving at Auschwitz from all over Europe increased steadily. The transports frequently arrived at night, one after another. The camp seemed to swallow up the new inmates as fast as they came. More barracks were being built, and more beyond those. It was said the new camp would be ready for business at the end of the summer.

As the number of men in the camp increased, the women were given lighter work in the kitchens or cleaning out the barracks. They were driven as hard as before, but it was not the soul-destroying physical labor they had first experienced.

Dvoyra lay on her bunk and closed her eyes. She wanted only to sleep. The others were talking and it was impossible to ignore the sound of their voices.

"The guard told me it was a bathhouse," Paula said. "A bathhouse for Jews."

They were talking about the remodeled peasants' houses with their sealed off windows.

"That's what the Nazis have now, is it?" Hannah said scornfully. "The only secret bathhouse in the world?"

"That's right," Eva said. "If it's only a bathhouse, why is it off limits? Why has it got a sign that says unauthorized persons found in the area will be shot?"

Dvoyra listened to the women talking, remembering Professor Hoffmeister's prophecy. *They will find a way,* he had said. A way to kill all the Jews in Europe. Whatever those ugly new buildings might be, they were certainly not "a bathhouse for Jews," but something infinitely more terrible.

One morning in late spring—Dvoyra knew it must be spring because the evenings had grown longer and the huge puddles that dotted the camp began to dry up—the women were confined to their block instead of being taken outside for roll call and assignment to a work detail.

At ten o'clock a squad of SS marched into the dormitory and ordered them outside. They were all lined up in three rows, then marched across the encampment to the remodeled peasant huts. Other women from other dormitories stood outside in lines, waiting. Off to one side a group of civilians, accompanied by SS officers, stood watching with unusually keen interest.

The SS sergeant in charge of the squad stepped in front of the rows of women and told them that a new facility had been installed, that these buildings were the new delousing center. Each woman was to take a shower and then be deloused. They would leave their clothes in the changing rooms in the small building alongside. These would also be deloused and returned to the prisoners after they had showered.

Dvoyra undressed and folded up her clothes, which were collected by one of the women and laid in a pile at the end of the room where they had entered. Now she followed the others out the door and on to one of the huts. There were two steps up to the door, which she noticed had a small peephole at the top.

She looked around the room. The interior walls had all been removed, and the doorframes were lined with rubber. Several shower heads protruded from the ceiling, but she observed, there were no drains in the floor.

This is no bathhouse, she thought, and the certainty of what was about to happen descended upon her, turning her body icy cold. She looked at the faces of her friends—Eva, Paula Mielewitz, Else, Hannah Rappaport—the women from the Biala-Podlaska ghetto had managed to stay together. Everyone was staring up at the shower heads.

They heard footsteps on the roof, and then hissing sounds came from the direction of the shower heads.

Suddenly Dvoyra understood. "Peninah! Annette! Yitzhak! I love you!" she cried out. "Please live, my children! Live!"

Chapter Thirty-seven

David could not believe his eyes. Maurice Asher and Mordechai Anielewitz were still alive. It had been over a year since the young Jews from Warsaw had stopped at Biala-Podlaska on their way to Brest. Since then they had been making their way through the countryside, trying to organize a Jewish resistance movement in the ghettos of eastern Poland.

David remembered that their entire arsenal had consisted of two revolvers. It was Anielewitz who had told David that *how to die was more important than how to live.*

"So my friends, how goes the insurrection?" David asked after embracing the two men.

"We will shed Nazi blood," Maurice Asher said.

"There will really be an uprising?"

"We will fight in Warsaw," Mordechai replied.

"And Bialystok, and Lodz and Lvov?" David asked.

Mordechai shook his head. "They have nothing with which to fight. They will be massacred like sheep just as your people will be slaughtered here."

"And will the Jews of Warsaw live?"

"No. The Jews of Warsaw will not live either. We will die too. But we will die fighting."

David nodded. "You were right. How we die is more important than how we live. I think I actually envy you."

"Then join us," Maurice replied.

"What?"

"Join us. We need you."

"I'm needed here."

"You can do nothing here," Mordechai said. "In Warsaw you can make history."

"What do you mean?" David asked.

"We need help. We need someone who can carry on Ringelblum's work, and we need men who can lead when the uprising is called."

"His work continues?"

"It continues," Maurice said, "but the end is drawing near. The archives is our only chance that the world will know what happened in the ghettos. We need your help desperately."

"I need leaders, Berg. The final battle will be bloody. We will face an entire army. The Nazis must suffer in that battle."

"What about the Jews of Biala-Podlaska."

"There's no hope for them. Tell them what we learned, Mordechai."

Mordechai glanced at his companion. "There's no hope for the Jews here."

"What is Maurice talking about? What did you learn?" David asked.

Mordechai closed his eyes for a moment. "David, the Nazis are building killing centers throughout Poland. Some are already in operation."

"Please be specific," David asked, his heart sinking.

"Well, we know the Nazis have been gassing Jews at Chelmno. They're using vans in which carbon monoxide is circulated while the victims are driven to mass graves in the forest on the edge of the town."

David sat down behind his desk and lowered his head into his hands to control the nausea that swept through his body. "Go on," he finally said, lifting his eyes to meet Mordechai's.

"We believe they have just completed construction of an enormous killing center in Silesia at the city of Auschwitz."

"Auschwitz!" David cried.

"Yes, you know of Auschwitz?" Maurice asked, surprised at David's outburst.

"Dvoyra Hoffman—you remember her—I introduced you to her when you were here before. Botchermann sent Dvoyra to Auschwitz with five other women for trying to give bread to Russian prisoners who were camped here."

"How long ago?" Mordechai asked.

"They took her on December thirtieth," David said.

Mordechai looked down at the floor for a moment. "David, your friend is almost certainly dead," Maurice said. "And if by some twist of fate she is still alive, you should pray that death comes soon. Auschwitz is said to be a huge factory for murder."

David was silent. The fear he'd been living with since Dvoyra's disappearance now crystallized into hate, and despair. He barely heard the other man's words.

"They have also completed a killing center not far from Warsaw at a town called Treblinka," Maurice was saying. "It is not yet in operation, but we know about Treblinka. It is intended for the Warsaw Jews. Three centers have been built here in the east. One is at Sobibor, one is to the south of Belzec, and—"

"Belzec! Did you say Belzec?" David interrupted.

"Why, yes. You know of Belzec?"

"I had to select two hundred workers for Belzec."

"How long ago?" Mordechai asked.

"A year ago."

"Have they returned?"

"No."

"A year ago the death camp was not yet open, but there was a labor camp there. It's just as bad. No one ever comes back," Mordechai said grimly.

"I sent those men to their deaths," David said angrily.

"We know of another camp here in the east," Mordechai said. "Do you know the town of Majdynak?"

"Yes, it's just outsdie of Lublin. I know the area well."

"Majdynak is where the Jews of Biala-Podlaska will most likely be murdered. It's one of the newest of the killing centers. They intend to gas thousands of Jews there."

"Just like that! They intend to obliterate Polish Jewry?"

Mordechai nodded. "Only the Jews of Warsaw have the means to fight. Will you come with us, David?"

David thought for a moment before answering. "Yes, but there is something I must do first."

★ ★ ★

"What are you doing, Berg?" the Nazi asked impatiently as David bolted the door to Botchermann's office.

"I must talk to you in private. The prisoners. When will the women be returned to Biala-Podlaska? You must give me some word to take back to their families."

A dangerous smile played at the corners of Botchermann's lips. "So you want to carry news of the prisoners back to the Jews?"

David stiffened. "What has become of them?" he pressed, his tone of voice almost threatening.

The Nazi stared at David for a moment before responding. His taunting smile faded and his expression grew grave. "They committed a very serious crime, Berg."

"What has become of them?" David demanded as he leaned forward over Botchermann's desk.

"If I had not dealt with these criminals as quickly as I did, there could have been reprisals ordered against the entire town."

"What has become of them?" David repeated impatiently.

"They are dead, Berg. You Jews must be made to understand that we mean business."

David froze. "You killed them?"

"They were executed," Botchermann said coldly.

The Nazi's words cut into David and instantly he lunged across the desk at Botchermann. Botchermann, taken by surprise, tried to pry his assailant's hands from his neck, but David's grip was too tight. Botchermann struggled to get to his feet and nearly succeeded in doing so before David pulled him, violently, back into his chair.

Botchermann tried to twist his head around so that he could see David, who was now behind him. He was gagging and knew he would soon lose consciousness if he didn't do something quickly.

From the corner of his eye David saw Botchermann's fingers stretching toward the top left-hand drawer of the massive mahogany desk. He waited until the Nazi had managed to pull open the drawer enough to reach inside for the Luger he kept there. Then without warning and with all the strength he could command, David shoved his knee into the drawer, slamming it closed against the back of Botchermann's hand. Botchermann's scream was muffled by the vomit that rose in his throat and the ever-constricting grasp of David's hands. David pushed his knee against the drawer until he heard the snap of bone. The Nazi's eyes seemed as though they were about to explode and perspiration ran freely from his face. Botchermann's arm drooped limply toward the floor as David took his left hand from the Nazi's throat and removed the handgun from the desk.

"Don't be a fool, Berg," Botchermann moaned as he pulled his crushed left hand onto his lap with his free hand. "You can still save yourself. I won't tell anyone what has happened here."

"Oh, you're going to tell them all right. You're going to tell all the world."

"What are you talking about? Have you gone mad?" he asked between teeth clenched to control the pain radiating up his left arm.

David pressed the barrel of the gun into the nape of Botchermann's neck. "How many people have you killed this way?" David demanded.

"For God's sake! Be careful with that thing, you fool! It has a sensitive trigger."

"How many, Botchermann?"

"I'm an administrator. I'm here to maintain order."

"How long does it take for someone to die when you shoot them here?" David pushed the weapon even harder against the Nazi's neck for emphasis.

"Berg, listen to me. You can still save yourself. No one has to know about this," the Nazi pleaded.

"Oh, but they do, Herr Botchermann. The world has to know and you will tell them. You will be the world's best teacher." David reached across the desk and pulled a pen from an ornate inkwell and dropped it at Botchermann's right hand.

"Now, write what I say!" David shoved several sheets of paper, which he snatched from the stationery box on Botchermann's desk, in front of the Nazi.

"My God, man! Be reasonable. My hand is broken. I'm in terrible pain."

David kept the Luger trained on Botchermann as he moved around the desk and sat down in front of his prisoner.

"Does the pain hurt?"

"Look how swollen my hand has become."

"Do you remember Daniel Dienavitch, Herr Botchermann?"

"Who?"

"The young musician you hanged from the back of a tow truck. You remember?"

"Berg, he was the insurrectionist. I had to maintain order."

"Do you remember the hundreds of men you broke in half with your insane work details?"

"I had my orders, Berg."

"And the two hundred you sent to Belzec?"

"Orders, Berg, orders."

"Not one came back. Not one! You made widows of all their wives, fatherless children of all their sons and daughters."

"There are no wars without their casualties, Berg."

"Pick up the pen!" David commanded.

"Look, Berg, I know you're upset over the Hoffman woman's death, but—"

"Stop!" David hissed. "Don't you dare so much as utter her name. You are unfit to even whisper her name."

"I sent her to a quarantine center in Auschwitz. I did not know what would happen to her."

"She tried to feed the hungry."

"They were enemy prisoners. When she tried to aid them, she became the enemy."

"And now you are the enemy prisoner."

"Are you crazy, Berg? We are in my office. You are surrounded by my men. You are as much a prisoner now as you were yesterday."

David smiled. "No, Herr Botchermann. You are in my hands now and you will live only as long as I allow you to live. When I am through with you, you will die."

"For God's sake, Berg. Don't be a fool!"

"Take the pen in your right hand and write what I say."

Botchermann stared into the barrel of the Luger for a moment and picked up the pen.

"To the citizens of the world," David began. "I, as SS and Police Leader Hans Botchermann, Police Leader of Biala-Podlaska—"

"Berg, end this nonsense while you still can." Botchermann cut in. "What do you think you are going to do? Give this to the mailman and ask him to deliver it to President Roosevelt?"

"Write!" Berg commanded again. "As SS Police Leader Hans Botchermann, I am Lord and Master of the Polish city of Biala-Podlaska and the eight thousand Jews who are enslaved here."

Botchermann gripped the pen awkwardly and began to write.

"I am the prisoner of David Berg, head of the Jewish Council here, and I write this confession at his direction. What follows is the truth.

"Jews from throughout eastern Poland have been delivered to me to await their fate. We have made life a living hell for them through starvation, hard labor, torture, and arbitrary execution.

"I personally have ordered the execution or exile of hundreds of Jews, and I have administered this territory harshly, ruthlessly, and without mercy.

"I personally ordered the execution of Daniel Dienavitch. He was strangled and hanged in front of a detachment of fellow workers. His crime was to question the terms of the labor to which I had committed him on the day of his execution."

"Berg, stop while you can," Botchermann broke in.

"As SS and Police Leader, it was my responsibility to administer the rationing of food and fuel to the Jewish quarter during the winters of my command. I knew the rations I approved were insufficient to sustain life and that hundreds would starve or freeze to death each winter. I made no exceptions and was able to reduce through death the numbers of Jews under my command each winter."

Botchermann wrote each word just as David dictated them. "You expect me to beg forgiveness and to come crawling to you, don't you, Berg," Botchermann sneered.

David ignored the taunt and continued: "I ordered two hundred men to report to a work detail in the town of Belzec, knowing they would never return to their families. They were taken to Belzec in freight cars already crowded with Jewish men from other districts. All the men from Biala-Podlaska perished, as I knew they would."

"I did my job well that winter, Berg." Botchermann laughed.

"I also sent six Jewish women to a camp at Auschwitz for trying to feed bread to Russian prisoners of war." David spoke quietly, still ignoring Botchermann's commentary.

"I was ordered to send troublemakers to the new quarantine center at Auschwitz by Himmler himself," Botchermann protested.

"All six perished there!" David shouted ordering Botchermann to keep writing.

"Herr Botchermann! Are you all right? Is the Jew still with you?" a voice yelled from the anteroom.

Botchermann's face broke into a smile. "Well, Berg, your little game is over, isn't it?"

"Sign the letter," David commanded.

"Of course, of course. Gladly. I have nothing to be ashamed of." He scrawled his name boldly across the bottom of the letter.

David snatched the letter away from the Nazi and folded it.

"Herr Botchermann! We will break down the door if you do not answer. Are you all right?" the voice from the other side of the door demanded again.

"Well, what do we do now, Berg? You haven't the guts to shoot me in cold blood. You're not made of the stuff we Germans are," Botchermann said tauntingly.

"Open the door," David replied coldly.

"What?"

"Open the door!"

"Yes, yes, of course. Now you are using your head." Botchermann jumped to his feet. The Nazi held his left hand, which had turned blue, and began to move slowly toward the door.

As the Nazi reached for the handle of the metal bar that bolted the door shut, David raised the Luger and aimed just above the Nazi's right shoulder.

"Herr Botchermann, we're coming in," the guttural voice shouted.

Before the SS and Police Leader could reply, David fired several shots by Botchermann's right ear and through the door. David heard someone scream in pain on the other side.

Botchermann spun around and confronted David. "Are you crazy?" he screamed.

"There's a madman loose in there," someone shouted. "Fire through the door!"

Botcherman twisted around and lunged for the lock as the volley of submachine-gun fire screamed through the door like a thousand nail-size missiles. Botchermann flinched wildly for several moments as the bullets cut through his body.

David stood surveying the scene before him. Botchermann lay hemorrhaging on the office floor, taking his last labored breaths. The door to the office bowed under the weight of the SS troops hurling themselves against it from the other side.

When they finally burst into the room, they found their leader dead on the floor. Otherwise the room was empty. Nothing moved other than the heavy red drapes swaying by the open window.

Epilogue

My dear Cousin Rebecca,

Our search has ended in sadness. We learned that Momma was sent to Auschwitz in December 1941. There can be no doubt at all that she died there.

We started our search for Momma and Poppa in Oleck-Podlaska. There we found my father's grave in the village cemetery. Sadly, he died soon after Yitzhak, Annette, and I left for Palestine. From Oleck-Podlaska our journey took us to Biala-Podlaska, where we saw what had been the Jewish ghetto where Momma was sent by the Germans. Ironically enough, the ghetto was not damaged as much as the rest of the town because no one was living there when the Russians finally attacked in 1944. We met a nice couple, one of the last Jewish families left in the town, who told us everything that had happened. The old man, whose name is Isidore Zuckerman, took us on a tour of the ghetto and showed us where the Self-Help kitchen was located, and the school Momma organized, and the community center. He showed us where the Jewish archives of those years, which Momma helped to collect, were found in the cemetery after the war.

We had walked through the square in the center of the town earlier that day. When Mr. Zuckerman told me it was from there that the survivors of the ghetto were transported to the death camps, my blood ran cold. I will forever associate that little garden square in my mind with Momma—although why that should be so, I cannot tell you.

We returned to our home in Palestine and recited

Kaddish for our parents. I know that the news of Momma's and Poppa's deaths will grieve you, but in a strange way I am happier now that we have discovered exactly what happened. Now we know that our family heritage in Poland is in the past and we must look to the future both here in Palestine and with your family in America.

We think of you all constantly. It is as if you have been with us every step of the way on our journey. I will write again soon, and I know that someday we will all be together.

Love,
Peninah

At midnight on May 14, 1948, the British Mandate in Palestine came to an end, and the war between the Jews and the Arabs began. It was concluded by four armistice agreements, the last dated July 20, 1949. The State of Israel had become an established fact of history, and the Jews finally had their Promised Land.

The following spring Rebecca's dream came true. The family held a reunion in Israel, and they danced, each with an arm around the shoulder of a loved one, in a meadow bright with flowers.

Harold Gershowitz is a senior executive with one of Chicago's largest companies. He has written many trade and business articles. Mr. Gershowitz decided to write *Remember This Dream,* his first novel, upon learning of his great-grandfather's final plea to his children and grandchildren as they emigrated to the United States from a small village in Eastern Europe more than 75 years ago. "Remember me!" he cried out to them. Mr. Gershowitz and his wife Diane, who works as his research associate, live in Northbrook, Illinois.

THE LATEST BOOKS
IN THE BANTAM
BESTSELLING TRADITION

☐ 27032	**FIRST BORN** Doris Mortman	$4.95
☐ 26513	**PRIVILEGE** Leona Blair	$4.95
☐ 27018	**DESTINY** Sally Beaman	$4.95
☐ 26991	**THIS FIERCE SPLENDOR** Iris Johansen	$3.95
☐ 27235	**SOMETIMES PARADISE** Judith Green	$3.95
☐ 26990	**LABELS** Harold Carlton	$4.50
☐ 27283	**BRAZEN VIRTUE** Nora Roberts	$3.95
☐ 27284	**THE FORTUNE TELLER** Marsha Norman	$4.50
☐ 25891	**THE TWO MRS. GRENVILLES**	$4.50
	Dominick Dunne	
☐ 25800	**THE CIDER HOUSE RULES** John Irving	$4.95
☐ 27746	**BEACHES** Iris Rainer Dart	$4.50
☐ 27196	**THE PROUD BREED** Celeste De Blasis	$4.95
☐ 24937	**WILD SWAN** Celeste De Blasis	$3.95
☐ 25692	**SWAN'S CHANCE** Celeste De Blasis	$4.50
☐ 26543	**ACT OF WILL** Barbara Taylor Bradford	$4.95
☐ 26534	**A WOMAN OF SUBSTANCE**	$4.50
	Barbara Taylor Bradford	

Prices and availability subject to change without notice.

- -

CYNTHIA FREEMAN

Cynthia Freeman's spellbinding characters and stories have put her books on best seller lists across the nation. You'll want to follow all these magnificent sagas of human needs, conflicts, and passions.

☐	26092	**NO TIME FOR TEARS**	$4.50
☐	26090	**COME POUR THE WINE**	$4.50
☐	26161	**THE DAYS OF WINTER**	$4.50
☐	27377	**FAIRYTALES**	$4.95
☐	25843	**PORTRAITS**	$4.50
☐	27743	**A WORLD FULL OF STRANGERS**	$4.95

Prices subject to change without notice.

Special Offer
Buy a Bantam Book
for only 50¢.

Now you can have Bantam's catalog filled with hundreds of titles plus take advantage of our unique and exciting bonus book offer. A special offer which gives you the opportunity to purchase a Bantam book for only 50¢. Here's how!

By ordering any five books at the regular price per order, you can also choose any other single book listed (up to a $5.95 value) for just 50¢. Some restrictions do apply, but for further details why not send for Bantam's catalog of titles today!

Just send us your name and address and we will send you a catalog!